RAVE REVIEWS FOR THE STARBRIDGE SERIES!

"This series offers well-told tales with a welcome note of realism about relationships . . . Recommended."
—Roland Green, *Booklist*

"This is the type of rousing adventure story which Heinlein made so popular a generation ago . . . Excellent."
—Andre Norton

"These novels emphasize relationships and challenge our understanding among intelligent races. The series also raises interesting moral and social questions."
—*Library Journal*

"This is a space opera in the best tradition . . . just tremendous. I'm delighted to recommend it."
—Judith Tarr

"A. C. Crispin's publishers continue to shower glowing quotes on the covers of the StarBridge novels—and the novels continue to deserve them . . . So far, the series is batting a thousand!"
—*Dragon*

THE STARBRIDGE SERIES

STARBRIDGE by A.C. Crispin
STARBRIDGE 2: SILENT DANCES by
A.C. Crispin and Kathleen O'Malley
STARBRIDGE 3: SHADOW WORLD by
A.C. Crispin and Jannean Elliott
STARBRIDGE 4: SERPENT'S GIFT by
A.C. Crispin with Deborah A. Marshall
STARBRIDGE 5: SILENT SONGS by
A.C. Crispin and Kathleen O'Malley
ANCESTOR'S WORLD: A NOVEL OF STARBRIDGE by
A.C. Crispin and T. Jackson King

Also by Ru Emerson

The *Night-Threads Series*
THE CALLING OF THE THREE
THE TWO IN HIDING
ONE LAND, ONE DUKE
THE CRAFT OF LIGHT
THE SCIENCE OF POWER
THE ART OF THE SWORD
XENA: WARRIOR PRINCESS
THE EMPTY THRONE
XENA: WARRIOR PRINCESS
THE HUNTRESS AND THE SPHINX
XENA: WARRIOR PRINCESS
THE THIEF OF HERMES

VOICES OF CHAOS

A Novel of StarBridge

A.C. CRISPIN
AND RU EMERSON

ACE BOOKS, NEW YORK

For Doug - who not only survived the book but at least half a dozen leg casts . . . and the other way around, of course

And for my darling Roberta, who puts up with her cat-mom deserting truly adorable tiptoes for a keyboard

This book is an Ace original edition,
and has never been previously published.

VOICES OF CHAOS

An Ace Book / published by arrangement with the authors

PRINTING HISTORY
Ace edition / March 1998

All rights reserved.
Copyright © 1998 by A.C. Crispin and Ru Emerson.
Cover art by Duane O. Myers.
This book may not be reproduced in whole or in part,
by mimeograph or any other means, without permission.
For information address: The Berkley Publishing Group,
a member of Penguin Putnam Inc.,
200 Madison Avenue, New York, NY 10016.

The Penguin Putnam Inc. World Wide Web site address is
http://www.penguinputnam.com

ISBN: 0-441-00516-0

ACE®
Ace Books are published by The Berkley Publishing Group,
a member of Penguin Putnam Inc.,
200 Madison Avenue, New York, NY 10016.
ACE and the "A" design are trademarks
belonging to Charter Communications, Inc.

PRINTED IN THE UNITED STATES OF AMERICA

10 9 8 7 6 5 4 3 2 1

Prologue

The late-afternoon sun glared down on the Arekkhi equatorial city of Ebba and the Emperor's island just across the shallow bay. Most of the furred inhabitants of both city and island had already retreated into shade for the remaining daylight hours. Low tide moved sluggishly across green-slimed stones and lapped at the ancient mole where sleek hydroships rocked gently on slender runners.

Low, domed clerical and government buildings on the island shimmered in the heat: Emperor Khezahn, frugal for one of his ancient line, preferred to plant trees for shade, rather than sealing the island in a climate-controlled dome.

Khyriz, youngest of Khezahn's male offspring, slid from his younger cousin's air-cushioned personal transport and shook out the *zhona*-silk formal robe as the two-seat car settled with a slow hiss onto its padded parking blocks before the palace's public entry. He glanced at the great portals leading to the reception hall, then fixed his gaze on his hands; on long, pale-furred and blunt-nailed fingers. His cousin Zhikna punched in the vehicle's personal locking code and walked toward the narrow, moving walkway. The younger male's delicately spotted hands moved nervously, plucking at his long sleeves, twisting his cuffs, fussing with his padded hat, never still.

Khyriz stepped onto the carpeted transport-walk just in front of his cousin and braced narrow, gold-slippered feet as the thing began to move. He'd deliberately placed himself where he wouldn't have to watch the youth jittering. Zhikna worried about everything, but this time there was no cause. *This is the formal confirmation, nothing more: Shiksara and I will be on our way to StarBridge as soon as the Heeyoon ship is ready to leave.*

It was true that some Arekkhi—like Zhik's arrogant, conservative father—would have preferred it if the Heeyoons had never entered their solar system at all. But since that was beyond changing, most of the Council had accepted the odd outsiders, if only for the new goods and advanced technology they possessed.

Everything's changed, Khyriz thought. *Changed forever.*

The Arekkhi were no longer alone, though few of them had actually met any of the pale-furred, long-muzzled Heeyoons— and of them all, only the two candidates for the Academy would get to know any of the many other forms of alien life out there.

The Prince ran a casual-looking hand over his right cheek, making certain his whiskers were maintained at the proper distance from his face. The state media were invited; they'd be watching him closely. He wouldn't like being taped flat-whiskered, as if he feared this journey.

I'm not afraid. Unsure, but why not? We've only seen StarBridge via the holo-vids the Heeyoons brought us. All things will be new experiences. He closed lower teeth briefly over his full upper lip in exasperation. The walkway moved in little jerks just inside the doors and Zhikna was muttering to himself, as he fussed with his cousin's collar. The Prince turned to gaze into a face almost twin to his own—both had the same high, unusually wide cheekbones, and a classically broad, flat, bronze-colored nose; narrow black stripes flanked the nose and bracketed the mouth. Khyriz's deep-set, slanted eyes were a dark green, though, while Zhikna's were green-flecked bronze, and the fur around his mouth was white, Khyriz's a deep cream.

"Leave be, Zhik," he ordered quietly. The younger Arekkhi's ears flicked rapidly as he released the bright red fabric; he was embarrassed. Khyriz forced his whiskers to curve forward in a smile. "I look acceptable; you dressed me well. Father will be astonished."

Zhikna stilled his ears with a visible effort. "You know these things matter," he insisted. His own robes—a bronze that brought out the color of his eyes—were faultlessly draped, and his cap fashionably covered one ear. His mouth scarcely moved as he spoke, his voice was very soft: Like many Arekkhi of his class, he believed there were listening devices and vid-watchers everywhere, especially on this island and in the palace. *Possibly his father told him that,* Khyriz thought in amusement. *To keep him from spreading family secrets*. The young noble wasn't known for his common sense.

"To males like your father, clothing matters," Khyriz replied; he didn't bother to modulate his voice. Listening devices and lip-reading vid indeed! "Up there—beyond our own space—it won't be the same."

"Perhaps," Zhikna mumbled.

He doesn't agree, Khyriz knew. But Zhikna wasn't interested in learning.

The walkway carried them into a long hall that branched in five directions; it slowed for the central pillar containing entry-level security equipment. Khyriz paid no attention; his mind was occupied reviewing the contents of the small bag of personal belongings he could carry onto the Heeyoon ship. Hardly any room at all, but one wore special garb at the Academy, and there would be things from other worlds to personalize his room.

All he had to do was get through this one final ceremony, then he and Shiksara would be on their way.

Zhikna cleared his throat and touched his cousin's arm, indicating the small, gold-rimmed, remote-controlled eye hovering between them. Khyriz turned to face it squarely. The lens would compare his features to the digitized images of those allowed to enter the palace, would then transmit coded data to the panel mounted on the hand-carved pillar, and the panel would program the proper carpeted walkways to move them to their destination. One deep breath later, the eye shuttered itself and backed into its wall niche; the pillar lights flashed in a spiral pattern, bright yellow and dark gold. The walkway resumed normal speed.

Zhikna sighed gustily, a low, growling sound escaping as he tugged at the wide cap that crossed his cousin's black-spotted, cream-colored brow, covering one rounded ear. Khyriz sighed in turn, shifted the cap so it lay flat between his ears, and gave his cousin a look. "Please, Zhik! Father won't care if my appearance isn't flawless, so long as I don't shame him; the nobles and the press will certainly focus on the Heeyoons, and I do not believe they care about the angle of my cap."

Zhikna gazed up, eyes wide, politely waiting for him to go on. Khyriz gestured widely with both hands, fingers splayed, a movement meaning, "Nothing else to say."

Zhikna cast his eyes down in negation. "But the Inner Council? After the ceremony, you are ordered there. . . ."

The "secret" Council of advisers to the Emperor, Zhikna meant. Though everyone knew who the members were; after all, such an honor could hardly be kept secret. In Khyriz's opinion, the meetings were secret simply because they were too boring to interest anyone besides a councillor. Zhikna paid attention to too many of the old tales, from a time when the Emperor's private Council was also his executioner. Wild rumor still said it was. "Inner Council is important, of course," he said diplomatically—it was just possible some device or other was watching or listening. "But my father rules Council."

Zhikna's ears flickered once more: His own father was merely noble despite the distant cousinship between Khyriz and himself. Still, the honored *zhez* Zhenu was Revered Leader of the Noble Tier of both regular and Inner Councils—just as Prelate Nijho—once a common priest who had risen to noble class—controlled the Church tier in both.

Everyone knew that much; little from regular council ever reached the common Arekkhi, and no one outside the Inner Council knew what was discussed in chambers. Or how much the Emperor followed its advice. Inner members were sworn to rigid secrecy; new appointees were tested, and those who seemed open to bribery, or those who had ever spoken in their sleep, were dismissed. No servants entered the chamber itself: The room was dusted and polished by two of the Prelate's trusted priests under the watchful eyes of the Emperor's youngest brother and a representative chosen by the nobles. The Emperor's personal tech scanned for spy devices before each meeting, with the entire Council watching.

Zhikna gazed at his cousin unhappily; Khyriz let his whiskers curl forward until they nearly touched, and laid the backs of his hands on the other's wrists, a gesture of close friendship. "I will use my best manners today, Zhik." He glanced forward as movement farther along the pale yellow walk caught his eye: Shiksara stood regally tall, nearly unrecognizable in upper-class silvery-blue and surrounded by Heeyoons. "Besides," he added softly, "with Shiksara also present, who will pay heed to *me*?"

Zhik's eyes widened. "Oh," he murmured, his hands suddenly and astonishingly still. "Oh, how truly lovely she is!" His eyes remained fixed on the shimmering gown all the way to the private reception, where the ceremony would take place. *Preserve me, O Holy Two, from my kit-cousin's romantic notions,* Khyriz thought with amused tolerance. He had to prod the youth whenever they shifted from one carpeted moving walkway to the next.

The ceremony with the Heeyoons was held in the silver room set aside for such public ceremonies, and was fairly brief, just as he'd supposed: The furred outsiders formally presented tiny translating devices called voders to the two young Arekkhi. The Arekkhi government, in the person of Prince Khelyu—Khyriz's eldest brother and the Emperor's Heir—gave them elaborately penned scrolls. In Shiksara's case, the scroll meant her father could rise one rank-level in merchant-class, and the young female would be allowed to wed outside that class when she returned home. If she wished.

Khyriz wondered what tale had been concocted for the Heeyoons to account for the small number attending the ceremony: Probably shyness, rather than distress at the thought or sight of such alien beings. Ten nobles who represented the noble houses, plus Zhikna, Prince Khelyu, and Shiksara's parents were the only participants in the ceremony. The only other Arekkhi present were members of the state-controlled media: ten of them.

So many reporters! Khyriz assumed the ten had been chosen—four of them female—so the Heeyoons would think the Arekkhi had open reporting, and sex equality, as the outsiders did. Khyriz fought a smile and kept his whiskers where they belonged with an effort: The four female reporters were probably the entire female press on the planet, the station, and both moons, and aside from the Emperor's sanctioned media, there *were* no media in Arekkhi space, including the station and the small colonies on the two moons.

Once the ceremony ended, the media converged as one on Shiksara: It was purely astonishing that a female or a person of merchant-class should receive such an honor as this, and Shiksara was both. The Heeyoons wouldn't know that—or know that her clothing, and the lessons in walking and gesture, had likely cost her parents half a year's earnings.

The Prince turned as a hand descended on his forearm—future emperor Khelyu gave him a rather grim look and drew him away from the others; down an uncarpeted hallway, down another, similar corridor. His brother halted before the blue door that marked Council chambers. Candles in etched glass chimneys flickered in wall niches; the floor was varnished, slick under his slippers: Both, Khyriz knew, were part of the protection against hidden listening devices. In this place, with the cloying scent of wax in his nostrils and the light making odd patterns across his brother's cosmetically enhanced nose-stripes, he could suddenly believe in such devices.

"You know the etiquette," Khelyu interrupted his thoughts tersely. Khyriz nodded, not trusting his voice all at once. The elder brother tugged Khyriz's cap down over one ear and reached for the bell-cord dangling next to the narrow door. "You walk in, you take the seat in the lowest circle, you salute properly, and you answer politely and succinctly when questioned. Otherwise you remain quiet. Also"—his voice dropped even lower, now a whisper that tickled the younger Prince's ear—"also this: sensors!" At that disquieting warning, the door slid sideways to admit them both.

Khyriz composed his hands and whiskers and stepped into the dark-paneled and dimly lit chamber. It was surprisingly small. Four levels, made of concentric rings edged in plain, highly polished railings rose from the little circular floor. Arekkhi in black hoods stared down at him from three levels, only an occasional gleam visible through gauze-covered eyeholes. His father stood alone on the fourth tier—the robes familiar, a flat, enameled mask completely covering his face. The hand holding the polished stick was gloved.

Khyriz felt suddenly cold as he took his place on the

forward-slanting bench. His mind raced. Sensors! But that meant that the seat he'd just taken was set up to measure his pulse and temperature, to test him for truthfulness. *Who is doing this? And why?*

He drew a deep breath. Who or why were not his business. It might be the bench was always wired. Perhaps his father had arranged this. But maybe another member of Council had done so—with or without his father's knowledge. *Khelyu took a chance, warning me. Why? Because I know some Jhaknandu?* Often, dance masters used the ancient fighting discipline as preparation for the formal dances—Khyriz had first learned it for that reason. But it was also tied to the old religion from highland Dagona; it counseled meditation, inner control, concealed emotion and thought. He had assumed the lessons would be useful on StarBridge. But—here and now?

Above him, someone made a faint, warning sound; Khyriz gracefully covered his eyes with both hands, then his mouth with crossed fingers, indicating honor to the Council and a vow of silence on anything he might see here. His rank at least meant he could remain seated; a lesser being would have been required to lower himself to one fragile midleg joint in token of his helplessness below their strength, before assuming a place on the bench.

He did not look up again; to do so would be an insult—as though he meant to pierce the identities behind those hoods, or even see beyond that flat mask. *He is Emperor; I merely a young royal.* He let the words of calming from the first rite of Jhaknan-du flow through his mind; the tension in his throat eased and his fingers stilled of their own volition.

A harsh voice filled the chamber, the words without inflection or accent. The owner surely thought it anonymous, but Khyriz knew it was Zhikna's father. No one else had that unpleasant low resonance to his speech, and the prince had heard that same chill anger flay his young cousin. "You will listen, youth, and you will obey, nothing else. When the naked aliens came among us from beyond our moons, they offered us trifles from their technology, their goods, their ships, and their ways. In exchange for this, they say one day our world might be made part of their League. They do not say when;

even if we join them, they make clear it will be as less than equals. That is not acceptable to Arekkhi, and you will think each morning with shame upon what they have offered your people!''

Another voice, unknown to him. ''They then offer free education at this StarBridge as a sop: Send your young to us, they say, and we will teach them about the worlds beyond your own. We know they mean this as a way to separate our young from us. You will remember this daily, and vow each morning to remain Arekkhi!''

Zhenu spoke again, overriding whatever the other might have said. ''We denounce them—and their arrogance!—but only here, and in secret. They have technology that can be invaluable to us. We . . . trust you see the point of this, young Khyriz.''

An answer was required, Khyriz realized numbly. He flicked his ears, said ''Yes,'' very quietly.

''Good. They may be our superiors in goods, but we are greater than they in diplomatic skills: We see their plans, though they try to hide them. They will lure us in with promise of trade, then dictate to us how we run our worlds and our houses. Any advanced tech we receive will be rigidly supervised.''

Silence; to his distress, Khyriz realized he should have said or done something. Another voice—this one ironic. ''You have no question, no comment?'' He thought quickly.

''Yes. My part in all this . . . ?''

Zhenu again; he sounded grimly pleased. ''You took the naked aliens' tests and passed them. They claim pleasure at your intelligence, yours and that of the Lesser She Shiksara, and by this claim you for their StarBridge. But tests can be manipulated, young Prince.''

''My scores . . . ?''

''Not yours.'' The Emperor's brusque voice assured him. ''Though if it had been necessary—it was important that the aliens believe we do not separate our royals from the populace, or count our females as lesser. The written tests of the merchant-she were enhanced, slightly; she was heavily coached before her spoken tests.'' A pause. Khyriz wondered if he should speak again, but Zhenu continued.

"Understand, the Lesser She knows exactly what her duty is. She has been instructed how to behave on this StarBridge— if she wishes to see her people alive again. But the merchantess is, after all, a she, so we rely upon you, young prince, to make certain she does not forget.'' Another silence. Khyriz could only hope the bench beneath him did not betray his confusion and astonishment. *They want me to . . . to spy on Shiksara and to report on her!*

Another voice broke in on his thoughts: The Prelate's. The Prince had endured too many dull harangues during the twice-seasonal religious meetings to believe this to be anyone but the head of the Arekkhi Church.

"You, Khyriz, will temper your words to the situation: You will say nothing of rank, kind, and type, or how these things are determined among us. The outsiders do not appreciate the importance of classes as they exist here, and therefore you will insist that such things *do not* exist here. The matter of Asha will remain *utterly* unspoken. We have not permitted the Heeyoons to see Asha; they know nothing of Asha, and will not learn. Not here—and not from you, there. Swear it.''

Asha. Dear gods! Khyriz somehow managed to keep his whiskers and ears under control. "I swear it,'' he murmured.

Zhenu, his voice silken, smug, added, "You offer them nothing about our religion or our history, unless you give the answer the outsiders wish to hear; we know you have a royal's education and skill at this. Volunteer *nothing.*''

And then his father once more. But Khyriz had never heard his well-loved parent speak in such a hard tone. "Call no unwanted attention to us, or to Asha. You will promote the transfer of their technology and trade to your people—and if the aliens are not forthcoming with such technology, you will locate it on this StarBridge and transmit the information to your people. When you return to your apartment, you will find a list of those things we most want of the outsiders—particularly those they show no sign of letting us control.'' *Worse yet! They want me to serve as a spy! I'm not going to Star-Bridge to learn, except about things they want!*

The Prelate's voice. "It is your sacred duty to do all possible so your people have free access to outside trade. By accident, these Heeyoons let slip there are beings—entire peoples—who are not part of their alliance. Remember the name 'Sorrow Sector.' If the Heeyoons do not give us what we desire, then it may fall to you to contact the rulers of this Sector."

"Swear you will do this," his uncle's voice added softly.

"I—swear," Khyriz replied as steadily as he could.

"We will send a communication device with you—one of theirs, which they claim will give you a private link with your home world. Our station techs have modified it to be certain it is truly private. We will have instructions for you, as we learn more here. You will obey. Swear."

"Yes."

"You will do all these things," Zhenu went on flatly, "or you will find yourself home in no time at all, disgraced and exiled to your estates. If you are fortunate. Otherwise, you will serve with the guards tending Asha in the northern mines!"

Khyriz spoke past a very dry throat. "Revered members of the Council, I shall try my best to do as you order. Though bound by blood to the Emperor, I am no one without the blessing of the nobility and my Church."

They must surely know how frightened I am! But somehow he kept his voice level, his heart and breathing normal. The black-hooded figures surrounding him stared down in silence; finally Zhik's father spoke once more.

"We ask only that, young Prince. Go, speak with the media, pose with the wretched merchantess. Take with you our wishes for your success."

Liar! Khyriz thought sharply. The lean figure high above him stiffened, and he drew a deep breath. Zhenu turned away. "Go," he said dismissively. Khyriz faltered to his feet and somehow walked from the chamber. The door hissed closed behind him.

CHAPTER I

◆

Magdalena Perez stood very still in the middle of the Joyous Hall of the Church of the Fathers Washed in the Blood—the only room open to outsiders, especially NewAm government officials. The room was too cool, as always: a combination of the climate, the altitude of the Church's rolling land, the fortresslike thickness of the walls and roof, and the fact that fires were allowed only rarely, except for those that warmed the private chambers of the elders. Magdalena fixed her gaze on the bare, waxed floorboards just in front of her feet; despite the chill coming through thin-soled shoes, she was sweating. Perhaps if she stood very still and kept her eyes down, no one would notice her. Perhaps this once, she'd escape punishment.

Vain hope: With one exception, every person in the hall was gazing—or glaring—at her. The Council of Elders—the four gray-bearded men who sat on hard chairs against the wall to her right—were smiling like indulgent old grandfathers because of the outsiders present, but any Church child knew the Elders were as strict with the children, especially the maidens, as Father Saul himself. Her mother, mouth set in a tight line, watched from near the door that led to the vegetable gardens, two older widowed women flanking her (because of the outsiders, of course; one of them was male). Magdalena had glanced at her mother when the women entered, but there wasn't any help there: Her mother's black eyes were grim under the gray married-women's scarf. The grannies kept their eyes humbly on the floor just before their feet, their backs to

the outsiders, enclosing Sister Lilith—once wealthy widow
Martina Elonzo Maria Perez—between them.

The outsiders: It was because of *her* that the two NewAm
officials had demanded to see Father Saul, Magdalena knew.
They were the first non-Church people she'd seen in the seven
years since her mother had joined the Church. Their faces—
male and female, young and old—revealed nothing; but the
man's eyes were wide, moving constantly. He must have expected evidence of sacrificial altars or wild orgies. Father Saul
told them all often enough that the outside believed that of the
Church.

At her side, Father Saul shifted from one heavy boot to the
other; his feet scraped the wood loudly and the grannies
jumped. He was beyond mere fury, Magdalena knew. She
wanted to run from him, but she knew that would be a bad
mistake.

When he'd fetched her from the small room where she had
been translating a Calvinist text for him, his face had been so
white and set, she had thought at first he was sick—until she
looked into his eyes: If he'd dared beat her bloody then, she
realized, he'd have done it. He'd said nothing, merely hauled
her out of the hard plastic chair in the ice-cold room, dragged
her down the chill corridor, and, just short of Joyous Hall, had
slammed her against the wall, giving her a throbbing headache
and rebruising an already painful shoulder.

"Two busybodies from NewAm Education have come because of a Church lass named Magdalena, also called Abigail." His vibrant basso voice sounded odd through the ringing
in her ears; dread twisted her stomach. Hard, heavy fingers
digging painfully into her biceps, he'd added, his voice a
deadly hiss: "You vessel of iniquity! You *stole* time from your
duties and your *loving* family of this Church—you brought
those outsiders down upon us! You deliberately sought forbidden information on the computer! You took tests for that
space-based Academy, where not just the most unholy humans
are taught, but the very spawn of hell—did we not show all
of you children the images of such creatures?"

Magdalena couldn't decide whether to answer him or not.
Either course would mean a beating later, once the outsiders

were fed the right lie and sent away. "Well! You'll pay for your arrogance, Abigail! But for now, you will keep your slut's mouth shut! Unless I permit you to answer a question. You will make certain they realize you never meant to forsake your family for the evils of the outside world."

He'd taken a step back from her, waiting, fingers still digging into her arm. Sickened and terrified, she'd met his eyes; he beat the compound children for not looking at him when he chastised. "Swear it," he'd demanded, his free hand dropping casually to the thick leather belt that held up his work pants. "Swear!"

"I swear," Magdalena whispered.

"You will say nothing, do nothing—*show* nothing but what I have said! Better if the outsiders think this is your own decision, Abigail, but remember that you are a minor child and my ward by your mother's vow—and by her legal signature." He gave her a hard shake that knocked her head back into the wall again. "Satan and his imps are dancing in your heart, but they won't stay there long, for I will cast them out! Do not dare mock me before the unbelievers, or it will go even the worse for you!"

"No, sir," she'd whispered. He'd hauled her upright when her knees would have given way.

"Compose your face and your voice. Lie to them as well as you have lied to me!" He'd given her one last daunting look, then waited in chill silence while she fought for control. Satisfied, he then strode toward the door that led to Joyous Hall, towing her, helpless, in his wake.

But as he opened the door, the Change came over him—the astonishing lightning-swift mood change that made him the beloved, charismatic Father Saul who brought new members into the Church and frightened Magdalena almost as much as his temper. A bright, toothy smile shone above his thick gray beard, and his voice was deep and warm. "Our apologies, Councillors, to keep you waiting after such a long journey," he began smoothly. "But the girl was deeply immersed in the translation of an old Scottish sermon—the revered Brother Calvin, you know—and was reluctant to leave her work.

Weren't you, dear little sister Abigail?'' He drew her after him, stopped in the center of the room.

Magdalena let herself be led and stood where he put her, in the center of the room, so many eyes fixed on her. The rough-spun fabric of the ill-fitting brown dress that all unwed girls between thirteen and fifteen years wore was prickling her arms; it hung heavily from her aching shoulders.

The one quick glance to her mother, to the outsiders from NewAm—the awareness of the elders behind her. Father Saul's heavy hand pressing down on a too-thin shoulder. No help anywhere. She eyed the two strangers from under her lashes.

One of the outsiders stirred then: a woman of her mother's age and size, though she appeared younger, petite in a businesslike dark green skirt and jacket. The man next to her—not much older than a boy, really—sat back in his chair, one ankle hiked up on his other knee, gazing around him with keen interest. "Solomon—Father Saul," the woman began, her voice was almost as smooth as the big priest's, "you say this is the girl, Magdalena Perez?"

"Her Family Name is Abigail," Father Saul corrected in his soothing rumble. "But Magdalena was her—Worldly name, yes." He gave Magdalena a deceptively gentle-looking shake. "You need not be afraid of them, Abigail, your Family is here to protect you from the sins outside our walls. Tell them."

Magdalena nodded and kept her voice low and humble. "I am Abigail, who was Magdalena Perez. What the Holy Father tells you is true."

The woman fumbled in the large bag next to her chair and drew out a long, narrow sheet of flimsy. "Now, Mr. Smith—Father Saul, your pardon, sir." A faint smile twitched the corners of her mouth. "Of course your equipment is outmoded, so we know you'll want printed proof of the girl's test results. Magdalena," she added gently, "there's nothing to fear from us. We've come to seek you out because of those results. You can tell us the truth, and if need be, we'll protect you. You recently took the StarBridge exams, did you not?"

Her mouth was very dry, but Father Saul's thumb dug into

her shoulder, an unsubtle reminder. "There was a language section, and I thought I could try that, see how good I'd be. It was—like a game," Magdalena finished lamely. The outsider woman's eyes flicked from the too-thin girl to the vibrant elder, back again.

"Magdalena—Abigail, I beg your pardon, Father Saul." Magdalena caught her breath painfully as the hand on her shoulder tightened. The woman was misnaming them both on purpose, she could tell—and Father Saul didn't like it. "Well, young woman, I am impressed by your scores, whatever you intended."

"It was quite a game," Father Saul interposed neatly, "I am certain, finding such tests on our aged computer system." She could hear the undercurrent in his voice and knew he'd have hard questions to put to her later, just how she *had* tapped into any outside data on the old machine. It was strictly forbidden to even think of reading outside news reports, let alone what *she* had done. "Of course, we give all your required examinations to our school-age children, and the tests for outside universities and academies are available, once the children are old enough for them. I fear," he said with a gentle laugh, "we still think of our daughter here as a child, but even so, she's a year short of age—"

"She's fourteen, according to this," the woman broke in, the flimsy crackling as she waved it at him.

He won't like that, Magdalena thought in a panic. Being contradicted by an outsider who was also female—one who bared her hair and legs and spoke like anybody's equal. *But he'll never let me go, I was mad to think he would.* And to StarBridge, of all places. She bit back tears and swallowed, hard, as her world began to close in on her before it had ever properly opened.

The silence inside the hall stretched; an odd cough, almost a snort, broke it. Father Saul glared at the young male outsider, who gave him an apologetic smile, then transferred the glare to the woman. "Ms. Sayners, her years upon this world count for little, since we have kept her safe from its influences; she is a very young, innocent child."

"But she passed the tests—and with a very impressive score," Ms. Sayners protested.

"Oh, the child has talents," Father Saul countered. "Though it would seem she neglected her duties . . ." She could hear the anger in his voice. He coughed, smiled. "Your pardon, it is my fault if the child is delinquent in the execution of the few tasks we require of her."

"The tests, sir—"

"Oh, tests for an *outside* school. You know, Ms. Sayners, that children do so many things in mischief and a computer would certainly provide temptation to—hack, isn't that the word you outsiders use?" He actually laughed; Magdalena started despite herself, and the hand tightened on her shoulder. "Now and again, one of the children with a talent for the machine decides to find the forbidden areas, and certain of them explore—"

"What—the daily news reports?" the man demanded.

"Of course not!" Father Saul replied easily. "Mr. Daffyd, you must be aware how much offensive matter is out there! Foul language, revealing apparel—things we do not condone here." He shrugged. "Still, we know they, ah, hack. But early training tells, doesn't it? Because in all our years here, in this sanctuary, no child of ours has embraced your ways once they are old enough to choose. They reject you utterly." He released Magdalena's shoulder, patted her back.

Only because they're all too afraid to do anything else, Magdalena thought miserably, *or too lost to hope to care.*

"Never mind the other children," Mr. Daffyd said easily. "We are talking about this girl."

"I fail to see why. She has already told you she was curious how good her language skills were. Why, I doubt she even meant to actually *take* the tests, did you, child?"

Momentarily, she couldn't speak; she shook her head. Silence. *He's getting angry again, say something! Tell them no, go with them, they'll . . . !* What could they do, two people against the entire Church? Through a tight throat, she managed, "I didn't know they would be sent anywhere. Truly. It was—just for myself." Tears blurred her vision as the woman's mouth tightened.

"That's the truth?" she demanded. Magdalena hesitated, but Father Saul was right there, the woman an unknown and across the long room. "You are telling me that we came all this way for—for a child's game?" Magdalena nodded, swallowed as the woman viciously tore the computer printout in half, spun on one heel, and strode to the door, the younger man on her heels.

She opened her mouth to scream, "It's a lie! Don't leave me here!" But her voice wouldn't work and then Father Saul had her by both arms, pulling her back against him, enfolding her in his iron grasp, his hand clamped hard across her mouth to keep her from breathing. Then the outsiders were gone. The outer door closed with a crash that echoed. . . .

Magdalena frantically fought swaddling, smothering blankets, then sat up, gasping for air. *I'm awake this time. Really awake, not just the other bad dream where you think you're awake, but the nightmare still has you.* All too often, one of those followed the Church dream. *Something made a loud noise . . .* what had wakened her? She clung to the side of her bed, concentrated on breathing deeply until her heart slowed to a more normal rate.

Eyes closed, she fell back onto her pillow and felt cautiously along the floor until her fingers hit metal: the heavy little brass chest David Esterhazy had given her after their final performance the previous night. Apparently she'd fallen asleep before she remembered to move it off the foot of the bed. She shoved it aside so she wouldn't step on it when she got up, then eased onto her back with a long, relieved sigh. The covers were twisted, the sheet under her felt sticky, and wet tendrils of brown-black hair clung to her face.

Not just a nightmare, but one of the bad ones. *It's all right,* she whispered to herself automatically—the words Dr. Rob Gable had taught her to use her first few days here. *You're on StarBridge. Where you belong. You've been here three years, it's all right. The compound on NewAm is behind you, you don't ever have to go there again, your mother can't tear at your emotions, the elders can't bully you. Father Saul—no, Solomon Smith, who took his church—his cult—and left Earth*

*when I was eight because there were already complaints
against him for stealing money like he took Mother's, and for
abusing children—Solomon Smith can't hit you ever again. He
can't make you marry him at fifteen, like he would have if
you'd stayed there. It's over and done with.*

But what had brought this on? She hadn't had a Church
dream in more than a year. "Okay," she murmured. "Work
it out, just like Dr. Rob taught you." The mental exercise he'd
given her made bad dreams a puzzle to solve, instead of a
terror to keep her from sleeping again.

But her comp was beeping at her, a soft, insistent sound: It
was almost time to get up, and the blinking green light on the
small screen indicated messages. She sighed and sat up reluc-
tantly. Who'd have left messages this early? "Probably David,
wanting to apologize or to argue again, after last night. Great."
Just now, she didn't want to talk to David.

First things first, anyway. She stretched cautiously, then sat
up, pointing and flexing her feet. The dance recital of the night
before had been strenuous, and a wrong move the morning
after often brought on muscle cramps. Nothing hurt, just now;
a hot shower would take care of the minor stiffness in her
calves, and if she got up and washed now, there'd be plenty
of time for a good breakfast.

Several minutes later, dry once more, she sat on the edge
of the bed to comb her hair before plaiting it into one thick,
long braid, and considered the dream. Ms. Sayners and her
companion getting up to leave—that hadn't happened. *See it,*
she ordered herself as she flipped the braid over her shoulder
and felt along the foot of her bed for the jumpsuit she'd simply
dropped there the night before.

Even after so long and all Dr. Rob's help, it still wasn't that
easy. Her stomach hurt, and her hands were cold. *It's past, it
can't touch you,* she reminded herself. She gave the black one-
piece garb most students wore a hard shake and pulled it on.

Of course, Ms. Sayners and her companion knew Father
Saul had made her tell that lie; they hadn't believed a word
of it. But rather than confront him and risk him pulling her
from the room and beyond their reach, they had ignored the
man's visibly rising anger and questioned her at length: about

the computer, the tests—and to her astonishment, about her age. *They knew Church law allowed fifteen-year-old girls to marry—within the Church, of course.* "My fifteenth birthday was less than a month away, they knew I'd be legally out of their reach once one of them married me. Father Saul was going to make me his third wife." They hadn't known about the man's specific plans; Magdalena herself hadn't known—except the inner certainty she'd had when he looked at her.

"I just knew, like always." She straightened one sleeve and straightened the cuffs, then knelt to find her boots. That sixth sense that had warned her so often, which of the compound adults to avoid, when her mother could be approached. . . .

The sense had kept her from getting caught at breaking Church rules and taking outsider tests, as well. Just like it had told her to trust the two outsiders. "Bless you, Adelicia Sayners," she added softly. When the woman had finally beckoned, Magdalena had eluded Smith's grasp and run straight to her. Sayners left at once, a protective arm around the girl's shoulders.

And she'd had the foresight to bring that young man along: Solomon Smith and his elders knew better than to argue with an official of the NewAm Child Endangerment Department. She learned later that John Daffyd had drawn an ugly little pistol and backed out of the room, to make certain no one tried to snatch her back.

Past and done with. With luck, maybe she'd never have another of those awful dreams. "List messages," she said aloud; her voice was rough from talking too much at the after-recital party, trying to be heard over the general roar of conversation.

The first was from Ladessa Phillips, the fifth-year translator she'd been tutoring in Arekkhi manners and dance; the second, noted as urgent, from Dr. Rob Gable, the school's director and psychologist. But when she played it, the only message was, "Call me as soon as you wake up, please."

"No visual," she ordered as she keyed his number. After a moment, his familiar, warm—but sleep-blurred—voice came back to her.

"Magdalena? Oh, good, I was afraid you might still be out

with David, celebrating last night. I need to see you soon—no,'' he added soothingly as she broke in, "there's nothing wrong, it's a message from Khyriz, from Arekkhi.'' *Khyriz!* Magdalena smiled as she pictured her tall, cheetah-like royal friend. The smile faded almost immediately, though. *Why would he send word to Dr. Rob, if it's for me?* All Khyriz's letters came to her directly.

But Rob's next words put Khyriz completely out of her thoughts. "That will keep, though. Ladessa's been injured, a silly freak accident in the gym. She's not in any danger, before you ask, just—well, why don't you go see her? She's out of intensive and I'll okay you to miss your first two classes.''

"Intensive! Rob! You're certain she's not—?''

She could hear the smile in his voice; as always, she felt her nerves and muscles relax as she tugged the jumpsuit straight and began fastening the front. "Go on, she's hurting and worried and she needs a friend. That's your job, for now. I'll see you whenever you can get here afterward.''

"Of course, sir,'' she replied demurely, knowing her reply and demeanor would make him laugh.

"All right, Magdalena. I know you're a full test ahead of the rest of your study group in astronomy, so I don't think it will hurt anything if you and I talk instead. I'll program the servo for lemon grass tea and poppy-seed biscuits.''

"Thanks, I'll be there.'' The breakfast combination was a rare happy memory of her mother—the two of them sipping from thick pottery mugs filled with honey-sweetened clear red tea, and eating warm biscuits.

She knelt to clip her boots, as the second message played. Ladessa's normally resonant alto voice was tight with pain. "Hey—lady, I messed up. Last night, after the recital, I was too wired to sleep or study so I went up to the gym and checked out a low-gee glider and was trying that stunt, you know the forward roll over the bar you said was a really dumb one? Well, I tried it, and swear, I almost had it! But my left hand slipped and even at low gee my right wouldn't bear all my weight, and—well, okay, I fell.'' *Ouch,* Magdalena thought as she automatically straightened her bed. "Ah—and, um—well, I broke my back. And—well, I'd like to see you,'' she said in a forlorn little voice; a brittle laugh broke that. "Looks like maybe now you'll have more time to tutor me in Arekkhi formal language and manners now, doesn't it? Though I guess dance is out for now." Silence, broken by the girl's long-drawn breath. "Anyway, come see me when you can. Please?"

Magdalena gazed at the screen for a long moment after the voice cut off. That was a long drop, it must be—she didn't want to think how many meters. Even with the gee set for gliders, it was still a long way down, and the floor was hard. The Earth girl was lucky to be alive. Magdalena scooped up her jacket, shoved her comp into the pocket, and headed out.

The hallway was fairly crowded, which was normal at this hour. Half a dozen humans chattered excitedly in Mizari— StarBridge's common language, and the first one new students learned. Magdalena stepped back a pace, into her doorway, as two Heeyoons loped around the group of humans, on their way to the gym. A hint of cinnamon teased her nostrils as she keyed the door: Vardi had passed by a moment earlier, conversing in their unique olfactory-based language.

But as the door closed behind her, she froze; David was learning against the opposite wall, obviously waiting for her. From the look of him, he'd been there some time. Magdalena cast up her eyes briefly, shook her head, and slipped into the flow of rapid foot traffic; the tall blond boy eased his shoulders away from the wall and caught up. "Look, I *said* I was sorry," he mumbled. She eyed him sidelong, shook her head, then held up a hand for silence.

"David, look. I said I was sorry, too, remember? But that doesn't mean I'm ready to just forget the whole messy argument yet, you said some things that hurt. And besides . . . I don't have time right now."

"You never have time—not for me," he began sourly. Magdalena stopped short to scowl up at him.

"David, I meant what I said!" she snapped. "Ladessa broke her back last night, and I need to see Dr. Rob—nothing to do with you or last night, either," she added firmly as he stared at her. "Look, I've got to go. If you really want to talk about things, give me a couple of days, will you? I'm not ready to say it's all right, and mean it.'' He still looked resentful, but when she moved on, he stayed put.

Magdalena sighed as she edged into the first side corridor and found herself trapped behind three giggling first-year girls from Jolie who were trying to converse in Simiu, and laughing at each other's French-accented attempts. She managed a smile for them as she edged past and lengthened stride. The girls giggled and she caught her name, barely recognizable in French.

The smile slipped as she hurried on, toward the infirmary. Darn David anyway. And—poor Ladessa. *She was only just picked as translator for the Arekkhi team last month, and she was so excited!* But it was impossible to stay distracted and walk at this hour; after almost running into two Simiu who had stopped to argue about the last line of a verse of haiku, she quit trying. Besides, everyone recognized her, and half a dozen fifth-year boys wolf-whistled in unison as she went past them. She grinned happily and whistled back, leaving them laughing. *Remember when you were too shy to even acknowledge things like that?* That had been nearly four years ago, of course. Back when she could say ''thank you'' in only a handful of Earth languages.

Back when she'd no more imagined learning to shift effortlessly from Mizari to Heeyoon, to French to the clicks and growls of Simiu to Arekkhi to Chinese, than she'd imagined there would be dance on StarBridge.

Dance. Back on NewAm, when she'd stolen odd moments from her translating duties so she could take the StarBridge tests, she'd never even thought about dancing. *I gave up hope when Mother moved us into the old cult compound back on Earth, in the Mexican desert.*

Magdalena remembered nothing of her father—and little of what kind of person her mother had been before Father Saul. She could still recall every detail of the few ballet classes she took in Brownsville, Texas. But once her mother began the search for Truth, there was no time to find a new teacher, the way they'd moved around. Then no time for frivolity, and then—dance was all at once something the Devil had invented, forbidden utterly.

She took a side corridor, away from the cafeteria crowd. Hardly anyone in this hall, just two Simiu running on all fours, racing for the elevator that would take them to the lowest level. Repairs had only recently been completed on the pool after the explosion that had injured so many and killed Hing Oun. The first relay races in a long time were scheduled for this morning, if she recalled correctly. Of course, if the Simiu were headed for the pool, they'd be watching and not swimming; they felt the same way about water as cats did.

The infirmary waiting area was empty at this hour except for Znaaht, a second-year Apis earning premed credits; Magdalena told the young Apis who she wanted to see. The meter-long, beelike being darted out of sight and returned almost at once, her voder translating Apis to standard Mizari: "A short wait only, esteemed dancer."

"Thanks," Magdalena replied in Mizari; a momentary, slightly dizzying multiple view of her bronze-skinned, narrow, full-lipped face played across multifaceted eyes before the Apis quickly flew into the hall. Magdalena gazed at the wall, her dark, nearly black eyes fixed absently on a wallholo of a field of bright red flowers.

Esteemed dancer—how nice. Her Family chores on NewAm had been washing dishes, tending babies, and translating sermons and diaries—nothing physical; she'd been a very soft fifteen-year-old. It had taken hard work, long hours at the barre and on the floor, enduring pulled muscles and mornings when it hurt to sit up, let alone get out of bed. It had paid off wonderfully last night, though—four solo dances, two ensemble numbers, and three classical duos with David. *David. What am I going to do about him?*

She glanced up as footsteps came toward the waiting room from where the private rooms were located; the steps turned and went in another direction. Her calves were tight again: She flattened her palms against the wall and stretched them out, then began to pace, occasionally bending her knees and rising onto her toes.

Odd, how little of last night's recital she remembered: The first number, the jazzy solo, was a blur, and so was the second—half a dozen dancers in severe black against a white backdrop, moving in static, jerky steps to music from an old film of Dr. Rob's: *On the Waterfront*.

And then had followed the first of three ballet duets for her and David. He was the only human male dancer who could partner her, and even he needed the hall's gravity lowered so he could do the lifts from the original Russian choreography. Slender, blond David Esterhazy loved dancing "Aurora's Wedding" with her. Of course, they'd both loved it—that lush music, the classic choreography culled from one of Madame Elinka's impressive collection of old dance videos. And audiences and dancers alike adored the trick pose at the end of the duet: the Princess upside down on his leg with her ankles crossed at the level of his ear, both dancers smiling, arms widespread—no visible support keeping Aurora in place. Even knowing how it was done because she often practiced it a dozen times a day, Magdalena still found it amazing.

The footsteps came back from wherever they'd been and headed briskly back toward the recovery rooms. She glanced toward the outer hall as Znaaht flew back into the room and, with a flick of her antennae, vanished into the infirmary.

The Firebird ballet had followed—a small portion of it for her as a solo—then a short piece composed by Serge LaRoche expressly for this concert. Madame had put in a long number using all the dancers but herself and David, then, giving her time to change her costume and catch her breath for the finale: the balcony scene from *Romeo and Juliet*.

The footsteps were returning, and this time, a white-clad Dr. Rachel Mysuki beckoned her to follow. Magdalena swallowed. "Dr. Mysuki? How—how is Ladessa?"

"She'll be fine," the doctor replied, her voice clipped. Not unfriendly, Magdalena knew: just too busy to waste much time in lengthy conversation. "She's going into regen as soon as she's had the chance to talk to you, though."

"Keep it short, you mean," Magdalena said with a nod. The doctor's mouth twitched in amusement.

"Just so." She gestured toward one door. "Very short, in fact. I'll be back here in five minutes." Magdalena nodded and went in.

Ladessa was even paler than usual, especially with her short, dark red hair tucked behind her ears. A purple bruise covered most of her forehead, and her whole body was immobilized in some kind of plas-and-tape cast. Her eyes were black, all pupil, but she managed a cheerful-looking smile as Magdalena approached the bed. "Hey, you dancer! I was so proud of you last night!"

"Hey, you flyer," Magdalena replied dryly. Normally she hugged the girl when they met; now she didn't want to even chance touching her, stopping well short of the bed and keeping her hands behind her back. Ladessa cautiously wrinkled her nose in amusement.

"It's okay, they've taken care of the pain and nothing's gonna move because of the bodysuit, so you can touch. My nose itches, and I wouldn't mind a little contact that wasn't a doctor right now."

"I'm sorry about this," Magdalena said as she stroked a stray, damp tendril of hair behind the girl's ear, then carefully rubbed the tip of her nose.

"Yeah, so am I. I can't believe how fast it all happened. One minute I'm on top of the world—*and* the glider—and the next, well—here we are, I guess." She sighed quietly. "Thanks, that helps. It wouldn't be so bad except for Arekkhi, *you* know. They want the Interrelator on planet as soon as they can get us—and I'm going to be forever in here, doing regen."

"Not that long, surely. And not nearly as long as you'd be trying to heal without it," Magdalena reminded her.

"Well, no, I'm exaggerating. But the Emperor and his council have been fussing because everything is taking so long."

"I didn't know that."

"Well, but you know how they feel about even probationary status, don't you?"

She nodded. "They want full status. Period."

"Pride will do that to you," the girl agreed. "Scratch my nose again?"

"Maybe Dr. Rob can lend you Bast until you can use your hands," Magdalena suggested, straight-faced.

Ladessa laughed briefly. "Don't think so, her claws are a little too sharp for my tastes, and besides, I'm allergic to cats,

remember? Even if she'd let anyone but Dr. Rob close to her."
She frowned. "I hope that . . ."

Magdalena waited; Ladessa shook her head. "What?"

"Nothing. I think Dr. Rob wanted to—never mind." A tap
at the door brought the visitor around as Dr. Mysuki came in.

"Five minutes and a little more," she announced crisply.
Magdalena turned back to smile at her friend.

"All right, I'll go now. Ladessa—"

"I'll be just fine," the girl said. "And I'll—ah—I'll see
you when I get out of regen."

"Shoo," the doctor added firmly. Magdalena went.

The waiting room was empty as she left, this immediate end
of the hall deserted. But the general vicinity of Dr. Rob Gable's office was so crowded with students moving from one
class to the next that it took her a long time to get from one
side of the corridor to the other, to tap on his door.

Khyriz, she thought with a sudden inner warmth as he called
out, "Come in!" *I have a message from Khyriz.* She was smiling as she went in.

CHAPTER 2

♦

Robert Gable was heading for the door just as Magdalena
walked in. She jumped, then grinned. "Gee, Dr. Rob, didn't
even occur to me to wonder how I heard you all the way
through the waiting room!" The school's psychologist was
short and slender; and the barely lined face that made him
look younger than the gray hairs in his beard suggested, was
on a level with Magdalena's.

"A little too wrapped up in last night maybe?" he replied
with a warm smile as he gestured for her to precede him
through the small, currently unoccupied room into his large
inner sanctum.

Automatically, she checked the holos on the far wall as she
headed for the comfortable, human-shaped chair currently in
front of his desk. One never knew what old movie posters
would be displayed in here, but Magdalena privately figured
they were changed frequently, and according to whatever was
on his mind when an individual student came in to see him.
A holo-tank occupied the other empty wall—Rob's communication screen for the outside world, as well as where his
"movies" were shown on a weekly basis. Only five days ago,
she'd been part of a raucous crowd watching several black-
and-white Marx Brothers films; by the time *The Cocoanuts*
finished the session, she'd been laughing so hard she could
barely breathe.

"But I thought," Rob added from behind her, "that we'd
both agreed you'd call me Rob. Since I don't call you Prima

Ballerina Magdalena.'' She laughed, then dropped bonelessly into one of the visitors' chairs, slid down on her tailbone until the back of her head rested against the back of the chair, and stretched out her legs, crossing them at the ankles.

To her surprise, there was no poster from any of Madame's impressive collection of ballet vids: No *Swan Lake,* no *Romeo.* No *Kiss of the Spider Woman.* There *was* a very small, dark picture that she couldn't quite make out, neatly centered among four large holo-posters: *The Scarlet Pimpernel* (there were several versions, but this was the very old, crackly black-and-white version from the early days of ''talkies'' that was her favorite of those she'd seen); *Scaramouche* (the dashing hero of the French Revolution in his black-and-white harlequin suit, long-nosed white domino mask, sword and plumed hat striking a regal pose at the top of the poster—battling the silver-clad and silver-wigged nobleman who was also his half brother, at the bottom of the holo). Bracketing both, the two mid-twentieth-century versions of *The Prisoner of Zenda,* both of which she'd seen and adored equally: The acting in the black-and-white version had been somewhat better, but the swordplay in the second—and the black-haired actor from *Scaramouche*—had given her delicious chills. *Swashbuckling. Swordplay. Things that are not what they seem?* Magdalena eyed Rob consideringly. *Don't go romancing, you,* she ordered herself. *He put them up because he knows I like those particular movies.*

She settled her shoulders more comfortably as Rob dropped into his chair, leaned back to place crossed feet on the desk, and smiled at her. Bast rose from behind a stack of files, papers, and books—Magdalena privately suspected Rob assembled the chaotic mess deliberately, in order to relax students who were themselves often disorganized. The black cat stalked across the desk to walk down his shins and sprawl across his thighs. Absently, he stroked her plushy fur.

Magdalena's eyes went beyond the school's director to the posters, and she smiled at Leslie Nielsen, whose dark eyes seemed to meet hers. As did Ronald Colman's from the black-and-white *Prisoner of Zenda* poster. But the tiny holo-print defeated her. She sat up, leaned forward and peered at it.

Rob smiled lazily as he petted the cat. "Would you mind doing the honors? The tea and biscuits are already programmed. And go take a look at that." He nodded toward the small holo-print. "If you like it, I had a copy made and framed for you, in honor of last night."

Magdalena flowed to her feet and fussed with cups and plates for a moment, then set tea and warm rounds of black-seeded bread where he could easily reach his share before going over to study the little holo. She caught her breath sharply. "Ohhhh," she whispered. "It's a Degas!"

"Madame has a book of them—" he began.

She nodded, her eyes fixed on the small replica of a water-color print: a dark-haired young ballerina in a long, sheer skirt and pointe slippers. Her eyes seemed to be gazing at the floor, but Magdalena knew her attention was turned inward as she visualized the steps she must execute. "I know she does," the student replied softly. "I've borrowed it, several times. This particular dancer, though—she's always been my favorite." She gathered up her own sweetened tea and plate of biscuits, settled herself comfortably once more, and took a deep swallow of the warm, fragrant beverage before she dared trust her voice. "How did you know that?"

He shrugged, smiled, drank tea. "Madame lent me the book some time ago, and I knew you'd borrowed it. I didn't know you were fond of that particular print; but she reminds me of you, the way you concentrate on any task, including dance." He bit into a biscuit. "I know you'll be getting high marks in ballet for last night, and that ovation at the end must have felt terrific—but I thought a little solid something would be nice, too. I enjoyed the concert, especially the duets. You and David move so well together—what?" he asked as Magdalena sighed, very faintly. She shrugged, drank more tea. "Anything you'd like to talk about, maybe?"

Magdalena frowned; she couldn't help it.

"Keeping in mind," Rob calmly added, "that I've already heard about the argument last night, up in the Spiral Arm."

"You've been listening to gossip," Magdalena said mock-accusingly but then she groaned, set aside her cup and plate, and buried her face in her hands. "Oh, God, I didn't even think about people hearing *that*! I thought we were being quiet . . . !''

"*David* was," Rob replied with a faint chuckle. Her fingers parted so one dark eye glared at him briefly, then again vanished behind the fingers. "But your whisper carries very well; remember that one-act play last year?" He waited a moment; Magdalena didn't move. "Honestly, I only heard that you had been arguing, nothing more. Want to talk about it, or should I butt out?"

She managed a laugh, small but genuine. Leaning back, Magdalena cast her eyes ceilingward and said, "All right, I was rude, sir, and I apologize."

"It would have been rude if I *had* been listening to gossip," Rob said. He shoved the empty plate aside. Bast, to all appearances, had gone to sleep sprawled across his knees; as his hand gently stroked her shoulders, she emitted a faint, querulous mew, then settled and slept once more.

Magdalena looked from the black, furry blot to the still-youthful-looking psychologist's concerned face. "I know you don't do that, and I was rude to imply you did. It's just—all right. I wasn't going to bother you with something I can work through myself, but since I'm here . . ." She set her cup aside and sat up straighter.

"I had a nightmare this morning. It woke me just before the alarm."

Rob waited, and when she shook her head and swallowed tightly, he said, "One of those, wasn't it?" She nodded. "Back in that compound, no way out?" Another nod. "Sort through it after you woke up?"

"Just like you showed me; my heart rate dropped almost at once. But—with Ladessa down this morning, I didn't get the chance to work out why . . ." Her voice trailed off once again; she shoved aside the tea and got to her feet. Rob watched her pace, his expression sympathetic. "Thing is, I think it's—well, I *know* it was because of David. Because of last night, up in the Spiral Arm."

"But I thought you and David were a genuine item," he protested mildly. "All the time you two spend together rehearsing and outside rehearsals as well. And then the way you looked dancing together last night . . .''

Magdalena stopped pacing and faced him. ''Well—that's part of the problem. I—don't get me wrong, I've always *liked* David. He's a nice guy, smart, a good dancer. Particularly good since he didn't dance at all before he came here. He's dedicated, he likes the Old Russian Romantic era music like I do. He's easy to talk to. He speaks Spanish like a native and he was very useful in helping me teach Ladessa how to dance like an Arekkhi.''

''So? Sounds like a good combination to me,'' Rob replied neutrally.

''It is. It's just . . .'' Magdalena paused in midstride to search for the right word, finally shook her head and sighed. ''It's just not enough! Well—for a good friend, of course it is. But I never . . .'' She paused once more, then shook her head again and came over to drop into the chair and meet his eyes directly. ''I didn't realize until last night that David wanted more than friends. Special friends, I mean.''

''Well,'' Rob pointed out, ''he gave you his StarBridge jacket, it should've told you something—understand, I'm not laying blame on you. Misunderstandings happen, after all, or why would StarBridge Academy even be here?'' That rewarded him with a faint smile. ''And I know how busy you've been the past few months.''

''Thanks, Rob,'' she replied. ''Truthfully, though, I know I should have realized when he said that about special friends—when he gave me the jacket—that he meant a pair. Romance. I—can think back, remember the look on his face, and I just—at the time, I didn't see it was love or a crush or whatever, because I didn't want to.''

''All right, that's honest—and normal,'' Rob said. He settled his elbows on the chair arms, made a steeple of his fingers, and eyed her over them. ''But last night—the way you looked at him during that balcony scene—''

She shook her head, hard. ''That was *acting*.''

Rob grinned, urchinlike. ''*The Rocketeer!* That wasn't a lie—it was acting!'' he said, his voice soft and faintly English. His furred companion moaned quietly, shifted onto her side, and rolled into a tight ball. "Seriously," Rob added, sobering, "I think I understand, but explain for me, okay?"

"All right." Magdalena settled her shoulders, and her eyes wandered toward the Scaramouche holo-poster. "Dance is theater, too. Ballet isn't just dance, it also tells a story, like a play, or those gruesomely dull Arekkhi vid shows—what did you call them?—soap operas? Well, dance is acting, plus music, plus movement—even just the dancing up in the Spiral Arm." A sudden, sharp visual passed through her mind: herself and Prince Khyriz up in the Spiral Arm, both in plain blue jumpsuits, her showing him how to moon-walk to some twentieth-century music. *He was better at it than you were, once he caught on, too. Comes of dance being so much a part of their society, of course.* "Ballet is particular music, structured movement—and acting. Juliet—that was acting." She shrugged. "I—you feel joy at a good performance, or the music, or the audience. . . . but real emotion gets in the way of the performance, it cheats your audience, and it embarrasses them."

Rob kept the faint, quizzical smile on his face. "I understand. Go on, please . . . more tea?" Magdalena shook her head; Bast circled twice and finally jumped down to pad under the desk. Rob poured himself another cupful, took another, now cold, biscuit, and busied himself with adding sweetener to the tea, spreading pale marmalade on the biscuit. "So—what next with you and David? Or have you thought about it?"

She shook her head. "He wants to apologize, wants me to say it's all right. At the moment—well, it's not all right. And he doesn't want to hear the truth anyway—that I don't feel like he does. Not yet, at least."

"These things happen," Rob reminded her. "I'm just a little concerned about what looks to me like a pattern. Considering your background. You've had seven boyfriends since you've been here—but none of your relationships have gone beyond hand-holding."

"*You* were the one who told me I had the right to say 'No' at any level of a relationship," Magdalena pointed out. "Including hand-holding."

"I still say that. I'm not trying to push you into anything, Magdalena."

"And seven's not so many," she added. "Look at Ladessa, she's had at least nine guys that I know of! And Alexis—she's gone with maybe a dozen girlfriends."

"True enough." Rob laughed quietly, and a corner of his mouth turned up in an abashed grin. "That's not the point. A girl your age should be comfortable with her hormones, and her attraction to boys—all right, or girls, if she's Alexis. Kissing. If I recall, you broke up with Charlie Menarti, *and* Aldwin Cho, because you didn't like the kissing part."

Magdalena shifted, crossing her legs at the knees. "Kissing's just fine. I've kissed—well, I *have*," she added defensively as Rob eyed her. "Plenty of times, just—Charlie was first term and Aldwin is a sloppy kisser, all right? And if *you* had been me and David suddenly Frenched you without warning, you'd have yelled, too!" Her cheekbones suddenly red, she clapped a hand over her mouth.

Rob's eyebrows went up. "Secret's safe with me," he murmured. "You know that."

"I know that," she said, more calmly. "It isn't—I don't *think* it's because of nasty, awful Elder Perkins and his grabby hands. I know when something leaves me feeling dirty, like he did. And I come talk it out with you, Rob, you know I do."

"Sure. And *you* know emotions like that can disguise themselves, which is why I'm pestering you." He paused. After a moment, she shook her head. "Good. Keep in mind, you're eighteen years old, healthy—but you don't seem to feel the urges most girls your age feel."

Magdalena laughed; her face and throat were still flushed. "Look, honestly," she said. "The past two years, I've enjoyed hugging and kissing with a couple of different guys, but I didn't have enough in common with any of them to feel like doing anything more than that. Especially when I've got so little free time as it is. But my hormones are just fine. Fair enough?"

Rob ate the last bite of his biscuit and washed it down with cool tea. "Fair enough," he said finally. "I just want to be sure if you left the school tomorrow, say, that you'd be as mentally together as we can make you."

"I understand that," Magdalena replied quietly. "I know you can't make me a hundred percent, or make all my years on NewAm just—go away. But since I won't be leaving the school tomorrow . . . I *won't* be, will I?" she asked suddenly. "Ladessa's accident and then talking about David drove everything else out of my mind. You said, a message from Khyriz?"

Rob grinned. "Message from Khyriz, one for each of us. And no, you aren't leaving the school tomorrow, your grades and everything else are well above average, so no, we aren't kicking you out. And no, there's no outbound ship for at least a week, and none headed through Arekkhi space for almost a month."

"Arekkhi space?"

"Message first," Rob said firmly. "Here." He shifted his plate and cup to the other side of the desk and keyed the holo-tank. "I'll start it so you can see the message he sent for me, and then your own, unless you'd rather view it privately."

"Here is fine," she said and sat forward to watch him key the holo-tank. Her eyes went wide as the tank shimmered and Khyriz stood there, life-sized, tall and elegant in his StarBridge jumpsuit. His deep-set, slanting eyes stared into the distance. *My God,* she thought reverently, *he really is as gorgeous as I remember him.* She leaned toward the tank as he began to speak.

"My good friend Dr. Gable, I send this as the time nears for the CLS interrelator and translator to leave StarBridge for my world." *How stilted and unnatural he sounds,* Magdalena thought in surprise. She'd had a couple of taped letters from him since he'd gone home; he hadn't sounded like that at all. "I would like to request a favor of you and the School, to permit Magdalena Perez to also travel on that ship, and visit my world and my home for a short time. As you know, I had hopes she might be chosen as a member of the team . . ." Wide-eyed, she glanced at Rob, then turned back to the holo-tank. She'd missed a few words; Khyriz had begun to pace within the small area marked for taping a letter—very unlike his usual poise. "I understand your reasoning and of course I know the two women chosen. My father and his council will, I think, be pleased.

"But could the School not consider such a journey to be 'fieldwork'? In case there is an opportunity for Magdalena to come to Arekkhi as interrelator or translator at some future date?" His whiskers curved forward in an Arekkhi smile that flattened the upturned corners of his mouth; Magdalena's mouth was suddenly dry. "Since my motive is the very selfish desire to see my good friend once again, and be the one to introduce her to my world, I would, of course, gladly cover the cost of her transportation and any costs of her stay here. As well as the cost of your reply to this message, and any reply Magdalena will care to make to my appended letter to her." He bowed formally—actually an Arekkhi bow didn't involve movement of the back at all, and this particular movement of hands and arms meant, "One who knows little is privileged to salute one of rank and bearing."

The image flickered, then froze as Rob keyed a pause. Magdalena transferred her astonished gaze from the suddenly stilled Khyriz to the psychologist. "Well?" he asked.

"Well?" she echoed blankly, then shook herself. "You mean, the School might actually let me go there?"

"Perhaps something like that," Rob allowed. "You'd like to go?" Magdalena nodded enthusiastically; her eyes sparkled. "Well, then. You heard, just now: Khyriz lobbied pretty hard to get you named translator. And it would've been a good choice, except that you're third year."

She nodded once more. "I know. I didn't even let myself think about it." *Not seriously, anyway,* the wry thought intruded. "But a visit—I don't see how I could take the time, with my classload and tests, and—"

Rob leaned back, made a steeple of his fingers, and eyed her across it. "Say—say that we could work around all that."

"Well"—she drew a deep breath and let it out in a gust— "of *course* I'd love to go! I'd be mad to say no! But—"

"Even if it wasn't just a short visit?"

She considered this, finally sat back in the chair and folded her hands in her lap. "It's what you said earlier, isn't it? Me

being 'gone the next day'—something like that.'' Rob grinned
faintly and shrugged. ''I *thought* there was something, I could
just tell you hadn't said that by accident!''

''Your sixth sense is working just fine,'' he assured her.

Magdalena snorted inelegantly. ''Of course it is—it always
does—''

''Except with David, last night,'' Rob said. She rolled her
eyes ceilingward.

''Honestly, I begin to think I handled that pretty darned
well, Rob. I mean, I didn't freeze or panic or anything, not
when he started getting mushy on me, and not even when he
kissed me. Not until his tongue got too active and his grip too
tight, and even then, I just pulled myself away from him and
told him to cut it out.''

''You did at that,'' he agreed. ''All right. I know you know
a lot about the Arekkhi—your classwork, language study, and,
of course, a lot of time with Khyriz and Shiksara. So you're
probably aware of some of the ongoing political situation.''

''Some,'' she admitted.

''Such as, the Arekkhi aren't at all pleased they weren't
immediately given full CLS status.''

Magdalena got to her feet and carried her cup over to the
food selector, pressing buttons for another cup of tea. Her eyes
strayed toward the holo-tank as the cup filled. ''I know. Plus,
Khyriz told me some of the Council is extremely displeased
about learning they aren't the sole sentient race. Particularly
the Prelate and the more . . . hidebound religious types.''

''Well, you can't blame them—''

''And I don't, of course.'' Magdalena retrieved her cup and
got settled once more. ''They probably see it as the beginning
of the end of their religion, which would put them out of a
job.''

''Good point,'' Rob said, though privately—given her background in that awful, hidebound, NewAm cult—he wondered
if she actually felt that way. Of course, three years of living
among such widely diverse cultures tended to make students
extremely accepting of other religions—and those who came
here in the first place were those who showed a willingness to
deal with differences of all kinds. He shifted his legs, one hand

steadying Bast. "So when the Emperor and Council finally agreed to accept an interrelator—mostly because we made it clear that was the only way they'd get outside trade going—we moved as quickly as we could to set up the team."

Magdalena laughed briefly. "Two human *women*, because the Council assured you they have no problem with females in roles of authority. I roomed with Shiksara last year, remember? She wasn't supposed to admit that Arekkhi females aren't really treated equally, you know—but these things happen."

"We plan on that up here." Rob grinned. "And, of course, the Heeyoons who've spent time on the station have eyes and ears—the Arekkhi couldn't have really hoped to keep it a secret for long. So we decided to call their bluff. And when they took that challenge, we decided that having two females as the entire CLS team will get the Arekkhi used to dealing with all kinds. And, of course, Alexis Ortovsky is tough-minded enough to deal with any macho types she's thrown against. And Ladessa is . . ." He sighed. "Well, that's our problem right now. Ladessa is not going to be able to make that ship three weeks from now; she won't be out of regen for at least twice that long. But after all the fuss and negotiations and hassle back and forth, we absolutely *have* to deliver a team to the Arekkhi. And deliver what and when we promised."

Magdalena's mouth was suddenly dry once more; her eyes flickered toward the image of Khyriz, back to the desk just in front of her. "Um—all right. You're asking—if I can take her place, aren't you?"

Rob nodded. "Exactly that. Wait." He held up a hand as she set her cup aside, the steaming beverage untasted. "Let me give you the pros and cons, then you get a turn. Fair? Number one: You're very qualified." He turned down a finger. "You are good friends with a ranked Prince who has some influence. And this would not need to be a permanent placement, if you found yourself uncomfortable: Ladessa won't be in regen that long, and she could replace you, if necessary."

He paused. She nodded, her face suddenly rather pale. "On the other hand," he went on, "you'd be half of the CLS team; the Heeyoons have had a small trading company on the space station for some time, and there have been Heeyoons on the

royal island—but so far no off-worlders have gotten any farther than the island, and that was just for one brief reception.
So all we know is what we've seen in vid, and what we've
been told.'' He shrugged. Magdalena licked her lips.

"You don't suspect there's anything—''

"Anything wrong? There's no hint of it. We wouldn't be
sending two of our brightest and best there if we thought there
was any chance of trouble. My gut feeling is the Arekkhi government is simply doing what it says: protecting its simpler
and less sophisticated populations from contact with alien
races.''

But Khyriz says lying is a political art form, Magdalena
thought suddenly. *And that few things are what they seem.* She
took a sip of hot tea, letting the warmth loosen her throat. If
Rob thought she was afraid, he might not let her go. *And I'm
not afraid—just a little nervous. Surprised, because he just
sprang this on me. Anyone would be.* Besides, if there was
anything wrong on Arekkhi, Khyriz would have said so, a long
time ago. Shiksara would have.

Rob was probably right. And probably the Emperor and his
Council didn't want the outsiders to see how low-tech the
farming communities were; Khyriz said hardly any labor-
saving inventions made it outside the major cities, and that
most villages had one communication center for everyone—
phone, vid screen, and news channel. Aldwin Cho said his
China of three hundred years ago had been similar, and that
government had had very tight rules about what outsiders got
into the country at all, let alone where they went.

The Council might believe the CLS would consider such
unequal tech a bar to membership. *Maybe if you stay calm, or
at least look it, you'll get the chance to find out,* she told
herself and eased back in the chair. Suddenly, with the opportunity within her grasp, she wanted it more than she would
have thought possible.

"If you go as translator,'' Rob went on, "you'll undoubt-
edly have to be able to work with members of the Council,
talk to the Prelate or other high-ranking religious leaders.
Think you could do that?''

"I . . .'' she considered this briefly, then nodded. "I don't think it would remind me of NewAm. I'm older, after all, and the language is different. I'm not—I wouldn't be one of *them*, or under their thumbs. That ought to make a big difference."

"Mmmm." He was gazing at her thoughtfully, over steepled fingers once more, a finger tapping at the opposite thumb. Nervous energy: Magdalena could feel her nerves buzzing with the same stuff, but she wasn't going to show it if she could help it. *Bless all those weeks and months of dance, I can keep absolutely still without thinking about it.* "Of course," he said, "Alexis will be the one primarily involved with the governing bodies, but often the translator winds up assuming any duties the interrelator doesn't have time for."

"I know. As long as someone tells me what I'm supposed to be doing, I should be okay," she replied with a faint smile.

"You'd be a long way from the School," Rob added.

"Well, but we all expect that," she said, and took another sip of tea.

"True. And, of course, there's the construction and tech crew out working on the jump-point station; they're only a couple of days' travel from the planet. And there are Hee-yoons on the inner-system space station—I knew there was something else." He snapped his fingers; Bast made a low, grumbling noise, then subsided again. "You remember Silvermuzzle?"

Magdalena nodded. "Graduated last year, went back to Arrouhl, his homeworld, to write up Professor Greyshine's notes on that dig here."

"Well, he's finished that project and his family's sending him to Arekkhi; in another month or so, he'll be on the station, working on trade agreements."

"And there's always Dana," she reminded him. "You know: Dana Marshall, pilot and tech expert. She's two years older than I but we get on great; I heard from her just before the CLS sent her to the jump point station to get the communications network up."

"I'd forgotten about that."

"She'll be there a while, if I need more human company. But I bet I won't have time to feel lonely. I like Alexis, after all. And I won't feel out of place. There's Khyriz, and Shiksara's told me so much about her family that I already feel I know them.''

''Mmmmm.'' Rob stared off into the middle distance, over her head; Magdalena found she was holding her breath. *If he decides not to let me go . . . !* When the psychologist cleared his throat, she jumped. ''Tell you what,'' he said finally. ''I made a couple of FTL calls to Shassiszss Station before you got here—because of the unusual circumstances—and they told me that it's my decision, to send you or not.'' Another silence.

She slid forward, onto the edge of the chair. ''Do you want my input?'' *I can't believe I'm talking like this! Like—like I could convince him if he's already wavering, or something!* But her voice sounded just fine—neither scared nor excited. ''My feelings?''

''Sure,'' he replied, his voice noncommittal, but his eyebrows went up as she drew herself straight and began ticking off points with the fingers of her right hand, the way he had. It wasn't lost on him; he eyed her fingers, then winked.

Magdalena grinned, briefly relaxed. ''Well, then. You can send Alexis by herself for the time being, but since it's a new post, that would be an awful lot of extra pressure on her. You could ask the Arekkhi to wait for their team until Ladessa's well enough to travel, maybe let her finish her physical therapy on the ship, but it sounds to me as if the Council would see the delay as an insult, another indication that they're a second-class world. And that would make *more* problems for the interrelator when she finally arrives.''

Rob's eyebrows went up. ''Good point,'' he conceded.

''You could find someone else to send as translator, but there are only so many beings here who speak Arekkhi with fair fluency, and only a handful of us who are fluent in language, gesture, intonation, and movement—dance. Silvermuzzle was good before he left, but he's been away from it awhile, he'd be rusty. And he's got two left feet, unfortunately. And''—she shrugged—''I suppose you could send someone with a lot of skill at diplomacy *and* a voder, but a voder isn't good for movement, which is a whole major part of their language. Voders aren't great at the subtler bits of intonation shift, either, not with the Arekkhi language.'' She considered this; fought the urge to say something else that would probably sound rambling and disorganized at best, and desperate to go at worse. *Rob is in charge of a very serious decision here; he won't let you go just because you really want to and Khyriz wants you there.*

''Good points,'' he said finally. ''And, of course, we do have Ladessa to send in after her regen, if you feel uncomfortable, or in over your head. At the very worst, it would be a six-month hiatus from classes. Including ballet,'' he added with a wicked smile. ''And David. . . .''

Magdalena cast her eyes up. ''Sure, tempt me,'' she mumbled.

''You're aware Madame intends to send vid of last night's performances to several of the touring dance companies?''

''I—knew that. She told us at the pre–dress rehearsal. I—understand, I'd be very flattered to be asked to join a dance troupe. But I know I haven't had enough years to be *that* level of good.'' She smiled faintly. ''I know about Rudolf Nureyev, I've seen Madame's vid of his *Romeo,* and I know he didn't even start ballet classes until he was fifteen, but he was an exception. A prodigy.''

''You might be, Magdalena.''

She shook her head firmly. ''No—much as I'd like to think so, I know I'd wind up doing the third-act solos: Dancing the Bluebird or the Sugar Plum Fairy and getting paid for it would be nice, but . . .'' She sighed. ''Remember how I decided to take the StarBridge tests, back on NewAm? The Heeyoons had just discovered the Arekkhi, and there was a piece of vid of a high lord from their council. I—think I fell in love with the idea of the Arekkhi right then. The sound of the language, the way he moved. And after all NewAm did for me, getting me here; after all the school's done for me . . .''

''Don't base a decision on gratitude, Magdalena,'' Rob said as she hesitated.

''I'm not. Dance has been . . . wonderful. I'll keep doing all that I can with it. But the chance to go to Arekkhi as a translator, even if it's only for six months—it's been my dream for at least four years, Rob, and I've worked hard to see that I could handle the pressures if I ever got the chance." Silence. Rob finally got to his feet, gesturing for her to take his place behind the desk. Magdalena came around and sat, waited for him to cue the tank's privacy field and let the message continue.

Khyriz's gaze remained distant, his body unnaturally stiff. "If there is any way for us to manage this, Dr. Rob, I would greatly appreciate it. The remainder of this message is for Magdalena, but it is not of *that* degree of privacy." A momentary pause; then Khyriz took a step toward the holo-vid camera, his eyes suddenly warm, whiskers curved forward until they nearly touched; his Mizari rumbled, barely accented, tickling her ears. "Magdalena, my dear friend, if you have seen Rob's portion of this message, you know my hope. I know you have often said you would gladly journey here. If my fortune holds, perhaps we shall see each other before the winter rains. Remember, the Grand Autumn Ball will this year be in honor of the CLS staff. I would be proud to escort you onto the floor of my fathers to dance the Xherniz. Perhaps, another moment when we dance?" His ears flicked slightly— one of his shy moments, she thought. Her face felt warm as the holo stilled. *The fur along his chin, there—I remember it pressing against my face, up in the Spiral Arm.* Her face was warm as she finally remembered to clear the privacy screen.

"All right?" Rob asked. He came from the food servo with two fresh cups of tea, set one before her, and leaned against the wall to sip his. She nodded, drank tea. "You look a little flustered."

"It's—all so sudden," she managed. "Unexpected."

"Need more time to think?" he asked. She shook her head firmly and he laughed. "No, I didn't think you did." They drank in companionable silence, then Magdalena put her cup down and got to her feet.

"I have that test—"

"Excused for now," Rob broke in gravely. "You won't be able to concentrate right now, and there isn't much time between now and your departure to get everything done you'll need to do. You and Alexis get together as soon as you can;

anything you need help with, any concerns you have—let me know right away, will you?''

"Of course. I just—well, what if everything goes well, and I wind up staying? I mean, poor Ladessa, all the preparation she's done for the Arekkhi, and now . . .''

"A week or so ago, that might've been the case,'' Rob said as he eased past to let her into the outer office. "But since then, she's had an offer from Etsane Mwarka on the Na-Dina homeworld, to assist with the translations on those tomb walls. Ladessa met Etsane back on Earth, some student tour, and they hit it off pretty well; enough that she started following the Na-Dina digs closely when she heard Etsane had transferred there.''

Magdalena felt a shiver slip down her backbone as she eased into the hall, wedged in the between-classes press of students among three Drnians and a first-year Heeyoon trying to keep up with his companion's rapid Portuguese.

Everything's happening so fast—and just as if it were meant, she thought, and headed back in the direction of her room. A smile curved her lips as she reached the door and let herself in. "When we dance,'' she whispered. Trust Khyriz to remind her of that lush, wonderful piece of music she'd used to teach him to slow-dance, human-style. Just the opportunity to see him again, and so soon . . .

The smile slipped; nerves tightened her stomach. "I'm going to Arekkhi as Alexis Ortovsky's second-in-command; it won't even be a month, and StarBridge will be behind me for the next half a year, at least.'' Who was she kidding, telling Rob she could handle something like this? "Oh, God, what have I done to myself?''

And something else—that message, a full holo-vid letter. But Khyriz had always sent her voice-only up until now, and the last she'd heard there was still no way to send holo-vid, because the Emperor wasn't allowing the units in yet. The only holo-vid would be with the Heeyoons on-station, if they had it. Otherwise—clear out to the new jump site. She frowned, sat on the low couch, her fingers drumming the table. "He went off-planet, just to send that message? But why?''

Maybe he just thought he stood a better chance of persuading her, if she could see him. But it didn't *feel* that way. Something felt . . . wrong.

Alone in his office, Rob stared fixedly at the door Magdalena had just closed behind her, not really seeing it. "Something feels wrong," he told Bast. "Not wrong enough to hold the girl back. But . . ." He frowned, drained the last drops of tea from his cup. *But what?*

For a moment he wondered if Magdalena had reacted to the mention of Alexis and her preferences, but . . . no. Magdalena had been incredibly naive when she first came to StarBridge at age fifteen, so many of her opinions influenced by that wretched NewAm cult . . . and so even though she'd openly embraced the different alien races on StarBridge, she'd been shocked speechless the first time she saw two boys walking hand in hand down the hall. But Magdalena was adaptable, and she'd been able to learn tolerance and acceptance. She'd been able to quickly separate what Solomon Smith had taught those poor captive children, and what her own instincts told her about love.

The incident she'd described last night with David—that still left him a little uneasy, but he tended to side with Magdalena on that one: She'd been too involved in the upcoming recitals to pay much attention to the emotional state of the people around her, and she was literal-minded enough that when David said "friends" or even "special friends," she'd assumed he meant exactly that. If the circumstances last night were as she described them, with David forcing the issue, then she'd actually done very well—for Magdalena Perez.

But there's something . . . He finally shook his head and got to his feet, cup in hand. "Bast, she really lit up when Khyriz was talking to her. You don't suppose . . ." He considered this, then chuckled. Bast stirred, made a faint, protesting little sound, curled back into a circle, and slept. Rob shook his head again, then checked his com to see what other appointments his morning held.

CHAPTER 3

♦

The Emperor's morning room was located where it would be close to both the royal apartments and Council chambers. It faced south, taking advantage of winter sun and a view of the water. During the heat of summer, however, the room was shuttered, and on this day ancient wrought metal lamps shone on a plain table and two long benches. The Emperor sat in a pool of yellowish light, dexterously working two cross-hilted forks through a long, bony fish. Across the table from him, Khyriz drank pale, watered jhuris-wine and tore a chunk of seed-bread into increasingly small bits.

He hadn't slept much the past two nights due to outside activities. And when he'd tried to relax, he couldn't—too much anticipation. The CLS ship had passed the new jump-point station and would dock late today. *So much changed when I went out to StarBridge. And again when I returned. And now. . . .*

In just a few hours, she would step onto the Arekkhi station. . . . *They both will,* he reminded himself sternly.

Unfortunately, he wouldn't be the one meeting them; his father had just informed him of that fact. Disappointing, though hardly surprising. Still . . . "Why?" he asked. The question would be expected.

Khezahn looked up from his fish, chewed meat, and spat tiny bones into the bone-bowl, then crossed his forks on the platter before replying. "It was my decision as much as the main Council's," he said finally. His voice was unexpectedly high-pitched and reedy for a male of his size and station.

Khyriz flicked one ear, letting disappointment show. "I know you prefer to keep your offspring on-planet, but—"

"Accidents happen," the Emperor broke in. Both Khyriz's ears went flat: His father seldom interrupted him. "But it is a matter of appearance: The Council is displeased that you appear to care more for the Academy and your outside acquaintances than for your own kind. Particularly since these females will soon live in the old palace." His gaze fixed on his son's right hand, and the small, bright bit of red enamel fixed to his freshly blunted thumbnail. Khyriz glanced at the tiny adornment—only he knew of the inner workings that made it a sophisticated spy-device locator.

The Prince spread his hands in a shrug. "It was a gift from the translator-she Magdalena," he said stiffly. "If another Arekkhi had given it to me, it would be a breach of manners *not* to wear it."

"I know Arekkhi customs," the Emperor said with a growl and Khyriz, startled, fell silent. The elder royal ate fish, sipped his jhuris, spat bones. "Khyriz," he said finally, "I am not angry with you, though many of the Council are."

Khyriz gestured sharply to his right with one hand, the Arekkhi equivalent of a human nod. "I know. They believe I deliberately failed them, at StarBridge. But Father, the Academy is nothing like they envisioned! Nor are the other beings who run the Academy as—as—"

"As stupid as some of the Council believe?" The elder Arekkhi's whiskers curved forward in a sharp, brief smile. "They don't really believe that, you know. They merely hoped. Few of them really thought you would provide us with the technology we need to be seen as their equals, Khyriz."

"Then why . . . ?" He couldn't complete the thought; memory of that session in the closed Council chamber, all those hooded figures, still gave him nightmares, from time to time.

"Because it is hard to see something unacceptable, and not attempt to deal with it," Khezahn replied. Khyriz went very still, wondering if somehow his own deepest secret had somehow been found out. But the older male's next words reassured him. "Change is hard, especially on the elder of us. Many on the Council fear the outsiders and their influence." A dark eye fixed once more on his youngest son.

Khyriz privately doubted the *zhez* Zhenu had ever feared anything in his life, but he kept that to himself. "I could not make myself steal and sneak as they ordered, Father; you should know that much. I did not want to. Furthermore, I have no skills for such spywork; I would surely have been caught at once. And sent home in disgrace . . . much sooner than I was recalled. But so much study was required of the students, there was no time to even think of how to begin such thievery, let alone carry it out." He stared down at his blunt-nailed, cream-furred hands; his father waited. "And yes," he added in quiet defiance, "I *did* like the outsiders. I do, still."

"I could tell as much from the first day you returned home, if not before that. We are talking of appearances, however." The younger male kept his eyes fixed on his hands, to hide his astonishment. His father had *never* stressed the importance of appearances, unlike the fathers of his contemporaries—or the Council. *Has he fallen completely under their influence?* Khyriz wondered, suddenly afraid. If his father were to actually become the mask-faced Emperor who had sat silent in the secret chamber while the inner Council bullied him . . . ! But his father now spoke, suddenly, in a much lower voice. *As if he fears a listener on this chamber,* he realized, and his eyes flicked toward the nail-gem. No sign. He didn't dare tell his father so, of course.

The Emperor shoved his half-eaten fish aside, whiskers quivering with sudden distaste. "Khyriz." He paused, then lowered his voice even more. "I have carefully kept you from the inner workings of our politics. But it is time you know: The current Council is not all of my choosing."

Khyriz fought the urge to stare. Such a confidence was new and a little unnerving, especially when matched with the expression on his father's face. *Say something,* he ordered himself. "I know a little," he managed. "The Prelate and the Iron—and Duke Zhenu were appointed by my grandsire—"

"And your grandsire died young, leaving his eldest son—me—to assume the Arekkhi throne at least ten years before such an event would normally happen," the Emperor finished for him. His whiskers flicked forward and his eyes narrowed in a brief, abashed smile. "The Prelate and his advisers terrified me as a youth. And your cousin Zhik's father is no one to challenge."

Khyriz kept his own voice prudently low—the room might not be "bugged," as Dr. Rob's movie-actors would say, but servants came and went; any of them could be in the pay of the Prelate. Or the Iron Duke, as Khyriz privately called Zhenu. "But, Father, it is *your* Council, not the other way around! The Emperor's word has always carried, no matter what the vote of the nobles and religious leaders!"

"My Council, yes. And technically, the vote of either Council carries no weight. In reality—well, unfortunately, your grandsire never kept an army or even company of militia. Not even an armed household guard. He was a miserly old brute." The Emperor's whiskers flicked forward in a brief, fond smile. "Guards cost money."

Khyriz knew that as well; but the question would be expected: "Guards? I—know the Prelate has an honor guard. . . ."

"Fully armed, as is Lord Zhenu's militia. No threat is ever spoken, of course; but both Zhenu and our religious father know that I know their soldiers could overwhelm the palace at a moment's notice, once they reached this island."

"That is—unspeakable," Khyriz finally managed.

"No, my son. Unpleasant, rather. And you should also know, your brother Khelyu is working hard and in secret to increase the numbers of armed palace protection here, on the island, and about the planet. Everywhere. Still, my troops are outnumbered by those of the Prelate and Zhenu. And since they employ good spies, they both know it."

"They—surely, Father, they do not threaten you?"

The Emperor gestured a broad, harassed shrug. "No. They need not; they hold superior numbers. Also, they know I will never risk harm to our people by sending my forces against theirs in open combat."

"Civil war," Khyriz breathed, his ears flat to his skull. The Emperor cast him a sympathetic glance. "Not in my lifetime, nor yours, if we are cautious, son. The last such was more than enough. Zhenu and the Prelate will not openly cause such war, either—though more because of the outside worlds. Appearances, remember?''

''But if they believed themselves right, would appearances matter?''

''Perhaps. I hope so. Khyriz—do you ever wonder why I employed the best history tutors for you?''

''I . . . no. Why?'' He knew, but the question would be expected.

''Because violence in our history has always come from those who know nothing of their own past. The last Civil War, a hundred years ago, began when the controlling nobles repressed the lower ranks, who then rebelled. This threatened the Emperor's control; he quelled the uprisings and the nobles, but his coffers were quickly drained by his own armies, and then the Prelate's forces took control. In the end, the Emperor won—but a weakened Emperor. You know the result of *that*, Khyriz.''

''Yes.'' Certain of the lower classes had eventually regained their proper place in Arekkhi society. Others had not. *Do not think about them, not here.* Even a slight body movement or change of expression might give his thoughts away; his father was a master reader of such things. *I could tell him—I believe I could. But he has his own problems. And—if I misread him?* No. Too much rode on common knowledge that the youngest Prince was nonpolitical and interested only in his estates, his clothing . . . and the outsiders.

Khezahn was following his own thoughts. ''Most of the nobles loathed the Prelate of that day more than their Emperor, which was the only reason the Emperor's forces won. But because the war made great rifts—and because many such ancient hatreds still exist—the question of Asha has never been resolved. And now it has returned to haunt your father.''

''Haunt? Why, Father?'' Khyriz knew, of course, but the matter was supposed to be a Council secret. His father would expect the question.

''You know, of course, that several rebel groups have sprung up—out-of-the-way places such as Mibhor, and the back highlands of Akkherif.'' He glanced at Khyriz, who ges-

tured an affirmative. The Prince knew of at least two rebel
groups who did what they could to resolve the question of
Asha—either by killing them off, or by rescuing them. Best if
he showed no interest, either way. "At best, the matter of Asha
is a shameful secret. And a difficult one to hide; especially in
such outlying regions," the Emperor went on. "And it's tied
to the outsiders. It's common knowledge that the Prelate would
destroy the new jump station and order the Heeyoons and their
trading company from our space if he could. But others on the
Council see the wealth promised by outside trade; even Zhenu
sees the promised wealth as a positive factor, and counsels
Nijho to press for no sudden decision against the outsiders.
Since he is behind funding for the armed who would fight for
the Prelatry, Nijho must at least appear to agree with him.

"I try to argue for common sense. If we trade with the
outsiders, accept their system of integration, find a way to
become an associate member of their League, learn what is
out there and how to deal with it—see what we as Arekkhi
can contribute . . ." Khezahn paused. "We who urge common
sense are more voices than you might think, Khyriz . . . but not
enough."

"Father—I—I didn't know," Kyriz faltered. "Apologies."

"You weren't supposed to know," the Emperor replied quietly. "And remember that events discussed in secret Council
are never to see light outside that chamber. But discussions in
regular Council are likewise sealed—on this subject." *He's
reminding me to keep my mouth closed,* Khyriz decided.
"Also, you should know that Zhenu and the Prelate—and
those they could bring to a temporary alliance wanted to banish
you to your estates, hold you in communicado, until they
found a way to expel the CLS. That notion was so extreme,
even Zhenu couldn't hold it together, but I doubt he will give
up all hope of that."

Khyriz realized he was staring once more. "Father—if the
CLS pulled out of Arekkhi space entirely . . . !"

". . . then many of us would be greatly displeased, but Prelate Nijho would not be one. I think, Zhenu would not, either.
He is so wealthy already, I doubt he would note the increase
to his purse from outside trade. But no one, except perhaps

Nijho, knows what Zhenu wants." The elder glanced at his son. "The CLS will remain here, at least for now. And I am working to gain allies in council so the threat posed by the Duke and the Prelate is entirely removed. But this returns us to the CLS, and appearances. Khyriz, I told the Council I would speak with you about your attention to the outsiders. I have. I did not say I would put restrictions on you, and I will not. However, *if* you appear to act in such a way, then the Council will be appeased."

Khyriz gestured assent, and fought to keep his whiskers from going flat. "I . . . understand. Father, I shall."

"Good. You are the most intelligent and open-minded of my offspring, Khryiz. I . . . you should also know this: Since the Heeyoons came, the Prelate has raised the problem of Asha"—the older Arekkhi hesitated—"insisting we must destroy them all."

"Kill . . . ?" Khyriz stared, his ears now as flat as his whiskers.

"Essentially. Compose yourself!" The Emperor ordered sternly. His son forced ears partially erect. "Good. I understand the shock this gives you." He turned away from the table, yellow and brown patterned royal silk swirling, then settling in smooth folds. Khyriz watched him, still stunned. *How long has he known this, and kept it secret?* "As much a shock," the Emperor went on, "as when I learned by happenstance that Nijho would add *xezzik* to the water given to all Asha, along with the *ephana* worker-Asha are all already fed."

Xezzik—mind destroyer. Khyriz fought for control, but the very thought of the drug that created ahla-Asha and ahla-Arekkhi had the power to make him ill. The voice-killing *ephana* was bad enough!

The Emperor gazed long and searchingly at his son, who could find no words to say. "The drugs will not be so misused. Once I have sufficient allies, and enough armed, the stores of those drugs will be destroyed. Believe that, Khyriz." His father's ears quivered. *He likes this no better than I, Khyriz realized.* Impulsively, the Prince held out his hands.

"I do believe it. I want the same thing, Father." But if his father's count of allies was wrong! Changes of alliance were common among high-ranked Arekkhi. Like Zhenu. "Zhenu," he said aloud. "I never trusted him! If he plots treachery . . . !"

He hadn't realized such behavior was more than proof of a lack in the Arekkhi people, until Magdalena Perez had taught him something of Renaissance and post-Renaissance Earth European history. Manipulation, treachery, religious warfare, marriages for political gain, assassinations, circles within circles: Since those few sessions with Magdalena, he'd thought of his cousin's abusive, arrogant father as the English Iron Duke—Zhenu was, to him, very like the narrow and chill-hearted leader Cromwell, who'd battled to destroy a pleasant way of life, and behead a king.

Magdalena. *My Magdalena.* She was so near. But he dared not think of *her*, either. If his father knew his immediate thoughts, he'd have cause for concern. The Emperor didn't need the distraction. *Any more than I need to explain it or even examine it.*

His father was talking to him, his voice again at normal pitch. "I just want you to realize that matters are difficult at present, and more complex than you realized; I do not need arguments with either council over you." Anxious eyes met his.

Khyriz directed his gaze toward the floor and flattened one ear in token of submission. "Of course, Father. I won't go to the station to greet the outsiders. But"—he hesitated briefly, as if the idea were only just occurring to him—"if I might suggest that we send the pilot you hired for me, Bhelan? He flies into my estate, after all, even in the worst weather. He is one of the best we have."

"I thought my own pilot—" the Emperor began.

"But you never travel in adverse weather, Father," Khyriz replied smoothly. "And your pilot seldom has reason to leave Arekkhi atmosphere. One doesn't anticipate any problem on the descent from station, but in case . . ." He only just managed not to hold his breath as the Emperor considered this, then finally gave assent. A moment later, Khyriz had the small chamber to himself.

No need for his father to know that he himself flew the shuttle under the former actor's guidance more than Bhelan flew it himself. Or need for his father or anyone else to know that the two males had become firm allies: Bhelan's many-times-father had fought the Civil War among other impoverished Arekkhi tenant-farmers and their Asha coworkers; Bhelan was proud of the martyr's memory—and willing to aid Khyriz *now*.

I have coached him well, Khyriz reminded himself, *he knows what emotion to show, what answers to give. Magdalena may well wonder, but that is as it should be. . . .*

Khyriz left the breakfast room and turned left, heading for his old rooms; his mother, the Empress Neoha, had the tiny bedroom kept ready for him always, though he'd maintained a small suite of apartments on the top floor of the Old Palace for his rare visits here. From that squat, ancient building he could come and go as he chose.

His whiskers curved slightly as he stepped onto the moving walk that would take him most of the way to the family's wing. Amazing, how naive he'd been before StarBridge: unaware of the secret layers of government and astonished to learn how many of the ancient rumors were true. He'd been almost trembling in his new hide boots the day he walked onto the Heeyoon ship that would take him to the Academy: How could he dare obey the inner Council—but what if he didn't? And if he dared tell the StarBridge authorities what his people demanded of him? Nightmares had plagued him the entire journey: visions of the advisers at StarBridge deciding he was mad and sending him straight home. Or believing him, but then isolating the Arekkhi and informing them why, only *then* sending their unwanted Prince home . . .

You did the best you could, under the circumstances, he assured himself. The Council hadn't been overly pleased with his silence, his dearth of "secret" information, but they'd let him have nearly two years away. In that time he'd found friends and allies, something he'd never considered possible. *How could I have known there'd be a Rob Gable, a Mahree Burroughs?*

How could anyone have imagined Magdalena Perez? She *knew* about peoples like his. Her planet's history was rife with

times when government was all-controlling, when lying was
an art form, where manipulation was so much a part of daily
life. . . .

At least Arekkhi weren't as violent as much of human history. Not always . . .

Khyriz discovered that Bhelan was not in the Prince's old
bedroom. The Prince waited for some time, then decided to
head toward his personal flitter, in case they'd missed one
another: In a building that sprawled the way this one did, such
things often happened.

The pilot, Bhelan, had in fact been on his way to meet Khyriz,
when without warning a heavy hand gripped his forearm and
another covered his mouth. Before he could react, he was
jerked back against a muscular body, pulled off the moving
walk, and hustled into a small, dark storage room. The door
slammed, then locked behind him.

Bhelan cried out as his assailant shoved him against the wall
and held him there. As the light sensor adjusted, the pilot could
make out baskets piled high with pillows and shelves of body
cloths, and then the short, squatty form of Ulfar, Duke Zhenu's
favorite bodyguard. The solidly built male gazed up at him,
eyes all pupil, incisors bared in a mirthless grimace—a killing
face, doubly terrifying in this scarred male. "A message for
you, pilot," he murmured softly.

"Message" Bhelan repeated unsteadily. A steel fighting
talon tapped casually against his face; he closed his mouth at
once. The deadly bits of metal were formed to fit over blunted
claws, held in place with adhesive; they had been outlawed
for centuries, almost as long as real claws had been named
illegal weaponry. Bhelan tried to force his eyes away from it;
Ulfar's whiskers flicked forward as he pulled his hand back,
letting the room's dim light flicker on the shining, deadly
weapon.

"Be still, listen," Ulfar whispered. "The young Prince is
no protector for you and your kin, nor are the alien females
who arrive today. We know Khyriz will go himself or send
you to retrieve them. We know your family history, and your
family's softness for Asha." Silence. The back of the fighting

talon slid smoothly over his cheekbone—turned, it could lay
his face open, or kill him. Ulfar eyed him for a moment, then,
apparently satisfied, stepped back a pace. "You will say nothing to the aliens that might arouse suspicion. They will not
learn how to fly our ships, not from you. Nothing of our politics—nothing of Asha, not even the word."

Silence. *He wants me to say something,* Bhelan realized; but
his throat was too dry for sound. He let his gaze slip briefly
down and away, submissively; shame heated his skin. Ulfar
bared his teeth, then said, "Martyr yourself for the young
Prince if you will—but then your family is dead as well. But
not as quickly or easily as this—" Bhelan cowered back in-
voluntarily as the talon flashed past his eyes and flipped his
right whiskers forward, travesty of a lover's gesture. "Say
nothing! Remember . . . who is the strong one? Your young
Prince, the Emperor—or Lord *Zhez* Zhenu? Obey Zhenu, and
live—for now." Before the pilot could even draw breath, the
bodyguard was gone, the door closing silently behind him.

Bhelan stood very still. *Let him get some distance from here,
before you step out,* he told himself; in honesty, he needed the
time to get his shaking body and his face under control.

When he finally did ease the door aside and step into the
corridor, the walkway was moving, sign someone stood on it—
but when he would have jerked back into hiding, Khyriz came
into sight from the direction of the royal vehicle-storage. The
Prince's eyes met his, widened as he moved off the walk and
Bhelan took a step into the open. When the pilot would have
spoken, Khyriz flicked a hand and an ear in their private code:
Not here; someone may be listening. It was primitive, but all
Bhelan could have interpreted at the moment. He made an
alien nod of assent, then followed Khyriz back to the walkway.
Two steps along the carpeted platform gave the sensors direction; Bhelan concentrated on getting his breathing back near
normal, until they descended into the covered and guarded
storage area, and gained entry to Khyriz's enclosed vehicle.

The Prince settled into the nearest passenger bench, pressed
the controls that would seal the car, start the atmosphere-
adjusters and darken the glass; as Bhelan settled onto the
pilot's padded and high-backed seat, Khyriz pressed the en-

ameled outsider device and hissed in the foreign tongue he'd
called Mizari. The air in the fore cabin crackled; both males
felt their short, sleek fur stand on end as the energy field activated. It would prevent any Arekkhi spy device from over-
hearing them.

Khyriz touched his pilot's hand. "Something went wrong,"
he said quietly.

"I . . . yes," Bhelan managed. His voice sounded high and
thin to his own ears. "Ulfar—he had a talon. He said—"

"No," Khyriz broke in when it became clear his companion
couldn't speak. "Don't say it, I understand. Ulfar without a
talon is frightening enough."

"Threats," Bhelan said finally. "Against you, me, the outsider women, my family . . ."

"As I feared," Khyriz murmured. "But we expected this
from the first, the threat if not the form it would take. My
friend, this changes matters, a little. They have shifted the
odds, nothing more; we will match the wager. Let me off outside the old palace, take the flitter straight to the shuttle-field
and launch as soon as you can. Once I reach the safe-room,
I'll put a shielded-frequency call to my estate manager. As
soon as you reach orbit, call and I'll pass on what Lijahr can
tell us."

Shielded frequency. Safe-room. The outsider devices that
allowed Khyriz to make audio-calls without using Arekkhi
wires, and the shield on the barren little chamber that supposedly kept it both protected from Arekkhi spy devices—*and*
unnoticed by them. Such things felt all at once like magical
toys from old tales. "You're certain . . . ?" Bhelan began nervously.

Khyriz gave him an outsider nod. "My friend, I *am* certain.
The distance-speakers bounce their signals off the outer wall
of the station *and* off the second moon before reaching my
estate, and my First of House. Even if Arekkhi tech could
match the path of the signal, they'd never be able to follow
the unpatterned shifts in frequency. And both units—mine and
Lijahr's—are sealed against spying of any sort."

"I'm . . . sorry."

"Don't be sorry, Bhelan. Father's Council is years wiser

than we are, so far as intrigue is concerned—but thanks to my
years at the Academy, our side has an advantage in technology.''

"It won't save either of us if the Council moves against
us.''

"No." Khyriz's whiskers flicked toward his cheekbones. *He
is afraid,* Bhelan realized. *But he still goes on, and tries not
to show his fear.* "But someone has to oppose them. Father
confirmed to me today that if he could, Zhenu and the Prelate
would eliminate every single Asha from Arekkhi soil. Against
a need like that . . ." His eyes slid sideways in embarrassment.
"Well, the age-old heroes and gods must still be asleep, so it
is up to the rest of us, isn't it? And at least your family and
their farm-tenants are safe. I had a very short confirming message from Lijahr before I went to eat first-meal with Father.
All safe.''

"I . . . thank you, sir," Bhelan said formally.

"Not 'sir'," Khyriz replied with a smile. "We are equally
at risk here, after all. Now: What else did the Iron Duke's
Butcher say to you?''

"To lie to the alien females about the ship, Arekkhi, Asha,
language . . .''

"And who better suited than Bhelan, the actor?" Khyriz
spatted a sour little laugh. "Poor Ulfar! He knows nothing of
anything beyond Arekkhi space, does he? Still, Bhelan: I know
you can act—not just in the life-vids or in the ancient plays,
but anywhere that you must. So"—his whiskers touched—"as
my friend Alexis would say, 'these precepts in thy ear.' ''

The pilot eyed him sidelong; Khyriz had shifted into Old
Earth English, of which the actor understood barely a hundred
words. Khyriz's whiskers and ear tufts quivered. "It's an ancient human play, Bhelan. About a tragic prince who dithers
over his choices while dire events occur all around him and
eventually kill him. I think you would like the plays of this
Shakespeare; in fact, I'll have a copy translated for you, somehow—I owe you so much, my good friend. But"—the Prince
became suddenly very sober indeed—"apologies. I needed a
moment such as that. I meant to say, let me suggest to you
various things you might do, under certain circumstances.''

"Oh . . . of course." Bhelan glanced to both sides of the closed-up vehicle, then down at the gauges; the air was heating up, and besides, anyone watching the flitter would have expected it to lift off its padded blocks and move out by now. He flicked switches, spoke into the voice-tube—it took two commands for the thing to start up and the air cushion to lift it—then spoke again to turn the flitter toward the old palace.

"Nothing difficult to remember," Khyriz assured him as they emerged into bright early-morning sun. "For now, because it suits us, we will play Zhenu's game. Be careful. The CLS translator, the dark woman, will know if you lie to her, or if you attempt to misdirect her. She's sensitive to such things. You must be subtle. . . ."

"But not too subtle," Bhelan replied as Khyriz hesitated.

"Just so. The other, the female with pale hair, Interrelator Ortovsky—she's extremely clever and she knows Arekkhi well. Not just our language, but as much of our ways as she could learn away from our world."

"What of Shiksara? Will she be with them?" Bhelan eased the flitter across paved grounds toward the three-story building that had once been the Emperor's palace and now housed the clerical staff, the enormous blocks of underground computer equipment that ran the planet's vid, audio, and other communication devices, as well as private apartments for a few nobles and minor royals who held a presence on the island year-round. Khyriz kept a suite here; Zhikna had recently been granted a very small set of rooms. The new CLS team had been assigned the entire middle floor.

Khyriz smiled, a faint forward movement of whiskers. "Don't worry about Shiksara; I know your family bought goods from hers, and you count her a friend. She has another year to go at StarBridge . . . and she may not come home even then."

"No?" Despite his best effort to remain dispassionate, Bhelan could hear the concern in his voice; Shiksara and he had both been round-eared cubs when they'd first met.

"No," Khyriz said firmly. "She wants to do some translating . . . Mizari and other ancient tales to our language, perhaps some of our tales to their languages. She'll be safe there, never fear. Though she has done nothing to let Zhenu believe she's said one word he did not dictate."

Safe, the pilot thought as he eased the multifunction flitter above the ground cover, pausing only long enough to let Khyriz out a few paces from the old palace. His face was grim as he sealed the door and turned the machine toward open water, gaining altitude so he could reach the shuttle field as quickly as possible. *Would that we could all be safe. . . .*

Two hours out from the Arekkhi station, a midsized, alien cargo and passenger ship slowed and began the first of several maneuvers that would bring it into one of two recently built ports designed to berth outsider vessels. Magdalena felt the change in engine strength through the soles of her pink-slippered feet and stared at her companion. Alexis Ortovsky, who'd put in considerably more hours in space than the translator, smiled and shook her head.

"No sweat; they warn you if something goes wrong." Not always true, but it was a useful lie. "We're getting close to the station—but they'll warn us about that, too." Magdalena sighed with relief and reset the music cube she held in her right hand, then settled her shoulders against the bulkhead and sat cross-legged on the small bench seat, giving Alexis what floor space there was. Even with the beds tipped up and latched against the white-painted walls, and the two shelves removed and slid into the tiny head, Alexis had just enough room to manage four steps in any direction. Small steps.

Ordinarily, the two women held dance practice in the corridor, but at this hour the crew needed that space.

Reedy, bouncy Arekkhi music began again; Magdalena nodded vigorously for her companion to begin, then counted off beats with an upraised hand.

"Three, four—right arm high, back, step-step-step, to the side, bring the arm down—and—that's good! You got it!" She silently applauded the interrelator, who grinned up at her triumphantly. "I told you that you'd make sense of it," she added as the music repeated itself.

"I had a very good teacher," Alexis replied; she shoved loose strands of damp, pale hair off her temples and behind her ears. "Too bad you had such a lousy student." She grinned ruefully.

Magdalena laughed. "You do just fine. Except for Khyriz, the Arekkhi won't expect either of us to know which foot is which, remember?"

"Just as well in my case," Alexis said. The jigging little dance concluded and the cube clicked off. Magdalena crossed to the head, shoved the cube into her small carryall, and sealed the top. She resisted—barely—the urge to ask "Well, now what?"

Two more hours at least before they'd dock. Their personal bags were packed and set aside, taking up most of the space between the tiny shower and the toilet, and the room neatened. The only other passengers the entire voyage had been three electrical techs (two Jolie humans and a Heeyoon wearing an old-fashioned voder) who had mostly talked techie jargon, among themselves. They'd been set down at the half-completed jump-point station three days ago. The small ship's crew—humans who'd worked together for the past ten standard years—were entirely too busy at the moment to be any company.

Magdalena privately thought Alexis had invented the glitch in her memory on how to start the giguelike Eglidha dance, solely to give her translator something to do. Alexis had the kind of mind that picked things up quickly and retained nearly everything. "I don't envy you," the interrelator went on, "trying to teach a squatty broad like me to be graceful." The dancer merely laughed and waved a hand at her.

Alexis Ortovsky was short—not much above five feet by the old Earth-style measure Solomon Smith's cult had used. Solidly built like the athlete she was, Alexis looked like a girl who'd grown up doing hard farm chores. But her stocky build did not mean she was clumsy—on the contrary, Alexis was graceful, thanks to many years of gymnastics back on Earth. She'd taken two World gold medals in all-around—something Magdalena had learned only by accident.

She was almost a study in opposites to the tall, slender, dark-haired Magdalena. Alexis was fair-skinned, her hair so pale a gold it looked white in some lights, her eyes were ice blue ringed in a deeper blue, like a hunting bird's. Confident and poised, she was extremely competent.

"Nonsense," Magdalena said cheerfully. "Tall and skinny like me only counts if you're a European-style ballet dancer—and I'm almost *too* tall for ballet. And there are short, squatty Arekkhi, too, remember that, Madame Interrelator."

Alexis laughed and squeezed her companion's fingers. "You're getting giddy, Madame Translator. Too close to real gravity, I guess."

"Lead me to it," Magdalena replied fervently. This was her third voyage, and even though this ship—and the one that had taken her from NewAm to StarBridge—were smooth, well maintained, and clean, she still thought of space travel in terms of the flying disaster Father Saul had chartered to take his cult from West Texas to NewAm. *Maybe if I keep at this, I'll adjust,* she told herself. It didn't seem likely, not even after an uneventful journey of nearly three months, more than half of it in hibernation. She jumped again as the com above the door crackled sharply and the navigator's voice filled the area:

"We're coming around to approach the station from the planet side, and the mural will be in full view for some time. Captain says you can use the view-screens in Crew Mess, or come to the bridge if you want a straight view." The little receiver buzzed unpleasantly. Alexis cocked an eye at Magdalena and mouthed, "Crew Mess?" To date, the translator had avoided the small view-ports on the bridge the few times they'd been offered.

To the interrelator's surprise, the dark girl shook her head and said, "No, I want to see the real thing. I've really been looking forward to this."

"This," of course, was one of the wonders of all Arekkhi space: The thirty-kilometer-long station, suspended in geosynchronous orbit above the Emperor's Island and the capital city, was impressive, particularly since the Arekkhi had built it nearly eighty years earlier, just after the last battles of the long Civil War. After all, their technology level at present wasn't much above early-twenty-first-century Earth tech.

Being Arekkhi, they hadn't just made it practical, they'd

also made it beautiful. It had taken nearly twenty years for crafts-beings to attach the thousands of brilliantly enameled ceramic tiles to a stationary shield on the planet side of the station, a mural almost eighteen kilometers long depicting their Creation Myth.

Magdalena caught her breath sharply as she gazed through several thicknesses of clear plassteel and the interrelator automatically held out a hand to steady her if her vertigo had kicked in. But the translator was staring avidly, hands pressed against the wall, her eyes bright with tears. Alexis glanced quickly toward the crew—they appeared much too busy to worry about the mural—then moved over to the second port.

The background was a brilliant red that could supposedly be seen from the ground, with a good pair of lenses. There were the Holy Two in long hooded robes, creating life: fruiting trees, gray-brown, horned herd-beasts that reminded Alexis of wildebeests, and others that looked more like giant fanged and tailless lizards. Near the far end of the mural, as the ship swung around, she could just make out the two Arekkhi, a black-spotted male with a broad, sharply defined nasal stripe; the female slightly smaller, her stripes and spots a little fainter, her ear tufts highly visible—both covered in short, sleeveless singlets. *How odd,* she thought suddenly. *I've never seen so much as Khyriz's forearm, and not much of Shiksara's arms, either.* Was the current fashion modesty—or a change brought about by the drapers' guild to sell more cloth?

A sidelong glance at Magdalena showed the younger woman still motionless, only her eyes flicking across the mural. Alexis turned back to study the two Arekkhi as closely as she could. A small, round-eared creature something like a ring-tailed cat crouched at the female's feet—it wasn't an immature Arekkhi . . . she'd seen pictures of the young. So what was it? Next to the creature were two more thickly branched trees, heavy with long white fruit.

The two humans watched the enormous mural until it was no longer visible, and the ship slowed as it headed toward openings in the station. Behind them, Magdalena could hear communication coming up from the station. ''I think we'd probably better go strap in; sounds like we're about that far from landing.'' Alexis nodded and paused just long enough to gesture a ''thumbs up'' of thanks to the harassed-looking human navigator who grinned briefly before returning to his boards. The two women walked down the short corridor to the Crew's Mess, where the landing seats assigned them were located.

Magdalena's fingers moved automatically, deftly getting the straps on the high-backed, padded chair locked in correctly— her thoughts were some distance away, down on the station, on the other side of the docking bay. *I wonder if he's there.*

At her side, Alexis leaned back comfortably watching the view-screen as the small ship maneuvered slowly, finally easing into the bay. Engines cut off, all motion ceased. She glanced at her companion, but Magdalena hadn't even noticed. Just as well. Shiksara had warned them that docking at station could be rough, and it took time. Alexis stretched out her shoulders, got comfortable in the cushy chair, and prepared to wait.

CHAPTER 4

◆

The women unstrapped the instant the All Clear flashed on the small screen above the food-servo unit, but it was still another forty-five minutes until the ship was completely attached to station, and the entry/exit tunnel in place. Magdalena fought the urge to pace. *You don't want Alexis thinking she picked the wrong translator, do you, Perez?*

Finally, the All Clear flashed again and the door slid aside. Magdalena hauled a blue duffel over her shoulder, picked up the squashy carry-bag. "Guess—that's our call." She swore mentally; her voice sounded much too high.

Alexis scooped up her own pair of well-worn bags—the StarBridge logo of a rainbow joining two worlds was beginning to fade—and gave her a warm smile. "You aren't worried, are you?" The other girl shook her head. "Oh—wait. I forgot; you don't like the transition walks, do you?"

"Not really. It's a long drop if that first step isn't there," Magdalena reminded her. At least she was trying to be funny, Alexis decided. The Russian woman laughed as she strode toward the main ramp, which was now completely surrounded by black tunnel.

Three Arekkhi were waiting for them in the echoing hangar: two dockworkers stacking containers on a flat carrier, and a slender male in a black pilot's jumpsuit. Magdalena's heart leaped: Was it Khyriz? But as she emerged from the chill of the tunnel, she could see that while he resembled her friend in height and build, this was a stranger. *You knew Khyriz prob-*

ably couldn't come. Politics and safety—he'd mentioned both in the last sealed message he'd sent her, just before the ship left Academy space. It was still a disappointment not to see his familiar face and share the greeting gesture that was theirs alone. *What did you expect? This is what happens when you plan something out in such wishful-thinking detail,* she chided herself, and handed over her bags to the two rough-clad Arekkhi males in charge of an outsider low-grav carrier. Most of their other luggage had already been stacked.

She glanced casually at the workers and away, so they wouldn't think she was staring: The two wore loose trousers and jackets with the station patch on the band collar. This was very new: The latest Heeyoon vid from the station had shown such workers still in loose robes, the long sleeves snugged to the forearms. And the black jumpsuit . . . *Practical, sure. But the Arekkhi place style over practicality, and for at least a hundred years they've worn those long, loose robes that cover everything but their fingers and heads.*

She wondered how much Khyriz had to do with this: The black suit was cut along the same lines as a StarBridge student's jumpsuit.

Alexis had crossed to greet the young male—and give the baggage handlers a chance to look them over. Magdalena followed, smiling as much in Arekkhi fashion as a human could (no bared teeth; like the Simiu, the ancient Arekkhi had viewed teeth as a threat or challenge; it was still rude to expose one's incisors) and returned his gesture of "One who is pleased to make a new acquaintance." His speaking voice was higher than Khyriz's and more reedy; his first words—surprisingly—were English. "I am Bhelan, pilot to Prince Khyriz. He bids me welcome you to Arekkhi." One pointed ear flicked and he added in Arekkhi, "Apologies. I know no other human words."

"Thank you for the greeting. Your accent is very good," Alexis replied in fluent Arekkhi, and Bhelan visibly relaxed. It was a polite lie, of course; but without human lips Arekhi simply couldn't produce certain sounds.

"My thanks, Interrelator Alexis. I am told your ship was informed that the master of station will not be available to greet you. His sorrow if you perceive a slight.''

"Of course not,'' Alexis replied promptly. Frankly, Magdalena thought, they would have been surprised if the station master *had* come out to greet them: Most of those chosen to serve this sector of station supposedly tested low on xenophobic scales, but the master of station was a distant cousin of Duke Zhenu (who'd gained the appointment because of his bloodlines), and the aging male supposedly shared his noble cousin's disdain of outsiders.

"These''—Bhelan indicated the cart attendants with a wave of his hand—''will remain to fetch your goods. If it pleases you to ride, there is another vehicle that can be brought. Apologies that your ship must dock in this sector, and mine is housed a long distance away—it is that the outsider ships need special attachings, and any royal shuttle must rest in special security and its own bay. I can carry those bags if you wish.''

"No need,'' Alexis said. Arekkhi shoulders were somewhere between cat and human in forward placement; a medium burden for a human would be an uncomfortable weight to a similar-size Arekkhi.

"No apology needed,'' Magdalena said. "We understand the needs of your station and the safety of your Emperor. And after so many days inside that small ship, I would prefer to walk. We'd like to see as much of the station as we can.'' Bhelan's whiskers flattened to his face so briefly that Magdalena wondered if she'd imagined the pilot's discomfort. But Alexis glanced at her and raised an eyebrow as Bhelan turned away to speak to the cart attendants, one of whom pulled a small com-link from a pocketlike sleeve patch. Bhelan spoke into it at some length, too softly for either woman to understand, then returned it to its owner and came back to join them.

"A small matter—please, if you will excuse me.'' A wide door in the far wall slid open; the pilot walked quickly through it and into another lock, bounded by a high clear wall. Magdalena caught a tantalizing glimpse of the curved world of the station beyond, before the door slid closed once more.

"So—what was all *that* about?'' Alexis spoke Mizari, keeping her voice inflexionless and her expression neutral as she stepped into the open. The two attendants were already pulling the cart toward the foot of the ramp where the last of the luggage had been deposited. "The look on his face—like he was scared."

"You don't suppose they're going to restrict *us* the way they do the Heeyoon Trading Coalition?" Magdalena returned in the same language. "I thought Dr. Rob said that had been worked out."

"He did." Alexis glanced up as the final bags were stacked and the attendants began lashing everything down with pale-colored webbing. "And I glanced over the documentation before we ever left StarBridge, that particular matter's under control."

"Even though we aren't meeting with the stationmaster," Magdalena said.

Alexis shook her head and glanced toward the closed doorway where Bhelan had gone. "Well, I wasn't surprised. Were you?"

"Considering he's the Iron Duke's cousin? No. But a member of his staff, just for appearances . . ."

"Well, there's the unspoken part of it," Alexis said dryly. "Though they certainly made it clear enough: The implied insult if a minor station dignitary met us before the Emperor did."

"I guess. But what does that make Bhelan?"

"A servant, and therefore beneath anyone's notice, including ours." Alexis gave her a sidelong, keen glance. "Does anything feel wrong to you? The way he moved, or gestured?"

"Not that way, no," Magdalena assured her CLS companion.

Alexis's most recent lover had been a telepath, a young woman from Jolie. Marie-Claire had been fascinated by Magdalena's odd talent for "reading" body language and expression and had persuaded her still-dubious partner that it *was* an authentic talent, even if it didn't work the way telepathy did. "Just—it sounds like the kind of neatly tailored lie an Arekkhi politician would create." She managed a crooked grin. "I'm being paranoid, sorry."

"Doesn't mean they aren't out to get you," Alexis replied with a quiet laugh. "But I don't think there's a problem, really.

If there is one, we'll find out, soon enough. But since you and I are a wholly new life form here, it could be they're trying to avoid panic on-station. I'll wager you that conveyance to Bhelan's shuttle is fully enclosed.''

''Mmmmm—maybe.''

''And if he gets us clearance to walk, I'll also wager there won't be a living soul between us and the Emperor's shuttle, once we get out of this air lock,'' Alexis added; she gripped Magdalena's arm as the other girl swallowed, hard. ''Sorry, forgot you don't like the 'a' word.''

''Air lock? I'm all right,'' Magdalena managed.

''Well, we'll be just fine,'' Alexis reiterated. ''And there should be a few Arekkhi up here like those two,'' her eyes slid sideways, indicating the baggage handlers who were clamping the last mesh ends over the high pile of luggage; both males eyed the outsiders avidly whenever they dared take their eyes off their work. ''And remember, we aren't the Hee-yoon traders up here; we're going to be based on-world, and we get to talk to anyone we want.''

The Arekkhi government had been firm about the traders: The few Heeyoons permitted to deal here were limited to their own small, openly marked, quadrant of station. The only time they'd actually been down to the planet was for a reception at the Emperor's palace, and a very brief tour of the city of Ebba and the lands about it.

''Well, the argument *does* make sense,'' Magdalena pointed out. ''I mean, look what happened with the Na-Dina! The way that combine just moved in before the CLS could even establish a contact! If the Arekkhi heard anything about that . . .''

''Oh, I agree with you. And, of course, it's good sense for the CLS to really regulate trade here—the way the Arekkhi go for personal possessions,'' Alexis said. ''The black market in rare things like Rigellan sculpture would be—well, incredible, wouldn't it? Your argument—the Arekkhi argument—is just fine. If only I didn't feel there was more involved. Arekkhi politics,'' she added with a faint sigh.

Magdalena grinned wickedly. ''One good twist behind the first one, and two more behind that. But they can't use the same argument on *us*. After all, we're here to help them set up this trade they supposedly want so badly, and besides—''

The door hissed behind them; Bhelan, his ears canted side-ways as if he'd just finished a monumental argument, was with them once more. "We can go now, if you like. On foot," he said. "The luggage cart will go on ahead to my shuttle. Unless you would rather remain here to be certain of your goods?"

"No, that's fine. Let's go, now," Alexis replied promptly. She walked into the backup lock next to the pilot; Magdalena fell in behind them and a little to one side, her eyes moving constantly, one ear half-tuned to the conversation just ahead of her.

The station itself was a wonder to look at—surprisingly like old Earth renderings she'd seen of space colonies. *Given physics as a constant, what would you expect?* she asked herself. The vast station was an enormous tube, mostly open space, occupied by buildings and parklike spaces all the way around. Floors looked and felt flat underfoot, but curved to right and left, meeting overhead. Since their ship had landed near one end, only the closest kilometers—including a vast lake that apparently wrapped all the way around the tube—were visible. Beyond that, things were fuzzy with distance and atmosphere, and dwindled to a point. After her first, dizzying glance over-head, Magdalena swore she wouldn't look higher than the shrubs and low structures around them. *It looks flat—stick with that, all right, Perez?*

A broad avenue led away from the banks of docking bays and plunged into tall yellow-green vegetation—bushes, trees, and flowering plants, all contributing to a breathable atmo-sphere, Magdalena knew. Long row-buildings with evenly spaced doors made five-sided figures with gardens in the cen-ters—the Heeyoons had sent vid of that, and she could see as much in a single, unnerving glance overhead. They were all single-story buildings; Arekkhi knees weren't constructed for climbing stairs, elevators were nonexistent, and there wasn't enough room up here for ramps.

Some of the pentacles of buildings looked like living space, others might be shops or businesses—a few they passed had signs on the outer walls or goods piled on both sides of a door clearly marking them as specialty shops. *The Arekkhi don't*

know any other kind of business, she reminded herself. *Yet.*
Their tech might have moved into space, but their merchantile
processes hadn't moved beyond the Earth Renaissance model.

There were only a very few Arekkhi in sight and none close
by—just as Alexis had predicted—but she could sense eyes
on the other sides of those doors: They were being watched.
She glanced ahead where Alexis and Bhelan were talking animatedly—discussing Earth baseball and a similar Arekkhi
sport. She crossed her eyes. *Baseball.* Poor David had been an
ardent baseball fan; she'd never understood the thrill of watching team sports if you weren't part of the team. Still—good
for Alexis, coming up with a subject she and the pilot could
enjoy: Bhelan no longer had that slightly haunted look about
his ears and whiskers. *He's good,* she thought appraisingly as
they crossed a small square of yellow-green vegetation sepa-
rating one avenue from another. The stuff was springy underfoot and released a minty, soothing odor as they stepped on
it. *Khyriz might have shown him holo-vid of us, but he's never
talked to a human before this.*

It was too much to hope that everyone they met would be
as easy to talk to as this male. After all, he was Khyriz's
pilot—he'd introduced himself to Alexis that way—and he
was young. Magdalena knew from Khyriz about some of the
more hidebound older and noble Arekkhi. More than she
wanted to know, really; but since manners and good behavior
counted for so much in this society, she wasn't worried that
high-ranking nobles would be openly rude.

Privately offended by, or even afraid of—that she expected.
Which was a large part of the argument against any alien group
locating on the planet. Supposedly, the normally unclothed
Heeyoons had terrified and disgusted station Arekkhi, at first.
Furless (if clad) humans would be at least as bad, especially
if allowed to go wherever they pleased.

Or so the argument went. *But I don't believe it,* Magdalena
thought. *Ordinary beings adapt—especially if we don't have
any other choice. Now, the Prelate. . . .* The Prelate didn't have
to adapt to anything, if he chose not to. He barely had to
answer to the Emperor, and only on certain matters.

She really didn't want to meet the Prelate; she could only

hope any such meeting came soon and was behind her, so she could get on with being useful to Alexis.

But most religious beings here might not be as narrow of belief as all that: Human religious leaders often supported the CLS and StarBridge both. It was the fringe types, like Solomon Smith, who didn't want to adapt. Smith had used a spaceship to travel from Earth to NewAm, and still preached that the world was created (flat) by God in the year 4004 B.C.

She came back to the moment as Alexis laughed cheerfully at something Bhelan had said; the Arekkhi's whiskers touched and his ears flicked forward. *Khyriz chose us a good companion; let's hope he's as good a pilot.*

Bhelan turned left just past the little park. "Apologies for the lack of moving walkways on-station, but they require energy that the station cannot afford. . . ."

"It's all right, I need the exercise," Alexis assured him.

"The boundary for the trader's consortium is just here, at the greensward," he said. That meant the women were the first outsiders of any kind to walk through this part of station, Magdalena realized, and exchanged pleased glances with Alexis. Maybe it wasn't going to be so difficult after all.

Almost at once their surroundings became industrial: Solid flatbed hover-carriers fronted massive, squat buildings—warehouses and factories, Bhelan said. *The packers and transporters are inside the buildings,* Magdalena thought, with that strong feeling of being watched. The path to the shuttle down to the planet had been cleared for them.

They couldn't see far in any direction here, except overhead: Up there, Magdalena could make out more enormous buildings and plenty of activity—but it was too far away to make out much detail.

Magdalena gazed around her, ignoring Alexis and Bhelan, who were oblivious to the silence as they cheerfully discussed his sister's first daughter, who played *djiris*—something like baseball or maybe soccer, Magdalena didn't know which. She came back to the moment with a start as the interrelator said something about second-class citizens. "If you can believe it," Alexis continued, "females of my own species were once thought too fragile to play games, and not that far in our own past. It's nice to hear that your young females actually play sports that were once reserved for your males.''

''Ah . . . our females . . . ah, well, of course. Such things . . . well, they go without saying, don't they? After all, only look at my niece. . . .'' The pilot suddenly had that harassed look to his whiskers once more, and he was almost stammering. The tips of his whiskers flicked constantly, a nervous tic that reminded Magdalena of her own habit of drumming her nails on the nearest hard surface. Alexis didn't seem to notice.

Of course not, she reminded herself. *Alexis is a professional at this kind of thing, she knows when not to show surprise. She has two years on you, and she's been off StarBridge before now. Unlike you.* Besides, Magdalena knew from all those sessions with Dr. Rob that she tended to read more into small things than was necessary. It could be that Bhelan had a problem with his sister, or his niece, some simple family matter like that.

Still . . . she'd ask Alexis later. *Remember what you both say: You aren't paranoid if they're really after you.* Meantime, she'd let Alexis handle Bhelan. *Look around, inhale, pay attention. The tapes the school had, everything Khyriz told you— there's still a lot of information to sort out, and only some of it visual.*

The bags stacked nearby, for instance: She knew by the label the product they contained was *zhoris,* the wheat-like grain used for flat bread and breakfast cakes. But the off-planet hydroponics—here and on both moon stations—couldn't grow it, and the chemists had never been able to duplicate the grain, the flour, or the seed. So, *zhoris* was brought up from the vast fields in central Akkherif, largely from Duke Zhenu's lands. Back on StarBridge, she'd eaten fruit-smeared zhoris-cakes and an elaborately braided loaf full of dried fruit and nuts and enjoyed it; she hadn't realized then that the strong citrusy smell was the grain itself.

And down that way, a long, narrow space between warehouses—was that actually a prehover vehicle? She narrowed her eyes. Wheels! *That's an antique for certain!* The Arekkhi hadn't used wheels on-planet in more than a hundred years, not since they'd discovered a method for cheaply run air-cushioned vehicles. Of course, the station was old, but that old? Or were wheels somehow more practical here . . . ?

Her eyes shifted from the wheeled cart to movement beyond it, and she caught her breath in a gasp. *What kind of being is that?* "What . . . ? Alex, do you see what I see?"

Alexis came back to join her, gazed where the translator pointed. "I think—wait, yes. Bhelan, those aren't like any Arekkhi I've ever seen!" But the pilot, after one brief glance between the buildings, had turned away, coughing and fumbling in his sleeve for a nose-cloth.

"Too small," Magdalena murmured. "But—the distance—"

"No," Alexis said firmly. "It's not that far—maybe a tenth of a mile—sorry, a fifth of a kilometer. They're definitely not—good Lord," she added in English; Magdalena's jaw dropped. "Those are *tails!*"

"I see that. Maybe young . . . ?"

"Not young Arekkhi," Alexis said firmly. "Bhelan, what . . . ?" She glanced back toward the pilot; he was still coughing, rubbing at his nose. His ears were utterly flat to his skull.

They aren't young Arekkhi, Magdalena thought filled with curiosity. These creatures had the wrong-shaped ears and profiles. And . . . no spots. Even infant Arekkhi bore some spots. The long, thickly furred tails bounced in counterpoint to their steps. But, as she turned to say something to Alexis, one of the two creatures suddenly looked their way. Startled-looking, wide-eyes met Magdalena's across the distance; the smaller creature urgently pressed against its companion, who also looked. The hover-cart shifted awkwardly as the two leaned into it, then vanished behind the next building.

Magdalena realized she was holding her breath, and she let it out quietly; the whole event couldn't have taken more than a few seconds.

"What was *that*?" Alexis demanded breathlessly; she and the translator turned as one to eye Bhelan, who spread his hands in an Arekkhi shrug. "Those—the two little beings we just saw, the ones pushing that cart, Bhelan. What are they?"

"They . . . ? Apologies, I didn't see. The dust made my eyes water." Bhelan emitted a growling little sound: Arekkhi laughter, though he sounded distressed. Alexis gave Magdalena another sidelong look, which the translator interpreted as *Let me deal with this*. The interrelator smiled at their pilot.

"Well, they were moving quickly, after all. Still, *I* got a good enough look," she added, and neatly described them.

Bhelan's ears flicked, and Magdalena, who was now watching him from the corner of her eyes, wondered as his whiskers and ears came back to normal—she'd have sworn he was still scared. *Why?* she wondered. "Oh, those," he said. "I wasn't certain what you—um, they're . . . they are Asha."

Magdalena started. Khyriz had been kidding her about something not long before he left StarBridge, something silly. And he'd said that, out of the blue: Asha. *But when I asked what it meant, his whiskers touched, he was laughing that little purrlike laugh of his, and he said, "Asha? You mean, you don't know about Asha?"*

Odd. Thinking back on that evening, she had a sense of something that had upset or frightened him about the word. She'd never actually gotten a straight answer from him, either. Somehow she'd received an impression of something like knights-errant. Maybe Hobbits. Possibly the wandering samurai from some of Dr. Rob's better old movies.

"Asha!" Alexis exclaimed in surprise. "I heard about them from the first Heeyoons who came here—and Shiksara said something about them. But I thought—aren't they smaller?" She moved her hands apart, indicating something the size of a large house-cat. "And aren't they pets?"

Bhelan's ears flicked, then remained still. "Pets—well, of course, they're pets. Their ancient ancestors were similar to ours, they say—but that was when even the Arekkhi ran on four feet and ate raw kill. The Prince explained it to me: It is like you humans and your—ah, your *monkeys*." The English word, even accented, sounded very strange at the moment. "The Asha—they vary. So some are little and they become pets; while others—well, they can be trained to perform repetitive tasks."

"More like dogs," Alexis murmured to herself. "All right, I understand." *I think,* the glance she sent Magdalena said.

"They must have seen you and taken fright; it is mostly

because of the Asha that we keep the Heeyoons away from this part of the station, since the creatures do so much work in this area. They are easily terrified by anything new.'' Bhelan eyed her anxiously. ''The master of station would be very angry if he thought I deliberately showed you Asha; if he thought I caused them to be frightened.''

''Why?'' Magdalena asked. ''I mean, why use them here?''

The pilot's eyes flicked toward her, away, back again. ''Because of the size of this station: Resources are limited. Food, water, and air—we waste nothing. One day, perhaps, we will adapt this place to your outsider tech, but for now, we use Asha whenever we can. They are smaller than we, they are housed in . . . in kennels, and they eat less. What food they do eat needs less preparation, and they do not bathe as Arekkhi do, so less water is wasted.''

''Sensible,'' Alexis murmured. ''Well, then. Perhaps we'd better get moving again. No need to get you into trouble, Bhelan.''

''My thanks,'' the pilot said, his ears twitching as he turned and started walking the way they'd been going.

Behind his back, Alexis and Magdalena exchanged glances. *Too pat,* Magdalena decided. *Sure, he could know all that— but his delivery sounded as if he'd practiced it.* Alexis's look held a warning; she nodded briefly. *I won't call him on that—I wouldn't anyway. But why couldn't things have waited to get complicated until after we landed on the planet?*

As she walked beside the translator, Alexis shifted her gaze to the back of their shuttle pilot's black jumpsuit. *Glib. And Asha, are they?* They'd appeared clever enough—apparently clever enough to manage the task of delivering that cart of goods without supervision. Still, she'd helped her father train their sheep-herding dogs for years. And she'd been part of the precollege Ukrainian group that had tracked the sign-language-trained gorilla in Kiev.

So she knew better than to make assumptions based on a split-second look at a brand-new (to her, at least) life form. *Asha, though.* The initial Heeyoons had been able to pass on nothing but the name; Shiksara had seemed unusually vague about them. *I'll have to find out what Magdalena knows. . . .*

Alexis's eyes narrowed thoughtfully. Bhelan had been determinedly vague about Asha, also. But he was Khyriz's shuttle pilot, and therefore, probably, the charismatic Khyriz's ally. *Odd that the whole walk has been deserted except for those two Asha. Is Khyriz up to something?*

Maybe she ought to start rethinking things. Starting now.

The shuttle bays reserved for nobles and royals were clustered at one end of a long, closed-off corridor that paralleled the length of the station. Bhelan waited for the visual scanner to process his facial markings and for the door to slide open, then ushered his passengers through. The corridor itself was remarkably plain, especially for Arekkhi: No paintings, murals, or other artwork graced the curved walls, which were marked only by flat-screen scanners next to wide doors at intervals. No moving walkway here, either.

There was another pause at the doorway marked by the Emperor's personal *ducat*, while Bhelan was again scanned. Magdalena gazed at the gold-painted device and felt oddly goose-bumpy. It was one thing to have studied Arekkhi history via books, holo-vid, and talking to Khyriz and Shiksara. *The ducat, the Arekkhi token of ruling, isn't a crown, of course; it's a forearm-guard, rounded at the elbow end, tapering to a point at the other so it covers the back of the hand. It dates from at least a thousand years ago, a time when small nations warred, and all fighters wore such guards. And the rulers wore special ones, to identify themselves to their own troops—and to their enemies.*

The current Emperor, like his predecessors, wore a small, ornately jeweled version of the *ducat* for official appearances. The painted device marked official vehicles, buildings, and belongings.

The chamber beyond the door was vast and completely empty except for the silvery, sleek flitter-shuttle. *New technology, or at least a new look,* Alexis thought. "Wow," she murmured. Magdalena bit back a grin as the pilot gave the interrelator a startled glance, then an Arekkhi rumbling chuckle. Khyriz had picked up "Wow!" from one of Rob's old movies, and he seemed to have passed it on. Alexis turned to give her companion a grave wink as she added, "I was expecting one of the older models, you know: right out of *Flash Gordon.*"

"The color version, right?" Magdalena asked. They were both fond of the howlingly impossible space exploits of both the black-and-white serials and the slightly more recent version with a late-twentieth-century rock music sound track: The spaceships in both versions were incredibly elaborate—and those in the color version unnervingly similar to vid they'd seen of Arekkhi off-planet shuttles.

"Art Deco," Alexis agreed. She glanced at Bhelan, who looked baffled, switched back to Arekkhi, and gave him an apologetic gesture: "An old joke between us. The ship is beautiful."

"The new fashion," Bhelan replied seriously. "Most ships coming to station these days are still not 'wow,' " he added.

"I've seen vid of the others," Alexis assured him. "But why is the Emperor's shuttle so—well, so plain?"

Bhelan considered this as he drew a five-sided link from his sleeve and pressed the sides with his thumbs; a ramp descended from the nose of the shuttle. Magdalena went up first, entering the ship at midpoint, though she didn't reach floor level until she was nearly at the rear of the main cabin. Once Bhelan—last of the three—reached floor level, he pressed the link again and the ramp came back up, sealing with a "snick" that made the translator's ears pop; the ramp became part of the cabin floor.

"Khyriz prefers the simpler fashion, which also suits our Emperor. These craft are faster and safer; this vehicle is also practical on-planet, though it is bulkier than a regular flitter." He indicated the cabin with a two-armed gesture. "Sit wherever you choose. You know how to adjust Arekkhi seating . . . ?"

"We've seen vid," Alexis replied. She began a slow turn in place to look over the possibilities as the pilot went forward; a narrow door slid sideways and closed behind him. There were ten of the half-egg-shaped seats placed apparently at random in the open cabin: Forward-tilted backside rests fit into thickly padded shells that would cushion a body of any size. Though made for beings who were comfortable with a spine curved from tailbone to neck, they could also be adjusted to fit a more upright human. She turned again to look across at Magdalena, who was frowning at the larger of two vidscreens—the cabin was well lit, but there were no view-ports.

Alexis walked over to join her, but when Magdalena would have spoken, the interrelator touched her lips silently, then fingered the ear-cuff. Magdalena's eyes narrowed, then she nodded once. She and Alexis had already agreed to be sparing in their use of the little disrupt: Any Arekkhi listening for conversation might become suspicious not to hear any.

In the closed-off control cabin, Bhelan moved swiftly, checking only that the ship had been recharged for the trip down before he examined the few possible hiding places: The obvious spot behind the com rack—nothing new there, though when he'd boarded earlier in the day, back on ground, there'd been a flat sound-recorder stuck onto the rack. *I was meant to find that one*, he knew. He'd removed it, disabled the receiver, and tossed it in the waste bin. A more careful search had revealed the second machine, buried in the padding of the pilot's seat. After careful consideration, he'd used a small handtool to switch the sound off—mistakes happened, after all; whoever had arranged for the device would think his planter careless. There hadn't been a third. *Not the Iron Duke, then.*

Probably not. Now, a very quick check showed no new device on board, and the sound on the machine in his seat-padding was still disabled. He hadn't thought anyone would try to access the ship here, but one checked, of course. He leaned over the narrow rank of boards and began the brief sequence that would turn the platform where the shuttle sat. But as he keyed the sequence, the door to the main cabin slid open and Magdalena came in, closely followed by Alexis. Bhelan's whiskers went briefly flat to his face, but Khyriz had cautioned him about these alien women, and as he turned, his smile was back in place.

Humans are friendly and curious, he said. *Don't misinter-*

pret what they tell you; they're more open than we are. And don't underestimate their intelligence.

The interrelator gave him a pleasant lip-smile. "I hope you don't mind," Alexis said apologetically, "but we'd really rather ride up here with you. After two months of viewing the outside on vid-screens . . ."

"It's just the way Khyriz told me," Magdalena added eagerly as the other woman's voice trailed away. "His last letter, he told me about the landing you made on his plateau, Bhelan! About"—her eyes wandered the little chamber—"about sitting over there," she pointed to the chair nearest the larger of the side view-ports, "and being sick all over the view."

Despite inner dread—he could almost feel that steel talon tickling the short throat-fur—Bhelan laughed. "It took two cleaners to mop up the mess and a full nine days to remove the last of the smell." *I knew it would come to this . . . when I first swore to Khyriz, I knew it.*

The tension left him as he gestured toward the three other chairs and took the pilot's, snapping toggles as he ran the final check: rudders, fixed wings, seals, air supply, fuel, the locks on the forward heliblade that allowed the craft to land nose up in a very small space—it was the only way a shuttle could come down on the Emperor's island—and finally the com-link with station. Through all this, he was vaguely aware of the two women: Khyriz's dark-she Magdalena taking Khyriz's favorite seat, while the pale-furred (*no, pale-haired, that was Khyriz's word*) Alexis deftly fastened the mesh safety harness between her legs and across her shoulders. As she eased back into the chair, the door between the inner and outer air locks automatically slid up into the ceiling when all the air had been removed from the docking bay. Bhelan eased the shuttle forward.

The inner door slid shut behind them, the outer lock began to slide upward. Bhelan tugged his harness tight and glanced over to make certain Magdalena's was snug. "You were warned about the drop . . . ?" he began. To his surprise, Alexis laughed, a bell-like, human laugh.

"Khyriz said that this thing drops like a brick until it's away from station." She turned to Magdalena and added, in English,

"What that old Earth theme park once called an E-ticket ride. Ready?"

Magdalena grinned, though the whites of her eyes showed all around the dark iris. "Let 'er rip," she replied and leaned as far forward as she could to smile at Bhelan. "Old joke," she told him in Arekkhi. "We'll be just fine."

The very thought of that long drop had scared her half silly, and even given her bad falling-dreams on the ship coming here. The actuality of it was nothing at all: a slight shift as the little vessel went from station gravity to none at all. By the time she'd drawn a deep breath and let it out again, the pilot had full power on, and the shuttle was easing smoothly away from station, moving toward the blue-green ball of a planet below.

Bhelan knew his business, she thought appraisingly. Of course, the Emperor was said to be fond of his youngest son; he'd make sure Khyriz had a very skilled pilot. Entry into the atmosphere was slightly jolting, but only slightly; Bhelan took them on an easy descent that circled the planet twice before leveling out at perhaps two kilometers above the surface— three above the oceans. "A long flight," he said apologetically—the first words he'd spoken in some time. "There is less bodily stress, and . . . well, you see more of our world this way."

The dark-she gazed out the view-port, watching everything. The interrelator, he noticed, was intent on his every move at the controls. She was a pilot herself, Khyriz had said. She'd learn a lot just from observing. Well, he'd chosen his course hours earlier, by allowing the women up front.

They were on the night side at the moment, about to come into sunrise, half a world from the Emperor—over the Iron Duke's upland holdings in northwestern Akkherif. Another Arekkhi standard hour and they'd be on approach to the royal island. Another hour, he could walk away from his passengers and, with good fortune, learn how his family was.

"What's that?" Magdalena's sharp question broke into his thoughts. "Look! Something's on fire!"

Bhelan glanced ahead through the pilot's view-screen: The

sky was pale rose from the flaming inferno below. Bhelan glanced sidelong where the woman was pointing and took a swift look at his boards. One of the smaller villages—too small for the screen to show a name—was down there. Or had been. Flames roared high, consuming the grasslands for several *parths* around it.

Alexis eased her restraints and came partway to her feet, leaning forward. "I can't see—is that a *building* in all that?"

Bhelan hadn't thought so fast in all his life. "It's—oh, there, I see! So far from the capital, things are still not mechanized, and the old ways hold. They . . . the fields have been picked over and they burn what is left."

"Fields?" The translator sounded suspicious, he thought nervously. The two women exchanged glances.

"But—that building—" the other protested.

"Possibly an ancient fence, or an elderly grain-storage no one thought it worth the time to unbuild. My father's people had fields in such state of repair," he added smoothly. Silence.

They flew through the night, and the sun was a ruddy glow on the horizon before anyone spoke again. Alexis eased back in her chair and tightened the mesh.

"Oh. Well, of course, they used to burn fields on Earth, a long time ago," she said. "I just wouldn't have thought . . . at night . . ." She broke off abruptly, then added, "Of course, I know there's plenty to learn still. Now that we're here, we'll be able to travel to places like that, talk to people."

Bhelan kept his whiskers forward with an effort. "Of course," he murmured, then keyed the front-view darkeners as the sun came up. *Innocents,* he thought sadly. *Even if these aliens . . . these women . . . are able to somehow walk the world as they choose, the Iron Duke will never allow them within two days' journey of that place.* How many, he wondered bleakly, had died there tonight? At whose hands . . . and why?

CHAPTER 5

Khyriz shook out the sleeves of his favorite red robe—the one Magdalena liked best—and glanced at the reflective wall of his bathing chamber. Droplets of water beaded the outer edges; he could see the robe but not his face. *Good enough,* he decided. Odd to think how long it had been since he'd fussed this much over his appearance.

If he went onto his balcony now, he'd probably be able to see the shuttle coming in on the final up-swoop; perhaps the grapples would already have it on the ground, the hatch open. . . .

You promised your father, he reminded himself. Considering the current crisis from half a world away and the Council's meeting to deal with it, the Iron Duke wouldn't be anywhere except chambers at this hour, along with the Emperor, the Prelate, and the rest of the council. No doubt they would be there for hours to come, especially the Iron Duke. The Prince could picture him, bellowing about the damage to his lands, and the cost to his own purse for lost fields and buildings. *Of course, Zhenu wouldn't care about the loss of life except how it hurt his earnings,* Khyriz thought grimly.

But the Prince was no longer so naive as to believe no one kept spies on the royal island. And others supported various members of the Council—they'd report a Prince where he'd no business being, out of loyalty or for money. Or out of fear. No sense making problems for himself at present; give the spies no reason to suspect him of anything, except too much naïveté, and an unseemly fondness for outsiders.

His mind raced as he made a final adjustment to his sleeves and turned away from the mirrored wall. *I wonder who led the attack on that village—and why?*

They might never know, since the Iron Duke would have his own people investigate—and release only such facts as he wanted released. But the end result was the same, no matter why or who had attacked the village: A hundred common, farming, and herding Arekkhi were dead or missing, the land for two parths around the village thoroughly burned—and every Asha in the area had vanished.

That last information had been costly, Khyriz thought: One of his household who'd proven so clever with his outsider spy-devices would be a long time recovering from his burns, and the device was gone—destroyed lest it fall into the wrong hands. *The Iron Duke may well be aware of such devices; better that he never learn I have them.*

He could obtain more of the devices—all it would take was another journey out to the half-completed jump station, where two of his old friends from the Academy were working. *Odd, how things work out. I went there to be certain my message would reach StarBridge unaltered. Finding Dana Marshall and Khenazk' both there—that was pleasant, and useful.*

Thanks to them, his two-seat flitter could now cross Zhenu's lands without being detected, and on-board communications to the Prince's estates were likewise safe from interception. Most Arekkhi wouldn't even suspect such devices were possible, let alone in such tiny packages. Khyriz glanced at the glittering little device on his claw, and his whiskers curved forward in a smile.

The smile faded: that poor village. Well, if good fortune was his, he'd know why and possibly who, once his in-place agents were able to make contact.

The Iron Duke would be furious if he knew the Emperor's youngest son—the Alien-Hugger, as he called Prince Khyriz—had agents planted on his very lands. Extremely skilled agents: In two years, not one of them had been caught. *Yet. Do not grow complacent. But—set that aside for now. Magdalena will know something is wrong if you greet her in this mood.*

He shoved loose fabric above his midarm joint where he wore the timepiece that had really been Magdalena's parting gift and that he'd finally learned how to set to Arekkhi time—he didn't want to remember how many hours it had taken with the fat manual and an Arekkhi comp to both work out the numbers and translate the instructions. It should have been so simple: Arekkhi hours were roughly one and a half Earth standard; there were fifteen of them to a day, fifteen divisions to each hour. . . . *Never mind, it's done,* he reminded himself impatiently, and composed his whiskers carefully.

In ten Arekkhi-standard minutes, he could leave his third-level apartments and start down the ramp to the middle floor. The entire old palace had been redecorated ten years earlier, but now the second floor had been remodeled for the CLS team. For Alexis Ortovsky and Magdalena Perez.

Khyriz had personally checked the entire floor for "bugs," as Dr. Rob's old movies called them, late the night before: There hadn't been any.

He crossed his main room, went down the short hallway and into the robe-room, pushed aside brightly colored garments, and checked the little wall-patch hidden behind them. It was a very old patch, from the days when the Emperor and his family still occupied the old palace, but it still worked: If anyone had stepped onto any floor in the CLS apartments since Khyriz had reset the device, it would show here—and it didn't. Except, of course, the two servants assigned to the team: They knew about the patch and wore neutralizing markers.

Who would have thought all the exploring I did as a small one would prove so useful? At the time, he'd been young and bored, and permitted nowhere but the new and old palaces, and the grounds between them. The old palace had a wealth of such devices, hidden passages, unnoted doorways—only a few of them had ever been shown on the official plans, and most of them were long forgotten. Like the wall patch.

Thanks to the ancient wall patch, and his nail patch, Magdalena and Alexis would start with "clean" rooms; Alexis knew how to keep them that way.

He emerged from the robe-room, checked his watch once more. Time to go. But as he moved through the vine-filled

entry, the portal light flashed and hummed at him. "Zhikna?"
he murmured in surprise as he recognized the familiar sound-
code. Right now his younger cousin should be with the greeting team for the CLS, standing next to the landing pad with
Second Prince Khedan. He reached for the door toggle, jumped
as the portal light flashed again. Zhik was always impatient,
but even so!

The door slid aside as the toggle activated, and his cousin
was inside at once. Khyriz blinked, toggled the door to close
as he turned. Zhikna's visible fur was hackled, his whiskers
and ears flat and trembling. His hat hung precariously off the
back of his head, held on only by the strap, his robe wrinkled
where he'd clutched it. And at his feet . . .

Khyriz's ears flicked in astonishment and then anger. Zhik
had brought a pet, one of *those* Asha! "What are you doing—
and how *dare* you, cousin?" he said with a hiss. "You *know*
I won't have an *ahla* here!"

"I—Khyriz, I'm sorry, I didn't know where else to go, I
need help, your help. . . ." Zhik's trembling voice faded; the
Asha, clad in a blue singlet that matched the youth's robes,
crouched on its haunches, pressed against the young noble's
legs, eyes all pupil and tail flat to its side. It whimpered faintly,
nonstop. Zhik glanced down and his eyes momentarily softened; he touched the Asha's forehead in a gesture meant to be
soothing; the little being fell blessedly silent as the young noble swallowed and tried to speak more calmly. "Please, I know
you don't like . . ." He couldn't seem to find the right word
and finally gestured, taking in the crouching being.

"You know how such—pets—are created," Khyriz said
flatly, but he kept his own voice low: It wasn't the Asha's
fault, no use in frightening it more.

"I *know*!" Zhik's scream startled all three of them. Khyriz
backed down the entry and beckoned urgently.

"Come in here and bring—is it him?" He couldn't bring
himself to say "it," as most of those who owned such pets
did. The shape of the nose, the darkness of the fur across it,
the thickness of the tail, the tuftless ears—all that indicated
maleness.

"Him," Zhik mumbled. Khyriz could hear his cousin murmuring reassurances, convincing the little being to rise to full height and its hind limbs, and come into the main room. It wouldn't enter the lowered seating area with Khyriz and Zhikna, but settled warily on the edge of the "pit," dilated eyes fixed on the young noble who was supposedly its master and superior. "I *know* how you feel about them, Khyriz, but just *listen* to me!" He was rubbing his hands, palm of one against the back of the other, repeatedly; the fur was damp from sweating palm-leather, a sure sign of distress. "He's Ah-Naul, and whatever anyone says, he's my friend." Zhik eyed him defiantly; the motion of his hands stilled suddenly.

Confrontation, Khyriz thought angrily. "Your friend, I see! How foolish of me not to realize that! And did the med-techs and your father neglect to give him the full dose of *xhezzik*? Oh, yes, how foolish of me to doubt, clearly there is more to him than blind adoration and total obedience!" Zhik's ears flattened. "Let that pass, I have no time for this," the Prince snapped. "Just tell me!"

"Father . . . gave him to me, after you left for the Academy," Zhik stammered; his ears remained flat. "I didn't tell you . . . *you* know why," he added accusingly. "I remember every single word you said when . . . when I offered you an alha-Asha. Khyriz, I still can't believe that . . . but, but never mind," he added hastily as Khyriz shifted, his eyes angry. "It doesn't matter, Ah-Naul is . . . what he is. I didn't . . . didn't want to . . . but how could I tell *my* father I didn't want such . . . a gift?"

Khyriz ran blunted nails across his forehead; his own finger-pads felt suddenly damp. "I understand that. He would have thought you were going soft on him."

"Softer than he already thinks me," Zhik corrected him unhappily.

"Yes. And he'd have berated you, or punished you."

"And he'd have killed Ah-Naul; he said so. I couldn't let him do that. I've done everything I can to—Oh, what's the use?" he snarled into the cushions; the sides of his hands slammed into them, suddenly, scattering bolsters everywhere. "What you said, about the *xhezzik*—there has to be some truth to it, doesn't there?"

"I have never lied to you, Cousin," Khyriz said evenly.

"But if you don't really know, either? I mean . . . how *could* you know? No one knows that much about Asha, not since the war. But . . . but I learned something, about the drug . . . it's not what he said, what my father said, something to add to his food to keep him healthy."

"He told you that?"

"Yes. But the other Asha, the ones who work the fields in Mibhor, I've seen the records, *they* aren't given the drug, and if *he* needs it, wouldn't they need more? If it's . . . if it's just nutrients? And—and why would my father be concerned about Ah-Naul's *health* enough to send that horrid Ulfar at odd times to make certain that he gets the drug?

"But now . . ." His voice broke and it was some moments before he could go on. Above him, the ahla-Asha stirred and keened faintly, a high, mewling sound.

Khyriz fought his ears back upright. *No, they don't bother to feed it ephana once the other drug has taken effect, do they?* he thought savagely. Some who owned ahla-Asha claimed to enjoy the little mewing sounds their "pets" made.

What had this Asha been before someone fed him poison and deliberately robbed him of everything—including dignity?

The whimpering Asha-sound brought Zhikna to himself again. He slid across silky cushions and bolsters and placed his hand against Ah-Naul's jaw. Khyriz shifted his gaze away at once. There was too much emotion between the two—it made him feel ill.

"Fine, Zhikna. You've had a change of mind, thanks to what I told you about the process. I'm glad to hear that much, at least. But now you have this . . . this Ah-Naul, because you didn't want his death behind your eyes when you slept. Didn't you think your father might have kept him, or given him elsewhere?"

"It was a test, don't you see that? Another of his endless tests for me! He would have done it, I know he would. But . . . that's past," Zhik murmured; his eartips were trembling again. "It's . . . it's the outsiders, the humans. Father came into my rooms early—my new rooms down from yours."

"I know about them; you showed me through them, remember? And I said I was surprised he let you move out." Khyriz had been; Zhik's quarters for at least four years had been either in his father's summer palace or a single, barren chamber in the new palace, part of the Iron Duke's small suite.

"He came in just at sunrise, and—he was angry, I still don't know why, not with me this time, just terribly angry. And he said . . . said, the she-aliens who come to live on Arekkhi must *never* see Asha; they must not know such . . . such creatures exist. And—and he ordered me to . . . to dispose of Ah-Naul." He glared at Khyriz, terror temporarily buried under fury. "Dispose! As if he were a . . . a piece of . . ." He couldn't complete the thought. After a moment he drew a harsh breath and went on. "He said—to go away, far from the island, to do it somewhere the . . . the she-aliens would never know."

"The humans," Khyriz corrected him gently, but Zhik was miserably lost in his own memory and didn't hear.

"He said—not to dare turn 'it' loose, that he'd know at once, that I should bring him . . ."

"Proof?" Khyriz suggested finally. Zhik gestured assent sharply; his ears were again flat to his skull, and his whiskers trembled frantically.

"I can't—do murder, Cousin!" he whispered. "I . . . I've never hurt anything deliberately! To even think of it will make me vomit! But . . . but if I don't . . . don't do what he asks, then Father will send Ulfar to take Ah-Naul, and how *he* would kill—" The younger male's breathing was a harsh pant.

"Don't!" Khyriz broke in, his voice sharp. "That helps no one, not you, and not—not your friend." The word didn't want to form, but Zhik gave him a grateful look. "Calm yourself and calm him so I can think in peace. Though I can tell you right now, the best thing would be for you to give him a double sleeping-dose and fly out over deep water, drop him unconscious to drown in the middle of the eastern sea, he'd sink to die without fear or pain, he'd know nothing. . . . I understand you can't do that," he added quickly as Zhik began a wordless protest. "Go, up there, soothe him, and be silent, both of you."

He was vaguely aware of Zhik climbing out of the shallow pit, the alha-Asha coming around to him, standing gracefully on its hind feet to lean against Zhik's caressing hands. Its round-eared head came to his cousin's shoulder. *Disgusting,* he thought in a sudden burst of anger. He forced himself to then set his feelings aside.

Some moments later, he coughed gently; faint as the sound was, Zhik turned to eye him in wide-eyed fear.

"This may come back to you later, if the Iron Duke finds out," Khyriz warned.

"I don't care," Zhik replied defiantly, though his ears quivered just a whisker's worth above his skull. "I will chance it."

Khyriz gave him a human nod; the Duke's son shook himself at that shared outsider-gesture, and his whiskers eased nearer normal. "Your father is in the closed Council meeting?" the Prince asked. Zhik gestured assent. "And he left no one in the hallways or ramps to watch you?" Another assent. "You've tested your rooms recently?"

"The way you showed me, Khyriz. No devices of any kind in the bathing, one in the entry, among the vines. Another above the bedding."

"All right. You left your rooms as soon as he was gone?"

"No. I waited . . . I wasn't dressed, and I . . . I couldn't move at first. I . . . was afraid I would vomit, and then my attendant—Jild is *his,* of course, is Father's—Jild came with food and stayed to straighten the bedding. I . . . waited until he was gone, and I could see him on the walkway moving toward the new palace, so he could tell my father whatever . . . whatever he learned in my rooms."

Khyriz spared a sympathetic thought, and a back-of-hand touch to his poor younger cousin. *Imagine being watched so closely; imagine being aware of it.* But Zhik was learning: how to thwart tech intrusions to his rooms, and how to deal with spies. The Iron Duke would know nothing other than that a terrified Zhik had left his rooms, taking the "pet" with him.

"Go back," Khyriz said finally. "And think right now what you can say to . . . to Ah-Naul in the entry, so your father will think you started out of the old palace toward your flitter, but thought at the last moment about getting a strong sleeping dose and dissolving it in . . . whatever is Ah-Naul's favorite drink." Zhik made an unhappy little sound of protest, but a sharp gesture from his cousin cut him off. "Listen to me! You must do this so the Iron Duke will not wonder where you were, all this time! Between when the servant left and when you returned to your chambers! He must think only that you were dithering on the ramps between your apartments and mine, trying to find a way around his order."

Zhik stared at him, his eyes all pupils. "But if he . . . Khyriz, I didn't think, if he has devices here or in the hallway outside—!"

"There are none, I would know," Khyriz said grimly. "Return to your entry, sound upset . . . that will hardly surprise your father, who thinks you spineless and weak. Take Ah-Naul into your bathing, and make reasonably loud sounds, as if the Asha is drinking liquid, then lead him at once out and to your flitter. Set a course with the island flight-techs for a point north and east of here, a course that stays over open water. Thereafter, do not change course for at least an hour. Your flitter is clean?" he asked. Assent. "No 'bugs'?" Another assent. "Good. But check it again before you fly out. Once you are north of the Bright Peninsula, turn west and approach my estate as low as you can. You still have the skills to land in the tunnel?"

Zhik considered this briefly, then nodded, human style.

"I hope so," Khyriz murmured softly. Because of the off-winds that made landing on open ground so hazardous much of the year, Khyriz's estate boasted a landing ramp that descended immediately to an underground hangar. "Because I want you out of sight as soon as you touch down."

"But . . . but the weather for this whole part of the hemisphere is calm," Zhik protested. "I always check, because of the flitter." His father had given him the sleek little hover vehicle a year earlier.

"The weather doesn't matter," the Prince said. "The important thing is that I don't want your flitter seen on my grounds today, and it is imperative that *no* Asha be seen."

"Seen?"

"If someone who owes your father favors happened to be flying across that headland just as you and Ah-Naul left the flitter?" *If,* he thought dryly as Zhik's ears flickered. There were at least two small craft that flew over the headland on a regular basis; a royal with his own private lands expected such invasive actions. "Take no chances; fly the least-expected approach, come in fast and low, land, and get out of sight at once. Don't leave until full dark; your father won't expect you to return quickly."

"No. But once I land—?"

"Everything is provided for. My master of house will know you're coming; he'll find a place for Ah-Naul." Khyriz hesitated, finally shrugged a very human shrug.

There was more, of course; a lot more. But Zhikna was very much afraid of his father, and Ulfar could persuade anyone to talk, if the honored *zhez* thought a secret was being kept from him. The only son of the Iron Duke might talk in his sleep, or he might simply blurt out the truth. *He might have been sent by the Iron Duke to test me, with Alexis and Magdalena coming.* . . . But that was carrying matters too far, and Zhik was no actor. The past hour, he had been in true misery. *He's done enough for me, often without even knowing it. I can't turn him aside now,* Khyriz thought tiredly.

He eased his way free of the mounds of pillows, cushions, and bolsters, stepped out of the pit, and shook his robes.

"Cousin," Zhik said quietly, "I owe you many great favors for this."

"Keep silent about this entire meeting between us, and you owe me nothing. Remember, your friend's life will still be forfeit if your father learns what you've done."

"I . . . know."

"And so will yours, probably. And mine, if he learns—"

"He'll learn *nothing*," Zhik broke in, so forcefully Khyriz blinked in astonishment and the Asha huddled even more tightly against his legs than ever. "You think I don't know how to guard my words and actions around my father? You think I didn't learn that from my first years?"

"Zhik, I know you aren't the foolish, weak creature your father thinks he has made, and his comrades see in you." *I hope you are not,* Khyriz added silently. "I merely remind you this is no game, but a dangerous situation. If you go on—"

"I must. If not, Ah-Naul is dead, the blame still mine. I will be careful, Khyriz; my father sees in me only what he chose to create. If he saw beyond that, he might turn his attention to you, and to see . . . what, Khyriz?''

The Prince considered this in momentary silence. Perhaps he *had* underestimated his young cousin all these years. *Perhaps. Don't overestimate him now, not with so much at stake,* he told himself firmly and spread his hands in an Arekkhi shrug. ''He would see what there is: one who wishes to remain unnoticed by your father. A sensible being, that is to say,'' he said easily. ''Wait.''

Khyriz forced himself to walk over to the ahla-Asha, and beckoned. The little being rose gracefully onto his hind feet and gazed up into the Prince's eyes. The Asha's eyes were nearly round, dark gold flecked with darker brown. But there was no sign of the least intelligence behind them. Khyriz kept his ears up with an effort, then laid a light finger on brown nose-fur, as if in blessing. ''Go safely, both of you,'' he murmured and took a pace back, watching as his cousin led his companion back into the hallway. The door slid silently closed behind them.

The shuttle was over open water by the time the sun came up; Bhelan reduced airspeed twice during the next several minutes, fiddling with the wing angle as the machine dropped gently nearer blue-green waves. He still had plenty of speed to dump, Alexis thought judiciously, in order to land the machine upright on the Emperor's island in roughly another hour. She divided her attention between the world outside and the controls; Bhelan's ears flickered occasionally as he eyed her but he made no effort to disguise anything he did. *I was afraid they would be secretive with tech like this,* she thought. Perhaps no one had warned Bhelan—or they had and he counted on his status with the royal family to protect him.

She glanced in the other direction. Magdalena was quiet, her gaze fixed somewhere beyond the view-port, though at the moment there wasn't much to see but water and an occasional floating mat of grass-islands that formed around enormous plant-bladders broken loose from far below the surface. *I would like to see one of those up close, to walk on the surface of it.*

So far as she knew, the islands were unique to the equatorial Arekkhi oceans: integrated life forms that bound together around long-streamered bladders that grew deep but broke off during storms to surface and tangle together. Thereafter, underwater plant-eaters (as intelligent as Earth's octopi, though they looked more like fat fish with flexible, paddle-shaped arms) plugged the spaces between the stems with leaves, branches, and other bits from the ocean floor so they could build nests just beneath the surface, while air-breathing swimmers vaguely reminiscent of otters layered the upper surface with floating bits: leaves, feathers, anything that came into their three-fingered grasp, so they could have a sunning platform between trips into the sea to find food. The flyers built the surface still higher and sturdier, giving themselves corner view-points from which to hunt.

The ship shuddered slightly, and Magdalena quietly caught her breath. Faint as the sound was, Bhelan turned his head to look at her, his ears flickering.

"Is the translator-she Magdalena well?" he asked. "This look with wide eyes, the Prince tells me in humans this means fright. I do not mean to frighten you," he added anxiously.

"I . . ." Magdalena forced a laugh, but her voice was tight. "It isn't your flying. I've only done a planet-landing once before, apologies."

"Everything is under control," Alexis assured her. "That just felt like an air pocket to me. I forgot about your first landing, though."

Magdalena nodded and bit her lip. *I would just as soon forget it: seventy cult children and two terrified elderly women crammed into a too-small cabin with uncomfortable or non-working straps, no view-ports or vid—and storm weather to come down through.* They'd all been convinced the ship was crashing, and she could still remember how sore her throat was from screaming. The elders, who'd ridden down in comfort, had beaten all the children, days on end, for daring to doubt God would deliver them safely to their new home.

She tried to set the grim memory aside; Alexis's hand clamped down on her forearm, and Bhelan was watching them both. She managed a smile. "It's fine . . . oh, look, Alexis," she added suddenly as movement below caught her eye. "It's a *gneris* come up to sun!"

The interrelator peered eagerly around her human companion as the small, sleekly furred beast heaved its front end onto a huge floating mat, then rolled sideways across it; before they could see it flip onto its back, though, the shuttle was across the mat and well beyond it. Alexis briefly tightened her hand on the translator's arm, and when Magdalena glanced at her, she mouthed, "Good job," and let go.

On her other side, Bhelan's ears were upright and still once more. He made another adjustment—*right wings, easing us down and dumping speed,* Alexis thought. The waves below were a little closer and passing under them a bit more slowly. And then, in the distance, she could see land: a tall bluff to the craft's right, a low, tree-covered expanse just ahead of them.

Bhelan's hands were suddenly moving very quickly, but now he was talking, too, letting Magdalena know what was going on. "We lose more speed now, so I can release the rear air-cushion and the hind rotors. In a very little—when we pass that small fishing boat, you see it?—there, you may feel a movement, but it is only the fore-rotor emerging from the nose. It will not open, of course, until after we begin the upending process, and I will tell you before that begins. . . ."

Magdalena watched, bemused, as he worked rapidly, adjusting, shifting, occasionally leaning forward to give the red-enameled com a voice command. The flyer crossed low waves and open ground, heading toward a black patch of ground surrounded by brassy skeletal frames; they were now moving at normal flitter speed, barely two meters above the surface. Bhelan nodded a warning and Magdalena clamped both hands on the chair sides and closed her eyes as the craft swooped up and hovered for one seemingly endless moment. The ship then slowly, smoothly dropped straight toward the ground, guided by five rotors and Bhelan's skillful moving of the fins, slowed by the air cushion. Moments later, it stopped with a little jerk; the faint engine noises ceased entirely and the translator opened her eyes to see the frame coming up to clamp onto the ship. Once it was secured, the shuttle slowly leaned forward and gradually came to rest on its belly.

Bhelan flicked the last toggles to shut down the engines, and unsnapped his harness with the other hand. Alexis was already on her feet, gazing through the forward view-port. "Someone to greet us," she said. "No—three someones." Magdalena fumbled at the protective harness; it didn't help that her fingers were still trembling. Bhelan keyed the door open and bowed the interrelator though it—*a human bow he'd surely learned from Khyriz,* Magdalena thought as he turned to aid her from the harness.

"Khyriz gave me a private message for you," he murmured against Magdalena's ear; the low timbre of his voice so near her ear tickled. "That he will see you today, somehow."

She looked up at him, wide-eyed, then smiled. "Thank you for that message. I wonder who . . ." Her voice trailed off as she got up to peer outside. She shrugged, then. "It isn't Khyriz; I guess we'll learn sooner if we go out, won't we?"

The air outside was still and hot; very muggy, especially to Magdalena, who hadn't been out of a controlled climate in three years. *Should have kept a wide-brimmed hat with my hand luggage,* she thought. The air smelled faintly citrusy: like the elusive scent Khyriz used to soften his fur after bathing.

Someone was already beneath the shuttle with a hover-cart for the luggage, but she couldn't make out anything else: The difference between the sunlit landing area and the shadows beneath the ship was too great, and her eyes were still trying to adjust.

Alexis was already talking to the official greeting party, which seemed to consist of only three males: Even from five paces away, and even in the unisex loose robes, the lack of long ear-tufts was obvious. Two more steps and so were the white patches flanking the nose, and the longer whiskers. Two of the males were plainly clad and bore household color-stripes on their sleeves, which meant they were servants of some kind.

The other wore deep blue silk, one forearm of which was gold with green stripes: One as broad as her index finger was long, the other extremely narrow. *That is Khyriz's elder brother—but not the heir,* Magdalena thought.

What was going on here? The CLS team had been assured a proper reception committee: the eldest Prince, a representative of the Prelate and one to stand in for the nobility. Perhaps they were waiting inside the palace, and this harassed-looking young royal—Khedan, she suddenly remembered—merely there to escort them . . . ?

But as she came nearer, Alexis's slightly raised voice told her that wasn't it, either. "Message to our ship? But we didn't receive any message!"

"Apologies, sincere ones," Khedan replied smoothly. "The message was sent and acknowledged by station and my brother's ship." His bow, his gesture, and his whiskers were all very correct and very well composed. Magdalena turned her head aside momentarily, to hide her surprise and compose her face. *He's lying,* she realized. But this wasn't the place or time to show she knew it. "The Emperor and his Council know your awareness of our culture and our ways, so of course they assumed you would want the full day's time we would give one of our own to prepare for such a meeting—and our own, of course, would come no farther than the second moon base, while you—!"

"Well, yes, of course we have come a greater distance," Alexis replied, as smoothly. *She* wasn't fooled either, Magdalena decided. "But we have proper sleeping and bathing facilities on our ships, so there was no need for the delay . . . but, as you say, such things happen, communications do go astray, and certainly there's no need for haste, since we will be here a very long time. And personally, I am looking forward to a long hour in a proper Arekkhi bathing pool." She glanced at Magdalena, then gestured toward her.

"I am Magdalena Perez, the translator for the CLS," Magdalena said, her bow and hand gesture indicating "one who is of another class and who is pleased to meet." Alexis wouldn't introduce her, of course. Arekkhi didn't introduce others; it was considered a gross breach of manners. As Khyriz had explained, it dated from a time, not that far back, when vendettas and petty bickering were common: One did not risk presenting one being to another, when possibly there was spilled blood between the two, or one would not wish to be acquainted with the other for some reason.

"I am Khedan, son of His Exaltedness the Emperor Khezan." The Prince glanced at his two companions, gestured for them to speak. Ordinarily, servants wouldn't in the presence of royalty, of course.

"I am Rohf, who has served the Empress ten years."

"I am Edhal, who most recently tended the wardrobe of Prince Khyriz."

Khedan gestured once more; the baggage cart, now full, was easing from beneath the shuttle; Magdalena glanced that way as Bhelan went back into the shuttle and the lock cycled shut behind him. The servants gestured a very brief bow, then went after the luggage. Khedan turned to indicate a pale yellow stripe of color not far from where they stood. "That moving walk will take us to the old palace, where you will be housed." He was silent thereafter, unless Alexis asked him a direct question. In silence they boarded the moving walkway, then entered the main floor of the old palace and walked past the few silent, staring clerical staff who were in the vast open space that led to the ramps or to the various chambers of office.

The middle Prince's ears fluttered constantly, and his whiskers hovered a finger's worth above his fur. Magdalena wasn't buying it. *It's a lie, like his words; he's acting, so he won't have to talk to us. Not because he's afraid of us as aliens, or afraid of saying or doing something to bring shame on his family or his home world . . . but because. . . .* She frowned briefly. She couldn't begin to decide why.

He showed them how to operate the entry controls to their suite of rooms, then left them outside the beautifully carved double doors that led from the long hallway to the old royal apartments; he grudgingly made a promise to Alexis that he would carry her greeting to the Emperor and the Council.

The two women watched him move back down the sloping ramp to the main floor, then looked at each other. "Well!" Alexis said. "Shall we?"

Magdalena managed a lips-only grin; there just might be
spy devices outside the new CLS headquarters, after all. "After you, madame," she replied gravely. Alexis pressed the five-
sided buttons, waited until the two doors slid back into the
walls, then stepped into the flowering, vine-covered entry.
"Wow," the translator added dryly as the tangy scent hit her
and the doors closed with a faint "snick."

"Whole floor to ourselves, pretty impressive," Alexis said;
she sneezed, rubbed her nose, and strode quickly through the
entry and into the main room—this was where the emperors
of old had entertained guests, and where they would hold any
receptions, parties, group meetings. . . . "Very nice!" the interrelator added as she surveyed the vast, pillared room.

Magdalena gazed around them: dark-paneled walls, dark pillars, darkly timbered ceiling, with gold and iridescent filigree
between the timbers. The entire south wall was dark-glassed
windows (they'd be clear glass after dark, of course) and balconies galore. At least ten doorways were evenly spaced across
the east wall. And central to the room, a vast talking-pit: two
small steps down from the floor, the cushion-filled area where
Arekkhi could sit and talk, argue, watch vid. . . . (*Yes,* Magdalena thought as she looked around, there was the new holo-
vid center that held their own communications gear, as well
as a complete Arekkhi entertainment system, and planetary
communications.) The matte-black video, sound, and two-way
communications system fit surprisingly well into the corner of
the room above the pit, though it was a sleek contrast to the
ornate chamber and its furnishings.

Including the being who rose from among the cushions and
bolsters: tall and slender, red zhona-silk slithering into place
and a padded hat canted at a familiar, jaunty angle between
his ears. Magdalena laughed aloud. "Khyriz!" she cried out
happily, and ran to greet him.

CHAPTER 6

◆

But she slowed to more decorous pace almost at once. *Alexis will think you've got the mind and manners of a ten-year-old!* she thought. And Khyriz: He looked different. Older, of course. *Regal,* she decided, *mature.* Maybe he wouldn't want to be bounced into by an overexcited and too-young translator. She took a deep breath as she came up to him and held out her hands. "Khyriz, my good friend."

The Prince laid the backs of his hands lightly on hers, the Arekkhi greeting between close friends, then spread his arms wide. "Magdalena," he said very softly, and hugged her, human-style. Magdalena hugged back, burrowing her face against his chest, hands flat against his shoulders. *I was right about one thing,* she thought. *He's matured; his muscles. . . .* At StarBridge, he'd been so lean, she'd joked that she could count his ribs through silk and fur both. Now a layer of taut muscle covered them and bulked out his shoulders. "And Alexis," Khyriz added as the interrelator came up behind them. "Or should I say 'Revered Interrelator?'"

"Not in these rooms, you won't," Alexis retorted with a wide smile. "I'll think you're being sarcastic . . . or I won't remember that's supposed to be *me*. How did you get in, though? I thought all those fancy buttons on the outside door meant it was locked."

"I asked that your servants permit it; I came down as they were leaving to meet your shuttle. I thought it would be more . . . pleasant to meet you here, in private." Magdalena glanced up at his face as he hesitated over the choice of words; *he sounds tense,* she thought. "And to be certain that you would not need to immediately . . . ah . . . *clean* these rooms on your arrival." He held up a hand and wiggled his fingers. Alexis eyed the little patch on his nail, and touched the earring-disrupt she wore so he could see the gesture.

"And . . . we are clean?"

"You are," Khyriz said.

"Good. Not that I expected such a breach of manners, of course . . ."

"If you are sensible, on Arekkhi you always expect that," Khyriz reminded her evenly.

The interrelator nodded. "Well—thank you. Gaudy and handsome as ever, aren't you, O Prince?" Khyriz wrinkled his nose in reply, baring neatly pointed teeth in an Arekkhi attempt at a human grin.

Magdalena had almost forgotten the kind of ham-handed jesting these two had indulged in back at school. Khyriz lifted the hem of his robe to expose short, narrow feet in soft red slippers. "No glass shoes, even now," he said cheerfully. "But your teasing is still amiss: In that vid of Dr. Rob's, it is the Cinderella-she who wears the clear little foot-coverings; the Prince has boots to his second joint." Alexis laughed. "But if *you* brought such glass shoes, Alexis, unpack them soon. My father's council is arranging a special ball to honor your arrival."

"Oh? That's nice of them. When?"

"That is not decided yet. Soon, however. You should perhaps have allowed me to arrange the formal garb for both of you after all," he added. Magdalena looked up at him, puzzled, then at Alexis.

"Arranged . . . ? But we both have clothes," she said began.

Alexis briefly met her glance. "Not the fancy stuff. I guess I forgot to brief you on that, with everything else going on; Khyriz offered to pay for fancy dress since it's not normally a CLS expenditure—but, of course, the CLS can't allow that." *Of course not,* Magdalena realized after a moment. *That would have the appearance of a bribe, and the CLS is extremely careful about appearances. Considering just Earth political history, they need to be.* "But they did come up with a special clothing allowance," Alexis went on. "So we won't have to go to formal events in StarBridge jumpsuits." She glanced at Khyriz. "I don't imagine trousers on human females will be wildly popular here, will they? Though we did see the station baggage handlers in them."

"A few of the working females also begin to wear them . . . fish-hunters, and the like. I hope such things will change even more, now you are here," Khyriz said. Magdalena frowned. Why did he sound so formal? "Personally, I have hopes of someday wearing my denims outside my rooms." He shook down the red silky sleeves, wrapped an arm around Magdalena's shoulders, and drew her close to him. "I trust my brother Khedan was polite when he greeted you?"

"Very polite," Alexis said. "But it was odd: We were expecting the committee. You know, your eldest brother, a ranking member of the Prelate's household and one of the noble members of Council, plus a few others."

"Yes, I know; I heard. An emergency—"

"Oh? Oh—so was *that* what that fire was all about? We wondered. I know your pilot said field burning, but it seemed so out of control and such an odd hour. In the Ukraine, we'd've called a burn that size a disaster."

"I had not heard about . . . a fire," Khyriz said quietly; Magdalena, still pressed against his side, felt his heart thudding rapidly. Alexis appeared not to notice the slight hesitation in his reply.

"Well, an emergency like that would explain why we won't meet the Emperor today. Your brother gave us a rather garbled excuse, something about a message to our ship and the full day of recovery—we never received it, and I'm assuming it wasn't actually sent. It makes a good excuse, of course. Because, we said from the first that a full day off to recover from travel wasn't needed. We worked that out long ago."

"I am sorry; I didn't . . . I don't know anything about this," Khyriz said. His voice definitely sounded odd now, and his whiskers were quivering, very near his face. Magdalena eased away from his side to look up at him.

"Oh, I'm not blaming *you* for anything," Alexis assured

him. "It was just . . . an odd greeting ceremony."

"I've told you about Khedan," Khyriz remarked pointedly.

"Khedan . . . oh, of course. The would-be priest who can't quite manage to take final vows." Alexis frowned at her fingers and spoke as if to herself. "Odd they'd send him; if he's so xenophobic. . . ." She shook free of the direction of her thoughts and smiled again. "Guess that explains it."

Khyriz's fingers tightened on Magdalena's arm before he released her. "And this fire. . . . I had not heard about one; doubtless it was not as vast as it would appear from the shuttle. But Bhelan would know; his people come from halfway around Arekkhi, and they still burn stubble after a harvest, to clean the fields before reseeding. Of course, it may have been wildfire; if so, there will be coverage on the news-vid. Your system will access Arekkhi vid stations, but the standard vid is there." He indicated an enormous, framed mural that took up a large portion of the wall nearest the cushion-filled pit. "The control is built into the corner, just here," he added and bent down to point out the five-sided buttons.

"I know how to work the television," Alexis said, deliberately patient. "And I'll look for a report on the fire, of course; I just wondered what you knew. Since it was your pilot who brought us in, I thought he'd have told you."

"My pilot," Khyriz murmured; one ear flicked and he shoved his sleeve up to bare the watch. "You see, I wear it always, Magdalena," he said. "Apologies, I must go now; Bhelan was to return for me as soon as the shuttle was cleared, I am needed at my estates."

"Oh?" Magdalena asked, and she could hear the disappointment in her voice. So could he; he laid the back of his hand against her cheek briefly.

"Apologies," he repeated softly. "I hope to return by early evening. If so, may I join you for a late *edha*?" Arekkhi ate five or more meals per day. *Edha,* a light repast that was more like a snack, was often an hour for casual parties. They ate *zhner,* the last meal of the day near what would be human midnight, and it was only for family, though one might invite a betrothed.

"Of course," Magdalena said, and managed a smile.

"You can show us which of the sauces are which," Alexis added. Khyriz laughed aloud—a little spatting noise.

"I can keep *you* away from the hot ones, which I know you cannot bear," he replied dryly, and left them. Alexis followed as far as the entry.

"Hah!" the interrelator called out after him. Magdalena heard him laugh again, then the door opening and closing behind him. Alexis came back in, kicking off her shoes in the doorway. "He looks good, doesn't he, Mags?"

The translator nodded. "He—didn't seem strange to you, did he?"

"Not really. A little shy. After all, it's been more than a year since we've seen him, and we're here instead of at school. Why?" Alexis asked. "Now—strange is what I'd have said about his brother, or Bhelan when we flew over that fire. If Bhelan had been human, he'd have been stuttering and sweating."

"I know. That—and those Asha." Magdalena shook her head and managed a smile. "You'll think I'm paranoid, already believing that everyone's up to something."

"If *you* feel that way, I won't think you're paranoid, I promise you that. I'll at least listen, and test the air myself." She turned as a chime sounded from somewhere on the other side of the entry hall. "That's the servants' door, bet anything. Our things must be here."

Magdalena grimaced. "Servants. That's going to be so strange."

Alexis smiled. "Remember that the alternative is we keep this barn-sized museum clean ourselves, do our own cooking and washing, and still find time to do our jobs for the CLS."

"Yeah, I know."

"Remember, Arekkhi are like our own people, they choose what work they want to do, and they're paid for it," Alexis reminded her. "You're helping feed two families. Come on; we've got bedrooms . . . let me think, down the main hall, all the way at the end . . . here." The interrelator flicked two wall switches to open opposite doors. "Very nice," she added as she looked inside. "Human-shaped beds, tons of Arekkhi bolsters and cushions and enormous closets. Want first choice, or shall we flip a coin?''

Several hours later, Magdalena shoved her last pair of socks into one of the narrow bins that substituted for drawers and shoved pins into her hair to get it off her neck. Early afternoon sun poured through the open balcony doors and it was suddenly very warm in the small chamber. "Time to go somewhere else." Maybe find something to eat and drink; it had been a long time since her last meal.

Alexis had left the door to her bedroom open but had apparently finished unpacking earlier; she was nowhere in sight. The translator pictured the floor-layout map they'd both been given, and started toward the small eating room that was supposedly part of their pantry. On her way back up the hall, she passed the office, its door braced open by a large crate marked "Main Computer." Alexis sat cross-legged on the floor pulling components out of the box, her back against the desk that had been built to human specifications. Bits of gear were spread all over the floor.

"You look hungry," Magdalena remarked. "And hot. Things like that go together better when you're fed, remember?"

"Yeah . . . thanks. You know how it goes. . . ."

"Tunnel vision; I've been there. But the harder you work, the less gets accomplished. Except you've done a lot in here already," she added, looking around. Other than the computer and its various hookups and accessories, everything else they'd brought for the office seemed to be in place. *Probably we won't hold many meetings of any kind in here to begin with,* Magdalena thought; most things would go through the Emperor and his councils at the start. But the room looked efficient; the big desk had two human-shaped, comfortable-looking chairs, and room enough for two people to spread out. A set of shelves took up two walls; four of the forward-slanting Arekkhi chairs, a few small tables, and good lighting completed the furnishings.

"You said something about food," Alexis said as she got to her feet. "Lead me to it. And a nice cold mug of *rhi*-juice."

* * *

Khyriz didn't return for *edha,* and so far as the translator knew, he wasn't back in time for *zhner,* the midnight snack, either. Magdalena tried not to feel disappointed as she undressed for bed. Khyriz had his own life here, a vast landholding to take care of, probably official duties for his family as well. *For all I know, he was eating* zhner *with the family of his betrothed. . . .*

Though that wasn't very likely: His elder two brothers had taken mates, and the heir already had two young. The succession was covered, and the laws covering population control applied to royals as strictly as to any others. *More strictly. Most of the wars of the past five hundred years have been succession wars. But that's not your business, Perez, unless Khyriz wants to talk about it. You're just disappointed because you wanted to spend time with him right away. It may not happen; you'd better get used to it.*

She left the balcony doors ajar: After three years on StarBridge, it felt wonderful to lie in bed and feel the cool, fresh air moving across her face. It smelled nice, too: The vines coiled around the balcony were more of that citrusy-scented stuff.

She woke sometime later—by the clock-patch on the wall, two Arekkhi hours. The air was almost chill, a little damp. What . . . ? She heard the low hum of a flitter beyond the window; probably what had wakened her in the first place. She slid from beneath the thin woven cover and wrapped it around her shoulders as she got up and crossed the floor to gaze over the railing.

There must be one moon up at present, but it had to be nearly full; brilliant blue-white light illuminated the open grounds surrounding the old palace. There were a few sets of parking blocks at the far edge of the short turf, and a small flitter was settling into place with a faint hiss of escaping air. A tall Arekkhi in a dark jumpsuit moved with easy grace toward the main entrance.

"Khyriz," Magdalena whispered, and for a moment, thought of leaning out where he could see her. Something about the speed at which he was moving made her hesitate. He was deliberately setting his feet in turn, bobbing slightly as he came onto his toes, his arms away from his body, fingers splayed: stalk-pace. The near-flat cant of his ears indicated the anger; she'd seen vid of the emotion, but never seen a hint of it in Khyriz. She retreated into shadow, and was about to turn away when suddenly Khyriz stopped and raised his head; his arms fell limply at his sides. He seemed to be staring directly at her bedroom. Magdalena gazed back, knowing he couldn't see her, wondering what could possibly be in his mind. Eventually he shook his head, humanlike, and moved on. She heard the faint hiss of the outer doors opening and closing behind him.

She realized she was holding her breath, let it out with a faint sigh, and went back to bed. "That wasn't just me," she whispered. "That was *strange*."

Their first full day on-planet didn't start well. Alexis came into the pantry clutching her head and mumbling in English. "I forgot to take my supplements last night, can you believe it? My head's pounding like I spent the night drinking my great-grandpa's slivovitz—"

"His *what?*"

"Wine made from beets. You don't want to know," Alexis said with a moan. "Pills—I don't think I can see well enough to sort 'em out." Magdalena ran back to her own room as the interrelator sank into her chair with a groan; she returned as Rohf set down two large mugs of rhi-juice and two deep bowls of cold water, then quietly slipped from the room.

"Here," the translator said. "Headache—that's the B-supp, isn't it?"

"I didn't take *anything* last night," Alexis murmured, hand over her eyes. "Give me the whole packet."

"Without food? They won't absorb right. . . ."

"I know. Rohf is bringing dry bread. Don't think I could handle anything else for the moment." She waited while Magdalena tore open the clear pack of half a dozen pills, tablets, and capsules, let the translator hold her hand steady as she poured the contents out, then held the water to her mouth. "Swell. Thanks, Mags. How long before we have to be at court today, or have you heard yet?"

"Second afternoon hour," Magdalena said.

"Good. Means I can eat a piece of bread and crawl back in." The interrelator glanced up at her companion briefly before letting her eyes close. "Don't worry; I went through this my first time off StarBridge. Supp-deprivation headache. I'll be fine."

"I hope so."

"If someone had poisoned me, I wouldn't look this good," Alexis replied, then grinned feebly. "That was a joke."

"Bite your lip," Magdalena ordered, only half kidding. "Better yet, bite on this—here's your bread." She shifted to fluent and unaccented Arekkhi as the tall, pale-spotted servant hovered. "We do not blame you for this, Rohf... not last night's meals or drink. We need the packets, and the interrelator forgot to take hers." She held up Alexis's torn packet and another full one she'd brought for herself.

"The young Prince told us of the supplementals," Rohf replied softly; his ears quivered. "I shall remind the translator-she daily of the need, if she wishes?"

"Thank you, yes," Magdalena replied. "Remind the interrelator-she as well."

"Samples of food and drink were kept, of course. If it is required that I taste—?"

"Of course not!" Magdalena replied quickly. Rohf—who had just volunteered himself as a poison-tester, Magdalena realized—gestured assent and left the pantry.

"I'll never forget again, I swear," Alexis said, groaning.

"You won't get the chance," Magdalena replied good-naturedly; she gazed after Rohf, distressed. "Eat something and go back to bed. I'll wake you."

"Thanks," Alexis said weakly; she shoved aside the rest of her loaf and got unsteadily to her feet. "I'll be fine, honest. Did you take yours?"

"With you as an example? You bet I did," Magdalena said. "Shoo. I'll wake you in plenty of time for a bath."

"Good," Alexis replied vaguely and wandered away.

The translator wasn't fully convinced, but when she checked later, the other woman seemed to be dozing normally. She went back to her own room to sort through the contents of her

robe-room. Two jumpsuits with the StarBridge logo on them;
a jacket—her own, not David's; three brightly colored plain
ankle-length and long-sleeved gowns with beretlike matching
felt hats that would serve for their first meetings with the Arekkhi. . . . The pale blue gown would do for this first meeting.

She shoved those aside and fingered the two pairs of authentic Earth blue denims folded on the back shelf, the three
precious cotton short-sleeved shirts folded neatly atop them
and the music-cube she'd put together for Khyriz and herself.
It had all taken up precious weight—but Khyriz would be so
jealous of the "Levi's" marked jeans. "The Khyriz I knew
on StarBridge would have been jealous." He'd been so
strange. . . . She sighed and shoved the robes across the casuals. "Forget the blue, wear the red, it's your best color, and
you're gonna need that, Perez."

She closed the hatch on the robe-room and wandered over
to the still-open balcony doors: At this hour, outside light came
through the small diamond-cut windows at the tops and bottoms of the inward-opening doors. Outside, there was a flurry
of activity: clerks streaming in to work on the main floor or
the lower archive-levels; a long, skinny hover-tram, which
brought workers from the mainland. Only three flitters rested
on blocks at this hour: the one she thought was Khyriz's (it
rested on the same blocks where he'd left his), a brightly colored one she recognized from planetary vid as a recent model,
expensive and fully equipped. The last flitter had the practical
look of a governmental vehicle, like those they'd seen in vid;
it probably belonged to a master of clerks.

Wonder what they actually do, down there? Was this where
official laws were keyed into the new, planetwide computer
system? Or where smaller proclamations—or even the menus
for the new palace—were prepared? Maybe she'd have the
opportunity to find out after this afternoon's meeting with the
Emperor. Clerks and other common workers put in what she
thought of as Medici hours: early mornings, early evenings
when the air was reasonably cool—a long, midday break for
food and rest.

It might be good to talk to the clerks downstairs soon—
before she had the chance to get nervous about it. "Remember

you convinced Dr. Rob, *and* Dr. Blanket said you were ready.
Compared to them. . . .'' But some of these clerks might be
doing work for her, personally. *If I get into one of the libraries
here on the island, and get access to some of the old books
that haven't been translated in at least a century. . . .* Khyriz
had teased her about all the ancient books stored here, the ones
that were *original* hard copies of truly ancient works, the language scarcely known these days except for a very few words.
*Like Latin, he said. He knows that I taught myself Latin once
I had a grasp of French and Italian.* It hadn't been easy at
first, but it got easier, languages were like that. And here, she
had the use of good computers.

Khyriz had said he'd get her access to the ancient volumes
if she wanted it. *If there's time* . . . She could imagine few
things more exciting than translating a text from some lost
aeon of Arekkhi history: *not merely some sermon by a female-
hating Huguenot.*

That wasn't likely. But the opportunity to explore a huge
library, all those books.. . . . she'd feel like the drawn and an-
imated heroine of that vid of Rob's, yet another retelling of
the ancient *belle et bête* fairy tale. *Beast gave her his library,*
she thought with sudden amusement. Khyriz had seen that an-
imated vid also.

She laughed aloud then. ''*Beauty and the Beast,* is it? Well,
you've hardly that kind of beauty or intellect! And Khyriz isn't
going to turn human and dance into the sunset with you. Grow
up, all right?''

By midday, Alexis was awake on her own, headache gone,
and grumbling good-naturedly over more seed-bread and rhi.
''Okay, Perez, now you know my Achilles heel, guess I can
expect you to hide the vitamins on me and become super-
interrelator any day now, huh?''

''What—let you veg out in your nice, soft bed and make
me deal with the hard stuff?'' Magdalena retorted. ''Reminds
me of a mystery story I read a while back, a woman with a
hormone imbalance who's married to a jealous man. One night
she dances with an old boyfriend, and her husband substitutes
sugar-pills for her hormone tablets, and she—''

"*Thank* you for sharing that!" Alexis broke in sharply. She stared at her hands briefly, then shook her head; pale hair flew. "Sorry," she said finally. "I have a horror of things like that . . . I must have read the same story; some detective shows up in this primitive village, makes a lot of smoke and fire and then produces the hormone the woman needs to become human again?" Magdalena nodded. "It . . . spooked me. The way she became—beastlike. I mean, still human in some ways, but with her mind totally gone. And, someone had that much control over her, they could give her mind back or withhold it forever. . . . Hey, never mind, we have a meeting with the Emperor shortly, guess I better go comb my hair and look nice, right? Maybe we'll even have a few minutes to run over our strategy for this afternoon."

"Couldn't hurt," Magdalena said. The hairs on *her* forearms and the back of her neck were hackled. *What made me bring that up?* she wondered. That awful memory from the early days on NewAm, when the cult was battling administrators over the education of children and at the same time trying to feed everyone. . . . *They drugged the younger girls, kept us in a state for days at a time where we were given a little broth, nothing else. They stole chunks of our lives from us. . . .* She shook her head fiercely. That was over, done, past! Just because she'd never been able to tell Dr. Rob about it—she'd worked it out herself, it was all right. *He can't touch you, they can't hurt you anymore,* she whispered to herself. The whisper trembled.

The strategy was actually fairly simple, as Alexis reminded her companion on the moving walkway between buildings: "I do all the talking; they'll expect that, and besides, Khyriz taught you more of the political gestures. You fade into the woodwork as much as you can, look wide-eyed and naive, and watch the Council. Especially this character Khyriz calls Iron Duke. Remember, things may go just fine—but in case they don't. . . ."

"I know." Magdalena nodded, caught hold of her beret as a sudden breeze tried to lift it from her hair. "And if I need to talk to you, privately, I'll step on your foot. No one will see that."

"Better than coughing," Alexis agreed. "Or our own gestures. We don't want them thinking CLS politics are as untrusting as theirs—even if it means they think we're babes in the woods, right?" Magdalena nodded and the two fell silent as the walkway moved up the ramp and into the new palace.

The Emperor had center stage in a high-backed chair; he sat at the midpoint of a long table. Windows on three sides let in light, but any outside view was blocked. A high, domed ceiling with murals of seasonal farming activities, everything gold-leafed and edged in iridescent paint, shone above an intricate mosaic floor. It wouldn't be hard to look wide-eyed and awed, Magdalena thought, as Alexis introduced herself, then stepped aside to let the translator speak.

Twenty-two male councillors flanked the shimmercloth-clad Emperor, all brightly robed and hatted. Only one—the Prelate, Magdalena assumed from his plain, priest's garb—hid his face behind a featureless blue enameled mask.

Alexis waited until her companion was seated in the cushioned human-style chair on the near side of the table, then made a gesture that was the honorific of Emperor and Prelate both: "One who is not the equal of this one." She then offered the greeting of "One who seeks equality where such a thing is possible." To the translator's surprise, the Emperor responded with the same greeting. The Prelate made no move.

There was a faint murmur of conversation, two of the Emperor's councillors speaking to him so softly she couldn't make out the words. *Which is these Zhenu?* she wondered; apparently the councillors were not going to introduce themselves. After a moment, she decided it must be one of those nearest the Emperor—and after another long moment, she decided against the aging male clad in pale blue. His face showed open curiosity about the two women, and when she looked at him, his whiskers curved forward. The other—younger, lean-faced, and clad in severe white—had eyes nearly as chill as the Prelate's; his whiskers canted up smugly.

The Emperor was younger than either; she knew that much, but he looked it—there was no thickening fur on nose or hands that indicated a male over forty, no graying hairs around his nose, either—though dye was so commonly used, one could never be sure.

Khezan didn't resemble either Khyriz, or the son who had met them the day before at the shuttle. His heir—a solidly built male clad in deep yellow at the opposite end of the table from the Prelate—resembled him only slightly.

The Emperor suddenly emitted a faint, polite cough, and those around him fell silent. "It is the pleasure of the Arekkhi to welcome the CLS interrelator and her associate to our world. We look forward to a pleasant and profitable relationship between all of our peoples."

"The thanks of the CLS and all its member worlds for your willingness to associate with our League," Alexis answered him politely. Magdalena gazed about her with interest as Alexis answered questions—mostly about their newly remodeled rooms in the old palace, the food, the servants—nothing important, particularly since they'd only had an hour of the Emperor's time for this first meeting, and no second one had yet been scheduled. Alexis patiently responded to a query about the furnishings, and then, before anyone else could toss out a question, added immediately, "We are grateful for your concern regarding our comfort, Great Ones. But we should instead use your valuable time to speak of our reasons for being here." She paused politely, and only went on when it was clear no one chose to answer.

"The CLS has asked me to personally convey their hopes that the trade you and they envision with the other League worlds will be profitable to all and promote greater understanding. I was told that the officials on Shassiszs Station hope we can now finalize the documents to allow such trade to begin, which will in turn allow discussions to extend to the Arekkhi a unique place in the League as a trading world. The CLS agrees with the revered Emperor that the Arekkhi are well beyond any need for protected status." She hesitated briefly as the Prelate shifted on his bench; Magdalena glanced that way, then let her eyes wander over a fine piece of inlay on the table so that she could watch the white-clad councillor

from under her lashes. He had just signaled to the Prelate—
wait. . . .

Alexis cleared her throat and went on. "You yourselves
have requested that the CLS act quickly in providing a team
to work with your people, to assure the Arekkhi will not be
held back from assuming their voice. They send word by me
that they agree to this timetable, provided the requests they
have made are honored. Since the Emperor has agreed that
trade within Arekkhi space is based on a guild system, and
that such guilds are housed all across the planet, the League
requests that the translator and I meet with the leaders of such
guilds, where they are situated." She paused; the Emperor
gestured assent, and the white-clad councillor made a very
subtle movement of his thumbs to the male at his left. "This
was agreed to, but no document has yet been signed. The
League asks that I remind the Emperor and his Council that
both the document *and* the meetings are requisite parts of the
overall trade agreement."

Silence. The Emperor curved his whiskers in a smile. "The
document will be provided, signed and properly embossed, of
course. The Council felt it would be better to ask questions here
and now, than to attempt these things via the far-distance communicator systems." The whiskers quivered faintly. "Many of
us are not—comfortable with such means of speaking."

"That is understandable," Alexis replied, with a lips-only
smile of her own. "Though it may take longer this way, since
I must communicate with the League myself, of course, before
making any alterations to the document." She leaned forward.
"Since time is of the essence, Great One, I have taken the
liberty of making a list of places where the Translator and I
would first prefer to begin these guild meetings." She drew a
folded piece of laid bond paper from her sleeve and set it on
the table between them. One of the servants retrieved and unfolded it, handing it to the Emperor, who read, then passed it
to the male at his right hand.

"Good choices," he said briefly. "I admit, however, that
we are not . . . have not yet arranged proper transport off-island
for you and your companion. Though doubtless something

suitable can be arranged by the time the document is finalized. We, of course, agree that the sooner this can be managed, the better for everyone . . . shall we say, perhaps, in a nine-day?''

"Nine-day!" Alexis echoed sharply; she bit her lip and added, in a quieter voice, "Apologies, Great One. I had hoped, however . . ."

"We shall meet tomorrow—at this hour if convenient to you?—to discuss the details of the document. Meantime, I will see to it that the guildmasters in these areas are contacted, to be certain there will be no delays once we are able to send you off the island. Once the document is finalized."

He gestured; the white-clad male at his left side shifted and spread his hands in a gesture of conciliation that did not warm his eyes. "In the meantime," the Emperor said smoothly, "one trusts there is sufficient to entertain and amuse you here, or provide education, if you desire.

"You shall have free entry anywhere you choose," the Emperor added, "including my household apartments, since my Empress wishes to greet the outsiders who were kind to her youngest son. And that son tells me the translator-she is an expert of sorts on your world's history. Perhaps she will enjoy the libraries here: There is a small chamber in the old palace that the clerks can show you, a chamber here that holds the family history, and, of course, the Prelate has graciously offered the books-room in his halls."

"My thanks," Magdalena said. "I am extremely pleased to be offered such an opportunity." The Prelate looked even less pleased to her eye than Zhenu did.

Moments later, the two were back in the main entry. Alexis gestured for Magdalena to follow, stepped onto the moving walkway that would take them back to the old palace and laid a cautious finger against her lips, keeping it there until they were halfway between the two buildings. "So . . . what was your take on that?" she asked finally.

"Besides that the Prelate didn't like us?" Magdalena replied dryly. "And that *was* the *zhez* Zhenu, wasn't it—the white-clad?" Alexis nodded. "I could be wrong," the translator went on, "but I felt like they were stalling. I wasn't aware there was a problem with the trade papers."

"There shouldn't be," Alexis replied. "Most of the terms were set by the Arekkhi, except for the one about us talking directly to the guild heads—and even that didn't present a problem until CLS said we had to go to *them*."

"Oh. Well, they can't keep us on the island forever," Magdalena said, "no matter how 'entertaining' it is here."

"They'd better not try," Alexis said flatly. "They've been so open on so many fronts—until it gets down to either of us going out and meeting the common Arekkhi. It was the same when the Heeyoons set up shop on the station. The Heeyoons finally backed off so they could keep their toe in the door, for once trade gets moving out of the system." Her eyes narrowed. "That is not going to work with you and me. We have a job to do. And the Emperor and his Council better realize that."

The next day's meeting produced a few minor concessions on both sides, but the trade documents remained unsigned; and the same thing happened the day after. Alexis finally told Magdalena, "I'm going to try a new tack here; they may think we're double-teaming them somehow, so I'll go alone this afternoon."

"If you're sure—"

"I'm not sure of anything at this point. But it's worth a try."

Magdalena used the time to explore the old palace library, which turned out to have nothing more than hard copies of books and documents already installed on her computer. After a cursory examination of the shelves—the carving was more interesting than the contents—she spent a surprisingly pleasant hour talking to the clerks and arranging for basic Mizari lessons for those who expressed interest. When she got back to the CLS apartments, Alexis was in the talk-pit, a cool mug of rih at her elbow and a roughly handwritten document in one hand.

"Got it!" she announced. "I just sent holos to CLS, by FTL. If everything's okay, the Emperor will sign tomorrow, I sign for CLS with your initials, and I've been promised a flitter and pilot for two days after that, whether CLS has a holo of the final document back to us or not!"

CHAPTER 7

♦

Late that night, Magdalena woke to a strong wind banging her shutters and a roomful of dry, hot dust. She staggered to her feet, somehow managed to close off the room, and found the control for cleansing the air. Out in the parking area, servants—and what she for a moment thought was Khyriz—hurried to secure flitters to their landing blocks. One had already been blown off its base and lay, one stubby side-wing crumpled, against the barrier between parking and walkway.

Fortunately, the sound of the rising wind was muted by the thickness of outer walls and glass and by the air-cleaning system: Strong winds tended to give her nightmares.

If anything, the winds strengthened overnight; when she wandered into the small eating room next morning, Alexis was nibbling at seed-bread and scowling at a message. "I should've known," she mumbled gloomily. "Read it and weep; the Emperor says it's too dangerous for us to fly into Ebba with the winds up."

"Well, then, we can go inland, can't we?"

The interrelator grimaced. "Want to wager on that? It's another delay; Arekkhi weather's a precise call these days, they *knew* this was coming. Not that we won't try," she added gloomily. "I should've seen it coming myself," she mumbled around more bread. "I swear, any more delays, and I'm gonna locate the old causeway to the mainland and *run* to Ebba!"

"Ahhhh—reality check, Ortovsky," Magdalena said mildly, though her stomach was suddenly tight. "It's underwater most of the time, which means *slick,* if I recall? If it's too dangerous to fly in this wind, what's it going to do to you, running on wet, slimy—''

"Yeah, I know." Alexis cast her a crooked grin. "I'm kidding, Perez, I wouldn't really. After all, all those inoculations don't protect against whatever's in the oceans, they said to avoid the big water until they do more intensive tests, remember. My luck and some odd germ would rot my toenails and kill me messily.''

"Leaving me in charge—don't you dare," Magdalena said flatly, but she smiled as Alexis laughed. "They're still signing the document today, though, right?''

"Right—same hour, both of us. I'll get us that transport, too, or know the reason why," she added grimly.

But Alexis proved no match for the full Arekkhi Council. The Emperor contributed little to the discussion and, Magdalena thought, looked harassed—he intercepted more hand gestures than he gave, and most of those, she could not interpret. The *zhez* at his left side did most of the speaking—he and Alexis, who was exceedingly polite, but not about to back down if she could help it.

"I understand the winds create a difficulty for the new-style flitters, because of the weight and wingspan," she said patiently. "I only suggest that we find an old-style flitter that can make the journey safely.''

"We *had* such a flitter prepared," Zhenu countered smoothly, "but, apologies, the pilot chosen discovered the identities of his esteemed passengers and begged to be removed from duty, for fear of embarrassing himself and his family. You must remember, please, Interrelator, that this is a trait of our kind. It is very difficult to locate those who—well, you see the difficulty.'' He rummaged in the dish at his elbow and popped a small sweet into his mouth.

"Apologies," Alexis said softly, "but would it be possible to get both a more solid-style flyer *and* the pilot Bhelan, who brought us from station? He has the necessary skills to pilot a shuttle back into atmosphere and onto the ground here—and he seemed to have no difficulty in our company.''

"He was part of the number chosen originally," Zhenu murmured around his sweet. Magdalena, watching him from the corner of her eye, saw the subtle gesture directed at the Emperor, and the Emperor's equally subtle reply. *I have no idea what any of that meant*, she thought vexedly. "But there was illness in his family, he was needed elsewhere, and, of course, there is always the fear the Prince might catch such a disease."

Momentary silence, which Alexis broke. "Well, then. I notice all our clerks showed up this morning, wind or no wind. What if we were to take the tram over to Ebba, like they do?"

One of the older councillors from well downtable stirred. "But if there *was* an accident! The Arekkhi who utilize the railed-tram understand the dangers of the seasonal winds, and—"

"And of course," Zhenu cut him off with a slightly edged voice and a sharp gesture, "while Arekkhi who use the tram can swim in our waters, I am told those who were not born Arekkhi may face dangers from them. And, of course, an accident to the tram, while unlikely, is something the survivors and the families know is possible; they accept the risks . . ."

As he paused for another sweet, Alexis gestured apology and said, "And Magdalena and I are both capable of accepting the same risks—we begin facing them when we qualify for StarBridge."

"Yes—one admires such courage," Zhenu murmured around a mouthful of candied fruit. His eyes, Magdalena thought, were still the coldest she'd ever seen—except the Prelate's. *He* still wore that enameled mask. "But if the CLS sought to blame us? If they felt we had not properly warned you—or that an accident had been precipitated—?"

"The CLS wouldn't do that; they give us leeway, and accept that we occasionally must take certain risks."

The elder who had supported him, every meeting Magdalena had attended thus far, spoke up now. "But if your CLS decided not to believe? If . . . apologies, Interrelator, but if they saw in us neglect, to allow you to board a tram in high winds? Or thought it went beyond neglect, to active intent to harm on someone's part? We would be penalized in that case, would we not?''

Magdalena glanced at Alexis, who was momentarily at a loss for words. ''But . . . if we were to send messages, letting them know we had chosen to . . .'' She hesitated; the elderly councillor spread his arms in a gesture that indicated taking point in debate. He looked far from happy, though. Before Alexis could go on, Zhenu leaned forward; the Emperor touched his arm with the back of his own hand and tapped the long sheet of heavy blue paper.

''Then, if that is settled for the moment, if we might arrange to sign everything here that needs a signature? Or a mark? So that the document is properly completed—and once the winds die down you may, of course, have access wherever you wish, though, of course, one hopes you will discuss your choice of direction with us. To be certain there are no difficulties. Such as the outbreak of *yenif* fever in the back highlands of Ak-kherif, and in the city Ehnoyhe.''

Odd, Magdalena thought. *No one mentioned disease there, when I petitioned two days ago to visit Shiksara's family.* But this entire meeting was extremely odd; emotional currents from all directions, the Emperor himself as odd as anyone here. She watched as all the parties necessary signed the trade document, made her counterinitials anywhere Alexis had signed, and took the completed, sealed, enamel-ducat-marked and synth-packeted document to hold on to as Alexis tried once more to get permission for them to ride the tram to Ebba, at least. Somehow the two women found themselves in the outer hall again, the doors closed between them and the Council.

Alexis stood very still for a long moment; there was no one in the spacious hallway but herself and Magdalena. ''Wait a minute!'' she exclaimed. ''We didn't even get permission to ride over to Ebba with Khyriz, once the winds die down! What was I thinking of?'' She turned around, stared at the double doors. They were as solid-looking, and as uncommunicative, as a stone wall. Two hard taps with her knuckles brought no response; there were no entry-levers on or beside either door.

She scowled sidelong at Magdalena and shifted into English.

"So—what's *your* take on that? Wait—keep it to yourself, even in English, until we're outside."

"I don't know what to think," Magdalena admitted. She couldn't remember ever seeing Alexis so angry.

"I know what to think, all right—well, never mind. Let's go. I need to get back to the 'beg pretty' program and get us another meeting with the Emperor, to get us over to Ebba at least!"

Magdalena shook her head. "That about the tram—it felt like the truth to me, Alexis. Like it's normally safe, but in high winds, the clerks take a small chance—like, oh, back on Earth when planes were fairly new, flying in winter?"

"I'd give you the option of not going, of course. But if it's okay for the workers, it's fine for me," Alexis replied. Her cheeks were blotchily red. "Come on; sooner we get back to the old palace, sooner we can get a new date to waste more of our time." Alexis glowered at the blank doorway, swore under her breath in Russian, turned, and strode down the hallway of the new palace, ignoring the mechanical walkway. Despite her longer legs, Magdalena had to hurry to catch up.

Fortunately, there was no one anywhere in sight—certainly no one who would know by her body language and expression that the interrelator was furious. The two women clattered down the outside ramp practically side by side, but as they reached ground level, Alexis sped off across the ground cover, dodging the oddly spaced hover-cars and empty landing-blocks as she headed straight for the old palace at a near-run. Her pale hair stood nearly on end in the gusty wind.

Once in the shelter of the old palace, she stopped abruptly and let Magdalena catch up. The corners of her mouth twitched. "Sorry about the temper tantrum and thanks for putting up with me," she said in Mizari. "I needed that."

"Nothing of the sort," Magdalena protested. "You have every right to be angry! They're—I don't know what they're doing! What's going *on*?"

"I don't know," Alexis admitted. "But it doesn't feel right. Unsafe vehicles and conditions, my foot! I think they're stalling, but why would they do that? They've known all along that the team can pull out if CLS requirements aren't met."

Magdalena shook her head. "I know. It doesn't make sense! Why let us come at all, if they're going to try to keep us here on the island?"

"Well, I don't know what they're up to, but I *do* know what's going to happen next," Alexis said grimly. "When we get back to the suite, I'm firing off an FTL voice-only encrypted message to CLS headquarters and another to Rob. If he can't do anything to help, he can see Mahree gets it. We may need her—especially if this is all the cooperation we're going to get." She started walking again, but at a normal pace. "I hope it won't come to that, but we may have to pull out of here even before we get properly unpacked."

"I understand." Magdalena nodded, and hoped neither her face nor her voice showed her disappointment. "What do you need me to do?"

"I need for you to send word down to the ground floor, our batch of clerks. You prepare a petition for another meeting, tomorrow—and a letter to the Emperor detailing what happens and how fast, if we don't get that meeting, or if this not-so-little hassle isn't straightened out at once."

"You want *me* to handle that?"

"Don't worry," Alexis smiled faintly. "I'm not asking you to play lawyer—*or* interrelator. I'll be the one signing both documents, and I always read what I sign. But I think you'll do a better job than I would of choosing the right words and phrases so it's polite but they know we aren't kidding. Also, I need you to find Khyriz, get him down to see us as soon as he can come. He's the Emperor's son, after all. Maybe he can do something to help."

"Worth a try," Magdalena admitted as they entered the old palace and strode up the ramp.

The building was unexpectedly cool, considering the dry heat and wind outside, and the lack of air conditioning. The door to the second-floor suite opened as they came up; Edhal gestured a bow. "Interrelator," he said very softly, "the Prince asked permission to wait for you. He and his cousin are in the salon."

Magdalena looked at Alexis, who raised her brows. "Something going right, finally," the interrelator said, then turned to the servant with a lips-only smile. "Would you bring *rih*, please?" The servant gestured assent and toggled the door closed behind them.

The two males stood close to one of the open balcony doors near the cushioned pit, Khyriz again in red, his smaller and more slightly built cousin resplendent in deep gold. The cousin's ears flicked nervously as the two women entered the room, stilled again as the Prince murmured something in a low voice.

Alexis slowed and glanced at Magdalena, then whispered, "I'm going to collar Khyriz right now—soon's we've done the polite stuff. Can you manage talking to the cousin for a bit?"

"I can do that," the translator replied. *I can try,* she added privately. The cousin looked scared half to death. *His first aliens, wager anything,* she thought. But by the time the introductions were done and Rohf had brought refreshments, Zhikna seemed to have relaxed considerably. Magdalena caught the interrelator's eye and nodded slightly.

Alexis touched Khyriz's arm and said, "If you don't mind, I've got something you should see. We won't be long."

Khyriz gestured assent, his whiskers flicking briefly forward. "Of course. Magdalena, can I trust you not to eat my poor little cousin while I am gone?" Zhik went wide-eyed and still; Magdalena laughed easily and gestured amusement.

"He's safe with me, Khyriz."

"Oh—a jest. Apologies," Zhik said hastily. Alexis could hear Magdalena suggesting she and the nervous young male settle in the talking-pit; she led Khyriz back to her office. Once there, door in place behind them, she glanced automatically at the comp screen and the distort-icon in the lower corner that indicated no one could understand their conversation, then gestured toward one of the Arekkhi chairs as she settled on the corner of the desk nearest him. Khyriz remained standing and listened without expression as she told him about their morning; when she finished, he sighed in human fashion.

"I feared something like this, Alexis. The problems they mention are real—"

"They should have warned us before we ever came."

"I agree. You—what was your saying? You preach to the singers," he added in slightly accented English.

"To the choir." Alexis bit back a smile at the words; the situation wasn't funny and she wasn't going to let Khyriz charm her. For all she knew, he might be step two of the Emperor's plan to keep the team quarantined.

"The choir, yes." He shifted back to Arekkhi. "I warned you, back at the Academy, about my father's Council. He is surrounded by elderly beings—and our old ones dislike change as much as your own."

"I understand that," Alexis said evenly. "But documents were signed and agreements made, and certain rules made clear before the CLS arranged for us to come here. That Council knew what we expected. Khyriz, if they renege on the agreements, Magdalena and I will have no choice but to contact the CLS and arrange transport out of Arekkhi space, as quickly as we can get it. Is that what they want?"

His whiskers went flat to his face, but flicked out to normal almost immediately. "Of course not! Not my father. You have seen some of his letters to me at the Academy, Alexis. You know how proud he was for his youngest son to be chosen for StarBridge. And he sees the usefulness of the alliance the League offers, the new tech for us, the mutually beneficial trade agreements . . . though many of his councillors do not."

Alexis snorted inelegantly. "Then why does the Emperor keep them as councillors? Your father's supposedly an absolute ruler, and the Council's only there to advise him. Isn't that right?"

"I did not lie to you or to the CLS about that, Alexis," Khyriz replied formally. His eartips were quivering slightly.

"Khyriz, I wasn't accusing you of lying." Alexis sighed and drove both hands through her short blond hair. "Apologies. I'm angry."

"I understand that. I would be angry myself." He hesitated, eyed her oddly for a moment, then said, "You do not understand the difficulty. Oh, there is the ideal of the Emperor and his Council, but . . . but the way things are now. . . ."

His voice had faded to nothing. She couldn't begin to guess

what he was thinking. "Can . . . you tell me about it?"

"Between us, and in trust, yes." He paused, and when she nodded, went on. "You know my father's father died young, at least ten years before his time. So my father was suddenly Emperor. And while he had friends, colleagues—he had not yet formed the alliances a ruler must have. Nor had he chosen councillors. So he inherited the councillors of his father. And— many of those males are still on the Council. Oh yes, I know," he added as Alexis would have spoken. "He is Emperor. He can send them away and appoint new councillors."

"Why doesn't he?"

Khyriz glanced down at his nail-device, then sent his eyes toward the closed windows. He lowered his voice. "Swear to me this does not go beyond you and me . . . and Magdalena, if you choose, but only if you are certain of the security of these rooms."

Alexis stared at him. She finally eased away from her seat on the desk long enough to check the comp screen, then nodded as she resettled. "My word on it."

"Thank you. I asked him that, very recently. He is Emperor, yes, but certain of his nobles—and the Prelate—command great wealth. And my father has . . . very few armed."

"You—" Alexis swallowed hard, licked her lips and tried again. "Khyriz, are you trying to tell me that if he dismissed them, these males would *challenge* him? They'd . . . what? Fight?"

Khyriz's ears flickered, then dropped flat and stayed there. "Never that! Alexis, you know our history! That last war, a hundred years ago—it taught us that there is nothing worth armies fighting and people dying! But these elderly males would ally to strew barriers in the way of anything they do not like. Such as progress."

"Like this morning," Alexis said with a growl. "But the Emperor was no more helpful than his Council."

"If he were as strong as my grandsire, he would not have such problems. He could order his Council to conduct surveys of the hydroponics on the first moon and personally deal with you and Magdalena as was agreed. With things as they are, there are petty deals, arguments, bickerings—so much time wasted so he can get what he sees for the Arekkhi worlds and our people.''

''I . . . all right. It sounds like what *I* know of Arekkhi politics at their worst. It's a wonder the CLS agreements got signed at all, I suppose. Still . . .''

''Fortunately, it is not all of the Council. My father has some allies among the old as well as the few he has so far been able to appoint. Even stubborn old males die sometime.'' His whiskers flicked briefly forward. ''But those who oppose him are powerful. The Prelate and our Church are certain the new alliance will lead to wholesale abandonment of worship by the Arekkhi. And others, many of them with livelihoods depending on hereditary land tilled by tenant-farmers or grazed by the flocks of our herders—they fear such a sudden shift in monetary standards that they will find themselves landless and starving.''

Alexis shook her head, eased off the desk, and began pacing. ''Khyriz, that was explained during the negotiations,'' she said patiently. ''The League is *aware* of those possibilities, and they know how to avoid them. Provided they get cooperation—and right now, I am *not* getting the cooperation I need! In fact, I'm not getting any cooperation at all!'' Her voice had gone up; she drew a deep breath and spoke more calmly when she went on again. ''Apologies. Look, Khyriz, I know this isn't your fault. But I need to get back in to see the Emperor, talk to him about this. We got shoved out so fast today, I didn't even have time to ask if Magdalena and I could at least get into the city with *you* as an escort. They can't object to that, can they? I need to see your father again. Right away.''

The Prince's ears flickered and went sideways: He gave her an odd look, then turned away to gaze out the windows toward the new palace. ''Alexis . . . I cannot help you with that. There are rules, laws, protocol. Even I cannot just see the Arekkhi Emperor. Even I must file petitions with his clerks and wait the prescribed time for an appointment. And once excused from the chamber, *I* cannot simply return, either.''

''All right, I understand that.'' Alexis drummed her fingers on the desktop. ''I guess. No, I know, it's protocol. But you're not just a citizen or a mere off-worlder, you're his son. And I

know enough about your family life; you see your father often.
As a father.''

"I can't—''

"You *can*," she replied flatly. "Over *edha,* maybe? Darned
soon, though. Give him a message from the CLS interrelator
that either the translator and I are allowed free access to the
people of the capital city over there—within three days, wind
or no wind—or *we are pulling out*. They'll have one hard time
convincing the League to send in another team. And there goes
all that great trade, and all that new outside tech. And probably
that half-built jump-point station, *and* the Heeyoon traders on
your station, too. Khyriz, inviting us in, then acting like
they've got something to hide is *not* productive!''

He went as wide-eyed as pictures she'd seen of startled, very
young Arekkhi, blue-eyed babes with silvery manes standing
on end. "I . . . Alexis, I will do what I can. But . . . if you wish
entry to Ebba, I can take you now, my own flitter, no one will
know until too late. . . .''

Despite her anger and the odd tension in the office, Alexis
laughed. "Joy riding?" She'd done that once or twice as a
young girl, with her wild older cousin Nicholas. Khyriz's
whiskers quirked—apparently he was remembering the story
that made him laugh so hard, back on StarBridge. "I can't do
that kind of thing anymore, I'm sorry. I'm official now, remember? I have to work with planetary officials and with the
CLS.''

"Well . . . I am sorry, too," Khyriz said softly. His whiskers
quirked again. "At least, this time the vehicle would not be
'warm.' ''

"That's 'hot,' '' she replied with a grin.

The slightly silly moment had eased the tension in the office.
Khyriz nodded. "I will find my father before *edha,* if I can—
before day's end for certain. I will tell him your message and
do my best to convince him. Then I will send you a message
or come myself, tonight." His whiskers trembled. "If you and
Magdalena permit, for *zhner,* if matters are worked out.''

Alexi was surprised. *Zhner* was usually reserved only for
family. She raised her eyebrows. "*Zhner,* is it? Of course,
Khyriz: You're my friend and I know Magdalena thinks of

you as a brother." For some reason, this rather formal little speech seemed to upset him. Odd. Probably he was worried about keeping them on-planet. "Thank you, Khyriz, for your help. Remember, I'm here because I like you . . . I like Shik-sara, everything I know about Arekkhi. I don't want to argue with anyone, I just want to do what I was sent for: to learn as much as I can about everything here, so the outside worlds can understand you as well. And the other way about."

"I know. There is much to learn here that I could not tell you on StarBridge . . . never enough hours to talk. I hope it is you and Magdalena who are the outsiders who will"—his whiskers briefly touched—"learn all our secrets."

"Yes." Alexis blinked, glanced at her watch-patch. "Speaking of Magdalena, though, we'd better go see how she and your cousin are getting on."

We are getting on very well, Magdalena thought—after a few false starts and visible shyness on Zhikna's part ("Please, call me Zhik, everyone but my father does"). Mere mention of his father—it astonished her that this shy youth's father could be horrid Zhenu—seemed to make Zhik nervous. Of course, he might be high-strung. It took some moments to get him seated comfortably, and he remained tongue-tied until she mentioned dance.

All at once, Zhik responded with enthusiasm, discussing Arekkhi formal dance with her at intelligent length. She was surprised to discover he was a named Prime—one of the rare males who led the most difficult figures at formal balls. Primes were normally much older.

Odd that Zhenu seemed to take no pleasure in his son's impressive accomplishment. Nothing that the youth said, just the sense of. . . . She shook that off and talked about her own work on Arekkhi dance; he seemed both surprised and pleased that an outsider would learn such a thing and that the two women would actively participate in the upcoming ball.

"Of course," he went on, "it is not the only form of dance among our kind. I once stayed among my mother's people for a season. Her family's estate is near one particular village, so they attend all the festivities, and at the festivals, there is always dance. . . ."

"Folk dancing!" Magdalena exclaimed eagerly as he paused. Arekkhi folk dance had barely been touched on during her time on StarBridge: Most of what she knew she'd picked up from Shiksara. And among Shiksara's merchant-class people, folk-dance was considered low-class; the merchant-she couldn't demonstrate any of it.

Zhik nodded, human-fashion. "It occurs in almost all villages and local regions, though the styles differ greatly."

"That's true of Earth as well: We have many styles and I can show you some of them; we brought vid. And, of course, every world has dance created by those who work the land."

"They have?" This was clearly something that had not occurred to the young noble. "All those other kinds of beings— how wonderful!"

"I think so myself," she said. "I hope to see some of the Arekkhi folk dances."

"Truly?" He gave her a wide-eyed kit's look.

"Of course. This is the kind of thing the League does. Didn't Khyriz tell you?"

"Perhaps. Apologies, I paid no heed to his talk of the outside worlds. Until now, I thought I could have nothing in common with them."

"That's one reason I am here, and Alexis," Magdalena said. "But also I would personally like to see Arekkhi folk dance because, besides being a CLS translator, I'm a dancer."

His whiskers flicked briefly forward. "But I know this much. My cousin showed me a vid of your dance!"

Magdalena laughed and shook her head. "Oh, no! Not that concert! It's two years old and I was awful!"

"It seemed very fine to me," Zhik protested politely. "Khyriz says this . . . ballet . . . is human ancient formal dance."

"For one part of our world. Oh . . . I can't think why that reminds me, but I was hoping since I'm on a real planet again that I could have a pet of some sort. Your father said I should ask you about your Asha, he said that you keep yours on the upper floor—" Magdalena stopped short. "Are you all right?"

she asked, leaning forward in alarm. Zhik's whiskers had suddenly gone utterly flat to his cheeks and she could see white all around his eyes.

"It's nothing, merely an . . . an old injury." Khyriz's voice came from behind her; she started and whirled about as her red-clad friend came across the salon. She eased out of the talking-pit; his outstretched hands captured both of hers as she stood up. There was something curious about his face: she was suddenly reminded of the used-car salesman "Cal" in the "selling things" moments, ads, between one of Rob's bad monster-movie vids. *This isn't Khyriz—not the Khyriz I know. He's acting a part, trying to divert my attention—from Zhik? But why?* She eased one hand from his grasp, turned her head; Zhik's face was composed once more.

"Zhik has a place in his ear, an infant-he in his first teeth bit it and the nerve sometimes gives him pain. Cousin?" He released Magdalena's fingers and walked around the cushion-pit to bend over his young kin. Zhik looked up, blinking. "Your ear . . . the nerve-pain, isn't it, Zhik?"

"I . . . apologies, Translator," he murmured, whiskers quivering, and let Khyriz help him out of the pile of cushions. "As my cousin says, pain took me by surprise. And we were having such a pleasant discussion about . . . about dance."

"It's all right," Magdalena said slowly. Her eyes moved from one to the other, flicked toward Alexis, who had come up next to Khyriz. "I'm sorry about your ear."

"But surely your medical-techs can deal with something so . . . basic, can't they?" Alexis asked.

Khyriz spoke very softly against his cousin's other ear, then gave him a little shove. "Go ahead, up to my rooms, Zhik, I'll come shortly." Zhik gestured cautious bows to each of the women, turned, and walked unsteadily from the room. Alexis turned to watch him go, her brow puckered. "Poor cousin," Khyriz murmured once the outer door clicked into place behind the young noble. "You know his father is Zhenu. The *zhez* has no patience with pain; when Zhik was bitten, his father ordered him to pinch the ear to stop the bleeding, and not to whine. My cousin has never seen a medical tech for the injury, the Iron Duke wouldn't allow it." He looked from Magda-

lena's shocked eyes to Alexis's set mouth. "Apologies that I
have upset both of you. I will go tend to my poor cousin, I
have an oil that stops the pain." He glanced toward the outside
door, back again. "Alexis, I will speak with my father today,
without fail."

"Do that," Alexis said flatly. Her voice softened as Khyriz
gave her a wary, sidelong look, his whiskers twitching. "I'm
not angry with you, my friend," she added. "Just with . . .
things."

Khyriz nodded, human style. "I understand. I will try to
make my father understand." He touched the backs of both
hands to Magdalena's wrists, gave Alexis a neat human bow,
turned, and left.

There was a long silence in the room after the door closed
behind him. Magdalena finally cleared her throat. "I thought
the full moons were five or six days away?"

She'd meant for Alexis to laugh. The interrelator grinned at
her. "Well, today's been weird enough so far, hasn't it?" She
looked up as Rohf came in with a basket containing four mugs
and a dew-beaded jug of rih, and sweetened bread-fingers, gestured thanks to the servant as she took the basket, then settled
two large bolsters against her back, her feet dangling over the
pit. "Magdalena?"

The translator's eyes still looked worried. "I'll make that
call down to the clerk's office first. Save me something, all
right?"

"I'll try. But getting angry makes me hungry."

Middle night: Both moons, nearly full, sailed high in the night
sky, blotting out all but the brightest stars and the station.
Khyriz glanced down the table in the family eating-room: His
mother and sisters sat at the far end, stitching on one of their
endless hangings. Much nearer sat his father and, unexpectedly, his middle brother. Khedan normally ate a very sparse
zhner alone, or with two of the Prelate's high-ranking priests—
nobles his own age.

Khedan was talking again; Khyriz kept his expression polite.
This middle brother didn't converse, he delivered polemics.
He'd spoken brusquely earlier about greeting the CLS team,

and he was coming back to the subject once more, ignoring his father's attempts to maintain peace over food. "After I greeted the alien females—"

The Emperor interrupted him. "Khedan, those are uncouth words, not acceptable to your rank. The proper forms of address are Interrelator and Translator."

Khedan's eartips flicked. "This is private, Father. I know how to speak politely when I must."

"A thing forgotten in one place can be forgotten in another," the Emperor replied evenly. "And I will not have rude speech in this chamber, whatever is done elsewhere." For some reason, this seemed to enrage Khedan, who shoved aside his half-eaten dish of roasted sea-curls, got to his feet, and gestured a sharp, "One who is unwell and would leave before finishing his food." The Emperor's whiskers flicked in exasperation as he gave the assent. Khedan stormed out. At the far end of the room, the Empress glanced at the closing door, then met her mate's eyes briefly before she turned back to her needlework. The elder male's gaze shifted to his youngest son, then.

"Father," Khyriz finally murmured. He wasn't certain what else to say.

"I do wish Khedan would take vows and leave the household in peace," Khezahn said. "He is not happy halfway between, and neither are the rest of us." He lapsed into silence, lifted a sea-curl from his own plate between hand-carved wooden pincers, and ate the little sea-snail absently. Khyriz chose one of the dipping sauces at random, but set his curl down uneaten as his father looked at him again. "Your message mentioned a difficulty with the CLS, Khyriz. I thought our meeting with them went very well. They were anxious to begin at once, of course, but . . ." His voice faded.

"They can be polite also," Khyriz replied gently, and gave him a terse recounting of Alexis's message. The Emperor looked worried when he finished.

"But . . . Khyriz, you know the problems with allowing them free access to . . . everything."

"I know of the raid on Zhenu's lands, to begin. No one has claimed responsibility?"

"Fifty dead, more missing, an entire *parth* of Zhenu's land and its village burned? No one would dare claim such a deed. The Zhez is in a rage!"

The rebels must be very good, Khyriz thought, *to evade the Iron Duke, and his legions of guards.* Amazingly good, to attack without the Duke knowing about it beforehand—the noble's spies were among the best money could purchase.

Still, they're spies and guards, not gods. Fortunately so. There were beings alive this night because of that fact. But he didn't dare think about them—not here. "The women wish only to journey to Ebba for now," he said finally. His father hissed faintly.

"Khyriz, I know they cannot understand. But if they have free access of the city . . . if they spoke with certain factions, or learned of Asha . . ."

Khyriz let his ears flick back and remain low as he murmured, "Father, the outsiders already know of Asha." Silence. He kept his eyes averted and went on. "The Heeyoons saw two on-station when they first came to us; they were wearing small vid-devices, and so everyone knows of Asha, out there. At the Academy, I was asked about them; faced with vid, I couldn't deny they exist." He glanced up briefly: His father was staring at him. "Apologies. But such a lie would have achieved nothing, save my immediate expulsion."

"You told them—?"

"The backup lie; that they are pets. The two the Heeyoons saw were in the offices of the Master of Station."

"Zhenu's cousin. And Zhenu said nothing of this to me."

"Zhenu's cousin answers to Zhenu, who knows you do not condone such . . . pets. The CLS knows of Asha and so do these women." He gestured submissively and let his ears go flat. "Apologies, Father. An unranked son does not engage in such matters. Or . . . or instruct his Emperor. But when you deal with the outsiders, I am your best expert."

"Yes." The word had no emotion he could recognize. "Then tell me what you see of this situation, and what course you suggest, Khyriz."

More than he'd ever have dared hope. *This is your father, not just Emperor; an Arekkhi of sense and compassion,* he reminded himself as he passed on Alexis's message. "The interrelator was not in a mood to be put off, Father."

"I understand."

Khyriz gestured assent and cautiously went on: He had never lied to his father before. But, as the humans said, there was a first time for everything. "If the first Heeyoons had been told, 'Leave us alone, we want no part of you,' the Arekkhi would have been allowed isolation. But since we openly took their trade and technology and new goods in exchange for recognition and trade—world status by the CLS, since documents have been signed—we cannot now say, 'Bring your side of the bargain in full, but let us choose ours.' The CLS will assume all the wrong reasons for this; if the team leaves the planet in anger, the trading group on-station will also leave, very soon. We will lose the new jump-station. There might even be an . . . investigation," he added quietly.

"Investigation?" Khezahn's whiskers quivered.

"Because we must be hiding truly terrible secrets, and this would include a downtrodden underclass—a slave class. There would be terrible shame attached to such an investigation. Would even the Prelate welcome *that*?" Silence. "Father, apologies, let me suggest . . . an alternative. A report on the human women by the news-vid tomorrow. Limited to Ebba, if you choose." *For now.* "And then, the morning after, if I were to take them to Ebba, for a meeting with my clothing designer, Fahara . . . and if they were permitted to speak freely with Arekkhi whenever they chose . . . Well, that would certainly help. I assume that the Master of City keeps the same number of marshals, who could instruct the people who might come into contact with the women, how to behave. Or vid-messages could be sent to the households."

"That can be managed."

"Suggest that to your Council, and suggest that I pilot the flitter. I have one of the older, more wind-resistant ones."

"Zhenu will never agree to that, and his allies could override me, Khyriz. Remember that Zhenu still seeks a way to bring in the trade that will make him rich enough to take over all Arekkhi space and yet avoid any entanglements with the outsiders themselves."

"I know." The Prince considered. "Father, what about Zhik as a pilot? He can pilot the older flitter if the winds are still up, his own if not; he is an excellent pilot, and he trembles at his father's shadow. They may mistrust me; they will not doubt Zhik."

"Perhaps," the Emperor said, but then his eyes narrowed.

"But my son, this Fahara—I remember now; she has an Asha—a Voiceless!"

The Prince gestured assent. "So she has. But Fahara is cautious, and the Asha knows the rules of conduct—and when this Asha was sold to Fahara, the sellers reminded her that the fate of her remaining family rides on her actions. She will behave as a pet—or as a working beast." The Emperor's whiskers went flat very briefly. "Father, the women come from a world with clever working beasts. In two days, they see an Asha: It fetches, understands verbal and gesture commands. And they are told, "It is a pet." After a visit or two for clothing or fittings, they will react as we do under such circumstances: All Asha will be assumed to be a pet, or working animal."

Silence, which the Emperor finally broke. "Khyriz . . . you make sense. Still, remember the Council wishes to distance you from the women. From the Prelate and Zhenu together, this is more order than request."

"I understand. But the women are my friends, fellows at an exclusive school together. They will think it strange and suspicious if I avoid them. They already find things strange and suspicious enough."

His father seemed amused by something he'd said. "I will summon Council early tomorrow. *Very* early," he added with a malicious tweak to his whiskers, and Khyriz remembered that the Iron Duke had only just come from a moon-season on his estates, half a world away. What Magdalena called "serious sleep debt."

"Father, thank you," he began. To his surprise, his father stroked his cheek, the way he'd done when his youngest son was still growing—and had done something extremely clever.

"Thank *you*, Khyriz." He shoved food aside and rose. "I must give some time to your mother. You?"

"Apologies," Khyriz replied as he stood also. No usual word-games with his younger sisters tonight; he had matters to attend. "I need to return to my apartments."

"Go, then. I will send you a message tomorrow, once I have agreement from the Council for you. Say nothing until then."

"I will not." Khyriz sketched a brief gesture-bow, turned, and left the chamber. It was late—Zhik might be asleep already. Unfortunate; it was vitally important that they talk, at once.

The youth wasn't asleep—he wasn't happy, either, once Khyriz got him settled in the talking-pit. He looked quite distressed by the time Khyriz finished speaking. "Cousin—I cannot do this. Look what I did only today when the Magdalena-she asked about pets!"

"So that was it," Khyriz replied. Zhik hadn't been able to even talk about it earlier. "Zhik, listen, please." Khyriz pressed the back of his hand against his cousin's arm. "I was among all those outsiders for two years: I had to tell them many things—they had vid from the very first visit so they knew much more than any of us thought. They have seen Asha . . . as pets." Zhik's ears went flat and stayed down. "Zhik, I must have your help. The women will leave us for good otherwise, and so will the traders. My father will be able to persuade the nobles who back trade; we will only be able to sway your father if *you* pilot your flitter for us."

"He . . . will order me to spy on you, Khyriz!" Zhik protested. "And on the women . . . !"

"Yes. He knows you will do what he orders, and for that reason he will let the women into the city. The CLS will remain here. And if they do, Zhik, I swear to you on my blood that I will one day be able to reunite you with Ah-Naul."

"Because of the outsiders." Zhik considered this; his ears lifted slightly, then went flat again. "But I cannot lie to my father!"

"You will not have to. The women and I will not speak of compromising things; Father and the Master of City control the populace. But if need be, I can tell you the things to say to your father. He will assume your fear is caused by the outsiders.''

"Some of it." Zhik was silent for a long time. Khyriz kept quiet with an effort and waited him out. "I owe you so much, Cousin," he said finally. "Ah-Naul—"

"No. Do not do this out of gratitude, or because you fear I will undo our bargain. Ah-Naul remains safe, no matter what you decide. Do this for yourself, for all Asha. For the good of all our kinds.''

"And for this Magdalena-she," Zhik added softly. "You were right, Khyriz. She did not seem alien to me, once we began to speak of dance. All those worlds, out there—so many things to see. . . ." He was speaking to himself. Khyriz blinked. *Magdalena, you have created a small miracle with your words.* Zhik shook himself and smoothed his sleeves. "I will do this, Khyriz. I pray I shall not disappoint you.''

"You will not, Zhik. Remember that I will be helping you." Khyriz got up and held out a hand to help his cousin from among the cushions.

CHAPTER 8

◆

Three days later, under a dark blue presunrise sky, a clear-canopied five-seat flitter rose quietly from the palace grounds and turned toward the mainland. Zhik handled the controls of the new-model air-cushioned vehicle with a relaxed competence that surprised Alexis. Of course, she had seen him only once before and some beings interfaced better with machinery than with the living. Zhik might be one of those.

Khyriz and Magdalena had the back of the open cabin to themselves. Alexis caught very little of their bantering conversation; she had her seat turned sideways, so she could see how difficult the flitter might be to pilot. Zhik knew he was being watched: His head shifted slightly so he could glance her way now and again—but he had his hands too full to talk. He would have: An air-cushioned vehicle like this would require minute altitude adjustments so the choppy water between island and mainland wouldn't throw them around. And according to the wind-readout, what had been a light breeze on the island was much stronger over open water.

She kept a neutral face, but inwardly she smiled. *One to our side.* However he'd done it, Khyriz had got them their off-island trip. It helped that the winds had eased, but still, she'd fully expected another excuse once that problem had gone away, and thanks to Khyriz—and whatever he'd said to his father—the excuse hadn't materialized.

She had not been surprised at the Council's astonished claims that of course there had been no intention to isolate the team, that most certainly the women could visit the Prince's designer, they need only ask! And the interrelator would be allowed full choice of route and stops, both directions.

She withheld judgment, of course: *How far can we actually range on a day trip to a specific central-city location? And am I going to have to go through this every time?*

Still, for now, she had cooperation. And more importantly, she had broad access to the community: She and Magdalena had been interviewed the day before by an intelligent-seeming news team from the city. The interview actually appeared on the news-vid late the same evening, barely cut, and nothing important had been left out. Today the team had free use of this hover-flitter, and Zhik wasn't trying to keep her from seeing how easy it was to operate.

Had the Council simply given in? Her threat to pull out had been real, but she couldn't believe a mere threat would be enough. Had the Emperor and the Council—she thought of them as ''They''—really been that blind about what was expected of them, in return for the expected trade? More likely there was an unknown reason for the turnabout.

No point in trying to second-guess Arekkhi nobles and royals, of course. Still . . . They knew she was pilot-class, her bio listed her qualification, and anyway, Khyriz knew it, and had probably long since passed that information on. She was being allowed to watch the flitter's controls—but her pilot was the Iron Duke's son. *I'll bet anything They ordered him to spy on us. Maybe even on Khyriz, who's nutty about the Outside.* Still: *Look at him!* Foppish, jittery Zhik as a spy? *Reality briefing, Ortovsky,* she ordered herself with an inner chuckle, and shifted so she could look at the city. Time to look around, and give poor Zhik a break. She could fly this machine if she had to; it was all she'd needed to know. *Don't get caught in a strange place with no transport.* That wasn't a CLS warning, either: Her father had drummed that message into her head years earlier.

Gee. Emerald City is nearer and brighter than ever, Toto!

Poor Zhik looked very harassed. But then, his father was a known xenophobe; Zhik might be unnerved by her blue-eyed gaze—or by her black jumpsuit. But They hadn't objected to her choice of clothing; for the vid interview, she had worn the same jumpsuit, while Magdalena dressed in the same emerald green Arekkhi-cut robe she was wearing today. *Let them see we can adapt to their ways, but let them also see there are other ways unlike theirs.* Subtle enough to be Arekkhi, she thought, and bit back another grin. If Zhik saw her smile, he might think she was laughing at *him.*

The interrelator eased the seat around to see what Khyriz and Magdalena were up to: He was absently pleating the blue *zhona*-silk of his robe between his fingers, eyes on the translator. Magdalena was unaware of him; she was on her feet, balancing with a dancer's grace despite the constantly shifting flitter. Her eyes searched the rough water below. "Shouldn't we be able to see the old causeway?" she asked.

Khyriz shrugged, human fashion, then answered aloud when he realized she hadn't seen. "At this hour? With incoming tide and this storm-surf, Magdalena, it is under water of . . . of a depth above *my* head. Only when there is a very low tide can you see it. And no one has actually walked the stones in more than a hundred years," he added as the translator glanced at him. "Much too dangerous."

"Oh?" she asked, then grinned impudently at Alexis. "Just as well you *didn't* try to walk to the mainland, isn't it?"

"I planned on running, remember? I know you get only about one Arekkhi-standard hour when the stones are above water." Alexis laughed. She hadn't really been serious, anyway.

"You must not attempt the stones!" Zhik said anxiously; he looked alarmed. "Not at any pace! They are covered in growth that is horribly slick. And the causeway is never entirely dry, A-Alexis." He was still having trouble addressing the two by first names, as they'd asked, even though he insisted they call him "Zhik."

Alexis's eyebrows went up. "But didn't the Arekkhi use them all the time? Until the hover-flitter came along?" Zhik muttered anxiously under his breath as he turned back to his control panel. The ship dropped a little; leveled. Magdalena clutched at her seat for balance, then flopped gracefully into it.

"We did—wheeled conveyances and foot traffic both used the causeway," Khyriz said finally. "But it's been at least forty years since the last use. Remember the climate is in a warmer pattern, and the water, so, a little higher. Also, when the stones were used, there were no *eshkard* in the bay. You know about them?"

"Yuck." Magdalena shuddered. "Those things with nasty bulging eyes and stinging tentacles. The vid I saw didn't say the nasty critters were this far south, though." Not quite a question.

"They were not. Until very recently. But they have spread quickly, the past few years. Like your—spiny urchins? The purple sea-things from temperate Earth-waters."

"Sea urchins. They took over entire stretches of the western American coastline, yes," Alexis agreed. "Until more people discovered how good they tasted."

"Well, *eshkard* are unpleasant to eat, by almost anything on Arekkhi—which is part of the problem, of course. And the spines do not just hurt if they penetrate skin, they are also deadly to us."

"Probably to humans also, in that case," Alexis mumbled to herself. The DNA wasn't remotely similar between human and Arekkhi, but the crossovers of disease, vectors, and poison-susceptibility could often be surprisingly close between the two races. She shrugged that aside and smiled. "Well, doesn't matter, since I'm not down there sprinting ahead of incoming tide, am I?"

How very convenient. The water's too high, there are nasty critters . . . and no one's mentioned any of it until now, when Magdalena brings up the causeway and me talking about running it. Alexis shoved that aside, shielded her eyes, and gazed toward the mainland; individual ships were now visible in the harbor, before bright canopies and low buildings. No sign of the fabled causeway below them, either.

The causeway business might be just what They said, but like so many things she'd been told since landing, the answer didn't properly address the question. She'd received so many glib, pat-sounding answers that didn't quite match facts they'd had earlier. Or which, frankly, sounded made up on the moment. Answers that would keep her from doing her job here.

Winds that would keep the new flitters grounded—but suddenly, they were safe—and their pilot was the *zhez* Zhenu's son. The spread of poisonous water-creatures, handily between the interrelator and the only non-tech access to the mainland. Which, sorry, isn't accessible anymore.

She bit back a sigh. The planet *did* have cycles that created temperature changes, something to do with its orbit and the angle of its axis. A planet without good ecologists could easily develop deadly critters with no controlling predator. As far as she knew, there were no Arekkhi ecologists.

Fine. So I'm imagining some things. But not this new flulike disease in the western foothills of the main continent, right where Shiksara's family lives. Only mentioned when Magdalena suggested that she'd like to visit her friend's parents. A new mutation of an ancient virus that caused high mortality rate was ravaging the local populace, though Shiksara's family had not been infected. But the virus, and its mutation, unfortunately, had no prevention or cure so far.

Convenient. *Okay, maybe I'm assuming that people who treat good lying as an art form* are *lying to me,* Alexis reminded herself. And Magdalena agreed that *something* was wrong here. She just couldn't pinpoint what.

Alexis liked Magdalena—appreciated her dance and language talents, admired the courage that let her bounce back from an awful childhood. Just now, she wished she had Marie-Claire here instead, despite their nasty breakup: Magdalena was a much better translator than Marie-Claire could ever have been, but in Marie-Claire she'd have a good telepath on Arekkhi soil. . . . *Okay, so it's bad manners to scan the minds of other sentient beings—but I'd use Marie-Claire in a heartbeat, same as the Arekkhi would. There's too much going on here that I can't begin to fathom.*

Marie-Claire hadn't even come to the farewell party for the CLS team assigned to Arekkhi—she hadn't even spoken to Alexis since the breakup. *Better yet, why don't you wish for Stephanie?* Stephanie Kim wasn't nearly as strong a telepath as Marie-Claire, but she could receive, if she worked at it. And Stephanie was such a . . . a kind person. . . . Alexis's gaze went distant. The city was replaced by the well-remembered face of her first steady at the Academy: a soft oval face, hip-length, black hair usually worn in a severe chignon, serious almond eyes, and a mouth that could be set when the surgeon confronted pain and injury—but could soften around those she cared for. *Oh, Steph, there I was, actually wondering if a life-bonding ceremony was possible—and you got posted out before the end of my second year! Do you miss me, or do you even have time to think about me? And how complicated is* your *life these days?* The interrelator's own mouth softened in a tender smile. Stephanie was probably up to her elbows in the aftermath of some crisis somewhere. Her last letter had hinted at that, anyway. She'd be the serious Dr. Kim, with hard black eyes, a tight bun of hair, a firmly set mouth.

Alexis blinked and buried the personal thought as Magdalena spoke up suddenly. "Look, Alexis, some of those old-style fishing boats!" Alexis came partway to her feet so she could look out and down. Zhik had slowed the flitter as they neared land, and almost directly below them, the very first rays of sunlight caught five Arekkhi fish-hunters in their traditional green robes and broad-brimmed hats. They were about to launch an old triangular-sailed vessel that looked like a fat Egyptian *dhow,* except the triangular sail was painted in elaborate patterns to identify the family owning the boat. Alexis caught her breath: The ears showing above one hat were thickly tufted with long silvery hairs: a young female.

"Oh, terrific!" She glanced at Khyriz. "Can we stop here? Of course, if they need to get right out and catch the tide, or something . . ." To her surprise, he brushed aside the possible excuse and nodded.

"They will be glad of the visit. Zhik?" The younger male nodded human-style, which surprised both women, then brought the flitter around and down with one smooth maneuver. He kept it hovering just short of the ground.

"I will remain here, so the bottom does not scrape against the stones," he said, and he pressed a toggle to open the hatches. Alexis scrambled out first, aware of Khyriz handing Magdalena out, and the translator's splutter of laughter. *He's playing the courtly Scaramouche, right out of Rob's old mov-ies, listen to that line!* One would think they were flirting! As if Magdalena ever flirted with anyone. With that long-skirted green robe, of course, the translator might feel like she was playing the heroine's part from that movie—and, of course, with such full skirts, even she might need the help.

Silly . . . But the silly moment helped: Now that her first direct contact with ordinary Arekkhi citizens was at hand, Alexis found herself surprisingly nervous. A little shy, even.

The fish-hunters were visibly astonished to be approached by two of the fabled outsiders, but once Alexis introduced herself and began to speak, it was clear they were pleased to be the first chosen by the outsiders for conversation. Two of the males did nearly all the speaking: the eldest and his first son. The eldest only now and again looked at the aliens, though, while the second son and the other two males avidly eyed them, ears almost vibrating with excitement.

The female presented herself as Ehna, the once-wife of the elder's third son, lost in an accident the previous winter. In answer to one of Alexis's questions, the elder explained, "Our females seldom go on the hunting boats; it is harsh work, long and hard hours, and the odor mostly unpleasant. Though the females of most fish-hunting groups are involved in the ac-counting and often in the preparation of the catch. But our family is not attached to a cooperative and we have no guar-anteed purchaser for our take. So it is vital that we have suf-ficient hands to manage the netting and the spears."

"I come from the land myself," Alexis replied. "And from a family where everyone had to work the harvest. I understand this is hard work." The elder looked both pleased and aston-ished by this. Ehna gazed at the interrelator steadily from un-der the broad-brimmed hat, as if memorizing her features and what she said, but spoke very little.

After several minutes, Alexis stepped back and gestured a farewell. "We must not keep you from your livelihood," she said. The younger male gestured a reply farewell, then turned to help his fellow hunters launch the boat. Alexis and Mag-dalena turned away at once to follow Khyriz back to the hover-car: The Arekkhi made elaborate gestures or speeches of farewell, but once the moment was over, both sides were expected to turn away and leave.

Magdalena caught up to the interrelator. "It really *is* a lot like the Simiu," she murmured in Mizari. "If you add in some form of 'good-bye,' of course."

"Different from dealing with Khyriz and Shiksara," Alexis murmured in reply, adding with a faint smile, and in Arekkhi, as Khyriz came up behind them, "but of course, Shiksara and Khyriz are both half human. . . ." It was an old joke between interrelator and Prince, and she glanced sidelong at the young royal, who quirked his whiskers forward in a smile.

"We Arekkhi are just better at mimicry and acting than you mere humans," he replied loftily and handed Magdalena back into the hover-car with an even more courtly bow than before. "But that was a good deed; their catch will sell early and for good price; everyone who saw you just now will want to know what was said and what you are like."

"Good." Alexis clambered in behind them. "So—where next?"

"It is your choice," Khyriz said. "The designer is that way," he indicated with his head, "and we have until midday. Three Arekkhi hours for exploration, perhaps."

"Well, then . . ." Alexis leaned forward to study the city as Zhik brought the flitter up. "Then, that way?" For answer, the young noble worked the controls and brought the machine slightly around, heading south toward what she remembered from maps as one of the busier open-air food markets.

They stopped several times at different stalls, most chosen by Alexis on the spur of the moment: a baker's where a crowd of working-class Arekkhi waited for rolled-up flat loaves enclosing a spicy meat stew; a covered square where newsboards and vid-screens were set up. A shaded park where several females and one young male—an elder brother, they learned—watched small young at play. The encounters went much the same: The elder Arekkhi were careful not to be caught staring, while the younger were visibly excited by the alien females among them, and curious about the differences

in coloring and size between the two. Once some brave being—usually young—asked a question, others followed; some
seemed to want to know about how others lived and what they
looked like, though most questions involved what the alien
presence would mean to their families. Crafters and artisans
seemed particularly surprised and pleased that their goods
might be desired on other worlds.

Only once did Magdalena look up to see three youthful
males in priests' dark blue trousers and singlets scowling
across the crowd. One met her eyes squarely and challeng-
ingly, then all three turned and walked away. "Newly made
priests," Khyriz told her quietly.

"Unfortunate—but to be expected, I suppose," Magdalena
replied with a faint sigh, and was distracted by another comment before Khyriz could say anything else.

Their final stop before the designer's was yet another park—
a narrow, shaded walkway under trees, vines, and woven arch-
ways. Alexis had spotted two elderly females slowly pacing
under a vined arbor, a sleekly furred, elegantly collared pet in
a blue singlet between them.

Zhik's whiskers were trembling faintly as he brought the
flitter to a halt, and this time he remained at the controls.
Magdalena hardly noticed: She was out as quickly as Alexis,
first speaking to the females, then kneeling to stroke their
wide-eyed Asha and speak soft love-words to it. It seemed to
please the owners—even more than Alexis's interest in them.
Magdalena, denied pets most of her life, was delighted in the
Asha, and the little creature—actually, it was nearly Alexis's
size—openly fawned on her.

It was an odd encounter, Alexis decided as they returned to
the flitter. The females were pleasant but vague—they reminded her of a great-aunt back in the Ukraine. The pet had
reminded her a little of her own adored Roxelana, the herd-
dog that had been her closest companion when she was a
child—the way it moved its head against the translator's hand,
she decided finally.

Khyriz seemed distracted; ordinarily, he watched Magdalena
closely, rather like a proud parent. At the moment, his attention
moved between the street and the flitter, and he scarcely

glanced her way. One of his eartips flicked as if something irritated it. Or as if he were upset. *As if he'd had a pet Asha and it died recently?* Alexis wondered.

She remembered all too well how it felt when she'd lost Roxelana. Those awful final weeks, the tumor—not enough money for an operation that would have kept the dog alive. No money in the family for such indulgence for a mere pet. It might not be that, of course. But she couldn't bring herself to walk over and ask him. *Later, maybe, Ortovsky,* she told herself.

The elderly females gestured a farewell to the interrelator as she started back to the gently bobbing flitter, then turned to the translator, who still knelt, cooing love and stroking soft Asha fur while she asked about its training, its diet. *Poor Magdalena. At least I had Roxelana.*

Khyriz was already in the flitter, the rear hatch swung open for the women. Odd, that he'd abandon Magdalena here. Most of the Arekkhi so far had been amused by the formal gestures he made toward the translator. Khyriz had seen that, and played up to it, so far. But as Alexis set her foot on the low step, she hesitated.

The Prince was up by the controls, one hand on his cousin's arm as he spoke rapidly to a trembling, flat-eared Zhik: "It is all right, Cousin, don't fret so, we are nearly gone, *he* will not know."

"He'll . . . he'll learn, he learns—"

"No. I swore to you. You will be safe, Zhik. I am proud of you, so far. Ah-Naul would—"

"No! Do not . . . do not name . . ."

"No. I will not. But I think that—" Khyriz broke off sharply and his voice smoothed as the interrelator pulled herself into the air-cushioned flitter, rocking it slightly. "Alexis, you startled me! You walk as quietly as . . . as that . . . as the little creature." He gestured toward the two elderly females and their pet, who were resuming their slow promenade; but he didn't look in that direction, and Zhik's eyes closed. Alexis filed the strange moment for later consideration and moved aside so Khyriz could edge past her to help Magdalena. He murmured something too low for her to catch; Magdalena wrinkled her nose at him impudently and wrapped green fabric around one hand to free her legs. The Prince spat laughter that was somewhere between a hiss and a snarl, and let her climb back into the flitter by herself.

Zhik adjusted inner controls as Alexis resumed her forward seat; the canopy darkened to block most of the sunlight, the side-ports slid sideways to let in outside air. It was nearing midday out there and getting warm. Fewer Arekkhi on the streets, and the ones they could see were in shade and not moving much: under canopies, roofed-over pavilions, or the news squares, walking or sitting beneath the vines that covered the promenades and filled the air with a sharp, tangy perfume.

Magdalena was suddenly very excited, chattering because of it. "What a delightful creature that was! Ai-Fenha, they called her, Ai because female, they said, but what a pretty name! And so *sweet*. I wish..." She sighed. "Well, it wouldn't be practical, would it? I would never have the time to take good care of a pet, and I won't be on Arekkhi that long, anyway." From the corner of her eye, Alexis saw Khyriz's ears go utterly flat to his skull; he brought them back up with what seemed to be a visible effort, his eyes black and all pupil as he gestured sharply in Zhik's direction. It was hand-language, but something she didn't know. Private code? *Don't let them know you saw that,* she thought warily. When she dared glance at the Prince, his ears were where they belonged and he was patting Magdalena's shoulder but his eyes were still too dark.

"The little beings live as long as we do," he said sympathetically. "And they form life-bonds with those who ... who keep them."

"Oh." Magdalena sighed faintly, then managed a smile. "Well, the CLS won't let me stay here *that* long, I guess, so ..."

Khyriz rubbed the back of his hand against her green-clad arm. "You can stroke *me*," he murmured. "I won't object."

"You!" Magdalena laughed cheerfully and gave him a shove.

Alexis cleared her throat ominously and said, in English, "Okay, so they're more like our parrots than our dogs, as far as how long they live. But if you two don't mind, I'd like to keep my breakfast where it is. And my 'ewwwwwww!' meter just pegged.''

It was an old joke from her childhood that, once she'd explained it to him, Khyriz had adored. He broke into spluttering Arekkhi laughter once again. Zhik eyed them all sidelong, finally mumbled something dark under his breath, and turned back to the flitter controls.

A few Earth-minutes later, he settled the flitter neatly under a shaded roof, onto a pair of padded blocks marked in royal yellow, and managed a weak joke. ''How useful, having my Cousin Khyriz here. Alone, I must leave the flitter on noble-class blue-blocks—those, way over. But since Khyriz is with us—''

''Since that, you can settle the flitter on royal blocks. Though, it would be better to park upon the noble, since you and your cousin could both use the exercise,'' Khyriz retorted cheerfully. ''But—let it pass. Go pull the designer's toggle; it is the reddish one.''

''I can read the designer's name and craft,'' Zhik replied waspishly, but his whiskers were curved so far forward they nearly touched. He crossed the wide, deserted boulevard as Khyriz aided Magdalena out and offered a hand to Alexis— who stuck out her tongue at him.

He smirked, an uptwitch of his whiskers, and walked across the street between the two humans. Zhik had pulled the marker, and now a single note chimed; the outer door slid aside to reveal five corridors, the central marked by a row of small lights. Khyriz bowed the others ahead of him, and the door slid shut.

All done with vid, like our computerized systems nearly two hundred years ago, Alexis thought, and followed the lights down the narrow, plain hallway. A short, sturdy Arekkhi female—the interrelator recognized Fahara from the holo Khyriz had shown her—waited for them where the hall emerged into a screened-over patio lush with plants.

The patio itself was a statement of the designer's financial worth: enameled bricks and colored gravel in swirled patterns, the faint tinkle of water in the garden. A fern-like blue thing gave off a pleasant odor when Alexis brushed against it. Lizardlike creatures stalked among the blue ferns, seeking translucent flyers. The designer gestured a bow, then led the way into an open sunroom. Brightly colored cloth was everywhere, piled, heaped, and strewn on a long table against the far wall, where colored drawings hung haphazardly. Shallow glass cases were fixed to the wall in several places. Near one wall, a brightly enameled screen angled across a doorway, and before it, an oval talk-pit filled with cushions.

The designer was the shortest Arekkhi Alexis had seen so far. Even shorter than the interrelator, Fahara was much sturdier in build. Her ear-tufts were obviously dyed: silver and gold stripes. Her eyes gleamed an impossible shade of silver that had to be lenses, and her shaped claws were enameled in the same silver. Her robe was unexpected: white and utterly plain. No hat, no gems, not even a pleat.

The little being she beckoned to her side, by contrast, was as beautifully clad as a porcelain doll Alexis had seen in a museum: Silvery cloth with a subtle red thread that flashed as the little one moved, snug sleeves embroidered and bejeweled, a gemmed hat.

Alexis bit back a startled gasp: This was no child, but an Asha! Unlike the pet Ai-Fehna, it stood upright; she couldn't imagine the gorgeously clad little being crouched at Fahara's feet, or anywhere else. The designer touched the Asha's forearm with the back of her hand and gestured; the little creature copied the basic greeting-gesture, reminding the Ukrainian of her Uncle Vlad's spider monkey: its inevitable hat-tip. Though the Asha was more graceful (and prettier by far). And silent, of course—unlike Arekkhi, the Asha had tails, but did not have vocal cords.

At her side, Magdalena went very still for a long moment, then squared her shoulders and returned the gesture. *Ask her later what that was all about.* But then she saw it: fringe hung from the sleeves, from shoulder to fingertip, swaying nearly to the floor. "Fringe of Dancer." Only the talented few who performed "Fringe of Dancer" were permitted such a costume.

Khyriz drew the women forward to introduce themselves,

then caught hold of Zhik's arm. "Cousin," he murmured, "you *have* seen Asha before, surely?"

The young noble was staring, astonished, at the little creature, Alexis realized. The Asha gazed back directly into Zhik's
eyes, her own eyes wide. *I wonder what he's thinking. What
the Asha's thinking—if they do think.* It could be just reacting
to his stare.

Zhik blinked at his cousin's wry comment and flicked his
ears nervously. "A-apologies, designer; I know it is ill manners to stare so, but—but the garment! My father's garmenter
clearly should serve as his curtainmaker! If that." He brought
his whiskers forward and gave Fahara a proper greeting-
gesture. "I am Zhikna, of the house of—"

"One knows you from vid, noble-he," Fahara said as he
hesitated. Her voice was unexpectedly high and carrying.
"Also, An-Lieye and I came to the city from one of your
northern villages when my repute began to grow."

"Earned, beyond doubt," Zhik murmured, eyes drawn
again to An-Lieye's softly rippling fringe. He added, rapidly.
"There is a cap in my flitter, in a color I favor. But the robe
it once matched is four seasons old and long out of style. If
I—?"

Fahara was pleased. "Go fetch it, noble-he, and let me see
what I think of it."

"The robe really *is* beautiful," Magdalena said. "But why
is she wearing it? Apologies, Fahara, but this is the first Asha
I have seen wearing real clothing."

Fahara gestured assent. "It is uncommon. I may be the only
Arekkhi to do such a thing. But I have no young of my own,
and it both pleases and amuses me to clothe her. Also, those
who visit me are mostly wealthy; if they have offspring, they
will often purchase garments they see upon An-Lieye. I choose
with care, and craft; they buy; I am rich." The designer
smiled; a calculated movement of mouth and whiskers, though
her eyes remained warm. "She wears the fringe for you,
Translator."

"For me? Oh!" Magdalena smiled, but her eyes were wide.
"Fahara, you do me too much honor! The gown is wonderful,
but I could not afford to pay what it must be worth!"

"A gift—" the designer began, but Alexis gestured a negative.

"Apologies, designer, but we are not permitted to accept gifts. Khyriz can tell you. But if perhaps—"

Khyriz touched the interrelator's arm. "Not a gift, of course. But . . . if the robe were a loan? A loan like the gems the CLS has already granted that I can tender you and Magdalena, for my father's ball? Also, think of the good to Fahara, for Magdalena to wear such 'Fringe of Dancer.' At present, Fahara has few noble clients and only one royal. She needs a reputation to gather such clients."

"Well, if you put it like that," Alexis said. Khyriz was right; he'd first offered jewelry as an outright gift, and then as a loan when the CLS cited their "bribe-rule." "I'll have to make certain it's all right, but it should be the same as your offer of lent jewels."

"Which was considered acceptable," Khyriz agreed.

"But—but 'Fringe of Dancer,' " Magdalena began. The designer uttered a little spat of laughter.

"I have seen the Prince's vid," she said. Alexis smiled as Magdalena groaned and made a face at Khyriz, who merely smiled and wandered away to inspect the gardens. Fahara eyed Alexis with a professionally narrowed eye. "The quality of *our* vid is unfortunate. I chose colors for you both based on the news report, but they will not do." She talked almost nonstop as she positioned the interrelator midroom and used a small black box to measure height and armlength, pausing only to ask a question or answer them, or to move Alexis's arms or legs for additional measurements. The box emitted faint clicking noises.

"Refreshments, I forget my manners," the designer announced suddenly. She set the measuring box on a matching pad and scooped a black basket from under the fabric-piled table as she gestured sharply. The Asha came to her at once, seemed to take in her urgent hand gestures, then took the basket, and hurried across the room in a flurry of skirts and fringes, and vanished down the hallway toward the outside. Zhik, murmuring something about his cap, left moments later.

Alexis pulled her attention from the black pad, which was

clicking and beeping softly, and asked, "Your pardon, designer-she, but I am curious. We have pets on our world, often very clever and trainable—somewhat like your Asha, perhaps. But I know of few who could be trained to take that basket, go to the right place with it. How was she trained?"

Fahara's whiskers flicked, and her words sounded stilted, all at once. "The . . . that particular basket always goes to the common pantry the five corridors share. Dhejahl, who prepares the food and drink for all of us, he fills the basket. She knows to carry a filled basket from the pantry to this room." Whiskers curved in a smile. "And Dhejahl has a vid-screen in the pantry with my appointments each day, so he knows how much to send."

"Oh. Would've been my next question. Hmmm—that's easy enough," Alexis said. Her eyes went back to the measuring machine. "What is that doing now?"

"It makes a model for me—look there," she added, pressing two red points on the board with one hand and gesturing toward one of the clear cases. Magdalena caught her breath as a three-dimensional red-line-holo of Alexis filled the space. "For Arekkhi, it shows the complete figure, and soon, the creator of the device tells me, he will be able to show the complete figure of human women. Now . . ." She pressed something else on the surface of the mat; a basic loose robe in pale blue clothed the body. Fahara tinkered with sleeves, turned the figure partway around, moved its arms, changed the neckline, added a hat, made it larger and then smaller. Alexis's eyes moved avidly between the board and the holo. The designer gestured. "The Prince says you understand such tech. Will you care to experiment with it?"

"Would I?" Alexis breathed, clearly enchanted. She took the designer's place. "I can't damage or erase anything, can I?"

"The figures are stored," Fahara assured her, and turned her attention to the translator. "Not the white for you, no. The special red. I go to fetch it."

Khyriz seemed to break free of his thoughts; he came back inside and gestured—the very basic, "This one requires the toilet." *Arekkhi are unexpectedly direct about bodily functions,* Alexis thought wryly.

"You know your way about my apartments, Prince," the designer said, and gestured a quick bow to the women. "I shall not be long over the fabrics. Begin your refreshment if An-Lieye returns before I do." She crossed the room and disappeared behind the enameled panel, following Khyriz. Storage as well as private space back there, Alexis thought vaguely, her attention already on the designer's neat little piece of tech. There were enough press-pads here to keep her occupied for some time.

Magdalena glanced at her absorbed companion, past her to the sunlit (and hot, even though covered) garden, then moved over to the table to feel the materials there and look at Fahara's drawings. Mostly the drawings were of ordinary daytime clothing for hot weather, the kinds of things the Arekkhi they'd met so far were wearing. Many of the drawings showed subtle changes in style: uneven hemlines or doubled skirts, a square-cut throat. Changes to fashion that hadn't altered much in a hundred years would need to be subtle, of course. Still—here was a jumpsuit, though it was covered by a very long vest.

Beyond another of the shallow cases, there were more pictures: Mostly still lifes, similar to old-style photographs, though there were a few holos, all showing the designer's Asha in a variety of exquisite robes. *I wish I could think what it was about her,* Magdalena thought vexedly. Her direct gaze? The pet of those two elderly females hadn't even looked at her, though it had delighted in being stroked. An-Lieye—she couldn't imagine stroking the little beauty. It would be like . . . like petting a child.

It was quiet in the sunroom, the only sound a faint beeping from where Alexis stood, and a faint clacking cry: those geckolike creatures. *Ehnoye,* she remembered, pets, but they also kept the local crawlers in check.

She frowned. Off to her left, she could hear voices—the designer's unmistakable one and another, softer. Argument? She was right next to the enameled panel, which gaped in front of the doorless opening. Well, Fahara's private life wasn't her business after all, and she began to move away. The designer's next words froze her in place.

"I do not feel at all safe, Khyriz. We know what will happen if *they* learn—" A soft murmur; she exclaimed angrily. "Yes, of course, I understand why you asked this. But what if they *do* suspect? If they, or your cousin say anything to—" Another murmur. "I *do* trust you! Or I would never have agreed to this meeting, or to having *her* here. All the benefits to me and this shop are nothing if—well, you know who has the most to lose if this goes wrong!"

And then Khyriz spoke almost as loudly and angrily as the designer. "Fahara, the time is past for these worries! If we do nothing, and my cousin's noble parent has his way? You know?"

"I . . . yes, I know." The designer spoke more quietly.

"We have not given up the search, Fahara, and will not. It is unfortunate they were moved. But I know this much: The movement was not caused by anything done here, in your household. Remember, we were permitted to come here today, with no change to the . . . population, shall we say?" Silence. Magdalena became aware she was holding her breath and let it out quietly. "I will go back now; compose your face and follow." No further sound. The translator glanced around quickly and retreated to the table of fabrics; Alexis was absorbed in the black box and the robe she was creating—all the colors of the rainbow, it looked like.

Moments later, Khyriz came back into the room. He glanced at Alexis, smiled at her, and wandered into the open once more. Magdalena gazed after him, stunned. He looked utterly normal; as if the conversation back there had never taken place. Whatever it was about, she could think of no possible way she could ever ask him.

CHAPTER 9

◆

Zhik automatically smoothed his robe as he eased out of the flitter, the crushed cap clutched in one long-fingered hand: How could it have gotten so far down in the forward storage locker? He shrugged that aside; no matter, any more than the wrinkles. He only had the cap at all because he'd hidden it years ago, when his father had ordered his son's out-of-fashion clothing burned, as he did every year. The robe was gone, but Zhik had hidden the cap. The designer could perhaps create another robe in this color—bronze, of course, but the weave was unique: It had shimmered at his least movement.

Fahara could re-create the weave, he was certain: Only think of the costume for "Fringe of Dancer"! The material was a wonder, the shimmering fringes held the eyes. . . .

Eyes. He paused in midstride. The look in the Asha-she's eyes, when Fahara had named him, the—the *depth* of that gaze, as if she could know who he was, who his father . . . *Impossible*, he told himself flatly. *She is Asha. Voiceless. Trainable, capable of some learning, but not . . . but not . . .*

But that was wrong! It was more than the way she had looked when Fahara named him, and not simply the way her ears flicked as Fahara named his father. Even an Ahla could react to names; Zhenu's was known and feared, and Fahara and An-Lieye had come from Zhenu's lands.

No: There had been a wariness to her face, her features. That had changed to a warmth when she looked at Khyriz. Sharp-pupiled eagerness, her eyes taking in the human women whenever no one seemed to observe her, her whiskers quivering with excitement . . .

Fool! You would have given such emotions to Ah-Naul once! He loved you, you told your cousin! Knew you, shared a bond with you! He could almost hear his father's chill voice behind the harsh thought; he looked quickly around the deserted parking, eased back nearer his flitter, and waited until his breathing returned to normal.

Asha—what did he know of them? Those like—like Ah-Naul, the ones he'd thought of as pets, simple beasts capable of deep emotional attachment to the Arekkhi who cared for them. He swallowed, his mouth dryer than ever. *Or so I thought. So I was told.* So he'd seen, all his life: His father had always kept ahla-Asha in his private apartments in the ancient family holding—and Zhik knew that before the current Emperor, he had kept them in his palace apartments. Khyriz's father had banned them from the new palace, though nothing had been said against Zhik keeping Ah-Naul. *That I heard, at least.*

Now . . . he didn't know what to believe. More honestly, which of them to believe: his cousin, or his father.

But the working Asha, the Voiceless. Like An-Lieye. Khyriz had never spoken to him of them; his father, his tutors, and his personal priest had all said that Voiceless were a separate bloodline, bred for intelligence so they could be trained to take over tasks too repetitive or dull for Arekkhi.

"The bloodline broke, upon both sides. . . ." The line of verse caught him by surprise: He'd forgotten about the epic old Ysif had brought him, the last year or so he'd been tutored. He recalled so little; mostly because of his father's rage to find the youth poring over a trashy bit of cheap romance, as he'd called it.

It wasn't . . . it was exciting. Tragic. From the last war, Ysif had told him. When brothers fought brothers, and fathers against sons. Zhik hadn't cared about the historical accuracy, if any; he'd been captivated by the excitement of battle, heroic charges, brave deaths.

He hadn't paid much attention to the love story that was the epic's heart, either, though that was mostly what he remembered of it. Hyeffan, the young commoner who'd fought his way to leadership of the doomed side of the war; Ynala, a female of different class, though he couldn't remember if the epic stated what class. Their love had been doomed as well: They'd taken poison together. He still recalled how Hyeffan had described her the first time: "A gleam of palest fur within the shielding hood; upon her face, a single spot; black droplet like a tiny tear, blotted upon her cheekbone."

"Single spot," he whispered, and his eyes went wide. Was it possible? Ynala—an *Asha*? If someone had dared write such a romance! But if things had been different a hundred years ago? It would surely explain his father's fury over the epic!

But Asha aren't . . . but they can't be! He drew a deep breath and tried to remember the things Khyriz had said about Asha. Nothing outright, of course—but if there was such a secret, even Khyriz wouldn't have dared simply speak. Not to Zhenu's son. *If he feared I would immediately speak to my father . . .* Khyriz was sensible, and careful what he said, when he said it. Anyone could be a spy, under the right pressure.

He couldn't remember when Khyriz had first said *that* about the ahla-Asha. *That they are sentient, but tampered with.* Only much later had the Prince mentioned the subject again; he'd warned Zhik about the liquid supplements supposedly fed to ahla-Asha for their health.

"I told him," Zhik whispered to himself, "that it was impossible! Who would create a drug to destroy the mind, who would use it?" Khyriz had flatly told him—nobles like his father, with the blessings of Church and Prelate; of course, Khik hadn't believed it. Until . . . He swallowed. "Until Ah-Naul, and Ulfar being there to be certain the supplement was given to him. Why would my father care if Ah-Naul was healthy? Why would Ulfar?" He suddenly became aware he was speaking aloud, if only to a deserted parking area. Still, there could be vid and sound capture, even here. *It is known that Khyriz comes here; his enemies, or those of his father could arrange such devices. Caution, Zhikna.*

It could make him vomit: that even a cold-minded Arekkhi like his father could condone use of such a drug! If it existed. But why would Khyriz lie about it?

There was an easy test of the matter, of course; Khyriz had recently told him that Ah-Naul was beginning to recover. The reversal was slow but steady. Zhik could go to him, see him— talk to him. . . .

The young noble swallowed an evil taste. *I treated him as a pet: a loved pet, but a dumb beast, capable only of certain learning. . . . How could I ever dare face him after that? To see in his eyes . . .* What—*who*—had Ah-Naul been before the drugs had turned him into a whimpering, cringing beast? Zhik smoothed his cap with care and started toward the boulevard and the designer's outer door.

But just within shade, he checked sharply. *Whimpering . . .* Ah-Naul had been able to make sound, though not words. He had vocal cords. The Voiceless must also, then. Could they also make sound?

He didn't know; he'd never before now met a Voiceless, even though his father kept hundreds of them in highland Ak-kherif, and on Mibhor. "You will avoid them, Zhik," he'd ordered often enough. "Such contact disrupts the concentration their feeble minds need for their tasks, and they carry disease that can be transmitted to Arekkhi."

He'd been curious, like any young Arekkhi—but Zhenu's flat order had been enough to keep him well away from them. If there *was* a disease, and he'd caught it. . . . *My father would have murdered me, or let me die.* Zhenu would certainly have made his life miserable enough he'd have wished to die.

Zhik suddenly remembered something else: Fahara had come from his father's lands. Had she brought the Asha with her? But why would Zhenu permit that? And if Asha could infect Arekkhi, why would she be here at all?

Ask Khyriz. He wondered if he would dare.

It didn't matter anyway; Fahara was here and somehow so was a Voiceless, as a member of her household. A very much indulged and visibly cared-for member. Surely the designer was breaking a handful of rules daily! If Khyriz had made himself her protector? Or Fahara's *and* hers? Nothing made sense!

Except one thing. If Ah-Naul was capable of . . . of real thought, if he had voice. *You know the one thing is true, the other . . . may be,* he told himself. If Asha were simply Asha, as Arekkhi were only Arekkhi, no separate kinds among them. . . .

He had no answers; he hadn't expected it. *I am not clever enough to sort through such a complex matter. As my father so often reminds me, I am merely the weak and worthless son of a strong lord.*

The words, and the obvious insult, had never bothered him before; Zhik had simply accepted them as true. This time, he was shocked by the violent surge of outrage; he suddenly saw everything with painfully sharp vision. His leg muscles burned with the urge to leap, his palms and fingertips cramped—he would rend, would kill! He caught his breath in a low, rumbling snarl and somehow managed to retreat, stumbling back into the parking shelter, shaking violently, eyes closed. He'd never experienced attack-rage, but there was no mistaking it. It was several long moments before he controlled his emotions enough to defuse the terrifying fury.

Fortunately, the entire area was still deserted; he waited a little longer to be certain the frightening moment had passed, then blotted sweating palms on his nose-cloth. "They will wonder where you have gone for so long," he told himself sternly. "Go back inside. Give the designer the hat." It would serve as an excuse, a confused corner of his mind said; an excuse to return. To see—but he would not let himself think what he wanted to see.

Zhik hadn't sealed the outer door when he went out and the corridor lights still showed the proper entry to the designer's private patio. But there was another light coming from the wall just into the corridor. *Was that there before?* He'd been too distracted on his way out to notice, if so. A doorway at this end of the corridor would be one of the wedge-shaped storage areas for the building's tenants, or the pantry—and quarters for the pantrier if he lived in. He glanced at the opening as he moved past it: shelves in a dim light, stacked high with sturdy baskets, another open door on the far side. He stopped, as slightly tinny-sounding music came from the chamber beyond the storage. A cheap audio, perhaps the pantrier's, but the song was for the *eghlida,* one of his favorite dances. *And often, a*

dance piece for "Fringe." Zhik's mind went blank and his
eyes wide as the music swelled; he pressed through the narrow
opening and crossed the storage, hesitating in the entry to the
next room.

It was barely furnished—a plain lamp, a pile of cushions,
the ancient entertainment system from which the music came.
Another doorway behind a woven screen: He could see daylight out that way, smell a savory bread and other pleasant
odors from the open-air oven. He drew back a pace as a cheerful male voice called out, "Only a little longer, small friend!"
and a slender figure slipped past the screen and into the chamber.

The Asha stood very still for a moment, head tilted as she
listened to a closing phrase of music—then, to his astonishment, brought up her arms and twirled lightly, eyes closed,
arms moving with a grace that was only partly the fringes. She
moved nothing but her arms, but Zhik went cold with certainty. She was dancing! "Fringe of Dancer"—there was no
doubt! Few Arekkhi could dance any portion of *eghlida* with
such precision. The dance could never be learned by rote—
not by one of limited mind! As the music faded and came to
an end, he let his breath out in a faint sigh.

Soft as the sound was, she heard it, and whirled to face him;
the arm that had been overhead, blocking her face, dropped
limply to her side. "Apologies," Zhik stammered. An-Lieye's
eyes went wider, if possible, when she realized who stood
there; she brought fingers to rest against her mouth, urgent
gesture for silence. In the quiet that followed, he could hear
the pantrier talking to himself as he arranged the basket of
refreshments. "Apologies," Zhik whispered; his voice shook
. . . her fingers trembled. "I . . . heard music, 'Fringe of Dancer,' and I . . . thought . . ."

She crossed to him, laid the backs of her fingers against his
mouth as the pantrier called out, "Ready, little one!" then
gestured urgently with her other hand. The gesture was complex, unknown to him, but he caught the sense of what she
wanted and hurriedly stepped back against the wall, next to
the screen. The Asha gave him a dark-eyed look and went out,
returning moments later with the laden basket. He could hear

the pantrier, singing off-key along with the audio, his mind clearly on his next task. The Asha hesitated, then held out the basket, her eyes fixed on his. He took it, tried to think what to say. The words simply came out as a low stammer.

"They . . . my father . . . they lied to us. To me! About . . . about Asha!" She gestured assent; her eyes were very worried. She began a gesture, and to his surprise, moved her mouth—she was *speaking* to him! No sound came, of course; he couldn't understand what she was trying to tell him. "Apologies, I cannot . . ." She hesitated, her eyes searching his, again made the gesture for silence. That, and the look of her, whiskers and ears trembling just above her fur; he suddenly knew what she wanted. "Your secret . . . ? You fear that I . . . ? I will keep silence, I will not betray you."

Something of that must have reassured her; she beckoned, drawing him into the storage, sealing the door behind them, crossing quickly to the doorway that led into the corridor, and sealing that as well. Zhik's eyes were fixed on her face, hers on his. *She is afraid. But what can I say? She knows I am Zhenu's son.* To his astonishment, she drew a pad and stylo from an inner sleeve-pocket and began to write, covering the surface with neat lettering. Zhik stared, astonished. *True proof; no beast can write!* But he hadn't needed the proof. She held out the pad.

"This chamber, Fahara's rooms, all safe, the Prince tests them often. Fahara—a friend. Protector. Prince wants the alien-she to learn the truth of Asha."

Khyriz? Nothing made sense! His confusion must have shown; she took the pad, erased the surface, and wrote again: "Asha are slaves, since the War, some well treated but most not. Few Arekkhi know what we are. With alien-she here, now there is danger to all our kind. The Prince says secret must be revealed with care."

"Danger—from the outsiders?" But she gestured a negative. He swallowed. "From . . . my father?" Hesitation . . . then assent. "But . . . but what can he do? Kill?" His ears went flat as she signed a tremulous assent. "And if he learns that I have discovered. . . ." Her ears quivered and sank. "No. He will not learn, never from me! I swear it." Her ears came slowly up; her eyes were fixed, very wide, on his. "There is no time now, Fahara will expect you and the basket. I . . . An-Lieye, I am *not* my father," he added rapidly. "I know nothing, but . . . but I would learn. If . . . I will come again, with the Alexis-she. And . . . and for myself, for garments. I . . ." His mind whirled, thoughts tumbling wildly; the words came unbidden. "If you will speak with me again? Teach me . . . the truth?"

She went very still for a long moment, and he couldn't begin to decide what she might be thinking. Her whiskers came forward suddenly, and she wrote briefly, "Come again, somehow we will speak." Still smiling, she tugged at the door toggle and took the basket from him. "Wait a little," she mouthed; to his surprise, he followed that.

"So we are not seen together—yes, I will wait." He watched her go, then leaned against the wall, his legs trembling. *You must show nothing,* he ordered himself. *Nothing of these past moments; nothing except . . . except pleasure, that the designer-she will begin to provide you with garments.* Such garments would include robes for the upcoming ball, new clothing for the next season . . . enough clothing to require frequent visits. The trembling in his limbs faded; he forced his whiskers back to where they should be and stepped into the corridor, the now thoroughly crushed cap dangling from one hand.

The next days went by so quickly, and were so busy, the two women quickly lost track of them, and later only specific events stood out. The trip with Khyriz and Bhelan to one of the living bladder-islands north of the royal island was a pleasant ride, but the bladder-island itself was a disappointment: Footing was treacherous, and the whole thing reeked of dung and long-dead fish.

Ebba's largest fish market had been interesting because they'd spoken with so many Arekkhi—most of them excited to meet the CLS team. Alexis and the Arekkhi didn't seem to notice the overpowering odor; Magdalena, who'd never been around fish in all her life, managed only thanks to her Star-Bridge training. She even ate raw *gnehyu* prepared specially for her by a stand owner: It looked like a work of art, tasted as bad as the market smelled. Alexis shared an enormous, reeking basket of mixed shellfish with Zhik, joking all the while about "hot-pepper-flavored, deep-fried rubber bands."

They'd taken one short trip into the countryside northwest of Ebba . . . unfortunately, the area was deserted except for a distant group building a stone wall. Zhik had looked scared, Magdalena thought, and stammered when Alexis asked if they could go talk to the workers. Khyriz had explained: Those were young males who were recovering from the fever in northwestern Akkherif, volunteers who had joined this program to see if exercise and drier climate would hasten the cure. The guards were there to protect outsiders; they wouldn't let the flitter close. It sounded "off" to Magdalena's inner sense; even Alexis had found the whole thing odd.

Khyriz had finally obtained the flitter-operations software for Alexis, so she could learn to operate a hover-machine like Zhik's; maybe by the time she'd passed the tests, the Council would have come up with a clean loaner for the team. Considering such a flitter would mean freedom of movement anywhere on the planet, Alexis doubted the matter would be that easily resolved. The Council was at least acting more cooperative these days, but there were still petty wrangles over any trip outside Ebba.

Magdalena had planned on a single small class in Mizari for the clerks who worked for the CLS team: To her surprise, so many of the staff had shown up, she'd had to make up three. Of course, most wanted to know about the outside, and only a few wanted to learn the language, so it broke down into one actual, serious Mizari session, a "words and phrases" group so the clerks could use a voder for serious communication, but speak greetings, basic questions and answers, and politenesses without it. The third class was cultural exchange, mostly question-and-answer stuff.

Empress Neoha had asked for Mizari lessons for herself and the little princesses—mostly cultural exchange, again. Khyriz dropped in on these sessions now and again; Magdalena could see the physical similarities between mother and son.

Magdalena seldom saw Zhik except when she could spare

the time for a trip with Alexis. The noble youth apparently intended to serve as their pilot until Alexis had her certification, though she wondered why he did: Most of the time, he seemed so tense when they started, exhausted when they returned.

Khyriz looked tired and worn whenever she saw him of late, and it worried her. Still, he often traveled to and from his estates to sleep in the old palace so he could go around Ebba with Alexis, or spend late hours with her.

Magdalena had never found a way to ask him about that troubling discussion she'd overheard at Fahara's. It still bothered her. But not as much as the incident in the high country outside Ebba.

Or the library incident: Magdalena was entranced by the puzzle-shaped old-palace library, though its collection of reading matter was clearly geared to clerks who liked the current Arekkhi vids: The shelves held mostly fiction in the same painfully predictable style as the ''soap opera'' vid. Still, when she'd tried looking behind the newer volumes—at Khyriz's suggestion—she'd found something truly old: a handbound, oversized book printed in an archaic type she could barely make out; the language was Arekkhi but so out of date she couldn't understand one word in ten—when she could decipher the ornate script, that was. It was fortunately mostly pictures: Ancient line drawings that reminded her of medieval woodcuts. And that enormous foldout, in the back! It had shown a near-life-size table, perhaps a tray, with a battle scene incised around the wide rim. It had intrigued and frustrated her both: The figures were small, the detail confusing, and the master of clerks had no magnifier. But when she came back early the next morning, magnifier in hand, the book was gone. She and a worried-looking master of clerks had searched everywhere, but the book was simply gone.

She'd let the matter drop only because the middle-aged clerk-she clearly feared blame would somehow attach to her. Still: odd. Where had the book come from—and where had it gone? And why?

*   *   *

Khyriz felt wan and exhausted to his bones, result of too many long, late hours with his father, planning how best to get around the Inner Council so the CLS team would get what seemed to them to be free access to ordinary Arekkhi. His mind swarmed late, sleepless nights with maps of routes that might be chosen by Alexis or Magdalena the next day; what he could say if such routes were forbidden by the Iron Duke and his allies; what different routes he could suggest.

It plunged him into Arekkhi politics, deeper than he'd ever intended to go: The Iron Duke didn't trust him, and Alexis was wary, having been burned once. She'd take herself and Magdalena off-planet without further warning. *Distressful to me; but we need this bond with the CLS.*

In the process of the nightly sessions with his father, Khyriz had developed a deep respect for Khezahn, who quietly worked for change despite so many of his Council.

Council meetings were becoming more tense: Two more attacks on the Iron Duke's Akkherif estates had been followed by a raid on coastal Mibhor, two fishing villages burned to the ground, and the small temple serving both bombed into rubble. Those responsible for the destruction of the temple had warned the priests ahead of time, and posted a notice afterward: ''Free the Asha!'' They had not otherwise named themselves.

So far, his method had worked: Alexis had work to occupy her in the CLS quarters, and there was plenty to see around Ebba and along the coast well to either side of the city. It wouldn't last long, he knew: The interrelator wanted to set up a trip to the lowland continent Dagona, another to Mibhor, and a proper visit to the station, maybe even a stop at the hydroponics labs on both moons. The Iron Duke, the Prelate, and their allies were utterly opposed to any of that, for their own reasons, but with the increase in raids on both continents, Dagona and Mibhor could actually prove dangerous. But the Council was nearly unanimous that they must keep any hint of fighting from the outsiders.

Late one night a nine-day short of the welcoming ball, Khyriz spread his hands in an Arekkhi shrug and sighed. ''Father, we cannot avoid it any longer, the women must be given a portion of the truth. The interrelator grows impatient; she is suspicious of the Council's latest excuses. And in a nine-day or a little more, she will certify for the flitter. What excuse will Zhenu give her then, for not going where she pleases?''

The Emperor pushed tiredly to his feet and shoved aside an untouched plate of bread. ''But to tell her there is danger . . . Will she believe it, or think it another excuse? And what of the CLS? If they see this as warfare, and simply remove their ambassadors, then all we have done is for nothing!''

Khyriz turned to look at him. ''If it were general warfare, CLS would insist the team leave. If they were in danger. But this is not everywhere. And they know from their own history that riots and fighting can be caused by fear of change. This has happened on other of the CLS worlds.''

''They will believe such a tale, after so many things we have told them?'' The older male sounded skeptical. ''That no word of fighting has been put forth anywhere and now, since no other excuse is acceptable, we give them a new and better excuse?''

''It would seem that way, so put,'' Khyriz replied. He paused to consider his words carefully—as he did every single night the two males came together like this. ''But if we . . . if *you* tell them that the problem has been ongoing from the first contact with the Heeyoons, but that we did not understand such problems are normal . . . if you tell them that many of the original groups now accept our relationship with the outside, but new groups have arisen recently that we do not know yet who all of them are or why they are angry . . . if you explain that you and the Council reason with them, rather than suppressing them, even though it takes longer to make peace . . . Alexis will accept that.''

''She will wonder why she has not heard of them before.''

''No; they know we have only one news-vid. Tell them, if need be, that you feared such news would upset the general population and encourage others to violence, and would solve nothing. If she sees all this as a cause for embarrassment by the Council, she will believe. And she will be willing to give you time to resolve the matters peacefully. She will not give up wanting to see all of our world, of course. But she will understand that certain parts of it are not safe at present.''

''And Zhenu may accept such a solution for now.'' The Emperor exhaled gustily, the sound vibrating in his throat. ''I will take this to the Council, Khyriz; I should have the support to force agreement, whatever Zhenu wants. I am reminded, Khelyu's First of House sends report from Hedessk that he has another full company of royal fighters ready to fight, though they continue to train. I am told they could be here, at need, within three hours.''

The Prince was quiet for some moments, adding in his mind. ''We are close to equal forces, then . . . at least in numbers. But Zhenu's are armed and the Prelate's may already have real combat experience. . . .'' His voice trailed off. To his surprise, the elder male showed no distress at the idea, but gestured a grim assent.

''I have my own ways of learning what happens on Arekkhi, Khyriz. I have long wondered who could possibly launch one ground attack after another against targets upon Zhenu's holdings here on Akkherif *and* in central Mibhor. As he tells us himself, his guards are well trained, armed, and placed where they can be the most protection to his assets. And yet the attacks hit his lands—and they succeed.''

''Perhaps he deceives himself as to the worth of his guards, or perhaps he does not realize that the more he tightens his grip, the more villages will slip through his blunted claws,'' Khyriz murmured. The Emperor's whiskers quirked forward briefly; he understood the meaning, even though he wouldn't have the least notion of Khyriz's reference—Dr. Rob's old spaceship vid with the blood-stirring music.

His father's affectionate back of hand against his cheekbone brought him back to the moment. ''Tell the interrelator, tomorrow,'' Khezahn said finally. ''I will convince the Council to accept this because it is logical, because it gives those who desire it more time, and because—because it is already done.'' He finished with a satisfied rumble, and for a moment his eyes didn't appear nearly so tired. Khyriz let his whiskers touch.

''Father, I shall.'' A short time later, he left, bound for the old palace—where Magdalena might still be waiting to share *zhner* with him. And perhaps some more slow dancing, Earth fashion, to the music-cube she'd brought from StarBridge. The fur at the base of his throat hackled as he stepped onto the moving walkway; he smoothed the fur with both hands, then composed himself to regal stillness. His image reflected on high windows, a being shaped like Magdalena but otherwise— so unlike her!

He touched the *zhona*-silk cloak—the long, bronze-colored fabric that crossed over one shoulder and under the other, fastening over his heart with a long, wrought pin, fluttering in the faint air-movement caused as he traversed the moving walk. The cloak was his most recent prized possession: near-duplicate of the one worn by the Romeo-he from the three-hundred-year-old Earth ballet video he'd watched with her back on StarBridge, just before he was called home. He had brought a copy of the vid with him, duplicated it to Arekkhi equipment. When he'd showed the dance to Fahara, she had practically quivered with delight at the music, the ornate fashion, the use of style, shade, and colors; she'd made him the cloak as a gift. He hoped Magdalena would remember it: The dance-mistress at StarBridge had used very different costuming for the balcony scene Magdalena danced at her final recital with pale-haired David.

David, Khyriz thought, suddenly gloomy. The human youth was so well matched with Magdalena, skilled at ballet. Khyriz knew he could never lift her as David did; not without special gravity. Arekkhi simply weren't built that way. Arekkhi couldn't stand on their toes, or spin as did that Romeo-he.

He'd always known there was no chance for him with Magdalena . . . To take a member of another species as his mate? His people would never agree to it! Besides . . . Magdalena cared for him but as a friend. She would eventually return to her own kind, find a mate like David. The thought depressed him beyond solace.

The moving walkway tipped down and a cool breeze flowed across his face: He'd gone the length of the new palace and started down the ramp, and barely noticed. Khyriz stepped off the pale carpet and gazed at the old palace; his heart sank. Certain things had always been impossible. He had known that deep down, but had never accepted it until now. *But friends . . .*

yes, friends. That, at least, is very possible . . . The Prince
glanced at the now-still walkway, stepped away from it, and
stalked toward the distant building.

There were few hover-craft resting on the blocks in the old
palace area this night: his own personal craft and that of the
chief clerk, who often left it on the island and rode the tram
with her team rather than expend the cost of fuel, air, and time,
all of which accrued charges. To his surprise, Zhik's vehicle
was nowhere in sight. Considering the hour, the youth should
be asleep; his father insisted upon proper hours, and still assured Zhik kept them by having the servant bring first-meal.
Jild, like most old palace servants, kept his own quarters, but
spent most of his day hours caring for his young master's
quarters.

Perhaps the flitter was being cleaned or repaired; Zhik was
using it a lot these days. Khyriz dismissed the whole matter
from his mind, and wove a path through the resting-blocks to
reach the separate door for the upper-floor apartments. Better
to make certain everything was prepared for *zhner,* his rooms
ready for a guest, before he called on the second floor.

Zhik's flitter sat on padded blocks well back in the unlit, common section of the nearly filled parking across from the designer's apartment complex. The young noble stood where he
could study the boulevard and the entry to Fahara's apartment.
He already knew her flitter was gone; *she* had said the designer
was gone for the night to the highlands, to choose specially
tanned leathers from Emhheru, master of hides. The renowned
Emhheru refused to sell in open market and would not send
skins on consignment, while Fahara, equally proud, would not
permit a crafter, however skilled, to decide what goods she
could choose from.

Even if she had been at home, Zhik would have eventually
crossed the boulevard, unafraid of being caught where he had
no business; the designer took strong soporific teas before re-
tiring, and slept in a chamber that was noise-sealed. It was
unlikely anything short of a fire or a quake would waken her.

He was still extremely quiet and always cautious—just in

case. But to stay away—no. He knew the risks, but went nearly every night.

She cares for me. She—she at least cares. He didn't dare hope for more, however he felt. She knew his kinship, after all. But the first gesture of her private hand-language she had taught him was the joining of thumbs, palms up. *Dearest friend and companion,* it meant.

He could be all that to her; as a protector, however, he had failed. He still could not locate her family. Zhik's eartips quivered faintly as he hurried across the boulevard and eased into shadow against the doorway. He didn't want to tell her that— but she deserved the truth—and he *must* see her.

The designer's marker was covered over by a plain plaque, a sign that Fahara was away. Before he could ease the plaque aside, the door slid into the wall and An-Lieye stood there, back in shadow, beckoning urgently. She was clad in simple, long-sleeved, hooded blue. He crossed the threshold and let the door slide to behind him, waiting until he heard it latch before following her down the lighted corridor. Just short of the patio, she turned to look up at him, her hands moving slowly. *Father . . . mother? My family?*

He gestured a negative. "I have tried, An-Lieye. Everything I knew to try, I have attempted it. I have failed you, worse than Khyriz, because I was so certain I could find them, because they come from my—from Zhenu's lands. . . ." His voice faded as she took another step toward him and laid her hands, palm up, against his dark gold robe.

You have not failed me, she mouthed. What followed was too complicated for him. Finally she drew out the stylo and pad and wrote: "You tried; the *zhez* is more skilled at hiding than you or the Prince at finding." He forced a smile, handed back the pad.

"I will still search, I will find them, if it is possible. But now, I must return to my apartments."

Her fingers tightened on his upper arms. *Fahara . . . gone the night. Stay.*

He gazed at her in astonishment. "An-Lieye—I dare not! If—if Fahara found me here, or my father's servant found me not in my apartments—!"

Please . . . stay. She gestured again, then moved her hands, laying them across his shoulders—palms down. Suddenly, and before he could respond in any fashion, she rose to tiptoes and tipped her head sideways. Zhik's throat-fur hackled as she drew her whiskers backward across his.

No one in all Arekkhi space had ever made that loving gesture with him before now. An-Lieye's eyes held his as she laid her hand across his nose. Gently. Palm down.

Those who trothed for affection rather than money or family ties made such a gesture, he knew. *Love.* What did he know about caring of any kind, let alone *love?* She stood before him, eyes still fixed on his, hands clasped before her. Asking nothing . . . and everything. When she backed away from him, a slow step at a time, Zhik followed . . . across the patio, and into the rooms beyond.

CHAPTER 10

♦

The day of the ball dawned sullen and humid. Magdalena, her hair in dozens of thin braids held back with a ribbon, prowled the main room, pausing often to peer out windows, where she'd seen heat lightning earlier. Even the seas were unusually sluggish: low tide and no hint of wind.

Alexis, flat on her back in the talking-pit, elbowed her way up and smiled. "Were you *this* jumpy before your last recital?"

The translator seemed to come back from a distance. "Hmmm? Oh—sorry, am I driving you crazy?"

"No. I'd've said so."

"It's the weather. I don't like lightning."

"It should be all right, the morning report said no storms this far east—no rain, and no wind." Alexis blotted her forehead on the hem of her loose shirt and scooped up the hand-held comp-pad, where she was listing points for her upcoming FTL call to CLS headquarters.

"I know. It's a little about tonight, too. The uncertainty, plus knowing how much perfection counts."

"Tell me about *that*," Alexis replied gloomily. "Watch me step on someone's feet. Like maybe the Iron Duke's—"

"The Esteemed *zhez* Zhenu—who does not dance, or participate in any pleasurable activity, according to Khyriz," Magdalena reminded her loftily.

Alexis grinned. "Oh? He seems to get enough fun out of thwarting us at every turn. But I'm thinking more kindly of

the Esteemed, etc. Ever since late last night, when he finally
agreed to sign off my flitter application.''

Magdalena stopped pacing. "He *did*? When was that?"

"Late—but before you came down from Khyriz's apartments with that silly smile on your face." She scooped up the
heavy Arekkhi two-handled mug and drank down cold coffee.
"Ahhhhh. Wonderful."

"Silly smile, indeed. Caffeine addict," Magdalena murmured with sarcastic sweetness.

"Music fiend," the interrelator retorted with a crooked grin.
"Dancing fool. Just because you spent *your* extra weight-
allowance on those music cubes and dance-vids." Alexis had
used a little of her allowance to bring two old-fashioned 2-D
framed pictures of Dr. Stephanie Kim—one cheerfully smiling
shot of Stephanie and Alexis on vacation at a Black Sea resort,
the second an enlarged news-vid shot of the doctor grim and
glowering at the destruction on Trinity after the Anuran in-
vasion. The rest of the interrelator's "free weight" had been
taken up by vials of freeze-dried coffee, which she broke out
on rare occasions to brew strong and drink cold, black, and
unsweetened.

Magdalena, who had never seen or smelled coffee before
StarBridge, wrinkled her nose. "Smells almost as wonderful
as that *ghneris* from the fish market."

Alexis laughed. "Raw, or my deep-fried spiders? Hey, this
is a lot better than my Great-Uncle Vlad's homemade beet
booze!"

"I'll stick with *rih*."

Alexis eyed her human companion more closely. "So, how
well did *you* sleep last night? Or how long? Looks to me like
you could use a nap already. And when do all those braids
come out?"

"Ask when I finished putting the last one in."

"Sometime after you got down from *zhner* with Khyriz."

Lightning flashed in the distance. "It's not really *zhner*.
Just—we mostly talk. But I wasn't that late; he had to leave
for Embriagha, some problem on the estate he couldn't dele-
gate. He'll be back by midafternoon, though." Magdalena
smiled, her gaze distant.

"I hope so. After all, he's the leader of our seven-male escort."

"Mmmmm. Same number as a royal would get—flattering. The braids come out after Fahara dresses me; I really thought a plain dancer's chignon would be better, but Khyriz insisted. Said everyone's fascinated with the length of my 'mane'—so I decided I might as well 'foof,' too."

"Good. Keep their eyes off my dancing," Alexis said as she turned her attention back to the electronic notepad and the growing list.

Magdalena came over to peer at the screen. "Didn't we already set up the points for today's call?"

Alexis glanced up briefly. "Minor addition. Zhenu didn't say in so many words, but I could tell the flitter approval was going to hinge on it: We get the flitter with no strings attached and no restrictions on travel—he's arranged that we'll get a report early each morning where the chance of rebels or fighting are, or any hot spots, so we don't go there."

Alexis drained the last drops from her mug. "In exchange, I said I would ask if the CLS will allow immediate import of three deep-search, heat-seeking satellites—something about there've been mining cave-ins and they don't have the tech to locate survivors from orbit. One of the Heeyoons on-station mentioned we have the tech, I guess. Anyway, Zhenu heard about it and thinks it would be useful."

"I can't see him being so altruistic," Magdalena began.

"He's not; he was very open about making a huge profit, he's had a lot of problems in his mines up in Mibhor, apparently—enough to warrant the expense of the outside tech. The Emperor cleared it, so everything's okay here. Zhenu says he'll pay for all three satellites up front, and he'll cover expenses for the techs who come to help get them in place and running, *and* he'll cover the cost of training the Arekkhi techs how to operate and maintain them."

"All that? Why?"

"I don't know. Maybe lost a bundle when one of *his* mines caved in. He wants it badly enough to turn us loose with our own flitter, though. The satellites aren't sensitive tech, so that shouldn't be a problem.

"I sent him a message saying as much, and said I'd apply to CLS this morning. He sent back by return messenger that the flitter and my operator's identikit will be here tomorrow, an hour before sunrise."

The dark woman raised her eyebrows. "Wow. Efficient. Odd, though. The Arekkhi have satellites *and* they can build heat-seekers. After all, that's how the collision-avoidance chip in the flitters works. So why can't they make their own . . . ?"

Alexis shrugged. "I guess it's different—locating something through dirt and rock. Not my field. But remember, on this world it's creative types who get free rein, not engineers. Tech is tightly controlled." Alexis glanced at the watch-patch she'd stuck to the pit wall, just under the media-center control. "Nearly time. With luck, I can get this out of the way by midday."

"Oops," Magdalena murmured. "Thanks for the reminder! I promised the master of clerks a special session in Mizari. I'll be back before Fahara comes!"

"You'd better!" Alexis called after her.

The translator returned to the second floor hot and headachy. She rinsed down in the showerlike *hruskeh*-closet, then slid into the enormous bathing pool. Rohf—seldom seen these days—had proven his existence by leaving the snack-basket filled with fruit and two kinds of bread—one sweet, and one made with smoked, dried fish. Alexis, already clean from her own soak, sat cross-legged on the edge of the pool to give her an account of the CLS call.

"So they'll get back to us tomorrow, but no one could find any reason *not* to ship at least one of the satellites, and a support crew. I'm expecting a yes."

"Good." Magdalena swallowed the last of a breadstick that tasted vaguely like bacon, and scooped cool, citrus-scented water over her shoulders.

"And Mahree said to tell you 'well done' on the translating classes. Particularly for the Empress. Sounds to me as if you'll be here as long as I am. Oh—she passed on a short message from Ladessa, via Rob: She's out of regen and hopes you won't be too pissed if she heads for Ancestors' World as soon as she's able to travel." Magdalena smiled and shook her head. "And you're out of time in there; Fahara is past due."

The translator sighed faintly. "I know. All right." She eased over to the far edge, where the drying-booth and her robe were. Alexis mumbled something about her hair and left.

Fahara arrived moments later, Edhal carrying the long, flat robe-baskets; her silver-and-gold-painted eartufts quivered. She dressed both women herself, adjusting, fussing, tweaking— hand-stitching when something didn't hang right. Magdalena stood motionless as Fahara worked on her robe for at least an Arekkhi hour.

"I don't know how you do that," Alexis finally said in English. "Play statue, I mean. If it's learnable, teach me."

"It's easy," the translator replied in the same language. "Madame—the ballet mistress on StarBridge—walked with a cane, and if one of 'her' dancers got jittery, the dancer got whacked." She glanced at her companion. "You don't need to look at me like that; it's not like being whacked in a 'spare the rod and spoil the child' commune. And it was good for me: I learned physical control, and by the end of the first year, I didn't associate getting hit with *anyone* but Madame. Thank you, Fahara," she added in Arekkhi as the designer-she bit thread and stepped back to observe the "Fringe of Dancer" robe. At the designer's sharp gesture, the dancer moved her arms, swayed in place, performed the first sleeve-gesture of the slow *emloah*.

"Wow," Alexis said, wide-eyed, as the fringes shimmered and changed colors.

The designer quirked her whiskers forward until they touched—Khyriz must have passed on his favorite English slang. "It would be truly 'wow,'" Fahara said, "if there had been time, and certain weaves—"

"It is a wonder, Fahara," Magdalena said firmly. "I only hope I do not shame the robe, or its creator." She stepped back from the holo-mirror as the designer beckoned Alexis to take her place. While Alexis tried to play statue and Fahara fussed with the pale blue *zhona*-silk that exactly matched the Ukrainian's eyes, the translator began unbraiding her hair.

Fahara was still fussing with drape and flow when Magdalena shook out the last plait and began untangling the brown-black, kinked mass with her fingers, but as she progressed, the designer gave up all pretense and stared avidly at the cloud of hair. Finally she came over to walk all the way around the Hispanic woman. "True-fringe," she said in a low, awed voice.

"What?" Alexis asked. "Apologies, but I don't understand."

Fahara blinked; her eartufts quivered. "Apologies, Interrelator," she said briskly. "You are unfinished. The translator-she's mane took my attention."

"It'll take everyone's attention," Alexis replied.

Magdalena laughed; her cheeks were flushed. "Sure! Make me more self-conscious than I already am!"

Fahara left soon after so she could change for the ball; Khyriz had obtained temporary use of a small room on the third floor of the old palace for her.

Khyriz came in moments later with a five-sided box—the gems he had promised for the evening. "With my mother's hopes for a successful ball. She personally chose them. This, Alexis," he said as he drew out a small hide pouch, "to match your eyes, she said."

Alexis slid the contents into her left hand: silvery mesh and ice blue, rounded stones. In place of the usual adhesive used by Arekkhi to hold such pieces to their heads, two Earth-style hair combs had been attached with that adhesive to the underside. Alexis bent her head so Magdalena could lay the mesh on the crown of her head, arrange the stones to hang across her forehead, then shove the combs into place. Two long, dangling ropes of stones and fine mesh hung behind her ears, along her neck, and lay across her collarbones. She shook her head cautiously; the piece shimmered but stayed put.

"The gold hoops that go here," Khyriz touched her earlobe. "Will you wear them? My mother was fascinated by them."

"If you say so." Alexis kept a hand ready, in case the headpiece fell off, and went out.

Khyriz turned to Magdalena; he looked suddenly shy. "For

you, my mother chose this.'' He freed the second *tyra*. Magdalena gazed blankly: gold twined with spindrift threads, like those worked in her sleeve-fringes. The stones were smoothly rounded—blood red.

"But—Khyriz, red stones are for a betrothed! I can't wear this!"

"You can," he replied softly as she hesitated. "You and I are . . . are friends, Magdalena. Red stones are not always simply for betrothed. My mother—she sees that in *your* company, I am happy. That you are my . . . my truest friend," he finished after a slight hesitation. "She sees this—she has seen the fabric Fahara chose for you and for me . . . and she picked this. It is her right to give you the honor." He touched the largest of the stones—smoothly rounded, like all Arekkhi gems. "Wear them, Magdalena, when we dance. Please," he added in soft English. Magdalena gazed at him wide-eyed for some moments, then bent her head so Khyriz could attach the combs. His fingers strayed over the thick mass of hair. "More rare and wonderful than true-fringe," he whispered.

"Khyriz? Fahara just said that word—*ahmakhneh,* true-fringe—and then she looked so odd! What does it mean?"

He smiled faintly and touched her hair again. "A myth. One that came as so many others, from the eastern continent Dagona. But then, so many things came from Dagona, once." But before she could ask what he meant by any of that, he leaned forward to press his cheek against hers and took his leave.

When he returned with the official escort, he was resplendent in silver and spindrift shot with red, the fabric an exact opposite of the translator's glimmering red. No fringes, but the royal *ducat* was stamped in platinum on both sleeves. His ears were nearly invisible, lost in the folds of his padded cap. Fahara came in with him, and her high-waisted silver robe, trimmed in standing black lace, oddly reminded the translator of cavalier garb from her own world eight hundred years earlier. The designer-she hissed Khyriz to a standstill just inside the main room of the second floor and tugged the cap low over one dark eye. Khyriz tweaked his whiskers momentarily flat in protest but let the cap stay where the designer set it.

Fahara's bright glance took in Zhik next, but the Iron Duke's son apparently wore his new fashion to please her: Khyriz blinked at the broad pleats and the glittering bronze sash that snugged them to his middle.

"So, Fahara and you choose to set a new fashion tonight," Khyriz murmured as he drew his cousin aside. "I admire your nerve, Zhik. Your father—"

But Zhik gestured a negative, then enforced it with a human shake of his head. "My father always desires that I wear the newest fashion. Well, he shall have it."

"Zhik, you know full well he does not mean it!"

"I know. In public, tonight, he will accept it."

Khyriz glanced swiftly toward the women, but they were across the main room, introducing themselves to the rest of their escort. "You must be mad! He will—!"

"He can use nothing but words against me," Zhik said flatly. "I am his only offspring. What will he do? Murder me? But I can bear his words. And if he threatens me, I will vanish."

"But . . ."

Zhik's ears flicked; he wasn't as calm as he sounded. "I will vanish, and he knows it. I have told him."

"Zhik, you frighten me."

The noble laid both hands, palm down, on his cousin's shoulders and smiled, his whiskers barely curled. "No, Khyriz. For once, you need not worry at all." The curl became pronounced. "The women gaze in our direction, and Alexis makes the . . . the *wrinkle* . . . between her brows."

Even though the sun had just gone down, the island was already lit with thousands of small lights that crowned buildings or lined the paths and moving walkways. The broad entry to the ballroom was crowded, but the low ramp that led down to the dance floor was unoccupied—tradition, Magdalena knew, and common sense. It allowed those arriving to see where friends and enemies were, to choose their own area for seating from the assortment of open benches, tables, and closed boxes—the latter for private meetings of all kinds.

Already, hundreds of Arekkhi made bright-colored groups on the vast dance floor. The Emperor and his family occupied the central platform, which was raised now, but could be lowered for the dance-figures led by one or another of the royal pair.

There would be subtle confrontations this night; spies were everywhere, of course, and reputations could be damaged by a poor performance. Magdalena glanced at Khyriz on her right, gave Alexis beyond him a discreet thumbs up, and let the Prince escort her down the ramp.

Alexis, as interrelator, should have gone first . . . but the Ukrainian had been adamant: "He's royal and you're a performer. And I'm nervous. You two show-offs take the heat off me."

Sudden silence fell as their party moved onto the floor and crossed it to the seating reserved for them: Someone had already arranged padded benches and cushions marked with Khyriz's *ducat*. Few actually stared or spoke while she could see them, but once they passed, Magdalena could hear the whispered comments. The translator smiled and gestured greetings with her free hand, but actually saw no one to recognize until after they were seated.

Close by, she picked out Khyriz's eldest brother and his lifemate, both in matching green; beyond them, several members of the Grand Council standing together, their mates seated in a group, avidly studying the robes of those seated across the chamber from them. Oddly, it reminded her of NewAm: The elders grumbling together at dinner over something while the women sat apart and cheerfully—and maliciously—gossiped. She smoothed spindrift-shot fabric over her knees and bit back laughter: NewAm had never been farther from her.

Laughter faded as her eyes picked up two more familiar beings, near the foot of the ramp: the Prelate, plainly clad as always, the enameled mask held over his face, and at his side, the Iron Duke. They were looking directly at her party, and she could almost feel the disdain in both pairs of pale eyes. She leaned close to Khyriz. "I thought the Prelate didn't attend such nonreligious events."

The Prince's whiskers quirked in a brief smile. "He *claims* he does not. Nijho's mouth and his body follow two separate paths.'' He laid the back of one hand against her shoulder, his eyes moving where she gazed. ''Pay them no heed.''

''I'll try,'' Magdalena replied honestly. ''But after this morning, I thought Zhenu was beginning to accept . . .'' She paused to choose a word.

Khyriz laughed briefly, but his whiskers weren't amused. ''Zhenu has more sides than the mirror-ball in Rob's old disco movie,'' he said. The English words jarred more than his tone of voice. ''Besides, *his* displeasure tonight is for Zhik.'' The translator glanced back at the bronze-clad youth, who was talking animatedly with Alexis and the rest of their escort. ''Specifically, for his robe, with its new fashion of pleats and sash.''

Magdalena rolled her eyes heavenward. ''I give up,'' she murmured. ''Poor Zhik, wrong no matter what he does!''

''Just so. Forget Zhenu. Look,'' he gestured with his chin, just beyond the Council. ''The master of music places several of the *idrika* players and two hand-drums just there. We begin soon.''

It took only a little longer . . . the master of music kept most of the musicians on the pedestal near the royal pillar, but set others in small groups around the ballroom. This arranging, Magdalena knew, was different each time, worked out by the master after the crowd arrived and settled in. The dances, sequences, and music never varied, but each ball was given a unique blend of sound. Once the last three horn-bags were settled into a niche beside the ramp, the master took his place on the pedestal and began the piping ''Iyida'' to clear the floor. The Emperor's pillar was lowered so he and the Empress could lead the first figure.

Khyriz led their group onto the red wedge of dance floor. Alexis gave Magdalena a resigned look and took her place next to Zhik, then eased a little closer to Magdalena as the males began their arrogant stalk forward to the heavy measure of basso horn-bags. ''Two returns and we go, right?'' she murmured in English.

''Watch my signal,'' Magdalena replied in kind. She had goose bumps, suddenly; warmth and a surge of adrenaline drove them away as Khyriz and the other males pivoted

sharply and strode back up the hall. A beat of three; ten males,
faces stern and arrogant, arms folded before them, repeated the
pattern. *When I first saw vid of them, I thought cheetahs who
walked upright and dressed like Medici. Then, I could not tell
Arekkhi apart . . . and it can still be difficult. But Khyriz . . . I
would know him anywhere.* The Prince's eyes warmed as he
pivoted for the third sequence. Magdalena held up a low warning finger for Alexis and prepared to follow the males.

Other dances followed. The two women performed only with
their hand-picked escort, but between figures, they talked nonstop to a wide variety of Arekkhi. Alexis wound up in a deep
discussion with the "gossipers"—the councillors' women—
about raising young on the land, dealing with climate, bored
young, and the difficulties of meat-herds. . . . The translator
had her own circle of new acquaintances, most of whom
wanted to know about her fringe: Would she really perform
with the planet's five best "Fringe of Dancer?" How had she
learned their dance? Would she show them some of her own
dance?

There was a pause about a third of the way through the
dancing, followed by a young figure: Child-Arekkhi of both
sexes clad in brilliant costumes affixed with banners performed
the creation-myth of Rain and Rainbow. Another pause, to
allow the young an opportunity to be praised before they left,
and then, "Fringe of Dancer."

Alexis gripped her hands and murmured, "Luck." Khyriz
took her place, and to Magdalena's surprise, leaned forward
to touch his lips to her cheek, Arekkhi attempt at a human
kiss. But before he pulled away, he murmured against her ear,
"Heed nothing beyond yourself out there. I just learned it was
Zhenu who chose you as sixth to the figure."

It took her a moment to realize what he meant. Five was a
lucky number, six not. She glanced down the hall toward the
ramp: empty. But among the councillors not far away, Zhenu
stood, an arrogant tilt to his chin and a smug set to his whiskers, black eyes fixed on her. *I will murder Khyriz for this,*
she decided as she stepped onto the floor, automatically moving with a dancer's glide so the fringes would remain utterly

still. Four other dancers—a male and three females—already
occupied the center of the floor not far from the Emperor's
pedestal. Magdalena considered them, thought momentarily
about Zhenu's look. It was surely a challenge. He expected
her to fail—to fall on her face. Fury filled her. *Zhenu thinks I
will fail, look foolish, and what . . . leave Arekkhi in disgrace?
Taking Alexis with me? How* dare *he?* For one so supposedly
clever among his own, he was certainly blind to anything non-
Arekkhi. And she wasn't going to fail. Not now!

She took her place among the other dancers—now five females and one male, his facial spots and stripes heavy with
dark cosmetic and his eyes anxious. Magdalena smiled at all
of them, lips only, then gestured a greeting of "one who is
honored to be among the great." It seemed to startle them,
especially the male, whose nose fur was dark with nerve sweat.
Probably *he'd* been told this was no place for him. *Like Solomon Smith telling me I "belonged" in that cult, that I was
female and so of no value. Like Zhenu letting Zhik know how
worthless he is. . . .*

She was still very angry, but her mind cleared as the solo
air-pipe began its slow introduction to the figure, and she focused on the dance to the exclusion of everything else. The
second air-pipe joined in—right arm up to make the sliding
gesture that set the fringe to moving from shoulder to fingers
and back again. Three reedy *evif*-horns took over then, along
with finger-drums from all around the hall. The music lilted
over a hushed ballroom; six beings moved as one and then in
sequence, letting the fringe ripple one dancer after the other
while the feet performed a dazzling sequence of steps.

Astonishingly, even after so many performances, it happened: She seemed to see herself from a distance while her
body moved with grace and precision, living the dance and
the music. The dance was everything. It was perfection. It was
joy. . . . Suddenly it was over, and the ballroom rang with the
soft nail-clicks of Arekkhi applause and the high-pitched hisses
that were the equivalent of a human cheer. Magdalena's face
felt flushed; the five other dancers crowded around her to lay
backs of hands on each other and on her, making no distinc-
tion. As she left the floor, the others came with her—all of

them united, dancers excitedly discussing a particularly fine performance.

Magdalena had questions of her own: How had the lead dancer moved her arm to create *that* exact movement of fringe, every time? Alniye demonstrated; she wanted to know then how an outsider had gained so much skill in this most exacting of dances. Magdalena explained, which drew more questions and comments. Only when the music began for the next figure did the group break up, but the five Arekkhi, including the young male Jheren, had Magdalena's enthusiastic permission to call on her, to arrange a dance exchange.

"Wow," Alexis murmured as the translator sank into her padded chair. "Sure know how to make friends, don't you?"

Magdalena laughed throatily, still flushed with triumph. "Common interests; works every time."

The interrelator switched abruptly to English. "I wonder if our friend the Iron Duke's as thrilled, though. No—don't look now. I'll point out something near the ramp; you can check him out."

"Got you." Somehow, the pleasure stayed with her despite the sinking feeling; when Alexis laughed and pointed, she moved naturally, let her eyes move across the Council without appearing to notice them, toward the Emperor's pedestal, which was once again half down so he could lead the next figure—a vigorous male-dance with ankle bells and staffs. "Mmmmm. I thought he'd be angry." The *zhez*'s whiskers still had a smug tilt to them; his eyes were narrowed; thoughtful.

"Should've watched his face change, the first time you set that fringe to moving. He figured everyone would jeer you for even trying 'Fringe of Dancer.' " Alexis frowned. "I can't guess what he's thinking. Hope it's not some variant of 'there goes our flitter.' "

"I don't know what to tell you," Magdalena admitted. Khyriz appeared at her elbow, then, out of breath from the morrislike excitement, to claim her for the slow, stately *yhenoia*.

*   *   *

Dance followed dance, up to midnight. At that hour, the music continued, but as background for the trestles of food brought in so the participants and observers could sit, eat and drink, and gossip. Magdalena saw Fahara at a distance, surrounded by nobles and a few wealthy merchant-types—their clothing bespeaking much money and less taste—all of whom were courting the designer's favor. "Good for her."

"I agree, Magdalena," Zhik said softly. It was the first she'd seen or heard him in hours. "The designer deserves much reward for all she has done." His eyes were warm; the translator had a sense of missing some hidden meaning, then dismissed the matter as Khyriz's servants came over with two baskets laden with special delicacies, tall cups of thin blue crystal, and a half-dozen beverages to fill them.

Time flew; the great hall grew quieter, the music slow and soft. Some had already left, Magdalena realized, and others were going. She glanced at Alexis, who smothered a yawn and said, "It's three hours until sunup, and I refuse to see the sun from here. In fact, I'm not going to see it at all, not even for my new flitter. I need sleep."

"We can leave," Khyriz said, and Magdalena nodded. Their escorts, duties over, had gone their own ways some time earlier—to bask in the honor, Khyriz said. It took some time to reach the outside, as they were stopped often to be congratulated and admired on the way out. Zhik led the way across the lighted ball grounds, then stepped onto the moving walk to start it toward the old palace.

Sound from behind them was muted; ahead, it was very quiet, and the old palace was dark except for one or two lit windows or balconies. The ground floor was deserted; the second, dimly lit and quiet. Alexis punched in the door code, and as it slid aside, held out both hands to the cousins. "Thank you for a wonderful time. Khyriz, apologies, but I'm not going to come up after all."

"Nor am I," Zhik murmured. Magdalena eyed him sidelong; he'd been quiet and distant for some time now, and at the moment he sounded like a sleepwalker. As if aware of her scrutiny, he shook himself, blinked, and bowed over both women's hands in a very old-Earth courtly gesture, soft cheek-

fur brushing their fingers. "Apologies, Cousin; my father will
expect me awake at the usual hour. Especially after tonight."
His whiskers quirked as his gesture took in the new-style robe
and the women. "It was worth every moment of lost sleep,
however." He sketched a brief farewell at Khyriz, turned, and
left.

"Well, I'm still vibrating," Magdalena said. "I'd never
sleep right now, I'm too keyed up. Just let me change into
casuals, Khyriz, and I'll join you."

"Good," he murmured. "I will go put on the casuals as
well, Magdalena, and set out food. . . ."

"Please do!" She laughed quietly. "I guess you saw I
didn't dare eat much for fear of ruining this robe, I'm fainting
from hunger!"

"That can be dealt with. Bring, please, the music cube?"

"Of course." She touched his arm with the back of her hand
and followed Alexis into the darkened apartments.

"Odd," Alexis said; she was most of the way downhall to
her bedroom. "I thought Edhal said he would leave a few
lights for us."

"Probably forgot," Magdalena replied. "Wasn't there a
separate ball for the servants and their families tonight?"

"Mmmmm. And half a dozen in the city—remember not to
plan on doing anything before midday tomorrow. Everyone
has half day after a party night like this." Alexis yawned
loudly. "And I'll need it." She vanished into her room; Magdalena entered hers and closed the door, quickly slipped out
of the "Fringe of Dancer," and carefully laid it flat in the
carry-basket, then dragged jeans and T-shirt out of the closet.
She kicked off the black synth-leather ballet slippers she'd
worn under the red and spindrift robe, eased the short socks
off with her toes, and, barefoot, scooped up the music cube
and went into the hall. Alexis, already in her nightshirt, waved
as the translator passed her. "Don't stay out all night," she
said mildly.

"Yes, ma'am," Magdalena said with a grin and lengthened
her stride.

*　　*　·　*

Half an Arekkhi hour later, she collapsed back into the cushions of Khyriz's talking-pit, bare feet propped on the edge, and blotted her mouth. "Saved my life," she said. "I don't know how you dared eat in that white thingie."

"Practice—and fear of making a spectacle of yourself by spilling in such circumstances." Khyriz, clad in one of several Arekkhi-shaped sets of blue jeans and T-shirt he'd had made before returning home, got to his feet and stretched. It really hadn't taken that much alteration, Magdalena thought appraisingly: Arekkhi legs tapered more than human ones, hips and waist were approximately the same measure. The shirt needed more material across the back and less across the front, unlike her shirts, which were equal fabric on both sides: They needed to compensate for shoulders that came forward more than human, and for a narrow chest that still had something of a "prow" of ribs—but not much of one. Still—very attractive.

She got to her feet and let him help her out of the pile of cushions, then bent down to program the music cube. Warm, lush notes centuries old eased into the room. As she straightened, Khyriz smiled, whiskers touching, and held out his hands. "When we dance," he murmured. The musician Sting began the slow, warm ballad that Magdalena had long considered theirs; she moved into his loose embrace, settled her cheek against his shoulder—he was really no taller than she— and let the music take her. *When we dance. Khyriz, my truest friend,* she thought happily as they moved with smooth precision around the room. *Remember the first time we tried human close-dance, in the Spiral Arm on StarBridge? Both of us so self-conscious, and then this song came on, and there wasn't anything but dance.*

She wondered if Zhik had seen his cousin in jeans and T-shirt—poor Zhik, having to fight a parent like Zhenu over a mere set of pleats and a sash, never mind bared forearms! Well, it was good the young noble had found some backbone. She only hoped it wouldn't come back to haunt him. Possibly Fahara was serving as his mentor; Zhik certainly spent enough time there these days.

The Sting-song ended; another slow old song began: "I Can See Clearly Now," the bouncy-beat reggae version. Somehow, she was reminded of her conversation early in the day with Alexis. "Khyriz?" she said.

He leaned back to look at her. "Magdalena?"

"I don't know if you heard. Zhenu finally gave in, and we get our flitter. Today, early."

"I remember now what she said as we left the ball." He considered. "How odd, though. Because my father said two days ago that the matter was at standstill, the Iron Duke in full fury and utterly opposed to it."

"Well, that must have been early, because late yesterday, he and Alexis came up with a trade. We get the flitter, she gets her papers. . . . and Duke Zhenu gets the high-tech equipment he wants."

"There are hidden shades to this," Khyriz said grimly. "What trade?" Behind them, the cube clicked over to the next piece in the slow-dance program Magdalena had set up back on StarBridge—a sad instrumental adagio from a centuries-old weekly vid about a warrior woman, the instruments and music reedy and very Arekkhi-like. Both ignored it.

"I don't trust Zhenu either," Magdalena said finally. "But Alexis says it's all right, the tech he wants isn't secret—oh, I don't know!" she broke out impatiently. "It doesn't *feel* right! I can't believe he'd care enough about cave-ins to spend what he'll have to pay for deep-seek, heat-sensing satellites! You know, it's the. . . ." Her voice faded. Khyriz was staring at her, eyes all pupil, and his ears were flat. "Khyriz? What's wrong?"

"Deep-sensing . . . ? Dear gods!" He turned away from her.

Magdalena swallowed; her mouth was suddenly dry. "Khyriz? Have we done something wrong?" He shook his head, but his ears and whiskers were still flat. "Khyriz!" She gripped his arm. "Khyriz, talk to me! If we've goofed, we can fix it, Alexis has *asked* CLS for the satellites, but nothing has been done yet!"

For a long moment, she wasn't certain he'd heard her, but he suddenly took a deep breath, bent down to shut off the music cube, and turned back to face her. The silence was unnerving. "A—apologies, Magdalena," he said finally. "I have . . . lied to you."

"Lied?" she whispered.

His eyes were gold, dark-rimmed—suddenly very alien. "For the same reason CLS has been denied open contact since the first Heeyoons found us."

Magdalena shook her head. "Khyriz . . . I don't understand! I knew something was wrong here from the first! But what?"

"I knew *you* would know. I hoped you would grow to understand, slowly, and that your compassion . . ." He clutched the fur on his forearms and tugged. "Too late. Or it will be, if Zhenu gets those satellites. He and his allies will use them to hunt and destroy Asha."

"*Asha?*" Magdalena stared. "Hunt them? That doesn't make sense, Khyriz! They're aren't . . . are you telling me there are wild ones?"

"Not wild. The Asha Zhenu seeks have fled the compounds where they are kept, or have been taken away. Because . . ." He turned away from her. "Because they are sentient."

For a long moment, his words made no sense. Then she gasped, and caught hold of his arm, pulling him around. "Asha are . . . those *were* Asha, out on the plateau, weren't they?"

"Magdalena, I—"

She cut him off with a sharp gesture. "Asha—they were working—but not for pay, were they? I *knew* something was wrong! It looked . . . looked like a chain gang, that old movie of Rob's. Khyriz . . . tell me that wasn't what I saw!" His ears were very distressed; he gestured hopelessly and turned away again. "And An-Lieye . . . I wondered when I first saw her; her eyes were too *knowing*. . . . But why am I telling *you* this? *That* was what I heard, you and Fahara arguing over An-Lieye; she didn't want us to see An-Lieye, and you did, didn't you?" She was very pale. "Khyriz, damnit, tell me I'm wrong!"

He looked half ill, ears quivering near his skull. "You know about our last war . . . but not *why* it was fought. Though I hoped you might learn more from the book . . ."

"That book—you planted it for me to find, didn't you?"

"I . . . thought it a better way. . . . but someone among the clerks is paid by Zhenu, or an ally of his; the book was taken away before you could study it closely." He gestured sharply. "It doesn't matter. The last war was fought by one side to give rights to the oppressed. The wrong side won. When the war ended, the oppressed became slaves. The Asha, and their champions. *You* know who writes history after a war!'' he added bitterly. ''For nearly a hundred years, Asha have been kept apart from most Arekkhi. They are born intelligent—like your blacks, or Utes or Maori, they are Arekkhi who look different, though here, few Arekkhi know it. Because they never see Asha. Or those they see are made mindless, or voice-less, with drugs. An-Lieye is no less a *person* than you, or I. If she had not been fed the drugs from childhood, she could tell you so.''

''*Drugs?*'' Magdalena fastened on that one word. ''You *knew* this when you came to StarBridge?'' He glanced at her, turned away.

''I knew. I was ordered to say nothing.''

''But on StarBridge . . . Khyriz, you were safe there! You could have—!''

''I could *not*!'' He spun back to stare at her, his eyes mostly pupils and his ears trembling. ''Magdalena, I knew so little about CLS! Except that they do not tolerate a slave class! If they had withdrawn from our space, what good would that have done?''

''What good have *you* done by silence?''

He made a frustrated movement, quickly stilled. ''I have done what I could to save them, Magdalena. Rescued—''

She cut him off with a sharp cry. ''Damn it! Your father is the *Emperor!*''

''But my father does not fully control his Council, have you not learned this? Zhenu would kill every last Asha before CLS learns the truth, if he could! The Prelate quotes the Holy Two to support him, and their allies in Council and elsewhere care only for the bribes given them! Zhenu has hopes he can force the CLS to accept trade on *his* terms and keep the secret of Asha. And if not, he sees opportunities in Shadow Sector! The Prelate is his ally, and *he* would free us from the outside en-tirely.''

Magdalena hadn't heard him. Her face was pale and set. ''That ahla . . . I can't even remember its name! I—I petted it,

I wanted one, and you let me—you let me think it was . . . !''
She felt her gorge rise.

"Magdalena, I . . ." He couldn't go on.

"You could have told Dr. Rob, but no, you arranged for me
to come here . . . not for myself but for my . . . my sixth sense?
You arranged everything, all the hints and odd goings-on . . .
you, damn you, Khyriz, you *manipulated* me! Oh, God, I feel
sick!" She shoved him aside and ran, out the door and down
the ramp.

A glance over her shoulder at the turn; no sign of Khyriz.

Her stomach twisted and she tasted bile. *How could he?* She
ran faster. *Wake up Alexis and get her to send an emergency
message to CLS, now!* She reached the second floor, keyed the
door to open/close-lock, and hurried down the darkened hall.

Bright light to her left—the pantries. Odd, she thought;
Alexis must have gotten up, but the door normally closed itself, and the light shouldn't stay on like that. She leaned
through the opening. "Alexis?" The full battery of lights was
momentarily blinding. She felt along the wall for the controller
and keyed them down. "Alexis?" Dead silence and an unpleasant, metallic odor. She took another step, froze as her bare
foot came down in something sticky.

Rohf lay dead at her feet, Edhal just beyond him, against
the overturned table. Something had torn their throats out and
not recently: Blood had dried on them and on the floor; the
pool where she had stepped was congealing.

Magdalena caught her breath in a faint shriek; something
moved on the other side of the table. Back to the wall, she
eased to where she could see. Alexis—alive but bound, her
head and shoulders covered in a mesh bag that glowed a pale
blue. The interrelator's eyes met hers, then jerked sideways;
her lips moved, but no sound came. Magdalena took a step
toward her, but Alexis shook her head frantically and sent her
eyes to her left again. Magdalena looked up. Half a dozen
dark-clad Arekkhi, their faces hidden by dark masks, poured
into the chamber. She backed away, turned to run—too late.
Something slammed into the side of her neck, just below the
ear. Everything went black; she barely felt hard hands catching
her before she could hit the floor.

CHAPTER 11

♦

Khyriz stared flat-eared at the closing door, then spun away and snarled the worst curses he knew. "All these years . . . and in the end, you *still* ruin everything!" He considered going after her, but rejected the idea at once. She could outrun him . . . almost any human could outrun an Arekkhi. And by now, she'd have reached the second floor. She wouldn't respond to the door; wouldn't speak to him. "Tomorrow . . . no, this morning, early," he promised himself. "I will go and speak to them both, and undo what damage I can." *If* it was possible. He felt as ill as she had looked. But even if Alexis was listening to Magdalena right now, they couldn't possibly be gone before he could talk to them. At least, there was that.

He keyed the door closed, the lighting off, and settled, still clad, in the talking-pit. The servants would see him when they entered, he'd hear them and waken. To sleep until midday as one ordinarily would after a ball, that would be disastrous.

But sleep wouldn't come. He shifted his back, eased a bolster from under his legs—no use. Whenever he closed his eyes, he saw only Magdalena's face, pale with shock and fury. *She will hate me forever,* he thought miserably. *And I will deserve it.*

He had just slipped into a light doze when the servants' door slid aside and brought him blearily awake. But it wasn't Ihnoe. Two of his father's largest and most trusted bodyguards strode into the chamber, and before he could say anything, they had him by his arms, out of the talking-pit and out the

servants' door, down the back ramp, and out of the building.
Khyriz dangled between them, helpless as a kitten until they
reached the moving walkway. He eased free of their grasp with
what dignity he could manage. Both were staring at his out-
lander garments.

"What cause have you for this?" he demanded. For a wonder, his voice was steady.

The nearest guard flicked his ears briefly flat in silent apology but said nothing. Khyriz straightened his shirt as best he
could and concentrated on keeping his ears and whiskers up
and out. For his father to send guards for him . . . had the Emperor already heard from the CLS women?

Alexis might have called Zhenu directly to cancel the agreement once Magdalena told her about the Asha. *Things could
be worse,* he assured himself. *Zhenu would have sent Ulfar,
and my father might never know my fate.* Unlike Zhenu, his
father might be willing to listen to him.

To his surprise, his harassed-looking father waited just inside
the new palace . . . and so, it seemed, did nearly every other being who lived or worked there. Anxious clerks, frightened-
looking servants, cousins, the families of the Council, a few
priests clustered near the windows, staring toward the old palace
and whispering among themselves. Khyriz glanced back the
way they'd just come but could see nothing out of place. But
when he would have spoken, the elder royal sharply gestured
for silence, then beckoned, drawing him into the nearest private
receiving chamber. The doors slid shut, closing them in a bare
little clerks' room. "Father—"

But Khezan gestured urgently: "Spy-wires." *He fears the
room has unfriendly listening devices,* Khyriz realized. But . . .
his father did not suspect visual ones, or he would have used
a private family gesture. The younger male looked at the nail
patch and gestured a negative, then held his hand up so his
father could see the little device.

"There are none, Father. I would know."

The elder's ears flicked, and his whiskers came forward very
briefly; he spoke rapidly before Khyriz could say anything.
"A parting gift, was it, Khyriz? But a good one. However . . .
listen. An hour ago, armed rebels calling themselves the Pro-

tective League took control of the old palace, the second floor. They hold the CLS women hostage—''

Khyriz's whiskers went flat. ''Magdalena?''

''They are both alive and unharmed. We learned of the attack mere minutes ago, when this League sent a sound-only voice-call to warn what would happen if anyone tried to force entry to the second floor; the Council demanded to speak to both the interrelator and the translator, and we were able to do that. Jhue and his brother volunteered to get you out before there was another hostage.''

''I . . .'' Khyriz fought for calm. Anger and panic were no use. But his voice trembled as he said, ''Zhikna was also up there, Father. And the designer.''

''Your designer? No. She was seen leaving the ballroom among the last, and she left the island at once in that—that gaudy flitter of hers. And your cousin was not in his rooms; he had not been since the ball. Jhue sent someone to fetch him, but the rooms were empty.'' The Emperor's mouth twitched and he looked quite angry. ''The father did not think of his son, of course. But Zhenu is in a massive temper at the moment.''

Khyriz brushed that aside. ''Father, they will kill Magdalena and Alexis!''

''No. I personally sent back the message that either we see and speak via their communications center, every fifteen standard minutes, or I order *oriph*-gas piped into the old palace.'' It would kill everyone, Khyriz thought dazedly. ''Or *venhur*.'' The latter caused temporary paralysis; but its affect on the humans might not be the same. His father touched his son's cheek in a parent's gesture of affection. ''Calm yourself. This League is not here on a suicide mission; that was clear from their first call. They are undecided, confused, and I think unnerved by the strength we showed during that talk. Once they decide what their demands are, we can negotiate.''

''They don't even have a plan of—?'' Khyriz spun away from his father and blotted damp palms on his denims. ''We. By 'we,' you mean the Inner Council? Father! Zhenu and the Prelate care nothing about Alexis and . . . and Magdalena!'' He turned to meet the elder's eyes directly. "Permit me to go back in, the back way. I can—"

"No, Khyriz." His father's face was grim. "I had you brought out for good reason. You are safe here."

"But I know the secret ways of the old palace, you know that I do! I can—!"

"No. That is an order," Khezhan said flatly. "Your Emperor's command. Swear to obey—swear it!" he added as Khyriz would have protested again. The Prince sighed gustily and gestured assent. "Swear aloud, Khyriz!"

"I . . . swear it."

"Good. We—the Council and I—we will negotiate a way through this crisis. And if Zhenu and his allies seek to use the moment against me, they will learn who is Emperor." He stepped back and blinked; he seemed to properly see his son for the first time. "What appalling fashion is this? Go clothe yourself!" he added sternly, then turned and left the room. The door hissed to behind him, cutting off a babble of worried voices in the hall beyond.

Khyriz stood very still in the quiet little chamber and considered his options. His father's final order didn't matter, any more than the first. "What does clothing matter? And I lied to Magdalena, why not to him?" he asked himself bitterly. Of course, he wouldn't be able to simply attempt the old palace right now—guards would be on full alert, and no doubt his father had just warned them to watch the alien-loving royal. He was no use to Magdalena, shoved into a locked room. He must choose his moment.

Meantime, a sensible being would learn more about what was going on before he acted. And he would eat and drink something—for strength, as well as to bring himself awake.

Automatically, he checked the nail-patch as he stepped into the crowded hall: There *were* listening devices here; at least two, and only one was his father's. He expected that. He ignored the astonished and embarrassed stares at his alien garb and set off for the family apartments.

A full hour later, he had used the facilities in his original rooms to bathe, but afterward resumed his Earth-style clothing. He'd left no change of clothing here, and besides, the denims were practical. He'd eaten, briefly, sharing the family dining with a tense and silent eldest brother. Now, bread and *rih* made a lump in his stomach. He'd learned what Khelyu knew, but it was almost nothing.

There was no record of a Protective League; no one in the palace had heard of it before today. It might be an offshoot from one of the known groups, of course. Those displeased with their lack of progress often separated from the main group and took matters into their own hands. Generally they were more violent than the parent groups. He dismissed that; let the Council speculate endlessly. . . .

The scope of the raid proved nothing, either. A certain level of skill would be required to get into the old palace via the servants' entry, but nothing special, and last night, security had been concentrated on the ball. The old palace had been nearly empty since afternoon; anyone who had ever served there would know how to key into the main servants' entry, and once inside, this League would have hours to find a way to break the security codes that would let them into the CLS suite—if they did not already have such codes, thanks to a traitor. Thereafter they would only need to wait for two pleasantly tired women to return to their rooms; they'd be taken completely off-guard.

But why? The rebels could expect no gain from this. Despite what his father said, it could be a suicide mission, or an attempt to send a direct message to CLS. Though . . . the Heir had just told him there was no sign of outside transmissions to or from the old palace since before early yesterday. The Council couldn't tap into the transmissions, of course, but they knew when one was sent or received.

He paced, unable to remain still; servants and clerks milled, now more excited than frightened. The halls fronting the old palace were crowded, the noise maddening. But the back passages were mostly deserted. He ignored the few Arekkhi he passed; hesitated for some time outside the closed Inner Council door that had once so frightened him. Now, he would give much for entry. The Emperor's ducat affixed to the wall showed he was inside. But the hallway was deathly silent, and no sound came from behind the door. *No entry without invitation.* The Prince sighed heavily and went back the way he'd come.

Khelyu had sworn he would leave messages on the system in his youngest brother's old rooms if he learned anything. *I haven't been back there in more than an hour. Perhaps . . .*

A elderly servant was just turning away from the door as he came up. He gave Khyriz's alien garb a startled glance, then remembered his manners and gestured a bow as he held out a folded and privacy-sealed message. "From the designer-she. Fahara. I am told it is urgent." He gave the Prince's blue-clad lower limbs a final dubious look, then backed away and was gone. Khyriz stared at the thick paper, fingered the seal-tape that would destroy the message if anyone but the chosen recipient opened it.

Urgent—why would Fahara send him an urgent message so early in the day after a successful ball? If she'd seen the guards around the old palace, of course . . . But he would know the contents soon enough—if he still had a feature-scan in his old rooms; otherwise he'd be unable to open the message. His only other scan was in the old palace.

It took time to find what he sought; the chambers had been partly emptied, and many things were not where they should have been. Finally he discovered one of the little devices in a basket, under a few dusty writing tools. *It should have been kept in the lockbox; you are too lax with security measures, Khyriz.* He aimed it at the spots on his left cheekbone, then held it over the message. The seal-tape sprang apart.

He automatically checked the nail-patch as he crushed the tape, then unfolded the message and read, his ears slowly flattening: "Esteemed Khyriz, all is lost unless you can help me. You are the only one I dare tell. I reached my apartments at sunrise to find An-Lieye gone, a written message, in her hand and in our private code, telling me she has run away with your Cousin Zhikna! I only now learn that he has been to see her often since the first time you presented the CLS delegates to my house. I swear to you I knew nothing of this unsanctioned alliance between him and An-Lieye! He has told her he can find her family and get them to safety, she writes. He speaks of love to her and she writes that she cares for him deeply. She writes no word of where they have gone. What can be done? If the Esteemed *Zhez* discovers what has happened in my house, he will have me stripped of all and condemned to the filthiest of his farms; he told me that much when I came here. But he will kill An-Lieye!

"You must decide what is to be done; I cannot. Apologies for my ignorance . . . Fahara."

He stared at the message blankly, unable to take it in at first. *Zhikna—and An-Lieye? Impossible!* But no, the look on Zhik's face when he first saw her in "Fringe-of-Dancer." He'd been odd the rest of the day . . . strange and distant ever since, Khyriz suddenly realized. And how like Zhik to fall for a beautiful garment and bright eyes! He'd done the same thing so many times before now!

But . . . but to deliberately *court* An-Lieye? The Iron Duke's son professing love—to an *Asha*?

And . . . when had Zhikna become aware of An-Lieye as sentient? Khyriz clutched at his ears and growled softly. He knew his cousin spent much time at Fahara's, but he had the new garments to show for it. *It did not occur to me there might be another reason.* Well, it had not occurred to the designer, either. He reread the message. "Foolish, idealistic young cousin," he growled finally. "I have been directing the search for her family all along. And An-Lieye *knew* it!" Knew, and had not trusted him, for whatever reason. So when Zhik swore devotion and love to her . . . Zhik had learned about females from the dreadful fiction-vid so popular these days, displaying the same chivalrous, charming, protective behavior of the heroes in the vids. The vid females admired it, of course. And An-Lieye, cloistered in the designer's apartments, might see him as exactly an Arekkhi male should be . . . according to the vids. Khyriz swore. Two hapless, helpless innocents out there—somewhere. Unless they could be found, quickly, tragedy would surely follow.

And if Zhenu learned of this romantic alliance, then Fahara was right to fear. But not exile: She, An-Lieye, and Zhikna would all die. Khyriz prowled the small chamber. Nothing in the message to even hint where the two might have gone.

So . . . where *would* Zhik look for An-Lieye's parents? The hair on his arms hackled as a possibility occurred to him: Surely Zhik would not go to his cousin's estates? But Zhik knew that Khyriz protected Asha, if only because of Ah-Naul.

If Zhenu learned his son was gone, even if he knew nothing else, he would check Khyriz's estates.

I will have to put a call through to Lijahr, to ask him if Zhik has arrived or tried to—no, I do not dare! Khyriz swore aloud. One of his two protected coms was still in the old palace, the other in his flitter, up North! Any call he made to his master of estates could be overheard—especially if the palace calling system was tampered with, and it often was.

He couldn't leave the island, either; Zhenu would wonder what was so important as to drag Khyriz away from his precious alien-she. *But I do not abandon my Magdalena.*

What next? He read through the designer's message a last time, then glanced at his message center, but it was dark. Perhaps his mother had heard something, he decided. He needed to keep moving, anyway, and he could access this machine from his mother's quarters. He carried the thick fold of paper into the washing, filled the foot-basin with water, and dipped the message in it. When he pulled it out, the water was dark, the paper blank. He shoved it and the seal-tape into the disposing-unit and left.

But just short of his mother's private rooms, his brother Khedan lounged against the pale wall, talking softly and urgently with another dark-clad priest-initiate. The companion's eyes widened as they fell on outland-clad Khyriz; Khedan, alerted by that, turned, and gestured sharply for his companion to leave. Khedan moved to block the hall then, a squarely built figure the youngest royal male could not pass. "Go away, Khyriz. Mother will not see you."

Khyriz stalked forward. The priest had disappeared down the hall, unrecognized. "Move, Khedan."

"No. You are responsible for the dark alien-she coming here, to teach Mother and our young sisters outsider language and ways. . . ."

Khyriz interrupted him, the first time he could ever remember, by laughing. "Oh? Mother asked for the translator's presence. That is her right, brother."

"You would even *lie* for the alien-she! But you will *not* bring shame to our mother's chambers by appearing in such garb!"

With an effort, Khyriz kept his ears where they belonged. It was hard to remember just now that Khedan was large but soft; he had truly terrified the young Khyriz. "She has seen them before. Go away, Khedan." A grim smile quirked his whiskers forward. "I wear my trousers honestly—unlike you!"

Khedan's eyes were dark with anger. "How dare you ill-speak the holy garb of the prelatry?"

"Holy? The clothing is not holy—nor are the priests themselves! Only the gods are! You are arrogant, Khedan!"

"Arrogant—?"

"Who else wears priests' trousers and tunic but keeps a royal's lifestyle? Even Nijho acts outwardly as a Prelate should; he fasts at the proper times, observes the forms of worship. . . . You act as a priest only when it suits you, Khedan." Khedan's ears flattened. "You keep no priests' rules. Even a royal priest is expected to avoid certain excesses. But you are greedy, Khedan."

"Our mother spoils you!" Khedan said with a hiss. "And our father indulges you. You were granted three years among the aliens, and why? Because you are the last son—the pet! Well, little ahla-brother, the alien-she you dote upon *and* her pale-furred companion will die before this day ends!"

Khyriz closed the distance between them with a bound, fastening a hand in the other's tunic as he bared long incisors in an attack-smile. "What have you heard?" he demanded in a throaty whisper. Khedan, startled and badly off-balance, tried to free himself, but Khyriz was older now: larger, and better muscled than he had been the last time the two physically fought. The elder Prince gasped as his younger brother forced him back and finally slammed him into the wall. "What have you heard?" Khyriz asked with a soft snarl. Khedan closed his eyes. Khyriz exerted more pressure. "No one will save you, Khedan. I am the only one here, and there are no spy-devices in this passage. Where did you hear about the CLS team? From Zhenu? Nijho?'' Khedan started at the second name. ''What is Nijho's part in this, Khedan?''

''No . . . not your business, Khyriz!'' the other said with a hiss.

''It is. You spy on Father for the Prelate, don't you?''

Khedan twisted in his grip, subsided as Khyriz pressed against him. ''How dare you? The Prelate has every right to know—''

''He has *no* right, not in the Emperor's household. He can be removed as Prelate if Father chooses, do you forget that? Let us say, then, that you report to Nijho. . . .''

The dark-clad stirred indignantly. ''To the Revered Father of All! You speak as if he were common!''

''He *is* common, the son of *jnerif*-herders on Mibhor. Nijho may find himself butchering *jnerif* again if he is not cautious. If the Emperor replaces him.''

''He won't dare! Zhenu is—he has—''

''Oh, yes.'' To the elder brother's astonishment, Khyriz emitted a short spat of laughter. ''Zhenu! Zhenu the invincible! Zhenu is noble only. Wealthy and powerful—but these things change. And if they do—you have chosen a poor ally, Khedan.''

''You have chosen worse,'' Khedan said, hissing, his eyes black with fury. ''Do you think the outside worlds will protect *you*? Or their females? They are distant; the rebels are here. And do you think Zhenu cares greatly whether every one of his—?'' He caught his breath raggedly; Khyriz pressed both thumbs against his brother's throat, hard.

''I can kill you,'' the younger prince whispered. ''Or I might allow you to live. *Brother*. Zhenu *is* behind this raid, isn't he? The rebels he secretly funds—you look astonished. Did you think I knew nothing of the Arekkhi for Freedom group? AF is Zhenu's, their leader personally chosen by him. Is this League taken from their numbers, or are these different fighters? Zhenu knows the old palace; that knowledge got the League in, didn't it? *Answer me!*'' Khedan's eyes bulged; his whiskers and ears were flat with terror, and he hand-gestured frantic assent. The younger prince eased the pressure, but only a little. "Zhenu planned it all. I know. I saw the look on his face last night! The AF supposedly rescues and hides Asha; in truth, it sets fires, destroys villages, kills. *Exterminates.*" Silence. "Why? Just to destroy all Asha? Or does he also plan to make our infamy public, so the CLS will see our world is unsafe and uncivilized, and withdraw?"

"Why do we need *them*?" Khedan might be breathless, but he still sounded righteous. "These aliens? The naked ones onstation, these—these hairless females who wear our robes and speak our language and pretend to be like us! You wait, Khyriz! They have plans of their own behind those smiles. Soon, they will order our lives and our world to suit *them,* and it will be too late for us!"

"You know nothing," Khyriz replied flatly. "I lived among them three years."

"You are a sentimental dupe, and they play upon that! Zhenu is not fooled by what these aliens say, the Prelate is not—"

"Zhenu and the Prelate?" Khyriz said with a snarl, silencing his brother. "They know only what has always been! They fear the least change! The CLS seeks cooperation, alliance, honest exchange of information and tech. . . . that everyone has an opportunity for reasonable fortune! And that all intelligent beings be considered equal." Khyriz pressed his lips against his brother's ear; Khedan shrank from him. "The Asha, Khedan," he whispered. "CLS will solve the matter of Asha, given the chance. And that is what most angers Nijho and Zhenu—and you. Isn't it? Your estates, Khedan—how much of the labor there is performed by Asha?"

"They—they are—"

"Do not lie to me, I know how you treat your Voiceless."

"Alien-lover," Khedan said with a growl. "Asha-lover!"

"Add to that," Khyriz replied flatly as he released his brother and let him stagger away from the wall, "that I love the Magdalena-she. Do you understand that? She is *my* Magdalena! If any harm comes to *my* Magdalena because of you, we will finish this, Khedan. Do not doubt me, I will tear out your throat, and laugh as you die!"

Khedan's ears went flat; he struggled to right them. "How

dare you threaten me?'' he demanded harshly. ''I will tell Father that you . . . that you—''

''Tell him. Do. And tell him whom you *really* serve! Though I wager Khezahn already knows. Our father for long has not been the weak young Emperor whom Nijho and Zhenu once dominated.''

Khedan stumbled away from Khyriz, shook his garments down and glared at his younger brother. ''It would do you well—*and* our father!—to consider why he assumed the throne so early, Khyriz! I would be careful what I ate and drank, if I were you.'' Khyriz stared, but before he could move to intercept his priest-clad brother, Khedan had scurried down the hall and was gone. A distant door shut with a sharp click; the double clang of locks being set echoed up the silent corridor. Khedan had bolted himself into the safety of his private chambers.

Automatically, the younger prince glanced at his nail-device. ''It's not possible!'' he whispered. Was that fury and bluff, or did Khedan really know something? *Had* the previous Emperor been poisoned? Poisoning was an ancient weapon—there were safeguards against its use, bans on having, making, and using poisons. *That would scarcely stop Zhenu or the Prelate if they saw poison as a means to the end they wanted.* He paced anxiously, realized what he was doing, and forced himself to stillness. The bans were mostly truce, anyway: the old, ''I won't use poison if you don't'' agreement. Zhenu had privacy on his estates to do whatever he chose; the Prelatry was mostly off-limits to noninitiates. Those two councillors currently had more power than they would have under the old Emperor. It fit.

But that wasn't important—not just now. Khyriz turned away from his mother's apartments and walked briskly back toward the main Council chamber. It was improper, but he *could* get inside via the private passage used by his elder brother. With luck, Khelyu would be available, personally or via com, so Khyriz could try to persuade him.

But it proved unnecessary; a clerk came over as the Prince stepped off the moving walkway just short of the Council doors, and handed him a set-com enameled with the Emperor's ducat. "His Exaltedness asks that you use this at once. Your presence is required." He'd scarcely keyed voice transmission when the doors opened and another clerk gestured sharply for him to enter.

Only five of the seats were occupied. The Emperor gestured, indicating the vid-unit set midtable. Alexis's voice . . . Khyriz moved to a position where he could see the screen.

The interrelator sat cross-legged in the talking-pit. She was pale, her hair a wild tangle, and she wore a loose nightshirt with the StarBridge logo on one shoulder. But her voice was steady. ". . . and I continue to attempt a negotiated end to this situation from inside. I hope things progress outside. About the upper floor—as I reported in our last call, we were told that the third floor had burned, and all living there were killed. But an argument the translator overheard indicates otherwise. She and I are concerned, both for the effect such deaths would have on a peaceful outcome, and for our friends." Khyriz glanced at his father; Khezahn touched the edge of his note-maker—well out of vid-range, and moved it where his son could read what he'd noted there: "Khyriz: Say nothing to upset the captors. Assure the women. Extend the talk as long as possible. Something useful may appear when vid is analyzed." Khyriz gestured a spare assent, shoved the notemaker aside, and stepped before the vid.

"I am here, Alexis," he said. For a moment, he couldn't think of anything to say. A dark-clad, masked figure moved partway into sight behind her and was pulled sharply away. "You appear well."

"I could use some sleep," Alexis replied dryly. "I'm glad to see you safe, my friend. What about the third floor?"

"Undamaged. Is Magdalena—?"

"I—I'm all right, Khyriz!" Magdalena's voice was higher than normal, her hair pulled back in a twist of fabric; she still wore T-shirt and blue jeans, and her feet were bare. A thin line of dried blood ran down her neck and made a small dark spot on the shirt. "I'm fine. And I'm sorry—"

"No," he broke in, afraid of what she might say. "The sorrow is mine that there was misunderstanding. You are my good friend, Magdalena."

She smiled tiredly, but her eyes were warm, searching the image of his face. Behind her, a deep male voice snarled out something, but the voice was warped by a distort screen. *So we cannot understand their words, or identify them by voice-print*, he realized. Alexis touched Magdalena's shoulder and murmured something against her ear. The dancer nodded, then added aloud, "They say we've had more than our allotted time. My good friend. My . . ." she shifted into English, *"air venting system."*

Angry shouts from three separate directions at once. The translator huddled away from them, but Alexis eased onto her knees and put herself between her companion and the far side of the talking-pit. "It means 'special friend' in our language!" she shouted back. "Ask her or ask the Prince!"

Khyriz gestured assent. "She speaks truth," he added urgently. "It is the first alien speech I learned!" Mumbling in the background, warped by distort. Magdalena swallowed and licked her lips; her eyes were enormous.

"Apologies, Khyriz," she said finally. "I didn't mean to frighten you; I forgot they told us, no alien words—"

"Between you and me, they are not alien, Magdalena," Khyriz assured her, bringing a faint smile to her face again. Before he could say anything else, the transmission ended, and the vid-screen went dark.

Silence in the Council chamber. Khyriz stepped back as his father stood; two councillors, on their feet to see the vid-transmission, immediately sat. All of them, the Prince noticed, were doing their best not to stare at his alien clothing. The Emperor paid no attention. "What was the meaning of those words—?" Khezahn began; Khyriz gestured an urgent negative.

"Father, if I might speak to you in private?" He flicked an ear and addressed the restless elders seated behind the long table. "Apologies. A matter that . . ." He couldn't think of a diplomatic way to phrase it; to his surprise, his father emitted a short, low spat of laughter.

"My allies in Council know that a secret is best kept by one, and safer between two than shared by all. Wait," he instructed, then pressed through the drape and keyed the narrow door behind it. Khyriz found himself for the first time inside the barren servants' station kept for Council messengers. Three practical seats and a low bench with a notemaker and sheets of paper—nothing else, not even a window. Khyriz automatically glanced at his nail-patch.

Khezahn touched his arm. "This room is safe: It is distort-sealed, and the distort is tested daily. What was that between you and the Magdalena?"

"The words were English." He explained. "I believe she means the apartments were entered via the duct system. But there is more." He spoke quickly, laying out his argument with Khedan. "If Zhenu is behind this Protective League . . . ! But Father, I believe Khedan spies for the Prelate."

"Of course he does," the elder replied. Khyriz's whiskers twitched in astonishment. "I often tell him things I know will be passed on to Nijho, to be certain it *is* Khedan. This of Zhenu: I suspected it, but there is no proof. Still, if the women can be freed—"

"Apologies, Father—but Zhenu will not free them unless he is certain they will leave Arekkhi. Alexis does not sound ready to take that course of action. Has there been any change in the position of this League?"

"They still take no position. They hold the women and make threats. We counter with threats. They cannot leave, however—"

"Father—apologies, but they can. If Magdalena is right about the air passages, they must have entered the building from underground. There are at least ten ways out that I know: the Prelatry, the library, the old kitchens that now house Mother's enameler and her staff . . ." His voice faded.

"Yes." Unusual for him, Khezahn prowled the small room. "So. The station has full tracking-vid trained on the island, but that will be of no use if they use the old tunnels. If Zhenu *is* behind this, then Nijho is without doubt his ally. If the women are taken into the Prelatry, things will be much worse; there are other ways out of the Prelatry you do not know, Khyriz. Ways not even marked on the official grid."

"I know more of them than you might think, Father."

"Yes. I remember the small youth who explored the old

palace.'' He was silent for a long moment, then gazed into his son's eyes. ''When we go back in there, the Council will not be surprised to see you are distressed. You will excuse yourself to your quarters, and go there at once. Old Nhedro will carry food to your room at the proper intervals. You can trust him. If—you have other needs, Nhedro will bring those who can best assist you.''

He means for me to go—he gives me permission to take his guards and steal into the old palace! Khyriz swallowed, gestured understanding. ''Yes. Bhelan will arrive with my flitter soon.''

''Leave word with the clerk outside the council doors where Bhelan will find you.''

''Yes, Father.''

''We will speak again very soon.''

''Yes.'' He hadn't expected this; it was all he could do to keep elation out of his voice, and to remember to flatten his ears in distressed fashion as his father keyed the door open.

An hour later, the excitement was long gone. The permission to act was nothing; he'd have gone anyway. Now, he had to plan in detail. Fortunately, Bhelan had arrived just as he was keying the rooms' com-system. He sent the pilot out for his protected com and the portable flat comp he'd purchased on StarBridge: The portable unit would shield the in-room system from tapping, so he could access the island grid and make certain of the underground passages. It had been too many years since he'd last used them. He had barely finished explaining what he intended when Nhedro came in the servants' back door with a large basket of bread, meat, and dipping sauces, another basket holding a variety of beverages and cups, and at his heels, the guard Jhue and his equally enormous brother, Jhoric. Both wore synth-plas torso armor and were armed with small multifire stunners. Jhoric carried a box that held another ten such weapons. Jhue, to Khyriz's astonishment, openly wore a talon. Bhelan's whiskers went flat and he turned away; he'd seen the wicked metal claw as well.

Khyriz gestured, taking in the food Nhedro had set out. ''Eat,'' he said as he turned back to the comp and keyed the final command to bring up the grid, then went down through it, level by level, until he reached subground. "Nedhro, pour me cold juice—whatever you have. Plain meat strips folded into a flat bread, and a small dish of hot *pjor* for dipping. This side, please," he gestured with his free hand; the other was busily moving across the flat surface of his portable comp. He was aware of the two guards and his pilot, watching the room's wall-screen as he narrowed the search area and amplified. Finally he sat back, felt blindly for food, eyes still studying the screen. Nhedro turned his hand right-side up, set the bread there, and folded his fingers around it.

Khyriz finally stepped back from the screen, ate quickly, and washed down untasted food with a tart drink. He sent an occasional look toward the guards and suddenly felt very young. *Remember your words to the Emperor. You alone are so familiar with the old palace, and the connecting tunnels.* If this went as he planned, there would be no fighting. Finally he gestured, a greeting that meant, "I welcome those who have greater talents than mine." "Were you told why my father asked you to come here?" he asked aloud. The two signed a terse negative. Khyriz explained, as briefly as possible. When he was done, the two exchanged a look, then gestured an even more terse assent. *I cannot begin to decipher what they think . . . of this and of me,* he decided finally. It didn't matter; they would cooperate.

"I go as well," Bhelan said evenly.

"Yes. Have you light-sticks?" His whiskers quirked forward, and briefly, so did the pilot's: It was an old joke between them, how many portable lights Bhelan kept on his person and in the flitter, in case of late-night emergencies of any kind. "Good. Sort out one apiece for us. While you do that, I still must find the best way from these rooms and into the passage that leads to vehicle repairs."

"There I can assist," Nhedro put in softly. "One goes as I came in, and then—"

"Will you show us now?" Khyriz broke in. "You need go only so far as that."

"An honor, Prince," the elderly servant said, even more softly, and left the remains of the impromptu meal.

*   *   *

The servants' hall leading from the back of a closet in Khyriz's old washing room went straight for some distance, then jogged back and forth, plain doors on either side marking the service entries to other such chambers. The Empress's ducat graced the last of these; four steps later, the passage plunged down a steep ramp, and the air grew heavy with the smell of baking bread. As warmth from the ovens became uncomfortable, however, the elderly servant turned into a side passage. This was ill lit, the floor plain long tiles, the walls unpainted in some time. He could see and smell mold. Nhedro slowed, beckoned the Prince forward, and spoke in a breathy whisper close to his ear. "Go here, a hundred paces or so; there are five passages branching off. Take the second left. It will branch again, two passages only; again take the left. That will bring you into the vehicle-repair. You can find your way from there?"

"Yes," Khyriz whispered back. "If you are alone in his personal dressing with my father—but in no other place!—tell him only this: 'It goes well.' " *So far,* he thought, but did not add aloud. The old one gestured a bow of deep respect, turned, and left them. Khyriz gestured his three companions on and began counting.

A short time later they reached the repair center: It was dark, the air close and fragrant with the odor of old-style fuel, of the oils used to keep machinery meshing smoothly, of paint and the enamel-baking units along the far wall. Bhelan led here, a dimmed light-stick in each hand; the other came close behind him. Once beyond the chamber, Khyriz again took the lead. From this point he knew where he was, and how to reach his goal. Another five-branch; this time he took the fifth arm right, and fewer than fifty paces on came to an area surprisingly well tended—last time he'd come here it hadn't been. He retreated into the older tunnel and gestured for his companions to come close.

"That—where we go—is used," he whispered. "Can you see it? The tiles are swept, the lights all operate, the walls are clean." He checked the nail-device, held it where Jhue and his brother could see it. "This is alien, their latest tech. There are no spy-devices in this tunnel—those who use it do not expect outsiders here, perhaps. Walk with care. If anyone comes, one shout of warning is our undoing. And that of the CLS team.'' He gestured as they came back into the tunnel, which had once served the Empress and female royalty when they traveled from palace to worship-chambers. But when he would have led the way, Jhue touched his arm and immediately gestured contrition for the contact.

''Apologies, Prince,'' he murmured, his voice a low growl. ''You have proven your right to be part of the rescue. But now, let us lead; this is what we are trained to do.''

He was right, Khyriz knew; he stepped aside to let one royal guard move ahead of him; his brother took up the rear. A moment later, a flush of pleasure curved the Prince's whiskers. *Proven my right—and to Jhue!* But none of that counted—not until Magdalena and Alexis were safe.

There was another short pause directly beneath the old palace: The guards were out of breath; Bhelan needed to change light-sticks, and to take two stun-weapons from the box Jhoric had carried. And Khyriz needed to think where the closest hatch into the air-venting system was. Once he oriented himself, he accepted a pair of the stunners and again took the lead.

The hatch had been greased so it would make no sound when opened; the interior—synth-plas lining an older metal system—had been matted in places, lengths of woven reed to ease the discomfort of those who crawled through here. After a brief argument, Jhue again took the lead, Khyriz next with Bhelan right behind him, Jhoric, six spare stunners fastened to his shoulders and back, bringing up the rear.

Crawling is not a comfortable mode of travel, Khyriz thought gloomily. Arekkhi leg-joints did not have the shield of bone like human knees, and Arekkhi forearms were more tendon, bone, and nerves than muscle. It seemed to take forever, moving slowly on his belly, edging his way up a steep incline toward the servants' corner of the second-floor apartments.

Silence everywhere, except for an occasional scrabble on Jhue's part or his own, and once the sharp click of a light-stick against synth-plas. Jhue paused at that, listening intently, then finally moved on. A few breaths later he stopped and twisted so he could look back, then gestured upward with his light-stick. The repairs-hatch into the second floor was directly above them.

For some reason, it was difficult to move. Jhue, massive as he was, needed three attempts before the thing eased offside, leaving a dimly lit five-sided opening directly above him. Khyriz's nose sensed something unpleasant up there; the set of the guard's whiskers didn't help. Jhue pulled himself into the room above with one swift motion, then reached down to assist Khyriz, and after him, Bhelan.

It took a moment for his eyes to adjust; Khyriz clapped both hands over his nose once they did. The servants assigned here—males he'd known all his life—lay stiff and dead in a wide pool of dried blood. Bhelan stared blankly, then gripped Khyriz's arm, hard, as Jhoric passed them and hissed a warning in the pilot's ear. Khyriz spun away from the sight of so much death.

Magdalena! But these two had been dead for many hours; the blood had dried. Magdalena had spoken to him not two hours earlier.

Jhue reappeared at his side. "There is no one here," he said. "My brother and I checked each room. The cushions in the talking-pit are still warm, there is chilled *rih* in a cup beside it. There are marks on the back of the door, there, inside the toilet," he added. "It may be the outsider-language; it is no Arekkhi written form that I know." Khyriz sketched a quick thanks and bounded down the hall, Bhelan cursing and right behind him.

It *was* a message, written in the cosmetic Magdalena used to enhance her eyes, small, printed letters in English. "Good," he whispered as he studied the message. Written Mizari had been his weakest subject, and she knew it.

"Khyriz, they have let us each use this room separately, with the other held hostage so we don't jump from the balconies. They speak of moving us before full dark; while Alexis was in here, someone mentioned a cavern or a grotto, and another silenced him with a blow. I did all I could to appear foolish and too frightened to pay attention to the conversation.'' Below this, a scrawl of words. ''Khyriz, please please find us!''

Cavern. Grotto. Everything was suddenly clear; he shoved Bhelan aside with a growl of apology and hastened into the main room, skidding to a halt before the comp unit as he punched in the Emperor's personal code. His father's face appeared on the screen almost immediately—the background, unfortunately, was the main Council chamber, but it could not be helped. ''Father, they are gone!'' Excited babble along the table, which the Emperor's gesture silenced. ''But it may not be too late. Warn the station to track *any* flitter or shuttle leaving the island, especially from the old sailing-harbor within the grotto! And send guards there at once!'' He keyed the transmission off, turned for the main entry, and ran.

CHAPTER 12

♦

The passage to the naturally protected harbor had long been blocked, but when Khyriz entered the main clerk's chamber he could see that the panels had been hacked to splinters, and the passageway was open. The scent of ocean reached his nostrils as he plunged down the long ramp, both guards and Bhelan now well behind him.

Low tide: Waves splooshed softly against the stone pier where ships had once docked. Moonlight shone on water beyond the entrance, but in here, it was dark. Still, there was a dim light to both sides, and as he stepped onto sand, the motion-device triggered them full on. New lights. And two sets of portable flitter-blocks. No flitters; no Magdalena. No one here but himself, the two guards, his breathless pilot.

He pulled out his protected com and keyed in the Emperor's code again. "Father? Too late." He somehow kept most of the distress out of his voice. "What vehicles have just left from the old pier? And does the station track them?"

"Khyriz." His father's voice crackled because of the stone above his head. "At least seven flitters just left the island, all going in different directions and all at the same moment—no doubt part of the overall plan. The station was ordered to track, but councillor Franyoe is unable to reach the master of station—there is no response. Wait where you are. My guards have just entered the old palace."

Khyriz turned back the way they'd come. "I see them . . . No! these aren't yours, Father, they're Zhenu's!" Ulfar, unmistakable, led the twenty or more armed guards who suddenly swarmed into the cavern; they moved neatly off the ramp and across the sand, flanking the bulky assassin. The two guards who'd followed Khyriz stepped between the Prince and this new threat.

"Khyriz?" Emperor Khezahn's voice. Khyriz pressed the low-volume control and turned aside, com against his ear. "Stay behind Jhue and his brother; my armed have just dispatched four who guarded the head of the passage; reinforcements will reach you in moments. Tell Zhenu's armed this."

"Apologies, Father, a better idea," Khyriz murmured into the device, thumbed the "send only" button, and keyed for full volume. He shook off Bhelan's trembling grasp and stepped into the open. "Ulfar!" his voice echoed. "You have no right here, this is the Emperor's private land! Turn and leave!"

Ulfar gestured sharply and his guards moved, half-circling the four. "The alien females are gone, Prince," he said with a snarl, whiskers touching and his ears quivering with pleasure or anticipation. Khyriz fought to keep his own ears upright and utterly still. "Perhaps they have already been dropped into the sea? But what matter how they die, since *you* will not see them alive again!"

Fury almost sent him into attack-rage; he forced it away. *Let him speak. Let him build a pyre for his master with his own words,* he thought grimly, and held the com by his side, where its speaker could pick up Ulfar's voice. "You . . . you are responsible for this, Ulfar?" He let his voice rise to an undisciplined squeak. To their credit, his father's two guards stood like statuary, alert and weapons ready but their features impassive. Bhelan, he was glad to see, had already faded well back, behind the two. Sensible of him—Ulfar's flat stare promised death. "Those are my friends! What have you done with them, Ulfar?"

Ulfar's whiskers quivered forward; he was enjoying the moment. "Perhaps already dead, their throats cut. . . . or perhaps they will join the ahla, or be penned with the Voiceless, to work the master's lands!" He spat laughter. "But you will never know! When the outsider-shes are dead, the aliens will leave our world. Then your weakling father will learn what allies *my* master has!''

''Your master—Zhenu?'' Khyriz stammered; this time he wasn't pretending. Magdalena and Alexis fed *xhezzik*, turned into . . . His fingers held the com in a murderous grip. ''Zhenu planned this?''

''The *zhez* foresaw everything!'' Ulfar boasted. ''He has planned for this moment since the Heeyoon traders first came to live on *our* station.'' Zhenu's bodyguard was positively hissing with pleasure. ''Zhenu already spreads rumor that *you* were behind the attack on the old palace, that you and the dark-she have vanished together!''

''No one will believe that I would harm the CLS delegates—!''

''But if rumor spreads that you and the Magdalena-she would be mates, but even the Emperor who indulges you would not permit such heresy? It will be believed because there will be no other explanation. The two-she will vanish; and I am going to kill you here and now, Prince. With your body weighted and thrown into the sea, who will know what to believe? Until it is too late.'' He took a deliberate step toward the Prince.

The high whine of stun-fire and the shriek of a wounded guard; the bulky guard spun around as tens of armed Arekkhi, sleeve-marked with the Emperor's ducat, hurtled down the ramp just as two flitters roared through the cave entrance, lights on full. Ulfar and his followers were caught by surprise, surrounded and disarmed.

Khyriz's legs trembled so, he didn't dare move. *Do not let Ulfar see,* he ordered himself. The bodyguard's black stare was fixed on him, whiskers quivering with rage. ''I am the personal guard of the Esteemed *zhez*, you dare not touch me!'' he shouted, but fell prudently silent as power-braces were clamped around his arms and upper body. If he tried to move or speak now, the bonds would deliver a painful shock. But his eyes still glared through the swarm of guards and found Khyriz.

The Prince held up his hand, the com now visible, rekeyed

the receive, and spoke into it. "Father? Matters are under control here. Did you hear?"

"We all heard, Khyriz." The Emperor's voice boomed and echoed in the cavern, momentarily silencing everyone. "Have my guards bring them here."

Khyriz sighed; Council would tie things into a monumental wrangle, and there was no time for it. He turned his back on the prisoners and lowered his voice.

"Father, but Zhenu and Nijho will—"

"They will do nothing. Return here and have the prisoners brought. Zhenu's personal craft was one of those that left the island just now; both he and his cousin, the master of station, are missing, and Nijho has barred himself inside the Prelatry."

The shuttle was an older model, the pilot nowhere near as good as Bhelan. Magdalena sat very still, eyes closed, and concentrated on breathing deeply. Their captors had grown increasingly nervous, and panic on her part might send one of them over the brink. Alexis's bare forearm rested against hers, silent comfort. The interrelator was quiet, too, though she'd spent most of the day talking—trying to get the members of this so-called Protective League to see them as beings rather than tokens of exchange; trying to learn anything personal she could about any of them, so they would treat the women more kindly. One or two—something about the way they moved suggested they might be barely of age—seemed briefly sympathetic, but as soon as the leader realized that, he made sure they were no longer allowed near the prisoners.

Magdalena tried to think back to the ball, but it seemed like something she might have dreamed years ago. Even her fight with Khyriz felt ancient. *Thank you, Alexis, for insisting on that call.* At least she knew he didn't hate her for the awful things she'd said to him. He'd looked tired, frightened. Well, he had cause.

"Where are you taking us?" Alexis asked quietly. Someone nearby snarled, and she was silent again. Magdalena shifted uncomfortably in the Arekkhi half-egg seat as the shuttle tilted and pressure shoved her back: They were heading up, away from the planet.

*   *   *

In a small, private shuttle bay well downstation from the alien sector and halfway around the cylinder from the royal and noble landing and storage, Zhikna keyed the controls for instant departure, in case it was necessary, and prepared to wait. He had caught a little of an open transmission just before docking: The satellite bank was down, his uncle, the master of station, missing. Briefly he wondered what was going on? But he had his own concerns just now.

He closed his eyes and ran through the plan once again. Bring the flitter to station. Fortunately, it was space-capable. Zhenu knew that, of course, but Zhenu forbade him to travel off-planet. Perhaps he wouldn't look for his son here. And, of course, the flitter wasn't docked where it should be.

He needed to exchange it for a generic model, one of those the Emperor kept by the tens; no one would expect him to travel in such a vehicle. No one would notice one such vehicle traveling around highland Akkherif.

So far, his plan was working: Lhore's father had been one of his tutors; he and Lhore were nearly the same age, and the friendship had been close. Now the tutor's only offspring worked on-station as head of the repair-center for the four moon-shuttles.

I know he loathes my father. Zhik hadn't been able to think of anyone else he could trust with even a little of his secret. Khyriz, perhaps, but Zhenu would think of Khyriz immediately. Lhore knew only that his friend was seeking temporary escape from Zhenu's wrath, and he'd willingly agreed to help Zhik change flyers. Better: He'd agreed that if questioned, he would swear the young noble was hiding somewhere on-station; if necessary, he'd show the questioners where the flitter was. Meantime, Zhik would be long gone, back to Akkherif.

It will go right; it must. The only sticky moment would be when he and An-Lieye emerged from the flitter. There was no way to keep her out of sight; he'd have to hope Lhore would think her a servant or a pet; that he'd dismiss her presence. There were plenty of Asha on-station, after all; most Arekkhi who lived up here didn't pay much attention to them.

A gentle touch against his cheek roused him from gloomy planning. An-Lieye, her face shadowed by the blue hood, gazed at him anxiously. "Apologies," he murmured. "I forget that you have never been off-planet before. You are safe with me." She gestured assent, then pressed her fingers against his shoulder, taking comfort from the contact. He freed a hand from the controls to lay over hers, and settled in to wait.

Three humid, still days passed. The station satellite system was up again, but malfunctioning at odd times; whatever the master of station had done to it had been thorough. The Emperor fell back on prestation tech and had flyovers conducted wherever there seemed a chance the kidnapped delegates might have been taken, but there was no sign of them. Or of Zhenu.

Fortunately, news was tightly monitored, and everything went through the sole government source. Nothing had leaked about the attack on the old palace or the kidnapping. Even Fahara, who had plenty of contacts on the island, knew nothing but the official explanation for the quarantine of the old palace the day after the ball: an underground leak of something noxious-smelling that had somehow gotten into the air system.

Khyriz worried about the designer's safety and tried to persuade her to take shelter in the new palace, but she refused. "If An-Lieye returns, I must be here." The Prince had Bhelan fly one of his most trusted guards down from the North to stay in her apartments.

There had been no word from Zhik or from An-Lieye; no sign of Zhenu, though it was assumed by the Emperor, his depleted Council, and Khyriz that the *zhez* was locked down in his central-Akkherif estates. Most of that palace was very old, built to withstand siege or open warfare.

There *had* been a message, just after Zhenu fled the island—an encoded message to the Prelate warning him to take no action but to hold ready. From the tone of the message, Zhenu at least still believed their joint force to be larger than the Emperor's.

It *was* larger—but the gap was rapidly closing, and Khezahn had an edge in tech. Zhenu was known to dislike computers, certain that anything stored in one could be broken into by another, laying bare his privacy. Other than the flitter he'd purchased for his son, most of his vehicles were several years old, and though his communications equipment was the most recent, it was Arekkhi tech.

The Emperor's com-banks were also mostly Arekkhi, but some innovation had come with the Heeyoons, and he now had the use of the off-world tech Khyriz had brought home with him, and that he'd added since.

By the fourth day, Khyriz was finding it difficult to eat or sleep. *At least Father is not keeping me out of sessions,* he thought as he drew on a plain blue zhona-silk robe for the day and hurried toward the Council chamber. He was the only Arekkhi with close knowledge of the outside, the CLS, and their representatives; the Council listened to him.

The Emperor was already seated in his usual chair; baskets of sweetened breadsticks and jugs of herbed water had been placed along the table, indicating Khezahn had ordered another long session. No one else had arrived yet. "Father, I have a request to make."

The Emperor's eyes were tired as his own; he gestured toward the nearest basket and said, "Eat. You do your friends no service by going hungry. What request?"

He took bread, forced himself to bite into it, chewed, and swallowed without tasting and said, "Even when we locate Alexis and Magdalena, it may not be safe for them to return here. Station will be no safer. I ask permission to call the new jump station—I know you wish to keep this secret until everything is resolved. But . . . if there is nowhere safe for them here, or if war should follow—"

"Unpleasant, but possible. The Prelate shows no sign of unbarring his entry, and now Khedan is missing from his rooms where I had him confined. No doubt he has taken sanctuary, and tells Nijho everything he knows. But the delegates would be safe in the new palace."

"Perhaps, Father. I thought the old palace—this whole island—safe until it was proven not to be. Also, they may—may not wish to stay here, or to see any Arekkhi ever again." He hoped that would not be the case; he couldn't be certain. Magdalena's exhausted face from that short transmission hung in his thoughts. "There is an outsider FTL ship at the new station, and a woman I know from StarBridge. She works on the computers and she also can pilot that ship. I want permission to call Dana Marshall and ask if she will bring the ship to a point near the station or one of the moons, where a shuttle could meet it and take my friends to safety. Nothing Zhenu has would be a match for the CLS ship."

Khezahn was alarmed. "But Khyriz, what if the Dana-she warns the CLS that their Interrelator has been taken?"

"She might. Father, they will know anyway, from Magdalena and Alexis. Or if the captors find a way to send a message out? That isn't impossible. But CLS will not act immediately. They are far enough away, it would take some time for them to reach us. And I know they would not attack us without hearing what we have to tell them. They would not attack if Alexis and Magdalena were still missing. I . . ." He gestured frustration. "I worry that . . . when we find them, there will be such danger that we *must* send them away at once! Father . . . I do not trust Zhenu."

"Wise of you, Khyriz." The Emperor closed his eyes and considered this, finally gestured assent. "Yes. To retrieve them safely, only to lose them again, or have them killed . . . that would be a terrible sorrow, and a dreadful message to send the CLS. But Khyriz, Zhenu may already have ordered them killed."

The Prince wanted to protest that, but he knew better than to underestimate the cold-blooded *zhez*. "I know it. But he planned this, and he is calculating. He may guess how the CLS would react, but he can't know. He may hope to bargain with you for their two lives, or perhaps he hopes to negotiate directly with the CLS. But Alexis is trained for such . . . situations. She knows what to say to keep them alive."

The Emperor considered this. "You know the interrelator better than I. And her training. But Zhenu plays his silence as a most effective weapon against us. He surely counts on continued uncertainty to weaken and divide the Council." He picked up a breadstick, wrinkled his nose, and tossed the breadstick back into the basket. "Make your call, Khyriz. Then return; the station satellite begins to operate again, and the

techs promise we will have new images before midday.''
Khyriz made a respectful gesture of temporary farewell and
hurried out, passing two of the newest members of his father's
Council.

Both were between his eldest brother's age and his father's:
young to be given such honor and responsibility. And one was
distant kin of the Empress, a male who had schooled with Zhenu
and had frequent business dealings with him. The choice made
no sense to Khyriz, until Khelyu had explained it: Wahhr
openly disliked the Iron Duke and his methods of extracting
profit from his estates. Also, Wahhr was fascinated by outsider
tech; he had hopes of petitioning the Emperor and the CLS for
the right to establish a training school in Ebba to teach use,
maintenance, and repair of new equipment.

The other, Yuchne, was common, once professed to the Prelatry, but dismissed after years of service on lowland Dagona
for performing blessings on all pets and beasts brought for a
five-year ceremony. One of them had been an ahla-Asha. The
priest had justified his actions by asserting that Asha and Arekkhi were separated from each other, yes; but only by the Arekkhi lack of tails and the Asha lack of spots. And Khyriz knew
(as most Arekkhi did not) that many Asha were born with
shadow spots, just as occasional Arekkhi were born with ves-
tigial—or even complete—tails.

Yuchne's family had protested the dismissal, and the Prelate
had only then threatened to add a charge that Yuchne had
violated law by seeking to prove a genetic match between
Arekkhi and Asha.

The grown Yuchne had inherited a modest fortune and used
it to hire chemists who sought antidotes to the damage caused
by the voice-killing drugs.

Once inside his old rooms, Khyriz checked the nail-patch
before he keyed on the household computer, then his Star-
Bridge portable. The protected com he'd used to betray Ulfar
would not reach as far as the half-completed jump station,
unfortunately; that meant delay-time, which meant he'd be
dealing with an irritated Dana; the always-busy tech loathed
the waste of her valuable time. The only other time he'd dared
call her from on-planet, merely to check on the scheduled ar-

rival time for the incoming ship carrying Magdalena and Alexis, she'd set his ears quivering with her pointed remarks.

It took time to get the call programmed in, to make sure he'd taken all possible safeguards against interception. The call was voice-only: Easier to set up, faster response times, and he was aware how haggard he appeared just now. No point in frightening the woman.

He could picture *her* very well as her voice came over the system, fifteen standard minutes after he'd sent the initial call. Her Mizari was quick and unaccented, but her speech in any language conveyed the same thing: too much to do, and not enough time to accomplish it all. Black hair fell to her shoulders, thick and wavy, surrounding a slender face and a warm, full-lipped smile. Dana had snapping dark eyes and capable, long-fingered hands equally at home on computer boards or that wheeled sitting-conveyance that served as her legs most of the time. "Khyriz? Long time, no hear! What's up?"

"Dana, bad things. A . . . an insurrection the night of the welcoming ball, rebels entered the old palace and captured Magdalena and Alexis. We have not found them, but have hopes. The . . . they may wish to leave Arekkhi for good, or it may be that they must, for safety reasons, and at once. My father permits me to ask if you could bring the FTL to a point where my shuttle could meet it so you could get them safely away. . . ." His voice trailed off; he keyed the transmission and prowled before the com-system while he waited.

Fifteen standard minutes later, Dana's crisp voice exploded into his apartment. "Damnit, Khyriz! This better not be a joke! You know how much work I've got out here and how screwed up this stupid computer system is? Half the hardware's been dropped, and the software doesn't even begin to mesh like it should and . . ." A deep sigh. "All right, I know you wouldn't pull a stunt like that. It'll take me—let's see—nine hours Arekkhi to check the ship and get to either a point off one of the moons or a point near the station—I'm assuming you don't want me to dock, right?—and it'll cost you. Remember that hover-chair you promised me, back on StarBridge? Well, I'm getting tired of replacing batteries in this mechanical wheeled thing, the gravity-adjusters aren't working, and I don't have time to mess with it! And the hand-push chair is as big a pain as walking, out here.'' Silence. But just as he was about to key in *send*, her anxious voice came on again. ''You really think there's a chance we'll get them back? I did all four years at StarBridge with Alexis and if you ever saw Magdalena dance . . . sure, I know you did. Saw the two of you hugging and swaying in place on the dance floor in the Spiral Arm a few times. Tell me where, I'll be there.'' He waited, no further transmission came through, and he finally keyed in *send*.

''Dana, I will personally arrange for a hover-chair. You should have accepted my offer a year ago, the *ekrhos* to pull you around.''

She laughed at that. ''Yeah, all I need, a hard-to-train over-sized beast with an attitude. I remember what you said about how much they eat! I can't afford that and I don't have the space. Pull strings with the CLS and get me a service-trained dog, would you believe they're still listed as pets? And Earth won't ship pets. Anyway, I'll leave the direct-mail system on, you tell me where and when, and the ship will be there.'' She cut off before he could even key *send* to offer thanks.

The call to Dana counted as a plus, but that was the only one for the entire day. The station transmissions gave no coordinates and showed only fuzzy images that could have been nearly any part of the vast highlands on either Akkherif or Mibhor. The images couldn't be shapened beyond a certain point; the initial vid had been of bad quality.

One brief vid was intriguing: The satellite had picked up a low-flying generic shuttle. The machine had vanished almost immediately, possibly beneath a stone-tiled roof. Of course, there were such shuttles everywhere: Most of the noble households owned one, and these days so did the wealthier merchant families and cooperatives. Still: it wasn't often one would be landed in open country. That would take skill.

One member of the Council peered at an enlarged, blurry still of one stubby wing barely visible under the flat stones. ''It resembles the old storage barns for steam-flyers,'' he said finally.

Wahhr keyed up the same image on his screen, enhanced a

corner of it with a voice command, then gestured agreement. "If the Emperor permits, there are lists in the main clerks' system of old buildings. It may be possible to create from them a shorter list of specific kinds of buildings."

"Go," the Emperor ordered mildly and gestured to his Heir. "Send a message to the chief clerk that the councillor's task holds priority."

But by midafternoon, the councillor was back, a noticeable droop to his ears. He'd created his list, but there was no data for any of Zhenu's holdings: It had recently all been deleted.

At full dark, the Council was still at work, now over mugs of chill yellow *khref*-wine, spiced meat, and bread; the talk had turned military. Khyriz had listened with minimal interest to his brother Khelyu's reports on numbers, placement of camps and supplies, and finally left with a promise to his father that he'd eat and sleep.

He intended to sleep—but not here. Zhenu must be holding Magdalena and Alexis on his highland Akkherif estates; his own estates weren't very far from the Duke's eastern borders. He couldn't wait here any longer. He had to *do* something.

Alexis looked around carefully before she sat up and stretched. They were alone in the chill little cave with its blocked-off entry. She got stiffly to her feet. The stone floor was hard and the pad under them inadequate; the over-cover thick, but grimy. Half a dozen flattened, grubby pillows completed their most recent "bedroom." She ached all over and couldn't remember the last time she'd been clean.

It was still better than their previous "cell." Once that shuttle had climbed out of the atmosphere, it had immediately returned to the planet—but when they'd emerged, it had been to a place completely unlike where they'd been. The ground was hard, dry, the only growth in sight some stunted, tough-looking bushes. Rocks, boulders, jutting stones—and constant wind. There'd been a drafty hut partway up a dry canyon, three filthy rooms, and a tiny lavatory. The room they'd been locked in wasn't much larger than the toilet. Their captors had only provided a blanket after Alexis began shouting through the door that they were going to die of exposure. She and Magdalena had spent the night sitting up, huddled together for warmth and what little comfort they could get from the physical contact.

She still hadn't seen any faces; only one of the rebels spoke to them directly, and no one said anything *around* their captives. It had frightened Magdalena, almost as much as that rough shuttle flight and the ghastly landing. Or the way they were permitted use of the toilet One at a time, while the other sat under the watchful eye of a stunner-wielding Arekkhi.

Alexis tried not to think what that weapon would do to a face at such close range. It was enough to keep them from trying to escape. *Barefoot, and who knows where on this planet?* she thought gloomily. If there had been a chance, it would have been in the old palace.

She hoped Magdalena believed her explanation about the masks. *If they try to stay unknown, it means there's a chance you'll be let free. It's when they don't care what you see or hear that you know they . . .* She couldn't complete the thought just now. Accidents happened. Whoever was directing them could have a change of plans. *No good thinking about it. You do what you can, Ortovsky.*

And things had improved—a little. After a night and most of a day in that dreadful room, they'd each been given a thick, loose robe—something a herder-she would wear. The fabric was scratchy but very warm, and it partly blocked the wind. They'd been fed a bowl of hot soup: red-brown broth and some kind of meat, hardly any taste but filling.

After that, blindfolded and bound, they'd been loaded into a flitter that smelled like one of its hydraulic units leaked. The move took hours (Alexis still had on the watch-patch she normally wore to bed), but the machine was slow and the ride felt erratic. She wasn't surprised that the countryside didn't look very different, once they could see again: more dirt and rocks—and a steep cliff, riddled with shallow caves. They'd been taken to one that had a wall built across the front of it; the faint light had shown an unimproved interior, except for a number of sleep-mats along the back, and an enormous upright pillar.

                              *   *   *

They'd been here . . . three days now, Alexis decided after a moment's thought. She was still afraid but mostly exhausted. They'd been left alone most of the time, though one of their captors brought food occasionally.

The door to the outside was kept closed; there seemed to be no lock. *Hardly necessary,* Alexis thought sourly, and fingered the synth-plas strap circling her throat. It was fastened to the pillar, which was going nowhere. Alexis didn't try to take the collar off: They'd been warned about tampering, and she'd gotten a nasty shock when it was put on.

Magdalena lay at her side, eyes closed; the interrelator could tell by her breathing that she was awake. For some reason, the collar upset her. She looked . . . ashamed, Alexis thought. *That bloody cult, something they did to her. Talk to her. If she gives up now . . .* "Magdalena? I—I need to talk."

The dark girl opened her eyes at the English words and sighed very faintly. "I'm sorry, Alexis. I'm not being any use to you, am I?"

Alexis touched her hand reassuringly. "Of course you are. You were the one who figured out how to let Khyriz know how the bad guys got in."

Magdalena didn't even smile, as she usually did at her companion's ancient American slang—culled from Rob's movies. "I could've thought of it sooner."

"Okay, he didn't get there in time to rescue us. I'd've liked that. But we'll get out of this, you'll see, schweetheart." The translator laughed at that, and Alexis grinned impudently. "Made you smile. Remember, these Imperial Storm Troopers have kept us alive so far."

"Mmmm. So far. Alexis, if the Iron Duke's really behind them, why is he bothering to keep us alive? And if he knew what Khyriz told me. . . ." She swallowed.

"You aren't still blaming yourself for yelling at Khyriz, are you, Magdalena? I'd have yelled, too. I can't believe they thought they could keep a secret like that! Anyway, you remember what I told those goons while they were Super Gluing us to the standing stone over there."

"I remember. But the CLS wouldn't—!"

"They wouldn't. But the Iron Duke doesn't know that. I'd like to see the expression on his face when one of those masked goons tells him that if the CLS even *thinks* we're dead, they'll bomb the Arekkhi back into the Stone Age." She shoved unwashed hair off her forehead. "A bunch of poor rebels might not care what happens to the planet, but a filthy rich noble sure would!" She pushed to her feet and stretched cautiously. "Come on, walk around a bit. Remember, if we get a chance to run for it, we've got to be *able* to run."

Zhik shoved the thick door-curtain into place and dropped the long, weighted bolster across the hem, to keep it in place. He hadn't been here in at least a year—not since the last time his father had . . . He forced the thought away; not important. Fortunately, the two-chamber building hadn't deteriorated much. Dusty, but that could be borne. It was out of sight from the air and almost the same color as the surrounding dirt. They should be safe here.

Zhenu might not even bother to search for him; he never had before.

Zhik tugged at his eartufts. He hadn't known where else to go. *Bringing An-Lieye was a mistake.* He knew that now. But he couldn't undo his action . . . and he didn't want to.

The small town of Lho was close by; most of the villagers were kin to his mother. They feared Zhenu, and had no loyalty to him. After dark the first night, he'd slipped down to the back street and found the house where his old nurse's family still lived, returning to the hut sometime later in an ancient ground-cart with food, cushions to fill the shallow sleep-pit, and several thick coverings.

There had been no information about An-Lieye's family. That had been too much to hope for, but there was a chance something could be learned from trusted sources in the nearby villages. It would take time because his contacts would personally seek out those sources; the village com-centers would be monitored.

Three slow days passed. An-Lieye taught him more of her sign, writing messages when necessary and mouthing the words for him. Finally, late the fourth night came the hoped-for faint scratching at the wall panel. An-Lieye scooped the hood over her head and retreated into the sleeping area, where she could watch and listen in safety. Zhik scratched a reply, and the near-grown son—third generation from his nurse—eased through the curtain, automatically repositioning the bolster with his foot. "Rewo my father sends greetings. He spoke personally with our kin in both villages where Asha have been living, and sent a trusted one to the village beyond, where the Fahara-she once lived. The elder in Fajh sends back word that the family of the Fahara-she has moved to a village nearer Ebba, so they could be near her.

"But the *zhez* would not permit the family Asha to go with them, and a moon-cycle ago, the *zhez* had them sent away."

"Sent?" Zhik managed to keep his ears steady. "You are certain of that?"

"Sent. The elder protested the loss of labor—hoping to keep the friends in their protection, you see?—but the guard sent by the *zhez* said they were needed elsewhere." Zhik tried another question or so, but there wasn't any more information, and the youth took his leave. The young noble stared at the door curtain, until he felt movement behind him.

"I had hoped," he said softly. "My father defeats me again, without even trying."

She touched his arm so he would face her and mouthed, *No. Not your fault. And there is good; you and I . . . we are together.*

He touched her nose with his fingerpads. "An-Lieye," he said suddenly, "I can do something after all. Something Khyriz could not. If your family was sent from Fajh, there will be records. He keeps a record of everything." He was suddenly very afraid, knowing what he would do. "I can get into my father's holding, early, with the clerks. I can locate those records—"

Her fingers gripped his arm, painfully. *No! You must not go into such danger!*

"It will be safe, even if he is there. He never goes to his clerks, but I will not attempt the open files. He keeps a locked room for duplicates of all records; no one goes there, except at a certain hour each day to add the new pages."

She didn't like it; her ears were nearly flat. He had to assure her, over and again; she would be safe here. Nothing would happen to him. "The holding is my home, no one will question why I am there."

You will leave me alone . . . I am afraid. Her eyes were dark with that fear—he'd vanish, and she would be alone and utterly helpless, so far from Ebba, from Fahara. "No, An-Lieye. I will always come back to you, I swear it. But to assure you: The youth who just came is a friend of Asha. *My* friend. I have trusted his family with my life before now. Tomorrow, before I go to the holding, I will tell him that he is to come here at full dark tomorrow. If I have not returned, you can trust him, and any he trusts. And there are many like him on my father's lands. They will see you safely returned to Fahara." Her ears remained down. "Nothing will happen, An-Lieye. Nothing will separate us." He touched her chin, then slid his hand behind her near whiskers and flicked them gently forward.

Her ears still quivered near her pale-furred skull, but she moved closer so she could lay her cheek on his.

CHAPTER 13

♦

The greatest difficulty had been getting plain clerks' robes so he could enter the holding unnoticed. He would have to avoid the chief clerks who might know him, or at least realize he wasn't an underling. But it was easy to avoid the masters, since most of them lived on the holding grounds in a converted part of the ancient guard-wall. If he arrived with earliest, uniformly clad clerks, the higher-ranked should still be asleep; if he was able to find what he needed quickly, he'd be able to slip away while the entire staff was having the long break during the hot hours. *With luck,* he reminded himself time and again. So much depended on his father's insistence on a tightly ordered household—but luck would still be a factor.

Still, Zhenu kept such a large staff and had such a high turnover rate that Zhik doubted anyone would recognize him. Certainly not the clerical workers.

But his plan depended on him looking like just another such worker. Rewo finally obtained a garment from a distant but trusted cousin, who also supplied his ident-code and agreed to stay away on the day in question. Zhik could only hope for all their sakes that no one ever found out.

How to get *to* the holding presented problems as well: Low-ranking clerks from the outlying villages commuted by ground-shuttle, and they all knew each other. They'd wonder about a stranger—or worse, talk about one. But no low-ranked clerk could afford private transport, and he certainly wouldn't have permission to bring it into the holding. And it would draw attention if he walked—the nearest village was simply too far away.

Zhik hadn't wanted to involve his benefactor any further, but he had no choice: He'd have to take Rewo's offer of a predawn ride aboard the elderly transport-cart that delivered fruit and grain. Rewo knew a place near one of the old walls that would be in deep shadow at sunrise, where Zhik could slip from the cart and approach the clerks' doors as if he'd come from the apartments.

His own part of the plan was makeshift, but the best he could devise. He considered it gloomily as he settled his back more comfortably against a grain-basket and wrapped the dark blanket carefully around his shoulders. It was vital that no guard or spy-device of his father's see a clerk mixed in with the produce, where he had no business.

The cart was slow and ancient, the motor spluttering as it rocked along the narrow track. His palms were damp with stress and fear, but his cheek fur still felt warm from An-Lieye's parting touch. His whiskers curved forward. *Such small, delicate hands. Innocent hands.* An innocent himself, he was still surprised how they had been able to come together again and again and give each other so much pleasure.

Rewo roused him with a low word and Zhik blinked; somehow he had lost all track of time. The ancient wall was just ahead, and the rising sun was casting first shadows. The villager stopped his vehicle and climbed out to study something in its clattering works; Zhik eased from between baskets and slipped quietly onto the road, across the old watercourse, emerging in the deserted stone courtyard.

Hundreds of years ago these grounds had been a garden, one of the wonders of all highland Akkherif. But the climate had changed, becoming steadily drier. His father saw no purpose in the expense of gardens, anyway.

The courtyard was dark and deserted when he slipped into the ancient holding by means of a small door between the pantries and the clerks' chambers. Rumor held that the door was once used by prisoners on their way to the pens below-ground. *I hope that is no omen,* he thought, and paused near a long drape, one he could quickly slide behind if anyone came. Unlikely, even this far from his father's suite; the *zhez* despised noise, particularly in the morning, and his hearing was said to be acute. Most of the enormous staff avoided the halls entirely, and spoke in hushed voices behind shuttered doors until nearly midday. That was when Zhenu was in residence, and more often than not the past years, he was. *And if he is still in the new palace, Zhikna?* But he'd trust no "if" or "maybe" that might make him feel safe. This was no place to relax his vigilance.

Once his breathing slowed to normal, he blotted his palms on the white robe and moved quickly toward the nearest ramp that would take him down to the first underground level. The locked records-storage was down there. *I hope it still is. He said often the records would be safer a level lower.* He could only trust in Zhenu's unwillingness to alter anything that worked; he didn't have time for a prolonged search.

But probably nothing had changed. There were still no computers in the holding, and only the most basic of communications devices—including those used for spying. Zhik would have heard about upgraded tech, if only because his father would have carped bitterly about the expense; he'd have heard about moved storage because of the time and trouble incurred.

He'd forgotten how drafty the lower floors were, and the smell of damp in the narrow ramps descending to the cellars nearly made him ill. He finally had to stop, close his eyes, and wait for the dreadful taste in his mouth to ease. *Because your father ordered you locked in the pens down here for—for some youthful prank. For how long?* But he could not remember how many days, or the cause. *He robbed me of so much of my kithood, I remember so little of it!* Except the bad, now and again. Like now.

He forced himself to go on as soon as he was barely able: He knew he could hear anyone stepping onto the ramp at either end—but if his luck failed while he dithered here, and someone did at each end of the ramp? What excuse for a clerk belowground at this hour?

He hurried, fearful of that very thing, but stopped short of the ramp's end, listening intently. No sound. He finally dared to ease from the ramp to a nearby alcove that had once held a guard's bench. No movement anywhere, though he could hear two male voices arguing about something, down by the pens. They didn't seem to be moving; good. His goal was in the other direction.

As he'd hoped, the storage hadn't been shifted, and the door was closed but not sealed for the night; someone still came down at first light to ready it for the day. He could have worked the seal, given time—living here and being so often locked in some chamber or another, he had learned early how to manipulate the old seals. Better not to spend the time. Though probably the clerks still followed standard procedure; they would not come here with revision-copies until the end of the first work-session. That should be near midday, just before a light snack and the rest-hours. Zhik planned to be gone by then. *I hope I will be. An-Lieye* . . . she would worry until he returned. And at midday or just before, it wouldn't be unusual for a clerk-clad male to be sent on an errand, away from the holding.

His whiskers quirked briefly. *Who would believe that I would ever thank my father for his harsh insistence on rules?* Once, he'd loathed the very word "rules." Thanks to unvarying routine, he just might succeed.

The records-room was a relief after the lower hallway: The air was unscented, clean, cool, and dry. That was for the protection of the hundreds of years of records, but more important to Zhik's thinking, it was a relief after the old horror-laden scents of the ramp and the lower level.

Wood-bound, cloth-covered logs and registries with hand-written entries were everywhere, stacked ten high on deep shelves. No seats or benches, of course; no one actually worked here. But there was an unfilled corner behind a tall crate of rolled documents that must be more than five hundred years old. He eyed them briefly, astounded at the weight of years flung casually into a box, then turned away to locate the most recent registry-lists for the *zhez*'s Asha. It was near the door, between the registries for hall servants and those for individual villages. Everything logically placed and well marked. *My thanks, Father*, he thought dryly, and settled back in his hidden corner with the latest volume.

Of course, An-Lieye's family would not be listed by names; they were accounted by numbers and physical description. It took time, even with the list of numbers An-Lieye had written out, so he could memorize them. Even with the *zhez*'s efficient system. A good many Asha had been transferred from the noble's Akherrif lands recently—some about the time of the first contact with the Heeyoons. But since just before the arrival of the CLS team, transfers had increased dramatically. As had deaths—listed as by accident or disease.

The son's ears went flat as he read down one such list. "Jhrror fever? There has been no outbreak of that fever anywhere in all Arekkhi space in three hundred years or more! And . . . and a flitter accident that kills twenty Asha?" What Asha on *these* lands rode in flitters? His father was killing them! Destroying them, Zhenu would say. Zhik scanned the death lists and only drew a deep breath when he found none of An-Lieye's kin in them. Though he noted with a sinking feeling that no records had been added to this list in a nineday.

But so many deaths! He felt sick: the cold-bloodedness of it all. This exact accounting, balancing numbers, ticking off victims as if they were fish in a hunter's nets . . . *He murders Asha, for fear the outsiders will see them and—and learn what I know.* If Zhenu even suspected Zhik had the least hint of any of this, he would kill . . .

No. He would not soil his hands with such a low task. He would have Ulfar kill me. The hair on his arms and nape stood up; it was several moments before he could breathe properly, and refocus his gaze on the ledger. He must learn what he could and go, quickly; get word to Khyriz; directly to the Emperor, if possible.

But if the Emperor himself was involved in this killing, or if he knew and did not care? He couldn't let himself think those things, though.

Finally, under Egress, he found the transaction he sought: The family had been part of a shipment of about seventy Asha that went to Mibhor:

- 7A4, 5, 6, and 8: males, physical labor, strong but unskilled.

- 7A10: aging female, good vision and weaving talent.
- 7A13, 14, 16: young females, dexterity but no talent.
- Transfer completed to *zhona*-silk factory 2, pens 7, 8, and 9.
- 7A9: elderly male, destroyed: weak, past producing off-spring.

Zhik's ears and whiskers went flat. They'd . . . his father had ordered An-Lieye's father killed! Because he would not have the physical strength to harvest *zhona,* and because he was too old for mating. Her mother, the five sibs were all listed . . . all alive at the time they left the estates, at least. *But her father! How can I tell her this?* he thought bleakly.

Another entry in the same neat hand—a separate piece of note-flimsy attached to the back of the previous page—caught his eye:

- 7A15: young female purchased by designer-she Fahara now living in Ebba. 7A15 female has been left in place because of the visits of the two alien-she, who obtain ball-clothing, lest they become suspicious; 7A15 and the designer have orders to continue to educate the two alien-she, who so far appear to accept Asha as pets and work-beasts. However, 7A15 will be reclaimed as soon after Emperor's ball as practical to be reunited with other 7A on Mibhor, see below note regarding designer-she.
- For known crimes regarding treatment of Asha, the designer-she Fahara is condemned in absence: for failure to properly clothe the Asha; for failure to teach the Asha its place and give it the proper religious readings concerning its racial sins against the Holy Dyad, and the Arekkhi; for failure to house the Asha in a proper pen. Designer-she to be removed from Ebba and returned with family to village of origin, any land-holding or village-holding belonging to this family condemned back to the *zhez,* the twelve beings thereafter to be put to *iyfer*-harvest.

His hands trembled so, he nearly dropped the register. Beloved gods, he'd done the right thing, after all! *Iyfer*-harvest! Those few who followed the wild herds willingly, to harvest the rare and avidly sought hairs from spine-bushes were paid well—but even the skilled seldom lived long. The high plateau was a dangerous place, and the fanged beasts killed noble Arekkhi hunters as often as the hunters killed them. Those condemned to gather the hair seldom survived an entire season, though little was found to prove a death: a bone here, a little blood there. The *iyfer* ate their kill.

But the ball was past! Four days ago! Had Fahara already been taken? He must find a way to warn Khyriz, who could get her to safety. She and her family.

There was vindictiveness in these temporary messages that could weaken him, if he let it. *I will not. Zhenu will not win, not this time.* Zhik forced his whiskers away from his face and turned his attention back to the ledger page. He memorized the numbers of the holding pens, made himself take the necessary extra time to read the final entries to be certain no further action had been taken against Fahara and hers, or the clan "A7." Against helpless beings whose only real crime was being unable to voice the wrongs done to them.

He swallowed sudden, deep anger. *I will be their voice. To the Emperor, to the CLS women, to the CLS itself, if I must. On the Holy Two . . . on my beloved An-Lieye, I swear it.*

The vow calmed his mind.

He closed the volume and returned it to its shelf, squaring the corners so it was exactly as he'd found it, then slid quietly from the chamber and reached the alcove again, pausing so he could decide how best to leave the holding. And, though he loathed admitting it, he needed a moment to still his trembling hands and legs. Mibhor—of all the places her people could have been sent, the Mibhor factory had tightest security. His father bragged of that so often. *Aware that I knew nothing of the need for such security,* he realized. *He will not win, not this time.*

He would need help; such a rescue was more than he and An-Lieye could manage. *Khyriz,* he decided as he pressed damp palms against his robe. *I must reach Khyriz about Fahara anyway, as soon as I can. He helped me rescue Ah-Naul; I know he has a kindly heart and that he cares for Asha. How deep such feelings might reach, I didn't realize until An-Lieye. If I can tell him where An-Lieye's family is, perhaps he can aid me in that also. And perhaps he could even get the Emperor to intervene....*

But no. That would be dangerous. Spread a secret among two and it is no secret; among more and it is gossip. Everyone knew that. And what if the Emperor already knew about Zhenu's Asha, or even had his own copy of the ledger? What if the Emperor approved?

Besides, a secret message to anyone from these lands couldn't be guaranteed to remain secret, any more than one received on the royal island. If Zhenu suspected anyone was interested in any of his Asha, let alone the 7A family, *An-Lieye's people!*—he'd have every last one of them killed.

He didn't dare risk that. But Khyriz might have a suggestion on how to proceed. He could trust Khyriz.

The young noble was very tired, suddenly. *I am not fit for this kind of intrigue; I am weak and fearful. The small dots, where the whiskers attach to my face, ache from so much uncertainty. And I put my beloved An-Lieye in danger.* He would return to her at once, give her the good part of his news, then wait with her until dark.

Then she would have to wait again, while he went alone to Khyriz's estates; now that he knew Zhenu's plans, he couldn't chance anyone seeing Fahara's Asha, with her distinctive non-Asha garb. He knew the *zhez* kept spy-devices trained on the Prince's manor and the grounds around it; if Zhenu saw An-Lieye in his company, her family . . . But who would think it strange if Zhik went alone to visit his cousin's estates? He so often did.

His cousin might not be in residence, but the master of household knew Zhik; he could arrange a safe call, on Khyriz's alien-tech-protected com, to the old palace, or wherever the Prince might be at the moment.

He thought through it one more time—it was as good a plan as he could make at the moment. Now, to get back up the ramp, outside, and safely away. But before he could move, he heard the voices he'd heard earlier—coming rapidly this way. Thick soles scraped on the uneven stone floor. Zhik shrank against the back wall of the alcove, mentally cursing the pale clerk's robe that might give him away.

To his relief, the two males stopped short of the other side of the ramp; he immediately recognized the authoritative voice of Hyorr, his father's second-in-command. Curious. Normally, Ulfar would be the one to give orders; his father really must be away from the holding, then, because the bodyguard was always at his side. That was good; he almost relaxed. But the hair on his forearms stood on end as he realized what Hyorr was saying.

"Remember, when you make the vid to prove the two alien-she are alive, remove the synth-plas restraints and place them against the inner side of the blank wall blocking the cavern; the space where it is merely a dark surface, so that no one seeing the vid will be able to guess where they are kept, even if they enhance the picture. And warn the alien females! This time there will be no trick, as at the old palace, when the dark-furred one spoke to Prince Khyriz and suddenly used outsider words. Warn the females that any gesture, any movement of eyes or head, *any single word in alien speech!*—by either one of them!—will cause the immediate and painful death of the other! Have you a talon?"

"Guardmaster, no," the other replied. Zhik didn't recognize his voice at all.

"Obtain one before you return. Let them see what death awaits them if they try to be clever. Both females saw the dead servants, killed by talon; they will surely not wish to cause such suffering. Now! Be certain you take the most roundabout way in returning to the refuge! The *zhez* orders that you remember this. He will be very angry if any of the young fools in your 'Protective League' should learn who funds them and orders their actions."

"Guardmaster, I will use greatest care, as I always do." The unknown sounded arrogant, despite his humble words. "Still, they are young and easily duped; look how they were persuaded to take the old palace, the night of the ball—"

"The young have curiosity and good eyes," Hyorr interrupted harshly. "Be certain! Or face the *zhez*'s displeasure! Also continue to keep your—your dupes, are they? Keep them away from the alien females. The *zhez* says the females are persuasive, that even his son has become fond of the alienshes. Though to my thinking, anyone might persuade his weak offspring to nearly any course of action.''

''Guardmaster.'' Zhik heard footsteps moving up the ramp, and moments later, other heavy steps going back toward the pens. It was some moments before he could gather enough courage to look out, and his fur still stood on end.

It was almost too much to take in. *What has happened out there since I gathered in An-Lieye and fled?* Could someone— this League—really have captured Alexis and Magdalena? A League that seemed to think itself one of the new rebel groups, or so it sounded. But funded and directed by his father. . . .

My father has taken the CLS women? He will murder them, once he persuades the Emperor to do what he has these young fools ask in order to make the exchange!

He had to do something—but he couldn't think! Follow that guard-captain? No. Foolish. He couldn't be certain who the guard was, and the fellow had been warned to watch for followers. And he would be armed with a talon. If Zhik weren't killed on the spot, he'd be brought back here to face his father's fury, or taken where the women were being held and all three killed. . . . *Get out of the holding, now, before you lose your courage entirely,* he ordered himself.

It took time for him to reach the outside unobserved. Muttering apologies under his breath to Rewo—the elder he had planned to retrieve Zhik at full dark—the young noble pulled the deep clerk's hood over his head and went straight to vehicle storage. As he'd hoped, there were several of the plain, old, closed flyers his father kept, and neither the entry nor the combust-codes had been changed since he'd lived on the estates. As long as he didn't attempt to cross the borders of his father's vast holdings, he'd be safe. Flyers like this were everywhere on Zhenu's lands, used by clerks, servants, and guards alike. Recordkeeping here was inadequate and seldom up to date. It would be nearly impossible to keep track of all the flyers, anyway: There were so many of them, and the need changed daily. Hourly, even.

The old-style flyers weren't as useful as his own flitter would have been, but he didn't plan on needing anything but quick transportation away from the holding, somewhere near the hut. He entered the nearest vehicle, then hesitated: He could hide it. *No. You take this as a clerk, and you operate it as one would, leaving it in Rewo's village on the blocks outside the officials' hut.* It wasn't that odd for a flyer to be left, so: if two of the Duke's came separately to one place and went on together to another.

He *had* the shuttle, near the hut, if there was need for speed or another off-planet trip.

The single track into Rewo's village would be deserted at this hour: Field Arekkhi would be dozing under portable shelters out among the crops and herd-beasts until the heat of day faded. Those few who remained in the village would be inside their houses or apartments, shutters and doors tightly fastened.

He'd be seen as one of the *zhez*'s many clerks, piloting a flyer according to Zhenu's order. The flyer would settle onto the blocks provided, and a clerk-clad Arekkhi would enter the town center. That might raise a few pulses in anxiety but generally would cause no open reaction. Once inside he'd remove the highly visible white clerk's robe that he'd fortunately worn over the thin brown one he kept in the hut as a disguise, and leave a message with Rewo's she, if he had not yet returned. Someone would come to retrieve the clerk's robe well after dark.

And then—but he couldn't plan any farther than that. . . .

An-Lieye was as anxious as he'd feared, though he'd barely been gone half the day. "It is fine. I am all right, safe. And you are safe. Here, sit, let me touch you." She leaned against him as he laid a soft hand on her cheek and rubbed the backs of her hands in turn. "I found where your family is, An-Lieye. They are alive, but we will need help to rescue them." She looked up at him, eyes wide. "They were moved to Mibhor, the *zhona*-silk factory." Her ears quivered with distress again. "No, it is all right, they have only been there a short while, two nine-days. But to get into the factory pens—I will have to think hard how to do this safely."

She gently touched his face with her open palm to get his attention. *Prince Khyriz will help us,* she mouthed and signed.

The Prince searched for my mother, my family. But, he could not find them.

Zhik stared at her blankly. "Khyriz? You never said that before!"

She hesitated, then went on, so rapidly he had to get her to repeat. *It was not my secret. I swore not to ever tell, for his safety, that no one would know what he did. But now . . . Prince Khyriz has searchers, he goes himself. They find Asha, and move them to safety. For two years at least they have done this, all across Arekkhi. He has tried to find my family, but at the time Fahara brought me to Ebba, they were moved to a village where it was dangerous for him to send his rescuers. After that, they were moved again, and he could not find them then.*

"I didn't know," he murmured. "Khyriz? I had no suspicion!" He emitted a weak spat of laughter. "My pleasure-loving, nonpolitical cousin! Apologies, An-Lieye," he added hastily, and touched her face again. "That was not disrespect. Yes, Khyriz can help us. He helped—no, not important." He couldn't possibly mention Ah-Naul to her.

She brushed his hand to get his attention once more and signed, *Eat. Drink.* He gestured a negative; the very thought of food nauseated him. *Yes! Eat. Drink.* And she would not leave him alone until he swallowed bread, washed it down with lukewarm tea. She was right: food took some of the haze from his mind.

"There is something else I learned," he said finally, and told her what he'd overheard about Magdalena and Alexis. "I must talk with Khyriz as soon as possible, and I must go alone, tonight." She gestured an urgent *no!* at that. He tried to be firm. "An-Lieye, I must! It is dangerous out there for you. If you are seen—"

I am safe only with you! she replied, and now her eyes were angry. *I go with you. Prince Khyriz will help.* He would have protested, but she turned away from him and began to move around the room, touching things with nervous hands, clasping and unclasping her fingers on her wrists. Suddenly she turned back to face him and signed, *Tell me again, the women. What the guard said. Cavern?* He couldn't understand her swift change of thought at first; then couldn't follow the gestures for what she was trying to ask. She had to mouth it slowly and in exaggerated fashion, twice, before he understood.

"Apologies, An-Lieye. He said a cavern—but there are so many caverns in this part of Akkherif!"

Not just cavern. You said, a wall—where a wall?

He had to close his eyes, rethink the moment. "He said there is a wall blocking the outside—"

Her eartufts quivered. *Yes. Cavern. Enclosed cavern. I know it.* There was more, and it took even longer for him to understand.

"A place built by villagers, years ago, where Asha could escape and then hide, until havens were found for them." He stared beyond her. Zhenu's guard must have discovered it at some point. The Asha who might have been there; any who were helping them. . . . He couldn't think about it.

It would do the women no good, anyway. Alexis and Magdalena were his task. An-Lieye's family and Fahara. *And you are Zhik, the Iron Duke's weak offspring.* Even Hyorr dismissed him with contempt. No matter; he couldn't let that slow him, either.

Perhaps it would even aid him. Everyone knew Khyriz was a pleasure-loving, indolent young royal, fond of dance, the outsider women—particularly the translator—and fine clothing. He distanced himself from serious arguments, avoided politics, spent most of his time in his manor house by the sea, employing artisans to enrich the interior, gardeners to beautify the outside. *No one would suspect Khyriz, if Asha were missing. I only went to him for Ah-Naul because I knew he has a kind heart. No one will suspect Zhenu's weak son of—of what I will do now.*

Should he attempt to enlist Khyriz for this? No. His cousin's estates were hours away, and there was no way to know if he'd be there. Zhik knew better than to use any communicator on his father's lands to reach Khyriz; they were always monitored, and someone would know at once who called and from where. Besides, delay might prove fatal for the women. "An-Lieye, will you tell me where this cavern is?"

She gestured a firm negative. *No. But I will show you.*

He argued with her, but she countered all his fears and his logic with the same response. *I show you. I go with you. I am safe only with you.*

The sun was lower in the sky; he finally had to give up. "You stay with me, An-Lieye. We'll find a way to rescue the CLS women, and then I'll take us all immediately to Khyriz's manor. We can be safe there. Even my father wouldn't dare attack Khyriz. We can make sure Fahara is safe." He'd tried to use the threat to Fahara as an argument earlier. An-Lieye saw it as an even stronger reason to stay with him. It was only with difficulty that he made her promise to wait in the old storage, near the shuttle, where he donned the clerk's white once more so he could retrieve the flyer. A shuttle abroad on Zhenu's lands might attract attention, and the ground-cart would be useless.

As he tugged the hood over his ears, though, An-Lieye's fingers clutched his arm. *Swear,* she mouthed urgently.

He couldn't blame her for the fear that he'd simply choose to keep going, once he reached the flyer; he knew it came from who and what she was. *Still, that she continues to doubt me . . .* It was frustrating; he knew it wasn't her fault. "I swear it, An-Lieye. By my love, I swear." The set of her ears was no less anxious, but she let go of him and stepped back in deep shadow beyond the shuttle to wait. He checked the track leading to the village, and the land on both sides of it. What he could see of the fields beyond the village. No one in sight, except a few distant Arekkhi harvesting grain. Someone might see him coming from this direction and wonder—but no villager would speak to what they saw as a clerk, and no villager would speak of him to anyone outside their own, lest word reach Zhenu and the village be blamed for something.

He could hear the high, vibrant cries of young somewhere nearby but saw no one; the flyer rose smoothly from its blocks. He took it a short distance along the track to the next village, but as soon as the last hut was out of sight behind a ledge, he brought it as high as it would go above ground and turned it toward An-Lieye. He had to show himself before she would come out, just as he'd asked. Even the thought of her stepping

from hiding to find the flyer was one carrying Zhenu's guards
had nearly cost him his bread earlier.

It took time, which made him nervous. He tried to hide his
fears, knowing they upset her. But at first she couldn't tell
where they were. In the end, he had to pilot the flyer most of
the distance to her old village, silently reminding himself that
they would have had to go that far anyway. And from there,
things went quickly. The afternoon was still overly warm—an
hour most Arekkhi would still be at rest, and only those who
worked the land or tended herds would be about once more.
Zhik eased the flyer into the partial shelter of a wide ravine,
settling it as much in shade as possible. Back where the ravine
was too narrow for the flitter to go, An-Lieye seemed to think
there was a way up. He glanced her way as he shut down the
machine. She was bent over the small erasable writepad Fahara
had given her, drawing a rough map, mostly marks and written
description: cave, path, shelter.

He wasn't good with maps, he knew. But he studied this
one with care, then released the back hatch. An-Lieye brushed
down her robes, tucked the pad back in her pocket, and followed him.

She is not as fragile as you see her, he reminded himself.
An-Lieye had come from these lands. It was useless to argue
with her again, anyway. He waited for her outside the flyer
and lifted her down, brushed her hand through his near whiskers, and sealed the hatch.

For one who had only been here as a very young she, his
Asha had not forgotten much: The ravine was steeper than he
liked, and her blue was smudged with dirt when they reached
the top. She touched his arm, indicated *down,* and wrapped
the thin fabric around one hand so she could crouch low and
work her way across the open. The footing here was all rough
stone, pitted with deep holes. Zhik kept a wary eye around
them, but they reached the far side of the plateau without incident. An-Lieye eased herself cautiously into a shallow depression near the edge and, once he was next to her, signed
for him to look down.

The drop was even higher on this side. He could hear water
running somewhere down there, and the land that sloped gen-

tly up and away from the ledge was blue-green, dotted with brush and trees. Perhaps a hundred long paces farther, more red stone loomed, pitted with caves. An-Lieye touched his hand to get his attention and pointed down. A narrow track had been cut into the stone here; hard to see in the gloom, but his foot found a smoothed step just below their perch. She tugged at his sleeve, gestured far down the line of caves, and mouthed, *There is the wall.*

He had to stare for some time before he could see it; it was well back within the opening, far enough that only the contrast between rough stone and flat unnatural surface—and their angle here—let him pick it out. Movement caught his eye then, and he eased lower, pulling her down with him. A black-clad Arekkhi moved lazily into the open, looked down the line of caves and across the open, stretching and yawning, then went back out of sight. Guard, Zhik assumed. If he had a hand-weapon, it wasn't in sight.

Weapon, he thought suddenly. *I did not even think to find a weapon.* But his plan called for stealth; find the women and bring them out unnoticed. One young noble with very poor aim would stand no chance against trained guards anyway. He turned to An-Lieye, who was watching him anxiously. He edged down so he could whisper against her ear. "You must wait here—no, hear me, please!" he added as she signed a sharp negative. "Your robe would be seen at once. And when I free the women, I will put them before me. They will need you, here, to guide them toward the ship."

She considered this unhappily, fingered the pale blue cloth, and finally nodded, human-fashion. He hesitated but could think of nothing else to add, and each moment he delayed made it harder to move. He laid a palm against her soft-furred face, then turned away and started down the narrow steps, counting as he went. Thirty steps, a short incline, and the path ended behind a massive boulder, right at the edge of a shallow stream.

Remember what she told you, the best way to remain unseen, he ordered himself and hugged the shadows, moving slowly and cautiously along the base of the cliff, stopping now and again to watch for guards. He worked past the walled opening, far enough that he could make out four guards relaxing just inside the opening of a shallow cave two caves past the walled one. Another few cautious paces, and their voices reached him clearly, amplified by the stone around them. He stood motionless then, and listened.

Better than he could ever have hoped. The four were alone here, under orders to avoid the women; the talon-armed captain had taken the remaining three somewhere for supplies, and to give the vid of the women to someone who would pass it on to others. Two of them still appeared to be half asleep. Even the one he'd seen at first was more interested in the drink they'd been promised than in his watch. Zhik waited until all four had turned to look at something in the back of the cave before edging back the way he'd come, and he didn't step into the open until the opening of the guards' cave was out of sight.

The stream was shallow, the water unexpectedly cool. It soaked through his soft slippers. He forced himself to move quickly now, staying as much as possible in the shade of trees or behind bushes, but taking as direct a line to the walled cave as he could. He was certain he didn't breathe once, crossing the open rubble of red stone. Not until he'd hastened into cave shadow and fetched up against that wall.

A deep breath. A second. He eased along the wall to the point he'd seen from above, cautiously raised a hand so An-Lieye could tell he'd made it this far, then edged back toward the narrow door.

CHAPTER 14

To his surprise, the door's seal hung loose. The reason was simple, as he saw when he eased through a narrow opening and tugged it to behind him. Alexis and Magdalena sat on a filthy mat, staring at him. Both wore restraint collars, and leads of the same material fastened them to an immovable stone pillar.

"Zhik! What? How did you—?" Magdalena began in a hoarse whisper. Alexis hissed a warning at her and drew herself up straight.

"If you're a member of that gods-blasted Protective League, Zhikna, you can leave right now!" she said flatly. The words caught him by surprise; it had not occurred to him that they might suspect Zhenu, that they might think he served his father. . . .

There was no time for this. "Alexis, no, I swear it! I only learned of this . . . this outrage hours ago. To come alone— yes, perhaps foolish, but to reach help was impossible. So I came. There is a flyer—" He reached for her collar. Alexis leaned away from him, her eyes wary.

"Even if we *can* trust you, you better leave this thing alone. Because that guard warned me, when he put it on—"

"I know about the collars," Zhik broke in urgently. "My father . . . I . . . No time. Trust me. I can deactivate it. Trust, please, Alexis." The two looked at each other, Alexis openly doubting.

Magdalena murmured, "Trust him, Alex. I intend to."
Alexis sighed, but got to her feet.

"All right—do what you can, anything is better than staying
here." She glanced at Magdalena as the young noble eased
two fingers between the synth-plas and her throat and forced
a smile. "But just in case he kills me, don't let him touch
yours, okay, Perez?"

The noble gestured a sharp negative. "They told you this
strip would *kill*? A lie! These make a painful shock, but nothing more. A kill-collar is much thicker. . . ." Zhik's voice
faded as he began fiddling with the white strip. Moments later,
Alexis swore between clenched teeth, but the collar clattered
to the stone floor, and Zhik was already at Magdalena's side,
working on hers. The translator closed her eyes and bit down
on her lip.

"It's not that bad, Perez, just caught me by surprise."
Alexis hurried over to the door and pressed her ear against it.
A moment later, the translator joined her. Zhik scooped up the
mess of bedding and piled the smelly covers in a heap behind
the pillar, then dragged the collars over and dropped them on
the mat, out of sight. Alexis glanced at the result and nodded.
"That won't fool anyone for long, but it should assure any of
the regular guards if they just look in, like they do sometimes.
What next?"

He explained as briefly as he could. "The guards were that
way"—he gestured—"from here when I came, sixty paces at
least, and if they are in the other cavern, they cannot see this
one. There are only four guards. The rest went away in the
flyer. When we go outside, we check for guards and then you
run to the place I point out." He managed a quivering curve
of whiskers. "I will run as quickly as possible and then explain
the rest."

"Tell us *now*," Alexis said calmly, though to his eyes she
appeared nervous—that line between the brows was very deep.
"Something might go wrong."

His ears flicked. "Yes. Apologies, Alexis. There is a hidden
path to the top of the ledge. It cannot be seen from here, but
I can point near enough. There is a passage, and then steps."
He hesitated, then added, "An-Lieye waits at the top. She

can . . . she is . . .'' His voice faded; impossible to communicate *that* situation briefly. The women were staring; he had no
idea what they might be thinking. ''Unimportant. I will explain
once we are safe. We must go.'' He moved around them, listening as Alexis had, then eased the door open a whisker's
worth. No one, no sound. He hoped those young males were
deep in discussion about the fermented drink they'd been
promised. They were supposed to avoid the prisoners, anyway.

Young fools, he thought grimly. *To kill servants and steal
these women—if they truly believe they are guardians of the
Asha, what good have they accomplished for anyone by this
stupidity?* He pushed the portal wider, eased his way out and
along the wall, head moving cautiously as his eyes searched
the lower ground and then the ledge. Still quiet. He signalled
to let An-Lieye know he was safe for the moment. Beckoning
the women close, Zhik pointed: first down-slope to their initial
halt, then to a boulder not far from the one protecting the path.
That one couldn't be seen from here, he reminded them in a
breathy whisper. ''Go now!'' He waited, watching and listening nervously while they walked quickly through the loose
stone and onto springy turf. Alexis shoved Magdalena in front
of her, and they broke into a run. Zhik glanced toward the
guard-cave and listened intently. Silence, still. A quick look
back; the door stood closed as it had when he'd arrived.

He forced himself across the rubble of broken rock and hurried into the shade of a low tree.

The women were well down the slope; he could see Alexis's
pale hair bouncing wildly. A warning shout suddenly echoed
behind him: Someone had seen them! Zhik stopped long
enough to tear off the slippers; they were wet, the bottoms
slick, and he didn't dare fall now. Well behind him, he heard
more shouts, and the high-pitched whine of a weapon cutting
through the growth behind him. Somewhere, near enough to
make him wince, a branch tore loose and fell with a crash.
Nothing came near him, and he made the stream unharmed.

He splashed through the water, reached the ledge panting
and trembling, and gestured for the women to lead the way.
Magdalena moved as fast as she dared: It was much darker
here, and the footing was rough. Neither had shoes, he real-

ized. Bare human feet looked even more fragile than his.

He'd dropped the slippers. What if anyone found them? But no one except Zhenu would know them, and those slippers would have to reach his father first. Zhik planned on being safely off Zhenu's lands long before that.

The guards were still searching the slope, but it wouldn't be long before they came this way, and he wasn't surprised to hear one of them shout, "Fheru, guard the way across the stream! If the she-aliens reach those rocks, we may never find them!"

"Smart, aren't they?" Alexis said, panting, baring her teeth in a human smile. It briefly warmed him; the interrelator only used that gesture around those comfortable with human ways. "Yelling in Arekkhi, and telling us poor, stupid aliens where to go hide!" She got no answer; Magdalena seemed to be using all her energy to keep going, and Zhik was nearly beyond speech.

Another blast from the weapon; this slammed into the stones above them and fortunately some distance behind. A few pebbles clattered down. Zhik chanced a quick look and swore: Not enough stone had come loose to block the path. But now, one of the guards stormed through heavy brush, cutting across the slope. He saw them; stopped to aim his weapon.

"Go!" Zhik said with a gasp as he saw the weapon. "That stone—get behind it!" Magdalena vanished into deeper shadow, Alexis right behind her. The young noble made as much speed as he could, though he was long paces behind them. The high-pitched wail of a force-beam lent energy to exhausted muscles.

Zhik heard a high-pitched human shriek of warning and saw Alexis just within the shelter, beckoning urgently. The force-beam howled a second time, but that sound was buried by the ragged crack of the huge ledge being torn apart far overhead. He threw his arms over his ears and kept going.

Stones of all sizes cracked bruisingly against him, and shards cut his hands; a massive chunk slammed into his back, sending him staggering. And then he was under the over-hanging rock. Momentarily safe—but only for the moment. "Go!" he said with a hiss at Alexis, and urgently gestured up.

"I mean to. I wasn't going to leave you, though." She turned and started up the passage, limping awkwardly but still making good speed. "Magdalena's gone ahead; I turned my foot on soft sand." She swore in her alien speech as the foot came down awkwardly on rock. "It's okay, just sore," she added, and started up the narrow passage ahead of him, taking most of her weight on both hands and one foot.

Steps. Zhik's legs were trembling so, he wasn't certain he could make the ascent, despite the low angle of the individual steps. *Count them by fives and when you finish a count of five, you then pause, breathe, and begin another,* he ordered himself, and started up.

The guards' voices were muted, but he could hear the wail of another force-bolt tearing the ledge behind them apart. Rock splintered behind them, and the faint breeze that had cooled his back was suddenly cut off. Alexis glanced back, then started climbing again. "Stupid fools! They won't be able to come after us now that they've bombed the only escape route! Unless—Zhik, is that the only way up?"

"Unknown," he said with a gasp. "Hurry!" Alexis glanced down at him, nodded once, and picked up the pace. The passage slowly grew lighter, and she turned once more.

"Gods, Zhik! you're bleeding! Are you all right?"

"Climb, please. Yes, I am fine." A dubious glance over her shoulder; he could tell she didn't believe him. He hadn't expected her to. Blood dripped from his nails, matted the fur on his forearms. The skin between his shoulders stung, the muscles throbbed; it felt as if a huge patch of fur had been scraped off.

They were nearly to the top. He could see An-Lieye's anxious face, Magdalena's pale one just behind her. The translator looked up as the force-beam wailed again; then yelled out a warning and yanked An-Lieye back out of sight. Rock-shards sprayed in all directions, and the whole ledge shook.

The sound within the cut was appalling. Zhik caught his breath sharply as more sharp chunks of rock slammed into his shoulders; Alexis half-turned, stumbled as the hurt foot took her full weight, and fell backward. Her head slammed into the wall.

Magdalena peered anxiously into the depression, then scrambled down to the interrelator, who was fighting to sit upright. "Are you all right?" the dark woman asked with a hiss.

"Fine," Alexis said, but her eyes looked glazed and her voice was slurred. "Help me up." Magdalena managed to get her upright and balanced on one foot, her hands flat against the stones, while Zhik dragged himself over the edge. It took both of them to get the interrelator onto level ground. An-Lieye waited, visibly anxious, eyes moving from Zhik to Alexis, to the drop-off.

Magdalena got her shoulder under the other woman's arm; Zhik, murmuring apologies, caught hold of Alexis's waist, and between them, they got her moving. Alexis seemed barely aware of her surroundings, only now and again trying to walk. The force-beam howled every few minutes, but nothing else fell near them.

The ravine was a nightmare. Zhik ached; he was half sick from pain and fear, and increasingly certain the flyer would not be where he had left it. In the end, he had to go on alone; if the flyer was still safe, he'd need to get the rear hatch unsealed and fire the engines. Configuring the machine to reverse out of its narrow hiding would take some thought, in his current state. Besides, there was simply no room for him and Magdalena both to help Alexis down to level ground. An-Lieye waited at the end of the ravine to be sure they headed straight for the flyer—the least delay now could be fatal for all of them.

Once he settled at the control seat, pain flared from every cut and outraged muscle, and he felt appallingly weak. *I will not be able to move again,* he thought dully. But if he could find Khyriz; then Khyriz would take control. Then he could rest.

He could see the women coming now, Magdalena struggling with Alexis, An-Lieye pressed against her other side, the pale blue hood fluttering behind her, and her ears utterly flat. Alexis limped on the twisted foot, eyes closed.

It took both females—human and Asha—to get Alexis over the lip of the hatch. Magdalena talked nonstop, soothing the interrelator, urging her to hurry at the same time. Somehow the other woman revived enough to struggle into the flyer on her hands and knees before she collapsed onto her side. Magdalena hauled the hatch down and knelt beside her as Zhik began maneuvering the flyer backward into the open.

The translator touched her companion's arm anxiously, patted her fingers. "Alexis? Alexis, talk to me! Please?"

"Perez? I feel . . . damned odd." The interrelator sighed very faintly and went limp.

"Oh, *God*!" Magdalena whispered. She felt frantically for the other woman's wrist. "I can't—damnit!" She drew a deep breath and held it, laid her fingers against the interrelator's throat. Alexis fetched another small sigh; Magdalena sagged beside her. "She's alive," she whispered. An-Lieye stared down at them both, then flung herself up the long, open cabin.

Zhik held up a trembling hand and she froze, eartufts quivering. Blood dripped from his nails. "No, An-Lieye, I am not very hurt. I swear it. Small cuts from the stones, painful but not dangerous. Sit close to me, please. I need you here." She gestured assent, still visibly upset, and drew one of the narrow benches nearer the pilot's shell. He finally got the flyer turned and leveled, set it moving as fast as he dared, and latched down direction and speed keys before he eased himself painfully around. "Magdalena, how is Alexis?"

"She's . . . I don't know," Magdalena confessed. She almost had to shout to be heard above the noise of the racing flyer. "Where are you taking us, Zhik?"

"To Khyriz. Apologies, Magdalena, I have nearly ruined everything, I learned only this morning—"

The translator made certain the unconscious woman was as comfortable as anyone could make her, then got stiffly to her feet and walked forward. "This morning? No, tell me later. You're obviously hurting, and frankly, I don't think I'd understand anything you told me right now."

"This is nothing, bruises and cuts from the fallen rock. I have felt much worse. Bruises and cuts heal quickly."

"Good." He didn't think she looked convinced, and her eyes flicked sideways, toward An-Lieye; she understood the reasons for his lies, then. Good, he thought. But her next act surprised even him. The translator went to one knee and met An-Lieye's eyes, holding out both hands in an Arekkhi gesture of greeting between friends and equals. "An-Lieye, I know Fahara introduced us that first day in her apartments, when you wore 'Fringe of Dancer.' But I knew nothing then. I am honored to properly meet you. Apologies for any rudeness on my part. Ignorance is a poor excuse." She hesitated, then added, "You look as exhausted as I feel. We will converse later, you and I. When there is a quiet place and time." An-Lieye gazed at her for a long moment, then drew out her small writepad and stylo, and scribbled words as quickly as she could. She handed the pad to the translator, who smiled as she took the device and read aloud, as if to herself, " 'No apologies. You were not permitted the truth. You both were always kind and polite.' Thank you, An-Lieye. *You* are more gracious than we deserve. Zhik, how far to—I don't even know where we *are*!"

"We are in the high country of my father's mainland-Akkherif holdings, and we go as straight as possible toward the sea, and my cousin's estate." He studied the controls for some moments, then shrugged—and hissed as stiff muscles protested. An-Lieye leaned toward him anxiously. "Apologies, An-Lieye, it is nothing, this young noble is too soft. Magdalena, we should arrive a standard hour before the sun goes and darkness sets in."

"Thank you." She swallowed. "How . . . is Khyriz?"

"Apologies, I do not know. An-Lieye and I left Ebba the night of the ball. I only heard of your capture during a chance encounter in my father's holdings."

The translator considered this a moment, then shook her head. "Apologies of my own, Zhik. Nothing makes sense to me just now. I'd better watch over Alexis, even if I can't do anything for her except be there." But she hesitated again and finally asked, "But if we're on your father's lands—is that League his?" He nodded, human-fashion, eyes moving between the controls and the view outside. "I knew it! But that means they'll have access to his resources!"

"They do not know Zhenu is behind them," Zhik said. "So

they have only a single plain flyer—and it is halfway across Zhenu's holdings just now. And because they destroyed the way up that ledge, they could not follow us. They may eventually discover that a flyer came for you; they may not.''

Magdalena shook her head. "If theirs is gone, it won't matter, anyway. But—you're certain it was gone?''

"I overheard them saying it,'' Zhik replied. Magdalena touched his arm very gently with the back of her hand, and returned to sit next to Alexis.

Time crawled; Zhik keyed all the flyer's controls to automatic once he was certain they'd passed the last of the rock-strewn areas. He was taking something of a chance on wrecking the flyer by avoiding the meandering tracks and paths of his father's lands. But heading straight across open ground would save considerable time and might let them avoid accidental detection. *My wretched luck, and we would pass my father.*

It was tempting that same luck, flying cross-country. These flyers were unstable at much height aboveground, which was the best reason to follow the ground-vehicle tracks. One good-sized boulder could rip off the undercarriage and bring them down in the midst of Zhenu's lands.

But if he could avoid hitting anything, he'd save hours. Even minutes counted now. The possibility of a good com back in that guards' cave was beginning to haunt him. *My father may already have learned of the rescue from those guards, he may already have seen my slippers and know I am responsible!*

Logic told him that wasn't possible: The League guards were not supposed to know who paid them, and even if they did—or if their captain had received their information already—what guard of Zhenu's would call in an alarm before all possible hiding places in those rocks had been thoroughly checked?

Still, he couldn't trust that; young guards, an impossible situation, how would anyone react?

Plan for the worst, his father often said. *I am learning,* Zhik thought grimly.

He still had to watch the controls, and the landscape hurtling past them, but it helped not having to touch anything. An-Lieye went back to the storage behind the document box, and dug through it until she found the safety box. She came back with packets of cleaning pads and several bulbs of sealing liquid, and, ignoring his protests, began to clean and seal the cuts on his hands and forearms. Most were as shallow as he'd thought, but one swollen finger still seeped blood and he couldn't move it at all. She gently wrapped one of the cleaning pads around the finger with sealant, then looked at him anxiously. "Better," he assured her, and it was true, though the cleaning itself had hurt worse than getting the cuts had. She touched his face, then moved around him before he could protest again. So she could deal with his back.

To his relief, nothing seemed to be broken, other than possibly the one finger. But his legs ached. Not surprising: He could not recall any time in all his life when he had moved so fast. An-Lieye mouthed an offer to massage them, but he gestured a negative, then laid his hand on her face and drew her close so he could draw his whiskers through hers. "Thank you, my An-Lieye," he murmured. "The hurt is much less." He was aware of Magdalena at the far end of the cabin; her eyes were wide as a kit's. To his astonishment, she suddenly smiled warmly, then turned her back on them. *She sees, and she does not judge.*

He forgot her, then; An-Lieye moved the seat closer so she could lean her face against his narrow shoulder, her fingers gently brushing his throat-fur. "My An-Lieye," he murmured again. "I have ruined your blue." The pale fabric was smudged everywhere with dirt, and now his blood; a small tuft of his back hair lodged in the hood. He removed it. "I almost fear to ask: How much hair did I lose?"

Only that, and three more like it, she mouthed, then took the hairs back from him and shoved them into the pocket with her writepad, curving her whiskers. *My payment.*

He smiled tiredly. "A good joke. We will somehow retrieve your other clothing—"

No. Unimportant. She smoothed the blue against her legs, brushing lightly at the dusty sleeves as he turned his gaze to the open land before them. They passed over vast grain plantations, and crossed a flat, shallow river not long after that.

Zhik stirred. "Magdalena, we are near. This is the Uyokkh, the border of Zhenu's lands. Twenty *parths* now that belong to the smallholder who separates Khyriz and Zhenu, and another ten *parths,* I think, to the coastline." he said.

The translator scrambled to her knees. "Is . . . that close?" Magdalena asked. Her voice was too high.

"Close. Fifteen standard minutes—"

She made an odd little sound. "I don't. . . . Forget it, it's much better than the last time I heard that phrase. Is . . . if you don't know he's there, though . . ." She sounded so uncertain, very unlike the translator he knew. *Frightened.* She had cause.

"If my cousin is not, someone who knows me will be. We can then learn where he is, and use his equipment to make a safe call—"

"Oh. I see. Good." She lapsed into silence once more.

"How is Alexis?" he asked finally.

"She's breathing too loudly and she won't wake up. I'm afraid to touch her."

"We are close, Magdalena," he assured her. "I see the orange line of Khyriz's distort; the protect-field around his flitter-storage and manor." He saw something else, too: another flying machine, high above his. Its pilot must have seen the bulky flyer; by direction as well as appearance, it would be known for Zhenu's. His mouth went dry. If Khyriz thought the flyer his father's . . . *Almost as bad: That might not be Khyriz's machine. My father has bragged of his own flyers crossing above my cousin's lands.* He couldn't even tell what kind of machine it was, not with the late sun reflecting off it.

He couldn't decide this problem himself; it wasn't just his life. "Magdalena, I do not wish to use the flyer's com to call ahead to Khyriz, because such a call can be overheard and traced."

She looked up. "I understand."

"But there is a flyer above us. It could be my father's, and he may know that I pilot this craft, with you aboard. Or if it is Khyriz's, and the pilot thinks this some move of Zhenu's . . . in either case, we may have trouble."

"Trouble? You mean . . . they'll fire on us? But—surely

they'd try to send you a message first, wouldn't they? Whoever it is?'' Magdalena eased gently away from the unconscious woman and worked her way forward, clutching at supports along the way; she was walking stiffly, and the flyer was re-acting to the late-afternoon wind. She gazed up through the clear plas, eyes shaded against the near-level sun. "After all, the *zhez* is a high-ranked noble; no one would risk offending him—or killing him—if he was on this vessel. Would they?''

"Before now, no. But if the Emperor has some proof my father ordered the attack on your apartments, and Zhenu is named traitor . . .''

"I understand. What do you think we should do?''

His head ached; it was increasingly hard to think. "It could be anyone. Zhenu's spies, the Emperor's, Khyriz's. At some moment soon, I must call ahead to Khyriz's flitter-pad techs, to identify us and be certain we are welcome to land.''

"I . . .'' Magdalena nodded once, sharply. "Call. It would be foolish of us to get this far, only to die at Khyriz's gates.''

"Yes.'' He let An-Lieye hand him the com, talked her through setting the controls he couldn't reach without stretch-ing for them, and keyed the send and receive buttons.

Unfortunately, the flyer's com was as basic as the flyer it-self, and he'd grown used to his own flitter with its full voice-activation and precoded call and ident numbers. Finally the signal went through, and after several delays—he nearly forgot the private ID code used only between himself and the Prince—a rough voice patched in to confirm the code. Less than a breath later, Khyriz's anxious voice boomed out at him. An-Lieye keyed the volume down at his gesture.

"Zhik! Where are you, and where is An-Lieye? I need to—''

"Listen, Cousin,'' Zhik broke in sharply, "I am approach-ing your lands in an older plain-flyer, one of Zhenu's—''

"Yes, I am picking you up, Cousin. The system here picked your craft up crossing the Uyokkh. As things are now, we thought it might be some move on Zhenu's part.''

"I heard today how things are,'' Zhik replied cautiously. "That is your flitter, up there?''

"Our flitter, yes.''

"Good. Because I have An-Lieye, and the CLS women.
They are . . ."

"Magdalena?" Khyriz's voice rose abruptly. "They—
never mind. I will have the tech here send you a coordinate,
we'll drop security at that point on the perimeter, you can bring
the flyer across, and—"

"No." Zhik sighed very faintly. "I am injured—a little,"
he added quickly as An-Lieye's ears went down. "But enough
that I am beyond such thinking—either programming coordinates or keying the auto-sys for them. Your main gates are not
far; half a parth or less."

"We will meet you there," Khyriz said, and cut the con-
nection, but moments later, he sent a return-pulse. This time
An-Lieye held the com for him, buttons depressed, so he could
concentrate on getting the flyer to safety. The wind was much
stronger, all at once; he could see the rocky edge that marked
the headland, see the distant and distort-fogged manor and the
enclosed flitter landing. Khyriz's voice sounded different; Zhik
finally identified the change—his cousin was already on the
way. "Zhik, more speed if you have it; my overhead pilot tells
us there are two flyers coming full-speed down the track from
your family's holdings straight for the gates."

"My father?"

"We cannot tell; the machines are unmarked, similar to
yours. My pilot will create what diversion he can." The con-
nection went dead; An-Lieye returned the com to its clip, then
winced back against Zhik as the flitter that had paced them for
so long roared down out of the sky, then veered sharply toward
the sea. A shimmering line of heat stabbed where it had been.
Zhik keyed for more speed, but their flyer was already going
as fast as it could, and bucking dangerously. He still couldn't
see the flyers, just Khyriz's flitter, darting in and out of sight,
the heat-bolt firing in a vain attempt to bring it down.

And then the main gates: thick metal, topped with the
Prince's ducat. Zhik fought the flyer out away from its direct
path, so he could approach the gates head-on, but wind caught
the near wing and he had to swing it sharply back the other
way; An-Lieye clung to the sleeve of his robe desperately, and
behind him, Magdalena cried out.

A flare of brilliant red exploded across the forward view-port and the flyer shuddered violently as three voice-alarms shouted urgent warnings: *Downed coolant tank! Shattered Wing! Fire!* The machine jerked halfway around and suddenly he could see the flyers, nearly on top of them. His machine stalled and slammed into the ground, tearing his bruised fingers from the controls.

The cabin was rapidly filling with acrid smoke. He shouted, "Out! Everyone out, now!" and flipped the hatch control, then keyed off everything he could reach. He staggered to his feet, then caught An-Lieye up and limped toward the outside.

Magdalena was already outside the hatch, tugging at an unresponsive Alexis. Zhik let An-Lieye down and said with a hiss, "Move from the flyer and hide!" then caught hold of the interrelator's nearer arm. Somehow the two of them got the unconscious woman out, and into the long, shallow ditch that would be a small river in wet season.

The wind was a chill fury, ripping the heat from his body. He scrambled back to level ground and gazed anxiously toward Khyriz's still sealed gates. They were thirty paces beyond the nose of his burning flyer, but it might as well have been the back side of the jump-station. The two flyers had settled just outside the gates, between them and safety. Body-armored guards poured from the hatch of the first to form a double line, back to back, facing both downed flyer and the gates. They appeared to be armed with everything from stunners to force-beams.

From the second flyer, only five emerged. But Zhik felt the blood leave his face as he identified them: three senior guards, Hyorr, and in the lead—Zhenu.

Delay them. Khyriz was their only hope. An-Lieye gasped and snatched at the hem of his robe as he got to his feet and stepped from the ditch, onto flat ground.

The *zhez* hesitated so briefly, Zhik might have imagined it, then came on, his white robe snapping in the wind, stopping once he could clearly see his son's face. One hand held a small weapon of some kind, casually. The other hand was tucked into the snapping fabric.

Zhik blinked rapidly. But it was no trick of the light; his

father was virtually featureless—nearly as unspotted as an Asha. In his haste, Zhenu had come out without cosmetic. "Zhikna," the noble said with an ominous growl. "I have heard curious things about you since the ball!"

Zhik fought nerves. Part of him wanted to cringe away from his father, flee from his anger. But one injured young noble was the only barrier between the Esteemed *Zhez* Zhenu and three unarmed females. *I am their Voice,* he reminded himself, and took a deep breath. "Yes, Father. Tell me, please, what tales you hear, and perhaps I can sort out the rumors for you."

"Fool!" Zhenu said, a growl, low in his throat.

"Once, *perhaps* I was that, Father." He waited then, physically still, not stuttering, and this seemed to confound his father. "Curious it is, though: I have also heard many things about *you.*" He watched impassively as Zhenu's ears flicked. "Treason and sedition—" He got no farther; Zhenu bellowed a particularly filthy curse. Zhik swallowed.

"I will gut you for that," the *Zhez* said with a snarl, and freed his other hand from the white robe. Long, curved metal talons glittered on both thumb and first finger. Oddly, the threat and the weapons steadied the younger noble. *He can kill me, yes. He will not break me. Never again. And I must delay him. . . .*

"If you touch me with those, Father," he said evenly, "if you take one drop of blood, the Emperor will execute you. I may appear worthless and weak to you, but to Khezahn, I am noble, and of age. And therefore your equal under his rule!"

"And if I kill him first?" Zhenu rumbled ominously. "Or if I have already killed the she-aliens and he knows it? If I am already dead in his eyes, and all that remains is my execution? Then what does it matter to me who else dies here? Do you think that I would mourn your death, weak and foolish son?"

Zhik gestured a sharp negative. "And if the CLS team is already off-planet? Or safely back with the Emperor?"

"A lie," Zhenu snapped.

Zhik raised his voice slightly as the wind increased. "Shall I describe to you, *and* to Hyorr, the place where they were held? The guard-captain he gave orders to this morning, in your cellars? The vid to be made—?"

"You . . . *you* did that?" Zhenu stared blankly, then spat laughter. "Oh, perhaps you somehow overheard, but nothing more! I will beat you senseless for such a lie, Zhikna. Because you are incapable—!"

"No." Magdalena's resonant voice overrode his. Zhik gestured urgently: *Go back!* But the translator paid no heed; she came striding up next to him, her chin high. "The interrelator and I *were* rescued by Zhikna. From *your* guards. The son has honor, unlike his father!"

"You do not *dare* speak to me in such fashion!" Zhenu roared. Magdalena took another step forward, eyes boring into the elder noble's, and Zhik realized with surprise that her silence and her stance unnerved him.

"How *dare* you threaten *me*?" she finally demanded. "After all the interrelator and I have endured these past days, because of you?" He would have spoken then, but she interrupted him—surely the first time such a thing had happened. "I am not your son! I am not your mate, your servants—*or* your Asha!"

Zhik didn't dare look at her; that would mean taking his eyes from Zhenu, who was stuttering in his fury. "Fool of a human woman," the *zhez* finally managed. "I can order you killed, now!"

He gestured an order to Hyorr, who turned and shouted to the double line of guards, "Make certain none come from those gates! Kill those who do!"

"You can't kill everyone!" Magdalena shouted.

One of the guards near the *eroe* end of the arc shouted, "The gates are moving! I can see the Prince's ducat on the lead vehicle!"

"I will kill your precious, dandy young Prince!" Zhenu bellowed back at her. "And I cannot imagine a greater pleasure than to let you watch as he dies!"

"You don't know *how* to imagine!" she screamed, eyes black in attack-fury. "And that is why you will lose!"

"Perhaps." Zhenu emitted a spat of laughter, his own black, flat challenge-stare fixed on his son. "But you and he will not survive to see that moment, will you? And *you* carry no weapons, do you? *Son*?" His voice dropped; now a low, carrying

purr, travesty of a father's love-growl. "Think; if you had the
courage or skill for such weaponry, you might just have protected the alien-she. But poor Zhikna, he cannot kill. The test
I set you with the ahla—but you did not destroy it, did you?"
The younger noble strove to answer, but Zhenu snarled, silencing him again. "Do not lie, *I* know what you did. The
creature is here, where you took it." A gesture took in the
distort-fence behind them.

Zhik could sense Magdalena's puzzlement and felt sick that
An-Lieye might understand his father's words. "Ah-Naul is
alive. My duty as a noble is to all sentients, by your own words
and by the Prelate's teachings."

"A *sentient* would understand what the Prelate and his father *meant* by such words!" Zhenu said with a snarl.

"I see. My mouth is to swear, while my hands kill? I will
not! I do not have the honor Magdalena says of me, but I may
at least strive for it." Zhenu stared at him. Beyond the smok-
ing flyer, Zhik could hear the sounds of fighting, the sharp
cries of wounded. Khyriz was engaged there, but he couldn't
tell anything else. And then the elder noble brought up the
hand-weapon. A fire-bolt; smaller version of the weapon that
had destroyed the flyer. Magdalena didn't know what it was;
he did. *I cannot let him kill her!* But, to die like that. . . . Zhik
swallowed, and tried to force himself to move.

He simply couldn't. Then Magdalena cried out in surprise
and whirled away from him. "No—go back!" she yelled. A
small figure in pale blue hurtled from the ditch to catch at his
hands, the deep hood fallen forward over her face. Her hands
were trembling. But she eased from his grasp, and placed herself squarely between Zhenu and his son.

Zhenu peered, visibly uncertain who or what stood there.
"What . . . ?" He spat laughter. "*You* spent the past days with
a paid-she?" A gust of wind; the hood blew back, exposing
pale, golden, spotless fur. The *zhez*'s whiskers and ears went
flat to his skull. "You . . . you . . . ? This is that creature
bought by the designer-she!"

A sense of unreality filled Zhik as he stepped to put himself
between his beloved and his father. The fighting was louder
now—nearer. Still, if the *zhez* chose, the women and he, his

beloved An-Lieye, were all dead in less than a heartbeat. *Delay!* he thought again. Somewhere above them, at least one flitter shrieked louder than the wind, and a red flame-bolt struck just beyond his father's flyers.

"Her name is An-Lieye," Zhik said. "And she is my life-mate."

For a long moment, it seemed nothing moved, not even the dying flames on the broken flyer. Then his father leaped toward him, both hands steadying the flame-bolt, the pinhole of the weapon veering from him to her, then back again. Wildly unsteady. Zhik sidestepped, trying to press An-Lieye behind him; Magdalena tugged at pale blue fabric. An-Lieye shook both of them off and fought to put herself between Zhik and the ugly little flame-bolt.

He pressed her back again, and this time An-Lieye stumbled and fell. "She is *not* your mate!" Zhenu said, hissing. "She is dead!" The *zhez* steadied himself, centered the weapon on the Asha. Zhik met his father's eyes squarely and moved; the bolt caught him midchest.

The pain was excruciating. Zhik shrieked once, horribly, as the chemical spread over his body; the beam sliced through his chest and broke up against Khyriz's distort. Burning, Zhik fell, already dead.

An-Lieye tried to throw herself on him; Magdalena caught hold of the frantic Asha and dragged her back, away from the searing heat. Her eyes fixed on Zhenu, who gazed, stunned at his son's corpse. He snarled a curse, and brought the weapon up again. Magdalena tried to retreat, but her legs wouldn't move. It was all she could do to hold on to An-Lieye. The little Asha trembled violently but made no sound. Voiceless. . . .

One of Khyriz's flitters swooped low, a force-bolt tearing up the ground behind him; the *zhez* stumbled, and his next shot went wild. Before he could fire again, he was surrounded by armed guards, who tore the weapon from his grasp and wrapped him in force-bonds. Magdalena sat down hard as her legs gave out, taking An-Lieye down with her. The young female fought her way free.

Zhik no longer burned; but he was no longer recognizable

as Zhik. An-Lieye dragged herself to his side, fingers tearing at the blackened turf, lips moving soundlessly.

Tears blurred Magdalena's vision and slipped down her cheeks. . . .

CHAPTER 15

◆

The sun dropped out of sight; with a final gust, the wind died away completely. Magdalena could hear a few high-pitched wails of pain but no more fighting, and the flames on the Iron Duke's flyers were suddenly doused as jumpsuit-clad Arekkhi shot broad fans of liquid over them. As suddenly, the acrid smoke from Zhik's stolen machine was gone, replaced by a faint, sweetish odor.

Movement to her left; she wiped her eyes and blinked rapidly. Five armed Arekkhi clad in blue jumpsuits strode among the wrecks, Khyriz in their midst. She thought he glanced her way but couldn't be certain; she got stiffly to her feet, but he had already turned to confront the bound noble.

Seeing the Prince, Zhenu fought his bonds, but subsided at once. Magdalena winced, remembering her own brief experience with them in the old palace. *That must have hurt.* He glared down at the slighter Khyriz. A long silence, which the Prince finally broke. "The mouth-bond as well, one of you." He waited while an additional strip was formed over the noble's nose and clamped to the main restraints, then addressed him directly. "We both know how your long-ancestor from the last war bit his tongue and bled to death, Zhenu. I have heard you boast of his courage. You will not suicide as he did. You will appear before the Emperor and await his judgment. But that is my father's business, not mine.

"Here, you have committed crimes on royal land, any of which are such that I could order your immediate execution,

and even the Emperor could not protest. But I will not kill
you. Trial for treason, before all Arekkhi space and the outside
worlds, will humiliate you worse than any death even *you*
could devise. But I *will* try you, here and now. And you will
be allowed no voice. You murdered your only son in such a
barbarous manner that I name you *less than sentient,* who was
Zhenu. According to Arekkhi law.'' He turned partway
around; impassive eyes met Magdalena's. ''You three are wit-
nesses to this hearing.''

Her heart froze—dread of more bloodshed, more confrontation. But, his look! As if she could have been anyone. *He's
against the Iron Duke,* she reminded herself. Personal gestures
would be out of place; Zhenu would see them as weakness. *I
can be professional also . . . I hope I can,* she added more honestly, then took An-Lieye's shoulders between gentle hands
and urged her to her feet, whispering against her ear. The Asha
trembled but let herself be moved away from Zhik, to a point
where she and the translator could see Zhenu's face, and
Khyriz's.

They'd lost some of the proceedings, Magdalena thought;
Khyriz had just sent one of his circle back the way they'd
come, and he was speaking in an undertone to others. He took
a step back, then, and met her eyes. ''Magdalena Perez. We
have proof by confession of a personal bodyguard that this
male-being originated the plan, spoke the orders, and provided
weaponry and funds for the attack on the old palace, and on
the CLS team. Have you and Alexis any proof of your own
against the male-being?''

She swallowed. ''I must speak for Alexis Ortovsky. She was
injured during our escape from the—the male-being's under-
lings. She is unconscious.'' She forced herself to concentrate
on what she said, knowing Zhenu would see hesitation or confusion as fear; a little of the earlier anger steadied her. He
would not have that satisfaction.

She very briefly told Khyriz how Zhik had rescued them,
the few things he had been able to tell her that she could
remember, back in the flyer. More haltingly, she told him of
Zhik's exchange with Zhenu just before the *zhez* killed him.

''The male-being threatened death to all of you?'' Khyriz

asked evenly; he glanced away from her as the guard returned, and gestured for him to wait.

Magdalena nodded. "Yes. But he killed Zhik by accident; he intended to first murder An-Lieye. Zhik . . ." She swallowed, fought air into her lungs, and went on, as dispassionate-sounding as he. "But the male-being would have killed us all if there had been time, I saw it in his eyes. He swore he would kill you be . . . before me, after he defeated your guards." Zhenu glared at her. Her mouth was very dry, all at once.

Khyriz gestured; the guard handed him a writepad and stylo. An-Lieye flicked her ears upright, shook herself free of Magdalena's grasp, and came forward. The hand clutching the stylo trembled, though, and she looked only at Khyriz. To the translator's relief, he was gentle, and he questioned her only briefly about what she had heard and seen. But before he could turn back to Zhenu, she gestured urgently and again began to write, then handed the pad to him.

Khyriz read silently, ears flicking in surprise. An-Lieye shifted her gaze to the bound noble, her chin high. She stepped back, hesitated, then spun on one foot and walked away. This was surely a first in the Iron Duke's entire life, Magdalena thought. His features showed more astonishment than anger.

Fortunately, he could not see the Asha's face; her ears remained upright, but her eyes were slitted in grief; the dark stripes flanking her nose were wet—Arekkhi did not cry the way humans did but in extreme distress seeped moisture. The translator wrapped her arms around the grieving young she. An-Lieye started, forearm hair hackled, then subsided against her.

"How interesting," Khyriz said finally. "Zhik told An-Lieye about certain records he read this morning. Records kept in your lower storage." Zhenu started violently, forced himself back to stillness as the restraints flashed bright blue. When the light faded back to normal, Khyriz held up the pad where the other could read it. "Of course, I already knew of your orders to Hyorr, to murder Asha and the villagers who protect them. Hyorr will not be available to carry them out." Silence. "You seem surprised. I have had your communications monitored for two years. And the raids on your villages Nho Four and

Lirh Seven, Asha who vanished? I know where they are. Because *I* moved them to safety." Zhenu glared at him. "I have a team in place just this side of the Uyokkh River, ten flitters of my own armed, and four of the Emperor's flyers under the Heir's orders, ready to invade your—what *were* your estates at first light, and prevent those deaths. We will take control of those lands and restore order—a hundred years too late for many Arekkhi and Asha, but order nonetheless.

"Thanks to An-Lieye's warning, I will see that the holding is entered in secret tonight, long before the hour of attack. The main records, and the backup records belowground, will both be sealed before the clerks can destroy them." Zhenu strained against the bonds, and Khyriz spat laughter. "Hurt yourself all you please, play the mindless *iyfer* in a trap! I care nothing for your pain, and your actions change *nothing*!"

Zhenu glanced away from him, eyes hooded. Khyriz laughed again. "And I know your thought, just now. The restraints cannot be used for long, or death results; you remind yourself, 'At some time, they must loose the mouth-bond for food and water, and for air, and then I will act.' No. No escape, no easy death by blood loss or by suffocation in the restraints." He drew something out of a pocket and held it up—a small sniff-bulb, Magdalena thought; she couldn't be sure for the rapidly failing light. Whatever it was, she was certain the Iron Duke was terrified of the thing; he now desperately fought the bonds. But the guards had him.

Another clutch of five jumpsuit-clad Arekkhi came from the direction of the gates, followed by a female in the distinctive red of a physician. The guards moved to help with Zhenu at Khyriz's sharp gesture, but the physician ignored them all. Her bright gaze fixed on the translator, and she hurried over to her.

"You recognize this, don't you, male-being?" Khyriz asked mildly. The physician would have spoken to Magdalena at that moment, but the suddenly nervous translator gestured for silence. "When I first planned for the CLS team to tell the outside worlds about Asha, I obtained tubes of both drugs, so they would know what was being done by beings like you. And in hopes the outsiders could find antidotes. The tube of voice-killer goes to them intact. I hope the CLS scientists will be satisfied with one bulb of mind-death. Because the rest are needed here.

"Of course, *you* know the color and shape of the bulb, and the effects! If you are fed one of these now, by morning you will have difficulty remembering who you are. A second then, a third the next sunrise—and you will be ahla until the Emperor discontinues the dose. If he ever does."

The power bonds flared bright blue as Zhenu fought to free himself, but the *zhez* was helpless. Khyriz firmly squirted the contents into the Iron Duke's nostrils, then turned to his guards. "Put him in the locked sick-room," he said with a snarl. "Two guards, both changed every hour. Remind them all, nothing short of full alert until the drug takes effect. And even then be wary. My extreme displeasure if anything goes wrong!"

Magdalena turned away, sickened and trembling; she bit the side of her hand to keep from vomiting. An-Lieye took hold of her near arm, her own fingers shaking. *That drug is reversible,* the translator reminded herself as she fought for control. *He said so. And after everything the Iron Duke has done, just tonight* . . . After what he had done to An-Lieye, who came from his estates, like Fahara. "Apologies," she stammered, and laid the back of one hand against the other's arm.

"Magdalena-she?" The physician's voice was unexpectedly throaty; that as much as the unexpected sound brought her around with a gasp. She gazed blankly at the red-clad, then shook herself. Physician . . .

"Oh, gods, Alexis," she whispered; it hurt to speak. "I am unharmed, but the interrelator fell and hit her head. The bone felt solid to my hand, but she is unconscious, and I can't wake her."

"Concussion," the physician said calmly. "Which I can deal with. I am Unya—take me to her, please." Magdalena led the way, then waited on the far side of the slope while Unya shouted an order for strong light down in the ditch and descended rapidly to crouch at Alexis's side. As a glare of lamplight bounced along the ledge, then centered on the fallen woman, the Arekkhi deftly raised lids to check her eyes, tested her pulse, felt her arms and legs, and shot a rapid series of questions up at Magdalena. "She walked after this fall? The foot is enlarged—oh, yes, I understand, an earlier injury, a turned foot? She was able to put weight on it? Good, anything broken is small, then, more likely sprain. And the spinal column must not be damaged. We still use great caution here, to move her." *After the way we dragged her into and out of the flyer, it may be too late,* Magdalena thought gloomily. But the physician's words and actions, as well as her obvious understanding of human physiology, relieved her. Alexis was still alive. If there *was* damage, CLS had the med-tech to fix almost anything.

She shielded her eyes against the glare and gazed back toward the flyers.

Zhenu was gone, and so were most of the guards. Flames crackled in one of his flyers and were snuffed at once by the three covered in slick-cloth who watched all three machines in turn, chemical sprayers at the ready. She could just make out two jumpsuited guards beginning to move slowly toward the gates, struggling with an awkward burden. An-Lieye, her size as distinctive as the pale blue robe, moved back and forth behind them. *They are taking Zhik's body—poor Zhik. Poor An-Lieye.* Bright lights backlit guards and flitters well beyond them, and if she craned sideways, she could just make out the pillars of Khyriz's gates.

Khyriz himself was nowhere in sight.

Magadalena sank down on the edge of the ditch, tears running down her face, trying to pay attention as Unya shouted out an order for a hard carry-mat, then returned to her examination. No use; all she could see was *his* neutral face as he spoke to her, as he pronounced judgment; his hand pressing down on that bulb of poison. *He has things to do, important things,* she tried to tell herself. A high-ranking noble, an ally of the Prelate—and Khyriz had just arrested him and administered drugs that were used to create a slave class.

But the arguments did no good. What he'd said just now, raids on Zhenu's lands—Khyriz must have been working all along to help the Asha. And the things she'd said to him, the night of the ball. . . . *I was right. I knew I didn't have the skills to serve in such a . . . a sensitive position. Rob was wrong.*

Blanket was wrong. Father ... Solomon Smith was right about me all along. She buried her face in her hands and wept.

The physician touched her hair in concern, bringing her back to the moment. "Are you injured? The program Khyriz obtained for me explains this as human weeping and, like ours, it means hurt."

The translator blotted her cheeks, gestured a negative, and managed, "It's also for very tired. I'm not hurt." *Physically.* Reassured, Unya turned back to her patient. Moments later, two of Khyriz's household came up in a small ground-flitter, a narrow hover-cart in tow. Unya climbed out of the ditch to study the Arekkhi-shaped niche atop the cart, then ordered mats and bolsters pulled out, a hard-mat dragged from lower storage to be fastened on top, another hard-mat carried into the ditch by three solidly built males in the red and brown of assistants. The physician followed, growling orders. Magdalena climbed up near the hoverer, to be out of the way, and clutched the rough brown robe around her, eyes fixed on her unconscious colleague.

"Magdalena!" Khyriz's anxious voice brought her halfway around; he drew her into a tight embrace. "*Zhyoya* Magdalena—bright, beloved Magdalena, I thought I would never see you again." Closing her eyes, she clung to him.

He finally released her, but only so he could cup warm hands around her face. "You are not injured? Swear?" She shook her head, then nodded, unable to speak. "But you are so cold! Here—come with me—"

"I should stay," she mumbled through a tight throat. "Alexis—"

"Unya will manage better without you. Come, my flitter is close, and it is warm inside."

"Warm," she whispered, eyes still closed. She felt him bundle her into another garment—his own cloak by its thick softness and the citrusy odor of his favorite fur-softener. He wrapped an arm around her waist then and tugged.

"Apologies, I cannot carry you, you must walk. Unless the hoverer—"

She made an effort, opened her eyes, and stopped swaying

in place. "No, Alexis needs it. I'm all right, Khyriz. Just—
just cold and. . . ." She couldn't seem to find any words; his
fingers tightened on her arm. "I can walk, if there's a warm
place at the other end."

The flitter was almost stuffy; there was a jug of heated *rih* and
a basket of bread, another cloak to wrap around her feet. The
warm liquid eased some of the tension in her throat; Magdalena drank two cups but couldn't face food. As she set the cup
aside, though, tears rolled down her face, and she began to
shake uncontrollably. Khyriz held her, his face against her hair,
murmuring soft words—she could never remember what he
said, but finally the trembling eased. He settled her next to him
on a wide padded bench, waited while she dried her eyes and
drew a deep, shuddering breath. "Here," he said, and handed
her a soft damp cloth. "There is more warmed water for your
hands and face."

It helped even more than the warm drink had. "Apologies,
Khyriz. Everything's been stuck in my throat so many days,
since the ball, what I . . . what I said . . ."

He stroked her hair, and handed her another damp cloth.
"No . . . here, this for your arms and feet. My apologies, Magdalena. For . . . being foolish enough to ask for you to my
world. You could have been killed."

"That wasn't your fault, Khyriz. That was Zhenu, and those
like him. Whatever I said to you, after the ball, I didn't mean
it. And then tonight, I was afraid, you went away, just left
me," She gulped, fought tears again. "I . . . I thought you were
still angry. That you . . . hated me."

"No. I was afraid at first, when the flyer went down, if you
had been injured. And then to see my cousin, dead like that.
To know that . . . that male would have killed you next. Even
so, what I did to him . . ." His ears twitched. "I had to go
quickly, behind his flyers, and be sick. And after that, to send
the orders about his holding and the records."

"I . . . should have realized. I didn't think."

"Where you stood, I could not have thought, either. My
Magdalena, your eyes are so tired and your mouth still trembles." He drew her close again, his voice low and throaty. "I

wish we could stay like this, but I must go soon. And so must you.''

She leaned back to look at him. ''Khyriz . . . the things you said to Zhenu. The words I overheard between you and Fahara, that first day. What *are* you?'' she whispered.

He shrugged, human-like. ''When I returned from Star-Bridge, I saw so much with new eyes, but there seemed to be nothing one foolish young Prince could do. And then I re-membered: Do you recall Dr. Rob's movie, the truly ancient no-colors one about the noble who formed a band of friends to rescue those sentenced to death? That was the beginning.'' She gazed at him, astonished, then began to laugh. ''What?''

''When—I went to see Rob, when he named me temporary translator, guess what holo-poster he had up?''

''Not—''

''Yes. 'That demned elusive Pimpernel'!'' She wiped her eyes again, but this time the hand was steady. ''I needed that. But, Khyriz, *you* aren't going with the fighters, are you?''

He nodded, face again solemn. ''I must. Just as you and An-Lieye must go at once with Bhelan—no, listen, please, Magdalena, I have thought of little else since you were taken. And things have happened since then that may ruin any chances we have to join the CLS.

''You are not safe anywhere in Arekkhi space until all Zhenu's supposed rebels are taken. Before, you and Alexis were a symbol of the outside. Now, thanks to my foolish mouth, his allies know I could be stopped if *you* were taken again.''

''Khyriz, I can't—!''

''No, listen. Bhelan will take you to a rendezvous with Dana Marshall. She will get you to CLS headquarters at Shassiszss, you and Alexis, and An-Lieye. I learned from my father earlier today that the Prelate and Zhenu have found a way to send vid-messages—their words have possibly already reached Shassiszss. My father received copies this morning.''

She studied his face. ''You look—is it that bad?''

''It is bad. They justify treatment of the Asha, each in his own way. Both claim control of Arekkhi space between them, and they issue orders to the CLS to destroy the contract be-

tween us. If this is done, the outsiders are guaranteed the opportunity to recover the Heeyoon traders, the outsiders
working on the new jump station—and the interrelator and
translator. Provided they move quickly.''

"*Dios mío,*" Magdalena murmured and crossed herself,
something she hadn't done in years. "But Khyriz, Alexis is
hurt! She fell, hit her head when we escaped Zhenu's guards.
The trip off-planet might kill her!" He stared at her, ears quivering. "Apologies, there wasn't time to tell you."

"There is even more reason you must go, then—" he began, but she shook her head so hard that tangled, matted hair
flew around her face.

"Khyriz, you know I can't! Me, stand before the Planetary
Council? Me, argue against the evidence they've already received?"

"It is not evidence, Magdalena! You know they lie! But
you can do what you must, just as Mahree did! Remember
your pre-StarBridge history?"

"Khyriz, Mahree Burroughs was born to do just that. Look
what she is now! The Council won't listen to *me*!"

"You know better about Mahree, Magdalena. The Council
will listen, you can persuade them to listen. Think, please, over
your short time on Arekkhi, how well you now speak persua-
sively."

"To the clerks in the old palace, and to your mother, who
is gracious and kind," the translator protested.

"Dr. Rob will counsel you, and so will Mahree. And—if
you will permit the entry into your suite in the old palace, and
use of your codes for the CLS com-center, my father will be
able to send his own messages to CLS; that will surely aid
you." He hesitated. "Magdalena, *please.* An-Lieye will help
you prove the truth. You can do this. For all our sakes, you
must try."

She managed a weak smile at that. "Khyriz, Alexis would
say you're trying to charm me, and it won't work. Except . . ."
she sighed, somber again. "Except it will. Because there *isn't*
anyone else, is there?"

"There is not. But more importantly, you care for us, my
Magdalena. Alexis will be safe here, Unya has the physician

training-vids on humans that I obtained when it was certain you would both come. And surely the CLS will allow a patch to my com-center here, once they hear of her injuries, so Unya can ask any necessary questions for her care."

"Surely they wouldn't risk harm to Alexis. And, of course, your father can use our equipment to send a message! Maybe he'll be able to prove to them that the other two lie. And then I won't need to . . ." She sighed. "I won't rest on that hope, Khyriz. I'll do my best to persuade the Council not to quarantine you, I swear." She thought hard. "All right. My hard copy of the sign-on protocol, and my password, are in the back pocket of my spare jeans, in my clothes storage."

"I will let no one else see the hard copy, Magdalena. I will guard it personally, and serve as my father's tech, when he sends the message." He stroked hair back from her forehead. "An-Lieye is distraught, but I think she is persuaded she can best serve my cousin by going with you."

"Oh, God. Poor An-Lieye." Magdalena's throat tightened and she had to blink tears away. Her fingers tightened on his jumpsuit. "Khyriz, come with us! *You* can persuade them!"

But he was already shaking his head. "No, Magdalena. I am wealthy, a member of the royal family—I could have as many reasons to lie and promote my own cause as Zhenu. And I am needed here. I've . . . become good at what I do, Magdalena. I can't let more Asha die. And there are still Asha, and Arekkhi who tried to help them, locked away in Zhenu's hidden camps." She turned away with a shudder and bit the side of her hand; Khyriz held her closely, his cheek against her hair. "Apologies. Everything I say upsets you."

"No." Magdalena eased herself around so she could wrap strong dancer's arms around his slender body. "You don't upset me. Words don't harm. It's the things Zhenu and his kind have done." She laid a hand, palm down, against his face. "Swear to me you will be careful, Khyriz! Swear you won't . . ." She couldn't finish.

His hands cupped her face in turn. "I will be very careful, I swear. Remember, I am needed here. Dead, I am no use to anyone."

*   *   *

There was no time for anything else. Bhelan came moments later, and Khyriz had already gone back to his com-center. The pilot got her settled in a shuttle much larger and plainer than the one that brought her and Alexis down to the planet. *What—a few mere nine-days ago?* An-Lieye was already netted into a long, curved bench, curled in on herself, ears flat, and eyes closed. Magdalena took the bench nearest, automatically fastening the webbing. Bhelan had the machine moving before she finished.

Once the shuttle escaped the planet, the pilot came back into the main cabin. "The Prince said to warn you, we don't dare use the station for the transfer. Apologies, but that means suits and a portable tube."

"Oh, God." One of her own worst nightmares—but An-Lieye had surely never been off-planet before, she'd be terrified by the open-space procedure. Doubly terrified if her space-traveling companion showed panic. "All right," Magdalena managed to sound calm. "How soon? And . . . apologies, but I doubt I can fit in an Arekkhi suit, Bhelan."

"Dana has two adjustable suits. Once the tube is fixed to our airlock, I will fetch them for you."

To her surprise, the transfer went well. An-Lieye seemed half in shock and did not seem to care about the suit, or hard vacuum, or anything else. Once Magdalena was sealed in and checked, except for the helmet, she helped Bhelan run the suit check on her listless companion. The smallest human suit Dana had was a loose fit, but not so baggy it might catch on anything—and, of course, the wire tube was supposedly snag-proof. *I hope.* Magdalena touched the pilot's shoulder with the back of one gloved hand and said, "Keep him safe, Bhelan." He nodded, human-style, which was oddly assuring; he set her helmet in place and efficiently ran the clips down. Magdalena drew a deep breath, remembered the order of the buttons on her left glove, and pressed the top two: seals intact, air supply full and clean. She clipped the Asha's suit to hers with the short tether, stepped into the lock, and waited for Bhelan to unseal the outer side so she could clip the line from Dana's ship to her own suit.

The trip across was probably safer than half the places she'd been on-planet recently, but disorienting. The lack of gravity made her stomach flip-flop, and she was glad she hadn't eaten much in days. Magdalena kept both hands on the Asha's arm, assurance as much as safety, and tried to focus on the slender wire mesh of the tube or the line hauling them in, not the eternity of starlit blackness all around her. Concentrating on that, and her breathing, helped. It still seemed to take forever for the line to reel them into the other ship's air lock. *Dana has to keep it slow. You don't want to hit anything and rip . . .* She closed her eyes, swallowed hard.

Once she and An-Lieye were safely inside the lock, gravity restored, Magdalena turned and sat, feet wrapped around the ceiling-to-floor grip-pole, both arms clutching her companion.

The tube didn't look as long from this end. The view just beyond her feet made her dizzy, though; she focused on Bhelan's ship, now moving away from them. Then on the tube slowly collapsing in on itself, returning to the engineer's ship. The flattened circle of tube stopped just inside the air lock, then slid into its belowdeck storage compartment, which snapped shut as the outer hatch closed. Air hissed into the narrow space.

Bare moments later, the inner door moved sideways, revealing the storage chambers beyond and a suited and helmeted shape in a familiar chair. Magdalena unhooked from the safety, drew An-Lieye with her, and unsnapped the tether. The door snicked to behind them, but the translator waited until the engineer removed her own helmet before unclipping hers.

The dark-haired woman smiled up at her. "Hey, you made it, great! Khyriz had me pretty scared. Let's get . . ." Her voice faded as Magdalena tugged the other helmet off, and An-Lieye, ears and whiskers plastered to her skull, stared wildly all around. "Ahhh . . . I thought it was you and Alexis I was transporting?"

"Alexis is hurt. . . . I think she'll be all right, Dana, but she hit her head."

"Ouch," Dana replied feelingly. "No, don't think she'd have liked that trip off-planet. Not the angle Bhelan said he took."

"This is An-Lieye." Rude of her to introduce the other, but

the Asha seemed incapable of anything at the moment.

Dana began peeling out of her spacesuit, standing awkwardly to brace one-handed against the chair. "An-Lieye. She's Asha, isn't she?"

"Here, let me help." Magdalena pulled the suit off and bundled it and the helmet into an empty niche, then turned to help An-Lieye out of hers. "Yes, Asha. They aren't what the Arekkhi said, exactly."

"Oh? And what's Khyriz's part in all this?" Dana slid back into her chair, waited—barely—until Magdalena had her own suit hung, then gestured for the two to follow her out of the storage.

"He's trying to help them—the Asha—to keep them alive. The Prelate—" She didn't know where to start.

"Wait. Bet you two could use a meal and the cleaning booth before anything else." Dana got them into the elevator, up one level to the flight deck, and held up a hand for silence while she keyed in coordinates, then clicked everything over to auto.

"Okay," she said crisply as she swung the chair around. "Sorry I couldn't help you two through the tube, I know you don't like them, Mags, but the tube is worse for me than trying to walk in a dark room. In a dark room, I just lose all sense of up and down and I fall. I tried the tube just once, and I lost everything. Including lunch." She grinned suddenly. "You don't want to lose lunch in a space suit." She gestured a greeting as between equals to An-Lieye, who blinked and returned the gesture. Dana smiled, lips only. "Not what they said, huh? Okay, I think I get it." The smile faded as her quick, dark eyes studied the two. "You both look ready to fall down, yourselves. The cleaning booth is ready, it's straight across from the doorway in here. I left out a few of my clothes in the cabin just beyond that—it's for you two, by the way. About the clothes: You're taller than I am, Mags, but I'm more solidly built, so it ought to come out even."

Her eyes strayed to An-Lieye. "I suppose she—apologies, An-Lieye," she corrected herself with a warm, lips-only smile. "There is a washing similar to Arekkhi, clean clothing that will cover you, and a chamber where you can rest. Magdalena, one of my loose shirts is maybe the same length as her robe."

She shook her head. "Your brown thing doesn't look that bad, but that blue really needs to be washed—"

An-Lieye's reaction to that startled both humans—a violent, gestured *no*!

"Uhh . . . I can explain later, Dana," Magdalena said in Mizari. "She has cause." She switched back to Arekkhi. "An-Lieye, apologies, the engineer-Dana did not mean you must wash the robe, that matter and any other matters pertaining to your person are *your* decision. But I . . . I see why you would keep the blue as it is. I would feel the same."

"Okay, sure." The engineer looked puzzled, but shrugged that aside. "Go get clean, both of you, sleep as long as you need to. We're at least nine hours from the jump station, and it'll take at least two weeks to reach CLS, even with the new jump point I'm going to use, and the enhanced power boosters on this hunk of tin. That's assuming nothing goes wrong, of course."

"Nothing will," Magdalena said firmly. "It just can't. Thanks, Dana. I . . . after everything that's happened the past few days, I am going to do just exactly what you suggested."

She woke, clean and disoriented, nearly eighteen Earth hours later, her hair still damp and her eyelids sticky. As she sat up and keyed the lights from off to dim, she could see An-Lieye in the bunk across the narrow chamber from hers, a slight figure wrapped in Dana's oversized navy blue shirt, the stained robe clutched in her arms. She seemed to be very deeply asleep. Magdalena eased from the bunk, stretched hard, then wrote a brief message and left it stuck to the other's pillow. "An-Lieye, we are safe here, and here you and I and Dana are equal. You can go anywhere you like as long as the doors are not sealed. I will return shortly, to show you around the ship."

She found the galley after a short search—the FTL ship assigned to the Arekkhi jump station wasn't that big—and programmed the familiar servo for sweetened orange pekoe tea, steeped five minutes, and two oatmeal raisin cookies. The taste would be off in both cases, but she didn't care; it would be close enough to remind her of cheerful winter breakfasts with her mother on the sunny south-facing third-story balcony of their apartment. Before Solomon Smith. As she bit into the second cookie, a faint whooshing noise alerted her to Dana's battery-operated chair. She glanced toward the open doorway, smiled, and drank the last of her tea. "I didn't properly thank you for dropping everything to come to our rescue—" she began.

"If you don't talk fast for all of us, I won't have a job *or* a station," Dana cut in bluntly. "I just got a detailed message from Khyriz, everything that happened, I can't *believe*!" She took a deep breath. "Okay, never mind. Khyriz said he was uploading a separate vid-message for you, it's on the flight-deck-com, so you can read it in privacy. I need a *long* nap." She turned the chair and was gone before the translator could even open her mouth to say thanks.

Magdalena drained her cup, then programmed another, this time a slightly weaker brew, and carried it with her up the short, narrow hall to the deserted flight deck. She eyed the bewildering array of panels, switches, pads, and buttons, most green-lit to indicate auto-pilot, half a dozen others deep purple for slave-link to an auto. *Slave.* She shuddered. The word would never sound the same again. *But how am I supposed to figure out where the message is?* No surprise—practical Dana had fixed a red square of paper on the back of her spare chair, a penciled arrow pointing toward a separate, smaller bank of controls. The vid-system was separate from the rest of the panel and similar to the one they'd brought to the old palace, Magdalena realized with relief.

It still took her several anxious moments to get the system up, respond correctly to the series of control-questions that would supposedly keep a terrorist or even an ordinary Arekkhi from accessing such advanced outsider tech, then went momentarily blank when it asked for her password. Finally the screen cleared, and she caught her breath. Khyriz's face was so sooty she couldn't make out his familiar spots, and his whiskers sagged with exhaustion. So utterly different from the vid he'd send her on StarBridge, to urge her here.

"My Magdalena, apologies," he began, and his voice sounded dull—worn, she could only hope, not injured. But he

anticipated her fears. "The fight early this morning proved
harder than even I feared, but I am not harmed, I swear to
you, only tired. Perhaps you will think I should have bathed
and reclothed before sending this message, but I feared delay
would give you more cause for concern than my appearance—
and I must leave in moments for Mibhor.

"Alexis is still unconscious, but Unya says she is stable.
We have placed her in the safest corner of my manor, with a
ten of guards on duty at all hours. I swear to you and the CLS,
I will protect her life more closely than my own.

"I will rest while Bhelan pilots my flitter to Mibhor, leader
in a squadron of many flitters and flyers. Zhenu concealed
many Asha in various of his mining camps on Mibhor, but
thanks to my poor dead cousin, I believe we can locate and
free An-Lieye's family, as well as many others. The designer,
Fahara, is safe on my lands, in a chamber very near Alexis's
and with the same company of full-time guard. Fahara would
have been sent to one of Zhenu's labor-camps for daring to
treat an Asha as other than pet."

His eyes were suddenly very warm, as if he met her eyes.
Magdalena's gaze blurred; she rubbed tears away impatiently.
"I swore an oath to you, Magdalena, and I will do all I can
to keep it—to keep myself safe and alive. But things do not
always go as we wish them to. Not in battle. And if something
should happen, and I do not survive—I wanted you to know
that I will be most sorry not to see you once more. My . . . my
dearest of all friends."

He seemed to force his whiskers to curve; the smile did not
warm his eyes now. "Magdalena, I know you have a life beyond our world. I always knew that, even when I hoped it
might be otherwise. Your ballet is a dance form I admire but
could never perform. Of course you will eventually leave us
to pursue that life. Rob has told me about the dance companies.
I am selfish enough to wish you would always remain with
us, but I will not ask it. And—and unselfishly, I am pleased
for you. And proud."

Her eyes brimmed with tears. *Oh, Khyriz!* She had seen him
in a plain StarBridge jumpsuit; in *Zhona*-silk; in Earth-like
jeans. Resplendent in fabric the opposite of hers for the wel-

coming ball. Just now he was grubby, exhausted—and never more beautiful.

"Magdalena, I know Alexis would make the corners of her mouth curve and warn you, 'He's trying to charm you, Perez. To be certain you persuade the CLS.' " His accent and inflection were nearly the match of Alexis's. "I know you will persuade them, because it is right. And when you return, I will be waiting where your ship docks."

His image remained on the screen for a long moment after he finished speaking. Magdalena dashed tears from her eyes and studied the lower-screen information: No space for response—probably he was already on Mibhor, fighting. If something already *had* gone wrong, if this was the last she ever saw of him . . . *Don't think that!* she ordered herself fiercely and keyed, "Save Message."

CHAPTER 16

♦

Magdalena slept more hours than she was awake, until well beyond the half-constructed jump station. Seven days after the transfer, she woke hungry and almost alert. "Tea will get you the rest of the way there," she mumbled as she shoved the thick braid over her shoulder and pulled on a stretch-waisted pair of Dana's trousers. "You're wasting time you don't have."

The tiny galley was already crowded: An-Lieye, her whiskers still nearly flat in grief, was teaching Dana basic "Fringe of Dancer" sleeve gestures.

"Hey!" Dana exclaimed as Magdalena squeezed past them to program the servo. "I like this! I can dance without getting my feet tangled up!"

The translator smiled as she eased back to settle into the only chair. "Looks good. Hello, An-Lieye."

Dana sipped tea. "Did An-Lieye tell you her fringe is starting to grow?"

"I don't think I remember a thing either of you has said in . . . wait. Fringe?" The servo beeped; Dana backed her chair, retrieved a steaming cup of Earl Grey and a dark muffin, and wheeled them over to her. Magdalena automatically blew on the tea and took a sip. "Wait. An-Lieye—is that what the designer-she was talking about? Apologies, I forgot, you weren't there the day of the ball. But—is that what she meant by true fringe?" The Asha gestured a yes, then looked at Dana and gave a very human shrug. Magdalena transferred her inquiring gaze.

"She had to write most of it out for me," Dana admitted. "Too complex for what Asha-sign she's taught me so far. She's originally highland Asha; most highland Asha females grow a forearm mane." She drained her cup, shoved it into the wall niche, and eased forward. "Sorry to eat and run, but the manual override for docking hasn't worked right since I left the jump station. If I don't see much of you in the next few days, you know where I'll be."

"Headfirst in the hardware or cussing the software," Magdalena agreed. "Dana . . . thank you."

"For what, the ride? We did that, remember? That's what friends are for." And with that, she was gone.

Silence. Magdalena shoved her cup aside. "An-Lieye, I am unsure where to begin, or what to say to you. I don't know what Khyriz or anyone else told you about this journey. How you feel about traveling with me." The other held out both hands for silence, then began to write; the translator picked at her muffin and waited.

*The Prince said we go to a distant place where many outsiders meet. That you will speak for the Arekkhi world, and that I must go so the Great Lie is revealed. He says this meeting is not what Arekkhi or Asha would expect, and that the outsiders will not believe the *zhez* simply because he is noble and we are not.*

"I *hope* that is true," Magdalena said finally. *Her lettering is neater than mine—I guess it's still going to catch me by surprise for a while; Zhenu and his kind did their work very well. But bless Fahara for daring to teach her; communications could have been much harder.* "I will not lie to you, An-Lieye, not when what we have to do is so important. But if there is any way, we will convince them." An-Lieye gestured a sharp assent. "Have you found anything you can eat?"

Another pause, shorter. *Yes. Dana showed me the machine for food and drink. Some tastes are strange.*

The translator laughed quietly. "The tastes are all strange, even for humans. An-Lieye, as soon as I finish eating, I must ask you to teach me how to sign."

Dana had the ship's lights programmed for Arekkhi standard days, mostly for An-Lieye's comfort. Without that, Magdalena would have lost track of time entirely. The other woman spent most of her time isolating and tearing down the small block holding the manual override, then testing it one switch, wire, and chip at a time. Magdalena avoided the flight deck entirely, afraid to step on or move something that would short out everything, knowing also that Dana needed no breaks in her concentration. Magdalena slept through the drop out of FTL so they could make the final jump to Shassiszss Station; now that she'd lost her earlier fears, the flight was mostly boring. Especially now.

Anything could be happening back there. Anything could already have been decided in the Planetary Council, and we might not even be allowed to speak. . . .

Mostly, she sat in the galley or in their tiny shared cabin with An-Lieye, learning her gesture language, learning everything she could about Asha in general, and this Asha in particular.

Late one evening, Dana joined them in the galley and programmed the servo for what the machine claimed was Coke and a burger; she was smiling again. "Got it done, and just in time; we drop out of FTL in an hour. Once I can beam the station we're out here, there may be messages for us."

"Good." Magdalena forced herself to keep eating tuna salad; she'd abruptly lost her appetite. "How long after that until we reach—?"

The engineer grinned. "Long enough; finish your food, you'll need it. Come up to the deck when you're done; the station's impressive."

Shassiszss Station *was* impressive; two wheel-within-wheel shapes at right angles, like an enormous gyroscope. Magdalena and An-Lieye both stared through the view-port; the translator was pulled halfway around as the other woman swore sharply. "Hey, Perez, come here, there's a message from Mahree, voice only. I'll switch it over there."

"Oh?" Nervously, she took the seat before the com, then winced as the familiar voice of the Ambassador-at-Large boomed into the cabin. Dana swore again and keyed volume.

"Magdalena, do *not* respond to this message! Dana will get her landing bay ID at the end of this, I'll meet you there. Now, don't worry, there's no real problem. But I just received a transmitted statement from Khyriz; he had to send it to me via Rob. It's a minor misunderstanding, I'm sure, but you'll have to explain why a supposedly deposed Emperor has access to your private password and is attempting to contact the CLS from your rooms. End of message. Dana—" The voice cut off as Dana switched transmission back and keyed in a series of digits.

She sighed, then looked at the translator. "All right, we've got about one Arekkhi hour to go. Anything you need to do before we dock, better do it now. And when you get out there, make sure Mahree knows to let *me* know where you are."

Twenty standard minutes later, Magdalena tugged her borrowed shirt and pants straight as the air lock hissed open, hoping no one would notice she wore only socks on her feet—Dana's shoe size was much larger than hers. On her right, An-Lieye stood very still except for quivering eartufts, the ruined blue robe clutched to her. Fortunately, the translator had seen the guide-vid to Shassiszss that every first-year StarBridge student viewed; she was able to explain the sapphire-colored decontamination mist and get them both through it. Mahree stood just beyond, dark hair pulled back in a severe, braided chignon.

Magdalena suddenly wanted to run to her; to be comforted. Protected. *No,* she told herself. *That's not why you're here.*

"About time you got here, Perez," Mahree said in crisp Mizari, but then she smiled, and hugged the girl, hard. "I'm so glad you're safe. Khyriz said to tell you at once that Alexis opened her eyes very briefly yesterday, and he thinks he recognized him." She let Magdalena go and turned to her companion, gestured an Arekkhi greeting between equals.

An-Lieye returned the gesture, then mouthed and signed, *I am An-Lieye, of the world Arekkhi.*

"I am honored to greet you, An-Lieye," Mahree replied in Arekkhi. "I am Mahree Burroughs, and I welcome you to Shassiszss Station." Flawlessly done, Magdalena thought—but, of course, that was why Mahree was Ambassador at

Large. "Now," the older woman addressed Magdalena, still in Arekkhi for An-Lieye's benefit, "do you need rest? Food?" Both shook their heads, and An-Lieye gestured negative. "An-Lieye, are you prepared to . . ." She hesitated very briefly.

Magdalena broke in. "Dana Marshall keyed up pictures and descriptions of the other League sentients for her."

"Good. Then come with me; the Council has agreed to see you—immediately."

Magdalena blinked. "But, I thought there would . . . I mean, that they'd need time. . . ."

"Ordinarily, yes. I wanted to talk to you first, to brief you. I'll tell you what I can while we're getting there." She led them on down the corridor, stopped at an elevator, and waited until it closed around them and began to ascend. "It's the vids sent by this Zhenu three weeks ago, and then the Prelate last week. Some members are worried about the Asha question."

"Asha? Mahree! They can't *possibly* believe what Zhenu says about them without even *meeting* An-Lieye!" They moved out into a brightly lit corridor; Magdalena let the Asha precede her onto a moving walkway, just behind Mahree. An-Lieye's ears had gone flat at mention of Zhenu's name; the translator touched her shoulder with the back of one hand.

"Isn't that the one Khyriz calls 'Iron Duke'? He was very persuasive—talked a lot about training and what could be accomplished. Apologies, An-Lieye. These councillors have not met you; they will understand once they do. I'm sorry, Magdalena, one or two of our more stubborn types seem to think you and Khyriz could have schemed to prove Asha are sentient when they aren't."

"That's—that's utterly stupid!" Magdalena snapped, then clapped a hand over her mouth. Mahree grinned at her.

"Nice new backbone, girl," she said. "Of course it is. Why would you and Khyriz want an embargo on the Arekkhi? Don't be afraid to speak out like that if you need to; most of the Council will respect you for it. And . . . here we are." She signaled, and a portal opened onto a bare, round room. Once inside, she pointed up for An-Lieye's benefit. "The chamber is overhead." She glanced at Magdalena. "Ready?" Both human and Asha nodded; with a faint shudder, the floor began to rise, the ceiling irised open, and they came up into an enormous dome. An-Lieye's gaze went to the transparent upper arc of the dome, where she could see part of the station and a dazzling frost of stars beyond it. As the floor settled into place, she turned slowly, letting her eyes take in the open area all around them, the seats, benches, tiers, and closed cubicles rising along the walls. Many of these were occupied, as Magdalena had expected. Vardi, Simiu, three humans . . . too distant to tell if she knew any of them, though it wasn't likely. Several Mizari conversed close together just in front of the lower tiers, seemingly arguing with a Drnian. The snakelike beings' head tentacles moved gracefully, oddly reminding the translator of the patterns in the Arekkhi Rainbow Dance.

Just beyond the floor they had just ridden up, she could now see two benches, a podium, and a holo-tank. Mahree gestured for her companions to come with her and walked over to the nearest bench. But before they could sit, two Mizari and the Drnian detached themselves from the arguing group and came across to join them.

The Esteemed Mediator, Ssoriszs, led the way; once behind the podium, his golden, pupilless eyes moved from Magdalena to An-Lieye and back again. The second Mizari—female by the lack of vestigal dorsal ridge—remained near the controls for the holo-tank. The human-shaped but very nonhuman-looking Drnian stopped a distance from them and made a Mizari greeting-bow, followed by the deft finger-gesture of her own kind.

Magdalena copied both movements, then curtseyed deeply. *Make no move anyone could interpret as a command to An-Lieye for a rote-learned response,* she reminded herself, and felt the heat in her face.

The Asha managed a creditable Mizari greeting, came very close on the Drnian's finger-gesture, and added the Arekkhi gesture of ''One who is pleased to be present among great ones.'' She then moved her arms in a graceful movement similar to a motion from ''Fringe-of-Dancer.'' *An Asha greeting?* She blinked that aside; she could ask later. The Drnian Secretary-General was waiting—Fys, who had been Secretary-General when Mahree first came here to argue for humans, had recently been reelected, Magdalena knew; it was oddly steadying.

"Most Esteemed Fys," she said in Mizari, "I am honored to be permitted such quick access to the Council."

"The pleasure and honor are ours, Magdalena Perez," the Drnian replied. "And the matter was deemed to require swift action."

"I am glad for that," Magdalena said. She gestured. "As you know, Arekkhi are not introduced to others. My companion will speak for herself, in her own fashion. And if—I could request that the proceedings be held in the Arekkhi language, as she does not know any other."

"There is some question regarding this . . . knowledge. But yes, we can grant such a request." The Drnian adjusted her tiny voder and looked directly at An-Lieye as she said, in accented but clear Arekkhi, "I am Fys, of Drnia."

The Asha's eartufts quivered slightly, then stilled. She signed and mouthed, *I am An-Lieye, of the highland Dagona Asha.*

The Drnian seemed slightly taken aback. *Zhenu must have done his job well,* Magdalena thought grimly. But after a moment, Fys continued, and it seemed to the translator that she spoke to them both. "Some days ago, we received transmissions directly from the station orbiting the Arekkhi world, and not long after, from the royal island. You will be given the chance to see the vids and respond to them, but first the League requests an explanation from the team Translator, why her private access codes and password have been used by an Arekkhi."

Magdalena took a deep breath. "Because *I* gave them to the Prince, Khyriz. Is it permitted that I explain all at once, rather than respond to questioning? Because it will make more sense if I do—and it will take less time. I fear to waste *any* time, knowing the situation when we left Arekkhi space." Silence. Fys turned away to speak with both Mizari.

"That is acceptable, if you agree to answer our questions."

"Of course." Magdalena took a deep breath and launched into the entire story.

It took longer than she would have liked, and the subsequent questioning seemed to go on forever. Finally, the Mediator and the Secretary-General seemed satisfied, and Fys gestured for the second Mizari to key the holo-vid.

The blank space was suddenly filled with Prelate, and for the first time she saw his face—the spots and nasal stripes so dark, they must be enhanced. His eyes were pale yellow, barely a slit of pupil. His message was as cold as his eyes, though later she could only recall the last of it: "The Asha were given to us by the Holy Dyad to care for and protect, as They care for us. Throughout our history, there have been wicked and lost Arekkhi who look upon Asha as therefore equal to us, and seek to prove this false belief by mating with them. Such Arekkhi are denied their place in the last Feast, though the Dyad may take pity upon the poor beasts who are so ill treated. These females who have come from your worlds to learn of our ways seek instead to place their own interpretations on matters. On Asha, and their rightful place in our world. Did not the CLS tell us that our own beliefs would be respected? Who is this Magdalena Perez to demand that we renounce our religion?"

The Prelate spoke smoothly, and concluded with a chilly smile. Magdalena's blood ran cold. She had never seen such a calculated movement of Arekkhi whiskers, not even from Zhenu. Moments later, the vid faded to black; she had missed the last of it. Probably fortunate. *More lies,* she thought grimly. Solomon Smith would have been proud of his "demon brother" from across so many light-years.

The holo-tank brightened again and the Zhenu's image filled it. He sat on a low, padded bench the same white as his robe; two ahla crouched at his feet, and he stroked them, rather absently, while they fawned on him. An-Lieye gazed at him and then his companions. After one flat-eared look at the unfortunate "pets," she kept her eyes on the ex-noble's face.

So did Magdalena, who had to keep reminding herself that this message had been recorded before Zehnu's capture. Largely, his speech mirrored the Prelate's, except his voice was harsher, and he added two other threats: "Remember that the Emperor with whom you bargained is no longer alive, nor is the youth Khyriz, who brought back your ways to our people. The station cannot be reached by your kind without our knowledge, as you know; the planet is even less available to you. Your Heeyoon traders *and* your human females will remain with us until we can be certain of a bargain we can trust—and in which we are active members. If not. . . . life can be short and uncertain on an *uncivilized* world, as you name ours. And we know there is more than your League outside our space . . . we have heard much of a certain . . . Sorrow Sector.'' His whiskers curved; he stroked both Asha with every evidence of fondness in his eyes and gestures. The tank dimmed, went transparent. Esteemed Fys gestured for the translator to speak.

Magdalena swallowed; her mouth was very dry. ''Thank you for letting me hear these lies for myself, Most Esteemed Fys,'' she said evenly. ''But the claims of these Arekkhi are not true: The Emperor is still in control of Arekkhi space. The interrelator and I were captured by agents of the *zhez* whose words you just heard, with the active assistance of the Prelate. Their hope was that you would be moved to see them as barbaric and that you would remove us, sanction their world. Because of her!'' A sweep of her arm indicated An-Lieye. ''Because of Asha! For a hundred years, she and all her kind have been named less than sentient, drugged, and kept as pets like those Zhenu had at his feet, or drugged and left without a voice, with no way to speak against the injustice!

''When the son of that Zhenu would have spoken for them, and for her, his father killed him, before my eyes! He is now the Emperor's prisoner, and the Prelate who spoke so . . . so pityingly of those who engage in beastiality—he cowers within his own walls! Which of us has not seen something and mistaken it for what it wasn't, on our own worlds, not just on the worlds of our allies? Isn't that why we have the Academy? And still such mistakes can occur!''

''But if they do not lie?'' one of the Mizari asked her bluntly. ''And . . . and if this mistake is yours, and that of the interrelator?''

Magdalena swallowed, shook her head. ''I am not wrong, sir. And I am not afraid to ask that you test my hypothesis; and An-Lieye will tell you she is not afraid, either!'' Silence.

Magdalena swallowed again and said, "Emperor Khezahn still rules. The message sent to you from the old palace on CLS equipment is his; I entrusted his son Khyriz with my password because when I left, the planet was far from secured. We could not be certain the Emperor's transmission would reach this place in any other way." She eyed both Mizari and Fys in turn. "When the message was refused here, Khyriz had the wit to send it on to StarBridge Academy, so Dr. Rob Gable— who *knows* Khyriz—would send it on to Mahree Burroughs. I ask permission to let the Emperor of the Arekkhi answer the lies of his enemies, here and now!"

More consultation, but to her surprise, it didn't take long— just enough time for Mahree to grip her hand and whisper, "Good job! Keep it up!"

"We will grant this," Fys said. Mahree pulled a small hand-comp out of her pocket and spoke into it, forwarding the holo-vids. "But," the Drnian went on, "there may be those here who still doubt An-Lieye is a true sentient. If . . . An-Lieye . . . would consent to an examination?"

Magdalena opened her mouth, then closed it again. *Don't say or do anything that looks like you're leading her, remember?* An-Lieye gestured assent. *And that isn't enough to convince them?* She had to remind herself that none of these beings had spent the last weeks on Arekkhi, that none of them had seen the other side of the Prelate, or Zhenu. That the CLS would want to be very thorough, considering they might have to close off CLS access to an entire system.

Mahree stood up then. "Most Esteemed Fys, with your permission, I request Dr. Stephanie Kim as examiner. You are free to choose others, but Dr. Kim is a telepath as well as a physician, and she speaks a little Arekkhi."

"She is also an acquaintance of the Arekkhi interrelator," Fys replied promptly. "So you may have Dr. Kim, but there will be two others as well."

"That is acceptable," Mahree said.

The Secretary-General went over to converse with the two Mizari; the Mediator touched something on the side of the podium, and the Drnian gestured to the other to begin the messages.

When the tank cleared, she could see the Emperor standing in the middle of the familiar main room in the old palace. Unlike Zhenu, he was plainly clad, only the ducat on his sleeves to identify him. To the visible surprise of the three councillors, he gave a Mizari greeting-gesture before speaking, and his first words were in Mizari.

"I am Khezahn, thirtieth in my line to rule all Arekkhi. To the CLS, my greetings and my thanks." *Khyriz taught him by rote,* she decided, then shoved the thought aside as the Emperor went on in Arekkhi. He was succinct, blunt, and did not excuse himself or his line. "I knew nothing of Asha until I took my father's place at his early death. Since that day, I have worked to change the balance of the Inner Council, in hopes that before my death, Asha and Arekkhi would be one people. Now that the greatest enemies to that peace are removed from power, it is possible this union will occur sooner than could have been hoped.

"We know the CLS rules; we know we can be banned from membership for having made a secret of Asha. I ask, personally, and for my world, that the CLS not banish us entirely. That we be given one final chance to repair what is wrong here. This contact with outside worlds is a wondrous and valuable thing, and of great benefit to our people. All of our people."

The tank dimmed, but to her surprise, brightened again. Khyriz stood where his father had, slender in a dark blue jumpsuit. "I beg permission to speak before the Council, as a former StarBridge student, and as leader of the group that for two years has sought Asha and removed them from the reach of such as the once-*zhez,* Zhenu. As of the hour of this transmission, I can personally assure the Council that Zhenu is imprisoned for crimes against Asha, the abduction of the CLS team, and the murder of a noble Arekkhi. I have, and can submit to the CLS, proof that Zhenu was behind the recent killings and the attempt to incite an Arekkhi civil war. I also hope to soon obtain proof that Zhenu poisoned the previous Emperor to gain control, with the Prelate, over a young and untrained Emperor.

"I have proof that the Prelatry was involved in creating the drugs that have controlled and subjugated Asha for a hundred years. Translator Magdalena Perez has samples of both drugs. I humbly request they be analyzed so that their effects can be reversed.

"My brother, Heir Khelyu, leads the Emperor's troops against the remnants of the opposition created by Prelate and once-*zhez*, and I am assured by him that Arekkhi space will be secured within a nine-day. Two at the most.

"I ask that the CLS not accept the words of the once-*zhez*, nor look upon his 'pets' as being what they seem. Do not, I implore you, close your minds to the Asha named An-Lieye. Think, I beg of you, what might become of any of us if we unwittingly drank something containing a mind-smothering poison.

"Lastly, I ask that you contact Dr. Robert Gable at Star-Bridge Academy. You know him; he is well respected. Ask that he lay all these recent events before the student Shiksara, who comes from a merchant family in a town where Asha live. Shiksara has been at StarBridge four years and has had no outside communication at all in the past year. She and I have not spoken in two years; this can be proven. Ask that Dr. Rob say to her, 'The threat against your family is gone— the Prelate's house in Vehyon is empty, and your parents are safe.' Then listen to what she can tell you about Asha." He bowed gracefully, and the tank dimmed.

Magdalena blinked rapidly to fight tears. *That bow was for me,* she knew—it was Nureyev's bow as Romeo, to Juliet/Fonteyn on the balcony above him. Mahree eyed her curiously, but her attention shifted as a small, black-haired woman strode across the open floor.

She fetched up in front of Magdalena, held out a hand, and said in clipped Mizari, "You won't remember me. Stephanie Kim."

"Of course I do," Magdalena said. "But I'd know you anyway, Dr. Kim. Alexis has that picture of you both—"

The Chinese woman shook her head; her eyes were wide and dark. "Make it Stephanie. The woman will be the death of me. How is she?"

"She sprained that weak ankle ankle again, then hit her head when she fell. But I heard from Khyriz just before we docked; he said she'd come to—''

''Oh, God,'' the physician whispered reverently. ''She's been out all this time?''

''It—she hit hard, I'm sorry, Stephanie. But Khyriz's physician—Unya—is taking care of her.''

''Know her—indirectly,'' the other replied gruffly, her voice rough with emotion. ''Your fancy Prince asked me to send her training tapes.''

''She watched them, I could tell. I'm sorry . . . I didn't mean to scare you. You look so tired!''

''Just got in from Trinity,'' Stephanie mumbled. ''Not your fault. I just—Alexis—oh, hell. Let's get this mess cleared up, shall we? So I can get transferred to go take care of her.'' The other two examiners were introduced—a blue-black, gangly human male Magdalena vaguely remembered from her first year at the Academy, and a Shadgui. The doctor turned to An-Lieye, then, and in heavily accented Arekkhi, introduced herself.

Poor An-Lieye, Magdalena thought. Condemned to live as a nonsentient—and now doubted here? But the Shadgui spoke almost at once, via its voder.

''The female from the Arekkhi world has a complex pattern of thought, logic, vocabulary, and is certainly a full sentient.''

The young man—she now remembered him, Prince Palmer, from Sierre Leone—agreed, his Mizari flawless except for the slightly musical accent that had also marked his English, a lovely blend of Sorbonne French and Swahili. ''If the doubters continue to doubt,'' he added, ''ask that she *write* her responses; I see the pad and stylo in her sleeve. Greetings, An-Lieye! My many-times ancestors were also slaves, in our world.'' An-Lieye eyed him in astonishment, then came forward to lay the backs of her hands against his. He smiled and returned the gesture.

Dr. Kim was silent. As one, the Shadgui, the Secretary-General, and the other telepaths turned to look at her. Mahree finally cleared her throat loudly and said, ''Well?''

''Ah? Oh!'' The doctor shook herself. ''Well . . . *of course* she's sentient. She's also . . . pregnant.''

Pregnant—pregnant? Magdalena's vision blurred. "Oh, *gods*," she murmured in reverent Arekkhi. "An-Lieye, you and Zhik! Did you—?" She couldn't say anything else; the Asha's ears quivered and her whiskers curved forward so far they nearly touched. The translator's mind bridged the gap almost as quickly. "You did! Mahree—Most Esteemed Fys—I think we have our final proof! An-Lieye's unborn, DNA evidence! If An-Lieye is what the Prelate claims, then surely she could never create life with an Arekkhi, could she? But An-Lieye conceived her unborn child with Zhikna—only son of Zhenu."

Mahree frowned, and switched to Mizari. "But Magdalena, you said he was . . ." Her eyes flicked toward An-Lieye. "There wouldn't be any proof left, would there?"

"We have the proof right here." Magdalena gestured, tugging at a fold of the ruined blue robe the Asha clutched to her breast. "The bloodstains are Zhikna's, from injuries he sustained while rescuing Alexis and me. I swear to that, here and now. But a test will prove it."

The rest of the session was mercifully short; An-Lieye was given full rights on-station as a sentient, and apologies for any distress the doubt had caused her. She was gracious but remote; her eyes shone, and to Magdalena's surprise, she permitted Dr. Kim to snip one of the bloodstains from the ruined blue, then produced a tuft of hair from the pocket of Dana's oversized shirt. *His* she mouthed. *From the—wound on his back.*

"The DNA tests will show they match," Stephanie Kim assured her as she withdrew a single hair, then turned to Fys. "Most Esteemed Fys, I have heard enough to be assured of my safety within the Arekkhi system. I request permission to leave now; Interrelator Alexis Ortovsky has been gravely injured and needs my skills to be certain she returns to full health."

Mahree laughed, to Magdalena's surprise. "She'll find a way to get there, anyway, Fys!" The Chinese woman grinned, but was gone the moment the Drnian gave assent. Fys went over to converse with the two Mizari. Magdalena sat, and forced herself not to slump from fatigue and relief. Mahree patted her hand. "Almost done, dear. Alexis will be proud of you."

"Thanks—at least, I hope so," she added. But moments later, the Secretary-General came back.

"The full Council will need to meet to decide the fate of the Arekkhi system; it will surely consider the lies told the CLS from the very first—but it will also consider the present situation. When a decision is reached, Ambassador-at-Large Mahree Burroughs will be informed at once, as will Translator Magdalena Perez and the sentient An-Lieye." She gestured a polite farewell, turned, and left, the Mizari slithering in her wake. Magdalena closed her eyes in exhaustion, only opening them again when the floor began to move downward.

It took three days, but Magdalena was so busy, they passed very quickly. The human liaison had her fitted for two changes of clothes and shoes. Magdalena insisted on a new set of jeans and T-shirt. Messages poured in from StarBridge, including an FTL call from Rob, who was smiling warmly as she keyed it.

"I heard from Mahree how well you did."

"Just what I had to, Rob," she protested.

"Oh? And what about the story Khyriz got from An-Lieye, you trying to keep the Iron Duke-him from killing her—and his own son?"

"That wasn't—I got mad."

"You had every right. Just like you have every right to give it up and come back here. If you want."

She laughed, and his trick eyebrow went up. "Rob Gable! I'm not about to go anywhere but back to the Arekkhi, as soon as they let me! Alexis needs me, and I have translation classes to start up again; with the Prelate out of commission, I can probably get access to the unaltered, dead-language histories, maybe even translate some of them. With luck, I can find the book Khyriz left for me in the old palace library that someone stole when I wasn't looking! And there are five very talented 'Fringe-of-Dancer' performers who will be *very* disappointed if I don't give them a tour of the CLS apartments. *And* teach them some ballet!"

"Sounds like a busy schedule to me," he agreed. "I was just checking, not ordering, you know. I knew you'd be good with the Arekkhi."

"*Most* of the ones I've met," she retorted dryly.

"Oh . . . wait, you've reminded me of something." He waited; she snapped her fingers. "Got it. The dance troupe with the enclosed stage, the ones with variable grav? Can you find a way for me to get in touch with them—um, not for now, in case they want to know? But maybe for a couple of years or so from now?"

"Riddles?" he asked, but she smiled and shook her head. "All right, be a sphinx. I have a message for you from Shiksara. I tried to get her to come deliver it personally, but she's upset. She said, 'Tell Magdalena I am sorry I kept the secret from her, but the *zhez* and the Prelate both threatened not just my family, but also all my hometown with Jhrror fever. A death sentence for not just Asha, not just my father and mother and sibs, but also everyone I ever knew. I was weak, Magdalena.' "

The translator bristled. "She wasn't, Rob! You know that!"

"I know; we'll convince her eventually. She's got a genuine talent for language, though: Blanket thinks she'll be good with the Simiu; we'll have to see. Oh . . . I just heard from Khyriz— by the time Dana gets you back to Arekkhi space, it'll be safe." He looked away from her. "And I think from the transmission I just got from Mahree that the CLS is fixing to send you out."

Alexis was getting bored with just drifting. At first it had been pleasant, restful. *When did I last sleep so long?* She couldn't remember. There had been pain at first: Sharp pain in her bad ankle and her head throbbed. That faded, eventually, though it hovered behind her half-conscious thoughts, threatening to return.

There had been fear—terror, really; she couldn't remember why that was, either. Not at first.

She became gradually aware of her surroundings: warm, clean bedding and soft, reassuring voices that spoke soothing

Arekkhi. Arekkhi hands touching her, holding her, helping her to swallow soft foods and liquids.

She had no real sense of how much time had passed, only a few hard-edged images of the Grand Ball, a confusing montage of black-clad and masked, armed Arekkhi, of the deadly stunner held at her eyes, ready to fire. Of running with the high whine of weapons assaulting her ears . . .

She woke with a start from one such nightmare and lay very still, eyes still closed. Her head no longer throbbed; she cautiously moved it and nothing hurt. *Where am I?* When she opened her eyes a crack, light hurt and she closed them quickly, letting her other senses work for her.

I'm back in the Old Palace! It couldn't be anywhere else: Her fingers knew the rough spot in the wooden bed-frame, and she could smell the familiar blend of her favorite lilac-like scent and the citrusy vines out on the balcony.

"Anyone home in there?" A low, warm voice spoke close to her ear—in English. Alexis frowned faintly. It didn't sound like Magdalena—but who else would speak such good English? "Easy now, I'm going to help you move so you can drink this. You just relax, I'll do all the work . . ."

She knew that voice, suddenly; though she'd never heard that particular tone directed to her: The soothing patter of a doctor or nurse talking to a patient. Doctor—English—woman's voice?

"Here, I've got your head. Just relax, let me get a pillow behind you."

Alexis let the back of her head rest against a strong, capable, familiar hand. "Steph?" she whispered. "Steph, is that you?" She opened her eyes, blinked furiously. Dr. Stephanie Kim, her black hair pulled severely away from a dark oval face, gazed at her, her eyes worried indeed.

"You recognize me?"

Alexis managed a weak smile. "Every time. What're you doing here, though?"

Stephanie gently brushed a strand of hair from Alexis's face and stroked her cheek. "Came to take care of you, of course. Heard you knocked that hard head of yours into something even harder." Her voice was shaky. "How do you feel?"

Alexis captured the hand in both of hers, and held it. "Now that you're here, I feel—fine."

Less than a half day later, they were on their way back to the jump point on the edge of Arekkhi space. Dana was pleasant but remote; most of her waking hours were spent diagnosing the problems in the new servo. "Bad software—unless it's something as stupid as incompatible drivers between the hardware. Aren't you glad I convinced them to leave the old servo unit in place?"

An-Lieye was even more remote, her mood ranging wildly. Magdalena sympathized, but couldn't think of how to console a fellow female who carried new life . . . but had lost forever the one who helped her create that life. *She's lucky, in a way,* the translator realized late one sleepless night. *Just as I am. I haven't lost him—but he and I could never have his child— even if he wanted one. . . .* Her face flushed; she couldn't complete the thought. The blunt fact was, she and Khyriz were not compatible in *that* way. But hours later, she woke, overly warm, the dream still lingering in her mind. Her lips curved. *Some things aren't possible. Others . . . may be.*

A still very upset Dr. Kim had left three days before Dana's ship; the fast medical transport would drop her and a load of supplies on the Arekkhi station, where Bhelan was ready to retrieve them and her, before it went on to Trinity.

Dana's handwritten message was fixed to the old servo: *CLS sends word they may have antidote for voice poison, will send chemical notation to Khyriz via old palace com. Breakthrough possible soon on residual effects of ahla drug. We dock at station in 8 A-standard hours.*

It seemed a lifetime; in actuality, it was no time at all— barely enough hours to pack her few belongings, take one last shower, comb out her hair. Try to eat. Dana brought the shuttle neatly into the bay in the royal docking area; the hatch slid up, the deck pivoted 180 degrees, and the shuttle rolled forward, into the inner dock. Magdalena waited for the all-clear in the air lock, fingers pressed against the hatch.

Finally the all-clear beeped and the hatch slid sideways. Khyriz stood at the foot of the ramp. Magdalena swallowed hard, then closed the distance between them, to bury her face against his throat. "I was so afraid I would never see you again," she whispered.

"Magdalena." His voice was rough with emotion; his arms tightened around her. "Welcome back."

"No," she whispered, and eased away from him enough to draw a finger through his whiskers. "Not back. *Home.*"

Epilogue

The Emperor held a formal reception the next afternoon—in the CLS apartments, since Alexis was still too weak to be allowed out of them. For the first time, Magdalena was able to meet and talk to the members of the Council she had only seen in the formal setting before. She liked Khezahn's new choices, particularly the once-priest Yuchne, who was quiet and intelligent, sparking only when the interrelator and Dr. Kim brought up the antidote formulas. Magdalena left them to it and let Khyriz take her over to more new arrivals.

The initial fuss over, she had assumed she'd take up her translator duties where she'd left them. But for now, Alexis spent most of her days in the talking-pit or the office, dealing with everything from Arekkhi, who wanted outside markets for their crafts, to applications from young Arekkhi for StarBridge testing. For now, it was Magdalena who traveled the countryside, meeting villagers, talking to remote herders and city merchants.

It still surprised her—really being able to travel when and where she wanted. Of course, there were safeguards everywhere: She knew of three CLS advisers on-planet besides the two who stayed in the new palace and met regularly with the Emperor and his Council, observing as the Arekkhi began undoing generations of repression. One of them was a special envoy handpicked by Mahree—a high-ranked Heeyoon—who seemed to spend half his time shuttling between planet and station.

But the Heeyoon trading company was making headway with contacts among the artisan Arekkhi, and the new master of station, one of Khyriz's numerous cousins, was himself head of a society that created contemporary versions of ancient Arekkhi jewelry and was patron to several crafting guilds.

Magdalena could already see some of the fruits of the Emperor's initial reworking of the planetary communications network. During the last two stops on her most recent trip West—

an impromptu meeting in a village market, and a formal hall-meeting in another, larger town—she'd had to answer some pointed questions about Asha, about the Prelatry, and about outside intervention in both matters.

And the Emperor's secret Council had been disbanded. The room where it had met for centuries stood empty. The Council still debated whether it should be made a museum—as a warning—or destroyed.

Fortunately, few Arekkhi seemed to hold Zhenu's attitudes about Asha. *Or those who feel that way are keeping quiet around the aliens*, she decided. Not so good, if true. But she saw no sign of things turning violent again.

Magdalena returned from an overnight visit to Shiksara's family to find Alexis settled in the talk-pit, half-buried in Arekkhi documents and computer marks, with Stephanie Kim cross-legged on the edge of the pit, scowling down at her. "Hey, Perez!" the interrelator said with a laugh, "having fun with *my* flitter?"

"Oh, it's yours, all right." Magdalena smiled. "I have no intention of learning how to pilot one of those—or anything like it."

Alexis laughed again. "Yeah, sure! You have Khyriz to take you."

The smile widened. "He doesn't seem to object—when he has time, of course."

"Which seems to be just about always." Alexis twisted partway around to meet her companion's almond eyes. "I swear, I just gotta talk to her for a minute or two, then I'll go take that nap."

"*If* I come with you, I suppose?" the doctor inquired dryly, and cast up her eyes. "I only *thought* my usual runaround job-description was a hard one! I was just about burned out anyway, but this woman's going to complete the job." Her warm eyes rested on the Russian, who raised an eyebrow and gave her a wicked smile.

"We just got word from Fahara and An-Lieye," Alexis went on after a moment. "All the preliminary tests show the baby's healthy, due in about five months, male—and the match

is more than ninety-nine percent that Zhik's the father. They'll
do another after it's born, but—''

''I didn't doubt it for a moment. But I'm glad it'll be proven,
for her sake,'' Magdalena said softly. ''Then that means the
Emperor—?''

''His chief clerk sent me a preliminary copy of the procla-
mation and the documents as soon as they got the physician's
sworn statement—it's here somewhere, one of these thick
stacks. They must not have doubted, either. Especially after
your testimony and Khyriz's. Anyway, the *zhez*'s immediate
holdings and twenty *parths* around it go to the infant as Zhik's
heir, with that in trust to An-Lieye while he's growing. She'll
need a handful of advisers for now, but I wager she'll be fully
in charge before the babe loses his infant-mane. Everything
else—villages and so on outside the twenty *parths*—will be in
trust to the Emperor while Zhenu's ex-serfs learn to deal with
independence. Oh!'' She began stacking things on the edge of
the pit. ''I nearly forgot: The latest antidotes have come in
from CLS; the Emperor's Council is very excited. Ah-Naul is
nearly back to normal, I'm told; An-Lieye had the opportunity
to take him in, but she did the better thing: They've found his
family and sent him home, even though he doesn't remember
them much yet; she also pledged financial support for them
because of what was done to him.'' She got to her feet, swaying slightly. ''No—wait, Steph, it's all right. Change of altitude, but not nearly as bad as it used to be.''

''Hah,'' the other woman exclaimed sourly. ''You've got
the part, cut out the act; you're playing feeble to keep me
here!''

Alexis laughed. ''It's working, isn't it? So, Perez, you're
here for the next two days, if I recall right?'' She was letting
her partner lead her slowly toward the hallway, and her sleep-
chamber. Magdalena went with them.

''Well . . . maybe not. Khyriz thought this might be a good
time for me to tour his estates, and . . .''

''You and Khyriz . . .'' Alexis stopped abruptly. ''I swear,
are you two in love, or what?''

Magdalena smiled. ''It isn't 'what.' '' The smile widened as
the interrelator stared at her, open-mouthed in pretended shock.

"Don't worry, I'm not quitting on you. And it's not as if we could life-bond, or have offspring, you know."

To her surprise, the interrelator's cheeks turned pink. "I don't believe *you* just said something like that! Prudish Perez?"

"Hmmmmm. That was only my nickname in first year."

"But he *is* a Prince."

"And subject to his father's say, but he's talked to his parents. It helps he's a third son. But they let him know that as long as we don't flaunt ourselves and upset the conservative and religious types, they won't make a fuss. They care for him—and they like me."

"Well, *you* look happy," Alexis said.

Magdalena laughed, and twirled in place. "I am. I just got a response from the McKenzie Dance Company—the best of the touring groups that wanted me to join them before we came here? Well, I sent them a proposal from Shassiszss, suggesting a touring group of twenty dancers and a star duo and soloist to tour with them. There'll be Arekkhi dance of all kinds, including 'Fringe of Dancer,' solos like 'Bluebird' from *Sleeping Beauty,* and some of that Irish tap. And a new hybrid ballet: Khyriz and I have been working on it, when there's time, a way he can perform classical ballet with me. McKenzie is *very* interested."

"Magdalena! That's great! But I didn't have a clue. Why didn't you tell us?"

"I didn't dare, in case they weren't interested. And, well . . . in case I'd jinx the whole thing. It won't be for two years at least, so you'll have plenty of time to get a new translator." She glanced sidelong at Stephanie, who tugged at the interrelator to get her moving again.

Alexis nodded. "Hmmm. Anything is possible, isn't it?"

She paused in the doorway as their new pantrier opened the outside entry; Khyriz stood there. "I'd better get horizontal before this woman scowls me into a relapse, Perez. I think the caller is for you, anyway."